The Courtesan's Secret

The Courtesan's Secret

A Venice Beauties Mystery

Nina Wachsman

LEVEL BEST BOOKS

Historia
ESTABLISHED 2018

Author Photo Credit: Jake Wachsman

First edition

ISBN: 978-1-68512-348-2

Cover art by Level Best Designs

This book was professionally typeset on Reedsy.
Find out more at reedsy.com

To my eight grandchildren who always inspire me

Contents

Praise for The Courtesan's Secret

"A dashing English spy seeks a lost treasure and an imperious courtesan searches for a beloved brother in Nina Wachsman's electrifying thriller set in 17th century Venice. Wachsman takes the reader on a wondrous tour of the fabled city, from its glittering palazzos to Moorish salons, and the lives of three very different women. A riveting tale that is both high adventure and a vivid portrait of Venice's Jewish community in the late Renaissance."—Mariah Fredericks, author of *The Lindbergh Nanny*

"*The Courtesan's Secret* is a captivating story of deception, international intrigue, and love in glittering 17th century Venice. In lush, well-researched prose, author Nina Wachsman powerfully evokes a lost and dangerous world of beauty, bigotry, and political rivalry through the series' two protagonists, a rabbi's scholarly daughter and a celebrated Venetian courtesan. I cheered them on as their struggle to save a loved one draws the two unlikely friends into a conflict between England and Spain. A book to savor."—Mally Becker, Agatha Award-nominated author of *The Turncoat's Widow* and *The Counterfeit Wife*

"This engaging historical mystery features a wonderfully varied cast of characters – an English courtier, a Spanish assassin, an Italian rabbi's daughter, and a Venetian courtesan named Belladonna, Jewish by birth but a convert to Christianity. With impeccable and extensive research, Wachsman immerses the reader in early 1600s Venice— a world of brilliant jewels, secret portraits, lively taverns, flaming torches, and the glimmering waters of the Grand Canal—but also poisoned daggers, the dreaded Council of Ten, and a deathly plague. Against this rich historical backdrop, the forbidden romance between the courtesan and the pirate shines. This mystery will appeal to fans of romantic suspense, as well as those interested in the history of Venice."—Karen Odden, *USA Today* bestselling author of the Inspector Corravan Mysteries

Cast of Characters

- Sir George Villiers, *a flamboyant courtier and favorite of King James I, King of England*
- Belladonna, *a famous beauty, a former courtesan and a woman of influence in Venice*
- Isaak, *a corsair (pirate) and the son of the chief rabbi of Venice*
- Sarra Coppio Sullam, *a poetess of renown, and a wealthy patron of the arts in the Ghetto*
- Jacob Sullam, *her husband*
- Mirabella, *their servant*
- Roderigo Mendoza, *envoy from the island of Jamaica in the New World*
- Rabbi Leone di Modena, *scholar, author, poet, orator, and chief rabbi of the Ghetto*
- Diana, *his widowed, scholarly daughter*
- Mattia Correr, *a Venetian artist who has painted both Belladonna and Diana*
- Bardon Morosini, *a wealthy nobleman, and a member of the Council of Ten*
- The Council of Ten, *elected by the Senate, and the most powerful men in Venice*
- The Turk, *a trader and dealer of imports who once sailed with Isaak*
- Diego di Ribera, *the ambassador of Spain to Venice*
- Antonio, *a Spanish assassin*

Chapter One: Villiers

September 1612

Letter from GIROLAMO LANDO, Venetian Ambassador in England, to the DOGE and SENATE:

This night the masque is to take place, all the courtiers and cavaliers will make a brave show. Among them, Sir George Villiers, apparently, a great favorite of the King. The ceremony will be attended by an extraordinary number of ladies very richly dressed and laden with jewels. His Majesty will take part in the gaiety, no doubt to enjoy the agility and dancing of his favorite, Villiers, who will sit with His Majesty under his usual large canopy.

The masque took place on a cold winter's night, although Sir George Villiers was certain the invited guests would not be deterred by the winds that relentlessly buffeted the Thames. The boatmen would need to chip away at floating ice to make their way to the dock at Hampton Court Palace. It was Villiers' own good fortune to be in residence with the King at the palace from Christmas through the New Year. He pitied those who had to brave the cold in scant costumes, which would be damaged by wind and rain or the weight of heavy fur throws. Hampton Court Palace was ablaze with light on this freezing night, its festivities a beacon to all those seeking favors or status at the court of King James of England.

Villiers glanced at his image reflected in one of the palatial mirrors in the ball room, and he was pleased. He had spared no expense with his costume, and had real gold leaf sprinkled in his tawny hair. His ornate golden mask had been ordered specially from Venice. He was wearing a white satin toga with fasteners of gold which his valet had a devil of a time arranging so that enough leg and torso were revealed–enticing, but not vulgar. The costume was a success, confirmed by the frequency of ardent glances from the ladies.

He enjoyed being masked, rejoicing in the freedom it afforded him. It gave him the opportunity to mingle without being recognized, overhear conversations and make a few snide remarks, anonymously. He made progress through the ballroom to where the King sat on his magnificent throne, bedecked in a long, glittering golden robe, but unmasked. Beside him was a younger masked man in a plum velvet robe lavishly embroidered with gold. The golden diadem created a halo about his head, as it should for a Prince. Villiers took the envied position on the other side of the King and, like his Royal Highnesses, surveyed the masked and costumed crowd.

Villiers, like any courtier, held his head high, emulating his monarch. The small fortune this evening had cost him would be of no matter once he received the intelligence he was expecting. A treasure, ripe for the taking, soon to be in his hands. The threat of insolvency would be at an end.

The ballroom was filled with a large crowd of masked and cloaked revelers, the smells of perfumes, sweating bodies, and wet wool almost overwhelming. Chords of fine music penetrated the general murmur of voices and the tinkle of well-bred laughter. A figure in white velvet, masked with the head of a stag, approached and bowed towards the King and the Prince. The King nodded and said, "My dear Arundel, even such a spectacular mask cannot disguise you."

Arundel removed the stag's head and bowed to the King. "A recent purchase, your Highness, from my visit to Venice."

"Thank you for reminding us once again of your triumph there. Your gift of the glass boat and the plans for faster ships has greatly improved our fleet." The King waved Arundel to stand beside Villiers, who had to make room for him by stepping further away from the King.

A scoundrel, this Arundel, who had managed to position his rapid departure from Venice as a noble success. Arundel's fortune may be on the rise for now, but Villiers had plans to surpass him. Before he could issue a biting retort to his rival, a new arrival distracted him.

Many eyes followed the figure who approached the royal dais, because of the magnificence of his blue peacock-feathered cloak. Villiers, likewise, admired the bright blue color and the way its feathers seemed to glisten in the candlelight. The man was masked, though his identity was not a secret to Villiers. He had been told the man he was expecting, an envoy recently arrived from the New World, would appear in a magnificent blue cloak. He had been promised this envoy was key to uncovering a treasure trove of gold and a means to usurp the Spanish of at least one victory in the West Indies. The conquest of this island in the West Indies to take control of the trade routes did interest the King, but Villiers was interested in the treasure. He planned to reap a generous share of gold for himself.

"That cloak is spectacular," said Villiers as the fellow made his approach.

"A costume cannot outshine the most glorious visage of all, the magnificence of Royalty," answered the masked man.

"Well spoken," nodded the King.

Villiers added, "There is no time like the present to enjoy beauty."

The masked man gave a respectful bow, "My city and all it has to offer awaits your Highness."

Villiers was confused. The envoy was from Jamaica, an island in the Caribbean. What city could he possibly be referring to? The King looked as puzzled as he, so Villiers asked, "What city is that?"

"Apologies, milord. In the mask, you do not recognize me. Giralomo Lando. The ambassador from the great and wondrous city of Venice." The man raised his mask and, sure enough, revealed the sweaty red face of the Venetian ambassador. Not the envoy. Villiers coughed to suppress the rising of panic like a bubble in his throat.

"Where—where—did you get that cloak?" he said hoarsely.

The man raised the hem of his cloak to fan it out. "Ahh, magnificent, is it not? It was delivered to the man who had recently taken the room next to mine here in London, and I recognized its label from one of the best shops in Venice. My friend had departed, leaving me much of his belongings, and since I did not want such an item to go to waste..." he paused to tug at the neck of his cloak, "but it is so very warm in here, is it not?"

The Venetian began to fan his face with his hands. Villiers wondered how a cloak made of feathers could be overly warm when suddenly, the Venetian gave out a piercing scream. He continued screaming, and the music and the dancing stopped. All eyes turned to the screaming man who was now writhing on the floor.

Villiers was close enough to see why. The ambassador's hands were tearing at the fastening of the cloak to get it off. The blue cloak flapped open, and flames were everywhere, devouring the poor man's arms and legs trapped inside it.

Villiers dropped to the floor to help the ambassador, pulling at the cloak's fastening, but the clasp held fast. There was shouting around him, which Villiers ignored as he continued to try and tear off the cloak, but it only pulled tighter and choked off the man's screams. Desperately, Villers tugged at a velvet drape hanging beside the throne, and once it fell into his hands, he immediately threw it over the man on the floor, attempting to smother the flames. The screams had stopped, but there was the horrid smell of burning flesh and feathers.

Villiers stood, breathing hard from his exertions. He looked all around. The crowd stood frozen, watching him. The Prince held a lace handkerchief to his nose, and the King's eyes were open wide, and his hands clutched at the arms of his throne.

There was no movement under the velvet drape. Gently, Villiers lifted it away from the Venetian ambassador's face. There was not much to be done for Giralomo Lando; his face was bright red, eyes closed, but he was still alive. His breathing was ragged, and the clasp was still tight around his throat, but the velvet drape covered the damage below it. The man may be dying, but Villiers had to know more about the envoy.

Crouching beside the fallen man's head, Villiers spoke close to his ear. "The man in the room next to you. The cloak was meant for him. You see, someone is trying to kill him, and he must be found before they do. Did you know where he has gone?"

Was it possible the man could hear him or could answer? The Venetian surpassed his expectations when he opened his eyes for the last time and responded to Villiers' question. "To Venice. To Belladonna."

* * *

"Is he dead?" the King asked, sounding less concerned, but more peeved. "Who has the audacity to murder a man within a few steps from a King?"

Villiers had regained his place beside the King and spoke in low tones to prevent someone from listening in. "Yes, Your Majesty, though it seems the Venetian ambassador became the victim by mistake. The deadly cloak was meant for the man we were expecting."

"Can we really make that assumption? It could be the Venetian ambassador was the true target," the King said, "After all, those Venetians are known for their poisons. Perhaps this was an act of revenge."

"This death was meant to be a spectacle, perhaps as a warning."

"A warning? To the King of England?" the King snorted.

Villiers had to be cautious. His favoritism depended on delivering platitudes to His Majesty, not warnings. He quickly backtracked. "Not a warning to you, Sire. But perhaps, to the allies of the envoy, from the New World. A hideous death is promised if they reveal the secret of the treasure." He gave the King a moment to digest this, before continuing, "I have heard of such things. Pirates and corsairs, for example, are wont to do such ghastly acts to their own men to scare them into silence."

"Ahh. I see," the King conceded. "Well, if you are so knowledgeable about such things, I expect you will get to the bottom of this."

The courtiers closest to the scene had removed their masks, and the ladies were fluttering their fans. There was a steady hum of murmuring while Arundel was waving frantically to the attendants, who promptly appeared and took the corpse away.

Arundel annoyingly reappeared, so Villiers decided to take his leave. He bowed to the King and the Prince, who looked as white as Villiers' toga and said, "I will leave for Venice tomorrow. I will find 'Belladonna.'"

"May I perhaps offer some help, your Majesty?" Lord Arundel spoke up. "Venice is a city known for its beautiful women, which is why I had commissioned their portraits for my own Gallery of Beauties—"

"Yes, yes, we know all about that, so just get to the point," said the King with a wave of a lace-edged kerchief.

"Well, Belladonna is the name of the most beautiful courtesan in Venice." With his pronouncement, Arundel's arm went to his hip, and his chin jutted out in defiance of anyone who would challenge his assertion.

Villiers' eyebrows raised at the same moment as the corners of his lips. "A woman?"

The King glared at Arundel, who took a step back, bowed, and retreated. Then the King crooked a finger at Villiers. "Sir George, a word."

Villiers bowed respectfully and came closer to the throne.

"If the key to the treasure is in Venice, you must go and find it. Do not dally with a courtesan. I want that gold, and I want that island." The King's voice was low but clear, and Villiers reassured his sovereign he understood.

Chapter Two: Antonio

Antonio kept to the shadows, taking each step along with the boots of the man he trailed, so he would not be noticed. He was sweating, and the dampness settled on his shirt, chilling him, despite the thick wool of his cloak. The man he was following veered from one doorway to the next, and Antonio could not tell if he was drunk or ill or was searching for a place to hide.

Antonio had lost track of his precise location, thanks to the maze-like passages that ended in either a canal or a dead end. He would be forced to backtrack and, inevitably, lose time. Antonio had been told this man had never stepped foot in Venice, yet the poor devil seemed to travel by instinct, always finding the one passageway that went all the way through to a bridge.

He had been chastised once for taking liberty with his orders when it came to the envoy, the man he was now following. He had made a mistake when he killed the man in England with a poisoned cloak. *Capture, not kill.*

This time he would throw his knife only to wound, and he could see he had the right man, so it should be easy to capture him.

Antonio never failed his commissions. After a hasty return to Spain, he had endured a confrontation with The Master of Spies, a courtier with little morals and great power, and the Spanish ambassador to Venice. The Master of Spies was the only man who frightened Antonio, while the ambassador, Diego di Ribera, disgusted him with his pompousness and incompetence.

When the Master of Spies chastised him after the fiasco of the peacock-feathered cloak, Antonio took heed of his warning. "Though I admire your creativity in your use of the inflammatory cloak, you did not accomplish our goal. The envoy has slipped away, and instead, the Venetian ambassador is dead."

Di Ribera pointed a finger at Antonio, and his face was red as he spat out his words. "The death of the Venetian ambassador will cause me trouble, and this fool was clearly instructed not to kill the envoy. Precious time has been wasted, and now that the envoy has been alerted, he is gone—to who knows where."

It might be helpful for these two arrogant courtiers to remember how dangerous Antonio could be. "The lining of the cloak contained a substance that bursts into flame upon contact with heat. The inside of the feathers was coated with wax to keep it stable, but at the close quarters of the masked ball, with increasing body heat, the wax melted, and poof! The coated feathers ignited."

Diego di Ribera's eyes widened, and Antonio savored his fear. "You had charged me to prevent the envoy from providing his intelligence to the English lord. My source advised me the planned delivery was to be at the Masque, so I made sure the connection would not be made. In future, please be more specific in your instructions, and such mistakes will not happen."

"Your source!" Di Ribera said and then snorted, "Your precious source neglected to tell you the envoy had already gone, which is why he never received your deadly cloak. Did this same source advise you as to where the man has gone?"

"I do know where he is, and I will find him." Antonio kept his voice even and his eyes on the Master of Spies.

Antonio was reassured he would be getting a second chance when the Master of Spies looked to him and said, "You say you know where the envoy can be found? That is most reassuring. This time, remember we do not want him dead—we need to question him."

"The ambassador was from Venice, and his rooms had adjoined the envoy's. The ambassador's dying words were 'Belladonna.' The same word had been overheard in previous conversations between the two men. It is not difficult to assume the envoy will be found in Venice, with Belladonna."

"Belladonna?" The Master of Spies raised an eyebrow and asked, "A woman?"

Di Ribera's hand clenched along with his jaw, and it seemed as if anger had forced him to grind his teeth before he would be capable of answering. "A courtesan. An evil woman who has beguiled and wheedled many out of their fortunes. Her origins are a mystery, but wherever she came from, she must have known the envoy and still pulls on his heartstrings."

The ambassador was an egoist and a prig, and Antonio had supposed somehow this woman had wronged him. A point in her favor.

"Interesting. There is another angle for you, Antonio. Go with Di Ribera to Venice. Find the envoy or go after the courtesan. She is likely to be useful in flushing out the envoy, and perhaps as leverage to gain his cooperation."

Now, pressed against the cold, damp wall of the building, Antonio had to remind himself of the Spy Master's order not to kill. The man was in his sights. His hand rested longingly on the hilt of the stiletto. Then, the swish of the canal waters and the singing of a gondolier signaled the approach of a gondola. A man's voice called out to the gondolier, and there was a bang of oars as the gondolier aimed his boat to the small pier where his next passenger awaited.

Antonio knew he had to act before his prey escaped into the boat.

He pulled out his weapon, aimed, and threw. The desire to maim, not kill, guided his hand. Antonio grinned at his accuracy when his target fell to his knees as the stiletto landed in his thigh. Antonio rushed from the shadows to grab him, but the man surged forward, despite his wound, and launched himself into the gondola. The gondolier pulled heartily at his pole, and by the time Antonio arrived at the edge of the dock, the boat was already out of reach.

Chapter Three: Belladonna

The night seemed to crawl towards dawn, dragging her along with it. It was becoming difficult to keep up her expression of mild interest, as Belladonna slipped through her salon and the loitering groups of well-dressed and completely drunk Venetians.

She had nodded to Contarini, one of the most powerful and ruthless men in Venice. The nobleman stood behind the dice players, not watching the game, of course, his eyes following her as she moved about the room. Belladonna was used to his vigilance and kept an equally watchful eye on Contarini, although her observations were more discreet. She had a network of spies; servants and courtesans who owed her their loyalty and Contarini their hatred.

She moved her silken blue skirts aside as she passed another group clustered around a small fancily-dressed man with a pointed beard, Diego di Ribera, the Spanish ambassador. He engaged the attention of the men around him with his exaggerated descriptions of the latest shipment of gold and treasures arriving from the New World. Belladonna knew from her own sources that the galleon passing through the Punta della Dogana on its way to Malaga was but meagerly loaded with gold, and its crew reduced due to the hardships of their journey. She smiled to herself, knowing the cynical nature of the Venetians, who would tolerate his boasting only for their own amusement, but would never believe in its veracity.

She was moving towards a group of women and men lounging casually on her silken settees, when her eyes caught sight of a young man, standing alone, watching her over the rim of his glass of wine. She turned her head slightly to give him her usual benign smile, when she saw him raise the glass in his right hand and turn it, so that she could see the red ruby of his ring. He smiled and nodded and then lowered the glass to his lips and drank.

Belladonna forced herself to turn away from him and continue walking languidly to the settees. She recalled in flashes the young man's dark countenance, his wild curly black hair, and the silver thread of the embroidery in his waistcoat, which had caught her eye. The ruby ring was a sight she dared not hope for, a signal once promised but never before seen, arranged so many years ago.

She had the strength to keep her face impassive as she joined the next group and laughed appreciatively at the jokes thrown out by the drunken young men who lay upon the settees. They were attended by the most beautiful women in Venice, all courtesans like herself, and women she counted upon as friends and allies.

She signaled to them with her eyes or with a soft touch on the shoulder or the clasp of a wrist— it was time to move their escorts on, to stir their companions out of their lethargy and into their crested gondolas towards their own palazzos.

"It is late, Domenico," she heard Elena, a dark-haired beauty draped in red velvet who was as capable as she of influencing men of power. "It is time for you to rise."

She knew that her words would instigate another wave of bawdy remarks, but would result in departure. Belladonna secretly thanked her friend for her efforts, for the movements of one group preparing to leave sparked the same motion in others.

Belladonna turned to the gamblers, so intent on their game they had not noticed the others shuffling off towards the door and noticed the young man with the ruby ring had disappeared. As she placed her hands on the shoulders of a player who was sweating through his losses, she declared she heard the crowing of a rooster, a bad omen for any gambler, as well as the signal for them all that the night was over. The losing gambler's face relaxed as the playing stopped, and as the dice and ducats were gathered from the table, he rose and stretched, no doubt grateful to still have some coins left in his pocket.

When the last of the tapers in the salon had been snuffed, and the servants were resting in their beds, Belladonna retired to her airy chamber. The large windows were open to a star-flecked purple sky, and an early-morning breeze cooled her as she began to remove her dress and unpin her hair. As her dress dropped to the floor and she stepped out of it, she sensed she was not alone.

Belladonna always kept a dagger by her side. The dagger was easy to conceal in a specially made pouch at her waist and was always close at hand. It had once saved her life. The weapon, and training on how to use it effectively, she owed to a Turkish grandee. The dagger was thin, with a long, pointed blade and a short handle wrapped with strips of black leather. Unknown to her opponents, the handle was hollow and contained a deadly poison that would be released by pressure on the handle. The mechanism would ensure even the slightest prick would be deadly.

She was not a woman to be taken lightly nor against her will. Those who thought they could possess her by force suffered for their mistake. She kept her breathing steady as she got into her vast bed and drew the curtains closed, waiting.

Someone was approaching the bed, and she concentrated on the sound of his breathing to pinpoint his location. There was a swish as the bed curtains opened, and her eyes were fixed on the dark silhouette creeping towards her. The sound of his rapid breathing had ceased. He must be holding his breath now as he approached. Instantly, she rolled off the bed, landing in a crouch on the floor. Dagger in hand, she thrust at the dark silhouette by her bed. The figure pivoted sideways, and the momentum caused her to pitch forward, falling against the bed. A whoosh of air across her face triggered her instinct to roll in the other direction, as a dark cloth just missed her head.

Leaping to her feet, Belladonna slashed the air with her dagger to keep her assailant from coming any closer. Suddenly sensing movement behind her, she spun away just in time to avoid a hood nearly thrown over her head.

Sprinting closer to the window where there would be more light, she glanced over her shoulder to see the glint of a raised dagger. Quickly, she raised her own weapon to block it, but at that moment, a black-gloved hand shot out and shoved her aside. A cold gust of wind blew the hair from her face as she regained her balance, but all she caught was a glimpse of the intruder's back as he vaulted through the open window. Still clutching the dagger, she leaned out only to see a gondola pulling away, a dark figure visible inside it.

Closing the windows, she latched them. It was growing lighter as the night progressed towards sunrise. Belladonna's hand was still clutching the dagger tightly, and she had to take a deep breath and exhale before she could allow herself to relax her grip. Her home had been invaded, and her sanctuary violated. Her nostrils flared, and she felt her face flushing with her anger.

She had chosen her name with purpose, as a warning she could be dangerous. 'Belladonna,' a poisonous flower, could enhance beauty or deliver death. She had been threatened before and was not afraid to prove her point or to face any adversary.

How had this intruder penetrated her defenses, with the ever-faithful but odorous Zancani supposedly keeping vigil? What would have happened if the intruder had succeeded in overwhelming her? The hood, which he had attempted to secure over her head, could have been a means to strangle her, or to subdue her, to carry her away?

She sheathed the dagger, banging it into its case. Her blood felt as if were boiling, and she stood, tense and silent by the bed, listening. Had anyone heard the scuffling? It would not be wise to alarm the maids, who would stir up rumors and speculation. In the morning, she would interrogate Zancani, her faithful bodyguard, and find out where he had been and how the intruder had gotten past him.

Belladonna arranged the curtains and the bedclothes so they would not betray what had happened. She hesitated before climbing into her bed, her skin prickling and her hands trembling, certain it would be difficult for her to fall asleep.

As she lay flat on her back, her eyes remained open.

She sighed and closed them, settling herself deep into the soft bedclothes. She imagined herself aboard Isaak's ship, in his arms, rocking to the soft lull of the sea.

Chapter Four: Belladonna

The ruby ring was the signal, and Belladonna heeded its message. The servants had been informed no guests were to be admitted tonight. She sat by a window overlooking the canal, her cloak nearby. She had dressed plainly, and the leather sack filled with her most treasured jewels lay nearby.

Across the dark glistening waters of the canal outside her window, a light appeared. It arced once, then after a pause, arced again. She rose, fastening the cloak around her, and grabbing her gloves and sack, exited her chamber. She took a last look at the salon, which had been cleaned and restored after the previous night's activities, and hoped she would return soon.

The curly-haired young man who had worn the ruby ring now helped her into the boat. Neither of them spoke as the oarsman steered towards the lagoon. The lights and songs of the gondoliers began to fade as the Grand Canal receded and the boat moved away from the main island to open water. In the dim light of the half moon, Belladonna could see the silhouette of a ship. In a short time, their boat was bumping against the sides of its mother ship.

They had lowered a rope with a sling of a seat, and though tucking herself and her skirts into it was annoying, it was preferable to climbing the rigging. With the assistance of the young man and the sailors above her, Belladonna was over the side and landed on the deck of a ship which was not unfamiliar to her.

The ship, sturdy and swift, rocking slightly against the motion of the tide, was orderly and quiet, though there were many men busy at their tasks. The curly-haired young man took her arm and navigated her through the crew to the captain's cabin.

After the door was opened to his knock, her guide disappeared, and she took a step through the threshold. Inside, it smelled faintly of smoke and leather.

The white of his teeth in the dim light was the first thing she noticed about Isaak, the man who once saved her life, but sailed out of it years ago.

"Isaak..." she murmured and fell into his arms.

"It has been so long," he spoke softly into her ear, pulling her into an embrace.

Isaak's breath was warm against her cheek, and with his hands running up and down her back, her resolve to hold back failed her. Neither of them spoke as, with eyes closed, they clung to each other as if they feared being torn apart.

Belladonna forced herself to push away from Isaak. Eyes locked on his, her fingers tenderly traced the line of his cheek to his jaw until stopping when they reached his lips.

Her breath quickened as his lips opened, but what he said was not what she wanted to hear. "You are in danger."

* * *

She took a seat on the bunk inset into dark wood cabinetry, her skirts covering the worn coverlet pulled taut across it. Placing the sack of jewels in her lap, she leaned back, twirling an escaped tendril of her tawny golden hair around one finger. As morning dawned, she imagined her maid discovering her empty bed, the clothes and shoes of her wardrobe tossed about in a frenzy. Aloud she said, "They will think I have been abducted."

Isaak poured himself a small glass of brandy and handed another to her, which she accepted. "Perhaps. Or maybe there will be a rumor you have suddenly departed for a secret rendezvous. Speculation will work in your favor, Raquel."

At the mention of her old name, a name she had not heard in more than a decade, a coldness ran through Belladonna. As 'Raquel,' she had been a powerless refugee when Isaak freed her, chained and bound to be sold as a slave, from a Berber pirate ship. As 'Belladonna,' she was far from powerless, and Isaak must understand why it pained her to identify herself by her former name.

"I am now known as 'Belladonna,'" she stated in a voice hoarse with emotion.

"I know you have not been 'Raquel' for many years," Isaak said calmly, "but now you must become her once more. Our enemies, the Spanish, have set their sights on the courtesan, Belladonna."

She bit her lip and then told him of the assassin's attempt the night before. Then she asked, "Why now?"

Isaak pulled her from the bed and gathered her into his arms. "Your past has come to Venice. I have important news for you. About your brother."

She pushed herself away from him. "My brother? How could you know anything of Roderigo? I had never spoken of him, not even to you."

"You told me you were from Jamaica, and on a visit to Recife in Brazil, your family was taken by the Inquisition."

Images flashed—momentarily illuminated from the darkness of buried memory—of worn leather boots trampling delicate flowers, petals scattering, tables of food overturned, plates and glass smashing into small pieces scattering across the ground. Her father shoved face down into the dirt, her mother grabbed by the hair. Cruel laughter, barked orders, the slash of whips and knives as blood flowed. Sweat beaded on her forehead, and her muscles tensed as she remembered struggling against hands restraining her.

Her face felt hot, and she fanned herself. A sudden wave of nausea overtook her, and she faltered in Isaak's arms. He managed to get her seated on the bunk, and she took deep breaths as her ears rang, and his words and face were blurring.

The world faded to black until she was conscious of a glass pressing on her lips, parting them. The sting of brandy burning its way down her throat revived her, and she found herself half in Isaak's arms.

She frowned, trying to sift through the memories of terror and grief. "It is very difficult for me to recall my time at Recife. I had gone with my parents to the wedding of my cousin… the soldiers came…I was with Roderigo when they took my parents away, but not us. We hid. He went to find a way…he told me to wait, but he never came back." She closed her eyes and shuddered. "I thought he had been caught and killed. I found a ship to take me away."

Isaak explained, "I had sailed to Jamaica upon orders from the Jewish Brethren of the Sea. My mission was to transport an envoy from the Jews of Jamaica to England. I found the envoy good company, and we shared our stories. The envoy spoke of the death of his family in Recife at the hands of the Inquisition, a story which reminded me of yours. I asked if he had a sister. He told me of how he and his sister, Raquel, were separated while fleeing the Spanish soldiers. He assumed the Inquisition had consigned you, along with your parents, to the flames. He had managed to board a ship departing to Jamaica, where he would be safe from the Inquisition. Where he has been safe until now."

Belladonna took a deep breath and gestured to Isaak to help her sit upright. As soon as she was seated, and placed a hand against her chest, feeling the rapid thumping of her heart. *Roderigo is alive!*

"Roderigo?" she said softly, her eyes misting. A name she had last uttered in the despair of never hearing or saying it again.

"Yes, your brother. Roderigo Mendoza," Isaak began, taking her hand and cradling it in his own, "He is the envoy from Jamaica. His mission is to appeal to the English, to prevent the Spanish from annexing Jamaica."

"But the Spanish already control Jamaica," said Belladonna, with a dismissive wave of her hand.

"Not so. When Christopher Columbus discovered the New World and claimed it for Spain, he had but one request: the island of Jamaica was to remain his personal domain, independent of Spanish rule. His request was granted by King Ferdinand. Jamaica has remained the province of heirs of Columbus, which has kept your brother and the other Jews of Jamaica safe from the Inquisition. Until now."

Belladonna raised her eyebrows. "What has changed?"

"The heirs of Columbus are weak and greedy. Jamaica is no longer a windswept island suitable only for pigs. Spanishtown has become the largest port of trade in the West Indies, and Jamaica is the gateway to all the riches of the Caribbean. The Spanish are offering pots of gold to the heirs to take over governance of the island. The Jews of Jamaica would suffer greatly if that were to happen."

"Are the English planning on annexing Jamaica?"

"The English are wary of engaging the Spanish in battle, especially if they are not assured of an easy victory. The offer of great riches and the promise of the inside support of the Jews on the island should diminish any hesitation of sending English forces to take over Jamaica."

Belladonna's brow furrowed. "And the Spanish have learned about the envoy's mission and, I presume, that Roderigo is the envoy to the English. What has Roderigo to offer?"

Isaak disengaged himself from her and rose to pour himself another brandy, tossing it quickly down his throat. Wiping his lips with the back of his hands, he coughed before speaking. "When Columbus anchored his ship at Jamaica, he fell ill with a strange fever that had already killed many of his men. The remaining men mutinied and attempted to take over Columbus's ship and take all the gold they had found in the New World. A dozen young men remained loyal to him, and although they were young and outnumbered, they defeated the mutineers. These young men were New Christians, secret Jews whose parents had sent their sons to the New World to keep them safe from the Inquisition. New Christians were easy to denounce as heretics, so their fortunes could be forfeited to the Inquisition."

"And how does this connect to my brother and his mission?"

"It was rumored that in gratitude for their loyalty, Columbus entrusted his gold to these young Jews and advised them to hide it. The secret of the treasure's whereabouts has been a well-kept secret of the descendants of the young Jews who settled in Jamaica. Your brother Roderigo, has been given a map that reveals the location of the treasure, and he was to use it as a bargaining chip to entice the English to Jamaica."

Belladonna tapped a finger to her chin. "I now understand how the Spanish are involved and their motive for attacking the envoy. But why have they turned their attention to me?" Having voiced the question, she realized the obvious answer. "Oh no, do they know of my relationship to Roderigo?"

Isaak's eyes held hers for a moment and then looked away, as if he were embarrassed about what he was about to say. "No, they do not know Roderigo is your brother. However, they do know the reason he left England for Venice –you. They assume you were lovers."

No wonder he could not meet her eyes. She coughed to prevent her from laughing at the absurdity of it. "And so, I am in danger. They assume, as an accomplished courtesan, that I am in possession of his secrets."

Isaak nodded, keeping his eyes on the one wall comprised almost completely of windows and a full view of the open sea, "I do not judge you for having found your path in life. It is better they do not know of your true relationship. There was an attempt on Roderigo's life in England, but a different man was killed. Roderigo's insistence that we set sail immediately for Venice saved him. If you assume your former identity as Raquel and stay in the Ghetto, you should be safe. They will never dream of looking for Belladonna there."

Her nostrils flared, and she said. "That is your plan? To have me hide in the Ghetto?" She jumped to her feet to confront him. "You knew me once as a helpless refugee, but now I am far more capable of taking care of myself. I have powerful friends—"

Black brows descended over eyes of sapphire as Isaak interrupted her. "Roderigo arrived in Venice; I had brought him here myself. But since he arrived, he has disappeared. He may be hiding. You will be in a better position to find him, with the help of my sister, from the Ghetto. I have already sent a message to her, and she is fully aware of this plan."

"Why?"

"Though Roderigo has come to find you, he knows the Spanish are after him, and he would feel safer among his own kind. There are many who open their homes to travelers, and there is always talk of new visitors who have arrived, especially one from the New World."

He seized her arms and the muscles in his neck were strained and taut as he brought his face close to hers. "Please, trust me. By staying in the Ghetto, you will not only be safe from the Spanish, but you will be able to find the clues to where Roderigo may be hiding."

The wood creaked and groaned as the floor beneath their feet shifted and tilted. Isaak released her and stood back. "The wind has changed. We must get underway soon, and you must go."

His eyes were following her as she reached for her sack. "You must not be recognized when you return to the city."

"Then I am in need of something to cover my hair."

Isaak opened a panel and pulled out a tumble of brightly colored cloth, which he tossed to her. Belladonna pursed her lips at its tattiness, but wound it around her head, making sure to cover every lock of her golden hair.

She patted her skirts and was reassured when her fingers found the shape of her special poison-tipped dagger. Belladonna was ready to depart, but before she could, Isaak pulled her back. Relaxing into his embrace, his mouth lowered on her own.

His kiss was tender and awakened the pit of emotion she had kept hidden for so long. It was just the same as the first kiss they had shared, on board this very same ship, on their way to Venice, when she had shared the story of her escape. His kiss had chased away the fear and sadness, had given her hope for the future and the belief all was not lost.

When he released her, he said, "Go to the Ghetto, and be welcomed by the Sullams once again, but this time as the widowed Jewess Raquel de Mendoza. My sister will help acclimate you to the ways of the Ghetto, and help you search for Roderigo."

On deck, the men scurried around, hoisting canvas and pulling ropes. He nodded towards a thickset man who held the rope seat for her. He looked towards the city and then back to Belladonna. "Be careful, and take no chances. Stay away from your usual friends and from your palazzo, and avoid going near anyone who might recognize you."

Chapter Five: Belladonna

The shadowy dark entrance to the Ghetto gaped before her. With the first rosy glimmers of early morning, the guards had pulled open the gates, then shuffled off as fast as their tired legs could carry them. Belladonna jumped as the cold of the canal water sloshing over the stones seeped into her flimsy leather slippers. The platform shoes she was accustomed to wearing were sorely missed. They had not only kept her dry, but made her taller and feel more powerful.

More sloshing of the canal waters—a boat approaching. A small flat barge loaded with barrels and hoisted nets passed close by, leaving a strong odor of fish in its wake. As she took small, hesitant steps into the shadowy entrance to the Ghetto, other smells and sounds assailed her. Chanting in a muddle of tunes and voices, the long-forgotten sounds of early morning prayers drifted out of the two synagogues facing each other on opposite sides of a small *campo*. She angled her way around the covered well at its center, puddles of water darkening the cobblestones around it. It seemed greyer and dimmer than she remembered, the tall buildings crowding out the sunlight. Then the yeasty but tantalizing smell of baking bread and the sweet scent of crispy biscuits tickled her nose and she inhaled appreciatively. Now passing the bakery, she headed towards the Sullam mansion, right before the bridge that led into the Ghetto Nuovo.

She paused momentarily before the brick façade of the chief rabbi's office. Should she go inside? Tell him she had just been with Isaak, his long-lost son? Ten years ago, when she had first arrived in the city, a young girl without family or friends, the rabbi had been the first person whom

22

she had turned to. The rabbi, not having the means to take in another in his small drab rooms, brought her to the home of the Sullams, who had graciously invited her to stay with them in their luxurious mansion. She had been awed by their wealth as well as their kindness and had tried to be the gracious daughter they hoped she would become. But she had greater ambitions that could only be fulfilled outside of the Ghetto. Though a Jew by heritage, Belladonna had determined she would never be a victim again. If she identified as a Jew, it would always make her vulnerable to persecution.

She became 'Belladonna' the most influential woman in Venice and the owner of one of the finest palazzos on the grand canal, with servants and a private gondola.

Now, she had played the role of Belladonna for so long she had forgotten who she once was. Raquel Mendoza, a *Converso*, had been baptized and brought up as a Christian, but was still vulnerable to the Inquisition, who could proclaim her, just as they had with her family, as secret Judaizers and heretics. Her parents had been consigned to the flames of an *auto-de-fe* in Recife, and she believed Roderigo had met the same fate. *But he was alive!* He had escaped, and so had she. Now she was seeking what she hoped was a temporary asylum, in the Ghetto of Venice.

Diana, Isaak's sister, and the rabbi's daughter, was the only person in Venice who had earned her full trust. Diana had proved her loyalty and her mettle when the two of them had survived the plots of the most powerful men of Venice while unmasking a murderer.

Without her high shoes, Belladonna could not reach the high window of the rabbi's study to see if he was inside. The rabbi could be at morning services by now, with his daughter Diana keeping her difficult and complaining mother occupied. Shrugging, Belladonna clutched her sack of valuables to her chest and urged herself forward.

She had been delaying facing her former benefactress, Sarra Coppio Sullam. The Sullams were one of the wealthiest families in the Ghetto, and they lived in an elegant mansion, rivaling many of the noble's palazzos on the Grand Canal. Sarra was a woman of refinement and beauty and had earned renown as a poetess and patron of the arts.

Ten years ago, Sarra had welcomed her, a refugee from the New World, sharing her books and her knowledge and encouraging her scholarship. Belladonna regretted she had repaid this kindness with betrayal and scorn. She knew little of the Hebrew faith, and it seemed strange to persist in maintaining a culture doomed to deliver only scorn and persecution. Her parents had not identified themselves as Jews but as Christians and the Inquisition had put them to death solely because of their heritage. When she had decided to depart the Sullams and leave the Ghetto, which had sheltered her, she had chosen to keep her heritage a secret to avoid her parents' fate.

When she knocked on the thick wooden door, she never expected it to be opened by the mistress of the house. The smile on Sarra's face was broad and welcoming as she ushered Belladonna into her home. There was no sign from Sarra that she was recognized.

"Mirabella, we have a guest," Sarra called out as she led Belladonna up the stairs to the *piano nobile*.

"Your servant does not answer your door for you?" Belladonna was not pleased to see the lack of control the mistress seemed to have over her staff.

"No doubt Mirabella is busy, and Eduardo must be taking inventory of our supplies. It really is no bother for me to see to the door myself." She lifted her lush green satin skirt slightly as she mounted each step.

The large reception hall was just as Belladonna remembered it; a high vaulted ceiling with medallions of gold, thick Belgian tapestries adorning the walls. It was as lavish as the palazzos of the patricians on the Grand Canal, save for the absence of family portraits that usually lined the walls. Portraiture was not wholly accepted by the people of the Ghetto, despite being championed by Rabbi Leone di Modena, Isaak's father. Recently, his daughter, Diana, had been the subject of a portrait by the famous Venetian artist, Mattia Correr. Though the rabbi was proud of his daughter's portrait, he had not revealed to anyone within his community that it now hung in the palazzo of the city's most celebrated courtesan, Belladonna.

Belladonna followed Sarra across the white and black tiles into the salon, settling herself, like the mistress of the house, in one of the plush crimson couches.

"Now, suppose we introduce ourselves?" Sarra gave her a bright but distracted smile. "I am Sarra Coppio Sullam."

Belladonna took a long deep breath, delaying to exhale, while Sarra awaited her response.

"You do not recognize me?" said Belladonna in a soft voice she hoped sounded more like her younger self. "Raquel de Mendoza, who sought refuge with you ten years ago, and now must beg your hospitality once again."

With a great deal of sniffing and gulped down sobs, Sarra rose from her chair awkwardly. She startled Belladonna when she threw her arms around her. "You have come back to us!"

Chapter Six: Diana

7th day of Cheshvan, 1612, from the journal of Leon di Modena

It is Cheshvan, the month after all the holidays are complete. 'Mar cheshvan' the bitter month. There are no more holidays, and the time for atonement is at an end. Therefore it is with some trepidation I write today, as the month draws to its close. The sound of the shofar has long faded away, its eerie wail sent to remind all Jews that it is our last chance to pray for mercy and an abatement of our suffering.

Venice is still filled with golden light, reflected in the canals, gilding the sun-bleached stone of the palazzo and making them even more impressive. But I wonder what fate has been decreed for me and my family. The prayers from Rosh Hashana still echo in my soul:

"Who will live and who will die

Whose life will be cut short, and whose life will be extended..."

Though there was no sound of the shofar, the ram's horn blown by the beadle early this morning, both she and her father had woken early as the sun rose. The rabbi had scurried out after grabbing his prayer shawl and book, leaving his journal open, with pen and ink atop of his last entry, and completely cluttering their one table. Diana could not resist reading her father's last entry as she closed the ink and wiped the pen. She put all of her father's things away and hoped to dispel the gloom that overtook her and seemed to arise from his writing.

Her father had relished the High Holidays, which had just concluded, but she had not. The long hours spent in the synagogue, supposedly engaged in prayer, but more often in deep retrospection, were a blessing to some, but a misery to others. Diana had attended with her father from the start of prayers to their conclusion, unlike most women, who usually only came to services to hear the blowing of the shofar.

Every year the shofar would herald a time to consider one's actions over the past year, to feel regret, and atone by asking forgiveness from both God and man for the transgressions. While her husband was alive, she had done so with all her heart. Since his death, she had less enthusiasm for repentance and less clarity about sin and what she ought to regret.

Were all of her actions of the past year to be categorized as 'sin'? As a scholar, she was familiar with the arguments of the great rabbis on the topic of sin and redemption, in which wrong-doing was divided between transgressions against one's fellow man and against the Almighty. Of the first category, she was guilty of impatience with her mother, who harangued and complained, but could be dealt with in a kindlier manner. As to her secret escapes from the Ghetto and her friendship with the notorious courtesan, Belladonna, she was less certain of categorizing it as a transgression. She could not believe it was sinful to take the opportunities offered to overcome the limitations imposed upon her, since she believed the Almighty must have had a hand in presenting them to her. Besides, it had revived her spirit, which had been sinking ever lower as the years passed and her memories of her dead husband, Yaakov, grew faint.

Sins between man and God were the challenge. The concept jarred with what she had learned; that the Almighty invites questions and expects doubts. The great philosopher, Moses Maimonides, posed the question, *who is the more righteous—one who carries out the requirements and good deeds without knowledge and without question, or one who seeks the rationale and understanding and faces continuous challenge to fulfill them?*

Maimonides' question had been debated by rabbis for centuries, and it had been one of her favorite topics to discuss with Yaakov. Though she had taken up residence with her parents out of necessity, it was some comfort to have her father to debate such questions and argue against or in favor of her actions.

The holidays this year, as in the last two, had ushered in waves of sadness—it was the time she missed her husband most. Yaakov had been a brilliant scholar, and his death had occurred during the last week of the Hebrew month of Elul. *Before* Yom Kippur, before God was to have made the final decisions of life or death. *Who will live, who will die, whose life will be shortened.* Why had God closed the book on Yaakov's poor life early, without considering her prayers for his recovery?

The holidays heightened her sense of Yaakov, like a hint of a delicate perfume, each time she recited the special Prayers for Remembrance during the services. The words stirred feelings of vulnerability and regret, the hope for a second chance. With Yaakov, it was of no use, and her pleas to the Almighty had been for naught.

On his deathbed, Yaakov's eyes had been sad but satisfied, as if he had finally been granted the understanding he had sought through all his years of study. She had not been angry when she held his hand and felt life depart. At that time, she felt God's mercy had provided a gentle escape to her unworldly husband. How Yaakov would have suffered if banishment or persecution were to fall upon the Jews of Venice!

Opening the door with bucket in hand, Diana felt the first chilling hint of a damp, cold winter. Thankfully, their rooms were warmer than usual now, since her father had stopped his incessant gambling, and they had enough money for firewood. The reserve fund of gold, which had been payment from the English lord for her portrait, was still safely tucked away in a hiding place secure from her father and his gambling. It had been a well-earned compensation, since that portrait had nearly been the death of her, as it had been for the many of other women of the artist Mattia Correr's 'gallery of beauties.' The gold and entry into Venetian society were Diana's rewards from the experience. Posing for her portrait had changed the course of her life for the better. She had been careful to maintain her traditions, so should her actions be considered transgressions that required atonement?

Philosophical thoughts plagued her as she joined other women gathered around the well in the vast courtyard of the Ghetto Nuovo. Their ages varied from little girls to the old women. Each waited for their turn to retrieve the water for their households. They chatted amiably, though occasionally shouted at the young boys who kicked stones into puddles to splash them while they waited in line.

When Diana was recognized, one woman offered Diana her place in line, out of respect for the rabbi's daughter. Diana smiled and declined, which earned her pleased nods from the others. Many in the Ghetto esteemed her father greatly, for he was known as an *Ilui*, or a genius in Talmud, and a great orator, who could bring the congregation to tears with his speeches. His writings, both in Hebrew, Italian, and English, had garnered him accolades and financial support from scholars and notables outside the Ghetto as well as among the *Gvririm*, the wealthy and influential within the Ghetto, such as the Sullams.

However, like her, Rabbi Leone di Modena embraced the new rationalism. They both believed life could be shaped by the course of one's actions and decisions, rather than to an immutable Fate possibly divined from kabbalistic signs.

Many in the Ghetto buried *kvitels,* prayer notes, beneath their doors, and dangled talisman such as *chamsas* from their windows to protect against evil spirits, rather than relying solely on the Divine protection of the *mezuzah* on the door posts. Rabbi Modena had spoken out against such practices, growing more popular in the Ghetto and therefore earning him criticism.

As she filled her bucket and began to lug it slowly back to their rooms, Diana resolved not to be filled with doubts about her forays out of the Ghetto or her friendship with the courtesan. Since her husband's death, she had been sleepwalking through chores and social interactions, awakening only to study the Torah her husband had loved.

Then the artist, Mattia Correr had stepped into her life and told her she was beautiful. He had selected her to be painted among the twelve most beautiful women in Venice for a portrait gallery for a visiting English lord. Mattia had introduced her to the courtesan Belladonna, and to the

29

glittering Venetian society, allowing her to shed the final cloth of mourning for Yaakov.

When she thought of Mattia, she felt a quivering inside. There was no doubt he had awakened feelings she had missed in the three long years since Yaakov's death. As she placed her fingers to her lips to kiss the *mezuzah* at the entry to her dimly lit rooms, it awakened her memory of the artist's kiss at their first sitting for her portrait. She had nearly succumbed to a strange desire for him, but today, she was glad she had not. The pairing of a Jew with a non-Jew was prohibited by Venetian law and could have resulted in her imprisonment in the dreaded dungeons of the *Pozzi*, in the nether regions of the Doge's palace.

Though she continued to be interested in Mattia and his art, at the completion of her portrait, Mattia seemed to have lost his romantic interest in *her*. For Mattia, the women he loved existed solely on canvas.

Diana had one mirror in the little alcove which served as her room. A silver backed hand-mirror, a gift from Belladonna, along with a beautifully fashioned skirt and bodice, which the courtesan deemed necessary for Diana's appearances in her salon. The garments were lain over the footboard of her bedstead and were also worn to the synagogue on the Sabbath and holidays. She smiled at the contrast.

Diana opened the shutters by her bed to let in more light and picked up the mirror so she could see how she appeared in its glass. Her skin was clear, and her cheeks were rosy from the chill of the morning. Blinking her dark lashed eyes several times, Diana smoothed down her rich black hair. Did she look the same as she did in Mattia's portrait? Did she still possess the aura of calm, self-assuredness of her painted image?

Chapter Seven: Belladonna

Belladonna suspected the surly maid, Mirabella, would be in the crockery, scooping up foodstuffs she could stash to be sold later in the market when the pounding on the front door was ignored. It was appalling how the maid did not bother to answer it, knowing her master was not home to chastise her, and her mistress would open the door without sending any criticism in her direction.

Sarra kept calling for Mirabella, and finally, the maidservant appeared. Giving Belladonna a once-over, from her sodden shoes to the tumble of tattered cloth wound about her head, Belladonna could see the smugness in the set of the maid's mouth, as she assumed Sarra's visitor was of no account and would treat her accordingly.

"Mirabella, please bring some refreshment for our guest." Sarra barely looked at her servant, so did not see the maid's disdainful expression. "This is my cousin, Raquel, who has returned after a long absence. Some wine, please. Would you fetch it?"

Belladonna pulled off the scarf and let her unbound golden hair tumble down her back. Only a woman of distinction, who had the time and the balcony to bask for hours in the sun, so her hair could absorb its golden rays, could achieve this color.

She gave Mirabella a sharp look and responded with a polite yet barbed order. "Yes, please, bring some wine. Not too difficult for you, is it?"

At least Sarra had introduced her as a visiting family member, someone notable from some other Hebrew community. Belladonna wanted Mirabella to feel the sharpness of her gaze to convey the message that her surliness and dereliction of duty must now come to an end.

Mirabella hunched her shoulders and lowered her head, as if she were cowered by her words, but Belladonna would not be fooled. She had caught the maid's covetous look at the leather sack that held her belongings, before the woman departed.

* * *

"You do not ask where I have been these many years?" Belladonna's fingers toyed with the top of the leather sack after the maid's retreat. "Have no fear, I will not refer to it, and neither should you—for your safety and mine."

"What is it? What is wrong?" Sarra asked.

"My brother survived the Inquisition and has come to Venice."

Sarra's pale eyebrows raised almost to the edge of her satin turban. "That is marvelous news! I am so happy for you," she clapped her hands in her excitement.

"His reappearance has brought danger," Belladonna said, leaning closer to her hostess and keeping her voice low, "he is the bearer of a great secret and has powerful enemies who seek to discover it."

Sarra was no fool and asked, "Is he in hiding in the Ghetto? Is this why you have returned?"

"It is known my brother came to Venice looking for me, and so these powerful men are after me as well. Isaak thought it best if I stayed in the Ghetto with you."

Sarra sighed and looked towards the open window. "Isaak. There is a saying, *if you have not discovered your purpose in life, what kind of life are you living?* Isaak has his purpose of rescuing our people from captivity, and you are the proof of its worthiness." Her eyes were warm as she looked into Belladonna's. "If he has sent you to us, I am certain there is great good to come of it to our people."

Belladonna leaned back and noticed the maid had returned with a tray and a carafe of wine. The woman's shifty eyes glanced too frequently at the sack of jewels. *Not one to be trusted, a woman who could prove dangerous if she overheard too much.*

Changing the subject, Belladonna spoke to Sarra like the long-lost cousin she was pretending to be. "How is Jacob? Is he in Venice now, or abroad?"

Sarra beckoned to Mirabella, who poured wine into two gold-rimmed glasses, and then sinking into her seat without taking a sip, she placed a hand across her forehead. Sarra moaned, "Oh, I cannot face Jacob now. Something terrible has happened. I do not have the courage to tell him of it."

"Tell me what is troubling you," Belladonna asked.

"My brooch, the one Jacob gave me at our betrothal. It is missing. I must have pinned it to one of my dresses and lost it."

"When did you last recall seeing it?"

Sarra furrowed her pale brows and tapped a finger to her lips as she searched recent memory. "I believe it was last Sabbath. It had to be, since the only day I would wear it would be Sabbath, or it would be in its box in my dressing room."

Her breast swelling with anger, Belladonna struggled to keep her voice calm as she raised her suspicions to Sarra. "What about Mirabella?"

Sarra's eyebrows settled back in place. "Of course, how silly of me. I shall call her back and ask her to search for it."

Belladonna held up her hand. "No, Sarra, let me deal with this. Rest assured, I shall find it—with Mirabella's help, of course," Belladonna's fists clenched, with a good suspicion of with whom the brooch would be found. She would not be surprised if Sarra's servants sold silver objects engraved with the Sullam name in the marketplace.

Belladonna sipped the wine, keeping her eyes on the maid's face. *Sarra is a terrible judge of character.* Sarra, did not consider her maid capable of any misdeeds, but from Mirabella's frequent looks at her own sack of jewels, Belladonna suspected the maid of having stolen the brooch.

Mirabella's face was bland of expression, even though she was listening to the discussion of the missing brooch. *Cold and calculating, easily capable of villainy and deceit,* was Belladonna's assessment of the woman. She now had the opportunity to repay Sarra's kindness by protecting her from this

33

servant's dishonesty.

Belladonna's eyes met Mirabella's. A moment of understanding flashed between them, and the maid momentarily lost her grip on the tray, and it nearly fell to the floor. Belladonna dismissed the maid with a wave of her hand. At first the woman did not seem as if she would obey her, but after a few more seconds of Belladonna's deathly stare, Mirabella departed.

Chapter Eight: Antonio

The warmth of the day had been hidden away, and the night brought a crisp chill and a misty fog to swirl and caress the figure in the shadows. Antonio was a patient man and had spent many nights standing in cold worse than this and in much less comfortable clothes, but enough was enough. There would be other nights and other places to skewer the Englishman, and after the events of the past few nights, he ought to merit a rest.

He turned the blade he held and ran a gloved finger along its edge until he was satisfied by the clean slice it made through the leather. A cat whined nearby, and with a whoosh the knife shot out in its direction, clattering to the cobblestones as the cat meowed again, but from a different direction.

Antonio chuckled as he collected his blade. He did not like the cats, but admired their instinct for self-preservation, a trait he found lacking in too many humans. Dare he leave his post by the gambling den? The English nobleman was likely to spend his first night and his last dollar either at the gaming tables or with a whore. This was the same man who had witnessed the conflagration of the cloak and the expiration of the Venetian ambassador. It should have served as a warning to him—if he continued to pursue the envoy, he would be the next candidate for Death.

Antonio had gathered enough intelligence about the English nobleman to know he was desperate for cash, and the lure of the gaming tables and its promise of a quick return on the investment should prove irresistible to such a fellow. Which is precisely why Antonio had decided to keep vigilance by the Monte Carlo rooms, where the stakes were high, and foreigners were welcomed.

As he leaned against the cold, damp wall, he imagined himself back on the mainland, his feet up before a blazing fire, a tankard of wine at hand. Neither the Spy Master nor Di Ribera knew he owned a house and land near Venice, in a place he had chosen for his retirement. No more soldiering for him, and if they tried to call him back to Spain, he would disappear. Orders and assignments from Madrid did not always merit a confirmation of success, which had led him to a lucrative business. When Spain ordered him to kill or kidnap, he allowed the subject to make a counteroffer. The poor soul always paid up, and he was clever enough to find a subterfuge that would allow him to collect his official commission as well.

Antonio's boots, a source of great pride, were recently made, and expensive and now splattered with mud and dung. He hated nights like this one, where no such bargaining could be made, and he would have to sully a recently sharpened blade. This Englishman was too well known and too great an enemy of Spain to create a charade around this killing. Antonio never asked why a man merited killing, and he did not care. It was the job of a soldier to execute his orders, especially when so much gold was offered in payment. He had done his best on the battlefields of Flanders, and he would continue to do so in the narrow calles of Venice.

Brandishing his blade, he bent over to scrape some of the caked mud from the heel of one boot. When he resumed his position, he was startled to see Villiers approaching, illuminated in the light of the torches outside the gambling den. The man strode with a jaunty gait, so Antonio assumed the Englishman had done well at the tables. Antonio's mouth stretched into a wide smile as he readied his blade to take this man's winnings along with his life.

The Englishman kept a gloved hand on the sword on his left side, so Antonio's plan was to approach from behind as Villiers passed by him. A thrust of the blade, a shove into the canal, and using quick fingers, he could remove the pouch dangling from the Englishman's belt before he sank into oblivion.

Antonio gave a small salute as the Englishman passed by, but the nobleman did not acknowledge him. He continued to follow Villiers from a few paces behind him, biding the time for his attack until the Englishman was midway across the bridge. It would be easy to overtake the Englishman, and with a few swift moves, it would be over. The direction not to kill only applied to the envoy or his lover, Belladonna, but he had been given no such limitations in reference to the Englishman. Besides, Antonio had always hated the English, so the pleasure would be all his.

A few steps more, and he would be close enough. Under the cover of his short cloak, the knife was poised for death. There was a soft whoosh as it hit home, and the man in front of him fell to his knees. Too bad this bridge was one of the few with a railing, which the stricken man grabbed and held. Antonio intended to take the man's purse, pry him loose and shove him into the canal, but was interrupted by another figure on the bridge, who was fast approaching.

Unable to retrieve either his knife or the purse, Antonio ran, cursing his bad luck.

Glancing back to the wooden railing of the bridge, Antonio saw his victim use his last ounce of strength to fall into the other man's arms.

Chapter Nine: Villiers

Villiers's hand clutched at his side to keep his life's blood from leaving him. He had not seen the face of the attacker, but due to his well-tested survival instinct, he had turned in time to deflect the blade's aim at his heart. The ornate scabbard and his expensive sword were still slapping against his thigh, and the pouch of coins still jangled at his belt, so the primary goal of the attack had not been to rob him, but simply to kill him.

Villiers knew his good luck from the gaming tables was still with him when this Good Samaritan appeared in time. Throwing himself into the other man's arms, his fingers clung to the fine velvet of his savior's doublet as light-headedness, and then nausea overtook him. His last thought was of his new cloak and his regret it would be sullied if he fell with it into the filth beneath his feet.

* * *

When Villiers regained his senses, his first sensation was pain.

"Impressive. You are lucky it was not dipped in poison, as is the custom of Venetian assassins," said the Good Samaritan, holding up the stiletto to show him. Long honey-colored hair rippled across the shoulders of an unadorned black velvet doublet. Though he looked like a craftsman, the fellow spoke like a gentleman.

I am in Venice. In a sudden flash, he remembered the gondola taking him to a well-known gambling house and the footsteps behind him as he left it. How foolish he had been, thinking he was free of enemies outside of England.

"Damn those Spaniards!" Villiers snarled, and his hands immediately went to feel his wound. At the look of puzzlement on the other's face, he explained, "That stiletto's hilt had the distinctive design of Toledo."

"This will cause you more pain, I'm afraid." A dark-haired woman dressed unfashionably in grey turned towards him from the hearth. He blinked multiple times in quick succession at the flat-bladed knife which she held up and flashed in the candlelight and at the startling beauty of her face.

Villiers pulled backed from both the beauty and the blade, but he was held firmly in place by his benefactor. The woman lowered the heated blade to sear his wound. He gave a howl at the pain, until the beauty applied a cooling salve and wrapped his chest in linen. Villiers sighed and resigned his head to the cushions beneath him.

The long-haired man grinned at him. "Lucky for you, I won tonight, and I am feeling generous and benevolent. Had I lost," he waved a hand, "I would probably have stepped away from you on that bridge."

"Do not talk so, Mattia; you know you would never do such a thing," said the lovely lady, her dark-lashed, violet-blue eyes searching Villiers's face. Her brows were furrowed, and he was pleased at the sign of her concern for him. It was then he realized that she spoke in English.

"How did you know I was English?"

"Your curses, quite loud and eloquent, gave you away," answered Mattia.

"How do you know my language?" He struggled to his elbows to examine his benefactors more closely. "Do you know who I am?"

George Villiers was not a cautious man but a suspicious one, and his survival thus far was due to his vigilance in detecting his enemies before they struck a fatal blow.

The two looked at each other and then back at him. Eyebrows raised, the gentleman asked, "Should we?"

Villiers leaned back and stared at the ceiling. His cloak and doublet lay crumpled on the floor. His papers lay inside, he supposed, undisturbed.

"I am George Villiers, of the court of His Majesty King James of England, recently arrived in your city."

"Mattia Correr, artist, and portraitist," his long-haired savior gave a slight bow. "Welcome to my studio, in the Cannaregio section of Venice."

His beautiful companion lowered her eyes, but did not make her own introduction. Ignoring him, she turned to the artist and said, "It is late, and the gates will soon shut..."

The artist reached into his doublet and retrieved a few coins, which he placed in her hand.

"Thank you for coming so quickly, Diana."

With a quick glance back at the artist, she gathered up a cloth bag filled with what seemed to be paraphernalia of a medic and departed. The two men looked after her, but she did not look back.

Mattia wandered to a sideboard, returning with a bottle of dark purple wine and two unmatched glasses. Gratefully, Villiers took one of them and watched with fascination as the artist filled it with the rich-looking wine.

"You are not the first Englishman I have entertained," he said, after pulling over a chair and sitting astride it near Villiers' couch. "I had a commission from an English lord, just last year, a Lord Arundel. Do you know him?"

He looked expectantly at Villiers, waiting for acknowledgment of the acquaintance, ready to launch into the tale of their comradery. Villiers had no desire to hear the story, having heard it to utter boredom from Arundel himself in London. Ignoring Mattia's question, one arm reached for the back of the couch, as he struggled to raise himself, wincing at the pain it caused him. "Take me to the English ambassador. He must be advised of what has occurred."

"Wait, my friend, you must rest," said Mattia, coming to Villiers' side and forcing him to lie back. "I know Sir Henry well, and it is very late. He will not be appreciative of anyone interrupting his sleep. You should stay at least until morning. Agreed?"

Villiers sighed, and his arm fell back to his side. He did not have the strength to argue. Instead, his eyes roamed the room to get an appreciation of his surroundings. Always need to assess what weapons were at hand, the location of the nearest exit, and a secondary avenue of retreat. A large easel stood a few yards away, and upon it, an expanse of framed canvas, creating the impression of a mast and sail of a sea-faring vessel. It appeared the studio had been made out of the grand salon, with furniture replaced by a clutter of jars, fabrics, and rectangles of canvases propped against the walls.

"What are you painting?" Villiers raised an eyebrow.

His benefactor grinned. "A portrait of a beautiful woman."

"Diana?" Villiers had to ask.

The artist raised an eyebrow, and his eyes traveled towards the exit. "She is a great beauty, I grant you, but her portrait is already complete. I am now trying to finish this portrait of a most famous courtesan. It was a devil of a time to get her to pose for me, but now, just as it is nearly complete, the woman has vanished."

Villiers winced as he raised himself onto one elbow, intrigued. "What do you mean?"

Mattia flicked his hair away from his shoulders and sipped his wine. "Two days ago, she presided over her salon, as regal as a princess, and today, when I went to call upon her, she was gone. None of her servants had knowledge of a pending departure, and there was a great deal of hand-wringing over the lack of any direction or an inkling of what was to become of them."

The disappearance stirred his imagination, since the courtesans of Venice were notorious for their amorous skills and unrivaled beauty. "Is it unlikely to assume this courtesan had been taken away by a besotted lover who wanted to keep her charms exclusive to himself?"

Mattia shook his head. "Not Belladonna. No one would dare. If she has disappeared, it is because she has decided to do so."

Villiers winced again as pain shot through his arm as he reached out to Mattia for help in raising himself to a sitting position. *Belladonna.* The same name on a dying man's lips. She was the woman who held the key to the treasure he was seeking.

"A shame," he said, trying to sound casual, "I had been looking forward to meeting a famous courtesan on this trip, and I am sorry I will be denied the pleasure of meeting this one. What do you think became of her?"

Mattia Correr downed the last of his wine and put the glass down with a thunk. "Now that I think of it, there is one person who might know where Belladonna might be, but she has just departed."

Chapter Ten: Belladonna

Mirabella was in the pantry, just as she suspected, with her back to Belladonna.

"I require your help, Mirabella."

The maid sniffed when she turned, her hands hiding something behind her back. "And who do you think you be, that I should be taking orders from you?"

"Raquel Vasquez, a cousin of your mistress, and certainly your better." Belladonna faced her adversary with arms folded across her chest and a scowl on her face. She could demand the maid display what she held in those hands behind her back, but there were bigger issues to attend to.

"What do you want of me?" Mirabella picked at her collar while shifting her eyes away from Belladonna.

Belladonna's voice was cold with her intention to convey an order that brooked no refusal. "Show me to your mistress's chamber, where I am certain you will help me search for the missing brooch."

Left with no choice, Mirabella could make no argument and gestured to Belladonna to lead the way. The two of them trudged up the stairs, one filled with trepidation, the other with anticipation. Belladonna expected the maid to give her more trouble in Sarra's bedchamber, but was confident they would find the brooch.

No doubt the maid would claim Sarra had missed it, in whatever drawer or crevice they would be lucky enough to find it. Belladonna only hoped the brooch had not already been sent to the pawnbrokers and that it was still in the house.

Belladonna pushed open the heavy wooden door of Sarra's bedchamber. The walls and hangings around the bed were a deep red, and the curtains had not been opened wide enough to illuminate the room with the cold morning light, so the room was dim and gloomy. Mirabella led the way to a door inset in the wall beside the headboard, the entrance to Sarra's small dressing room.

A bright chaos of clothing, shoes, and turbans greeted her eyes. Mirabella pretended all was in order since it was her task to keep it tidy.

"Well, here we are," Mirabella announced, leaning against the door and planting her hands on her hips. "What is it you are making such a bother about and upsetting the mistress?"

Belladonna's nostrils flared, momentarily, and her face flushed. Taking a deep breath, she took a good minute or two before releasing it. She leaned against a cupboard nearly bursting with the tumble of clothes leaking from inside, and held out her hand, palm up.

"If you place your mistress's brooch in my hand in the next few minutes, I will not demand to have you immediately sacked."

Now it was Mirabella's turn to gape, and her mouth dropped open but she was quick to parry the accusation with a loud protest. "You are accusing me of theft!"

"Just restore the brooch from wherever you can *imagine* it has been misplaced," said Belladonna, pointing again to her open palm. "If you want to put this matter to rest."

Mirabella glared and tapped her toe purposely at the noisy floorboards beneath her feet. Then she swiveled on her heel and stomped out of the dressing room. Belladonna would not follow her up to her small attic room, nor watch her as she searched among her stash in the mattress.

When Mirabella returned with the brooch several minutes later, she stabbed Belladonna's open palm with its pin as she placed it there.

Belladonna flinched at the pain, but ignoring the small spot of blood, she closed her fingers around the brooch. "Excellent!" she said, "Sarra will be most relieved."

Before the maid exited the wardrobe, Belladonna called her back, pointing with her unaffected hand to the many shelves that were in turmoil. "You might also take a few moments to put this room in order."

Mirabella bowed her head slightly in response. Belladonna knew how the worst type of servant could pretend to be compliant while their behavior was adamantly defiant. Nevertheless, she had achieved her aim. The brooch had been found, and Mirabella had been forced to accept she must obey her new mistress's orders.

This woman spelled trouble; Belladonna was certain. Such a woman was like a cancer in the household, spreading disrespect and disgruntlement until the entire staff would have to be dismissed and a new staff hired to replace them.

Though Belladonna could understand a servant's ambition to amass enough gold to ensure a life free from starvation, she detested dishonesty and encouraged a forthright request for money to pay a creditor or to stave off poverty, if dismissed. Mirabella's attitude betrayed the contempt and disloyalty she had for her employers. With such brazenness, Belladonna imagined Mirabella had stolen enough to have built a comfortable nest egg for when she left the Sullam's employ.

Mirabella had relied on Jacob's absences and Sarra's lack of worldliness to get away with her acts of theft and defiance. Belladonna would have to catch the maid in the act of theft to convince the Sullams to dismiss her. For that, she had a plan.

Chapter Eleven: Belladonna

Belladonna sighed and smoothed the front of the dark blue dress which Sarra had ordered for her. It was to be her Sabbath dress, worn once a week or only for special holidays, styled with abundant white lace around its bodice and adorned with bows of black satin ribbon. The Sullam's mansion did not have as many mirrored walls as her own, so she had to rely on a large gilt mirror hanging over the washing stand to see if the dress suited her. Grimacing at her image, she patted her hair, which looked messy and unkempt because Mirabella was not adept at styling.

Tonight, she would be accompanying Sarra and Jacob to the Spanish synagogue to hear a lecture from Diana's father, Rabbi Leone di Modena. She had decided to attend so she might learn more of the ways of the Ghetto, but before this evening, she was relying on Diana to initiate her, so she would not make any glaring mistakes.

When Belladonna had first met Diana, the young woman had to hide her origins to gain entry into Venetian society, and Belladonna had guided her, protected her. Now the tables had turned, and it was Belladonna who needed Diana's help. She had not been in the Ghetto for many years and did not remember the customs or the rules.

Now, entering the rabbi's office, cluttered with books and scrolls, Diana's tutorial began.

"On the Sabbath, we refrain from any type of activity which is considered work—cooking, kindling a light, or drawing water from the well. We do not write, or carry money, or cut or tear cloth—anything associated with commerce or our usual employment."

"What *can* you do?"

Diana smiled, "We can spend time with our family. At the Sabbath meal, which has been cooked in advance and kept warm on the hearth or in the ovens of the bakeries. Men, women, and children dress in their very best clothes, and the men go to the synagogue to pray while the women cluster together with the children and gossip."

Belladonna raised an eyebrow. "I cannot imagine you gossiping. Nor Sarra."

Diana smiled, but continued, "Or we can indulge our minds by reading or studying the Talmud or the many books of the Torah. It is a respite from the world around us, a temporary escape from the pressing needs and burdens that oppress us."

Belladonna nodded. "I can well appreciate those benefits."

Diana sighed and looked down at her hands, rough-looking in comparison to Belladonna's. "Sarra and I are grateful of the Sabbath, for it gives us more time for study. Since Sarra and I are both childless, we have little need to congregate in the square, where the main purpose is to bring the children together for play."

"It must make the day seem overly long," said Belladonna, twisting the end of her hair. Her fingers ached to feel the smoothness of the pearls she usually wore. The pearls were a talisman and a means to help focus her thoughts.

Diana shook her head. "You shall see. The Sabbath is a peaceful day, and as complicated as life becomes, the more I appreciate it. But I must show you how to make the blessing over the candles; it is one of the tasks specific to women and how we usher in the Sabbath."

An image of a woman lighting candles, a lacy covering over her head, came to mind. A memory buried for so many years, she could not remember who it was. It was not her mother; of that, she was certain. Her mother had embraced Christianity and never engaged in any Jewish customs. Ironically, being a good Christian had not saved her from the condemnation of the Inquisitors in Recife.

She shared none of these thoughts with Diana as she watched her friend waving her hands above the candle she had set on the desk, her eyes closed as she chanted Hebrew words. Diana opened one eye and asked, "Are you following?"

Belladonna frowned. It was a challenge to remember the strange words and to mimic some of the guttural sounds. Diana sighed, no doubt realizing it would be too difficult for Belladonna to grasp, and offered an alternative. "Never mind. You can just mumble to yourself as you wave your hands and close your eyes, and no one will know the difference."

The tutorial came to an abrupt end when the rabbi crashed through the door, tumbling a tower of books in his path. He began to pull out the drawers one by one, picking through them, not seeing what he needed, and then banging them shut.

"What are you looking for?" asked his daughter.

"Willow bark. The *chazzan* complains of pain in his head and that he will not be able to lead the prayers. So close to the Sabbath, and I cannot find a replacement for tonight. So, I promised to bring him a remedy." Another drawer banged shut, and a squeak as another drawer opened.

"Ahhh, here it is. I must go to him."

He held up a small leather pouch and hurried towards the door. Belladonna was directly in his path, and he stopped suddenly as he noticed her. "Wh-what are you doing here?"

His tone was ungracious, and it stung. Unlike the Sullams, it was evident the rabbi had recognized her. "Isaak sent me."

There was smug satisfaction in speaking of Isaak, the son who had left him. Though father and son had not spoken in years, she knew the rabbi did not like to be reminded of the relationship she had with his son.

"Why?"

"To find my brother and to avoid being abducted by the Spanish."

Belladonna allowed Diana to explain, folding her arms.

"So, you bring danger to our door once again," the rabbi said after he had heard the entire story.

"You should not be disconcerted by risk. After all, you are a gambler."

Her barb had hit home, and the rabbi scowled at her. The rabbi was addicted to gambling and had nearly lost his position and his home because of it.

Diana stepped between them, ever practical, to remind them of the matter at hand. "Father, you have never shirked aid to anyone who has come to our door seeking it. Nor have you been afraid of any challenge, no matter how much danger was involved. You have stood up to the Council of Ten and do not tremble at the sight of the Men in Dark Cloaks. Raquel needs our help to find her brother before the Spanish. Isaak has dedicated his life to rescuing Jews from Spanish captivity, and he needs us now to save the Jews of Jamaica."

"The Spanish will not think of searching for me here," added Belladonna, hoping to reassure the rabbi.

The rabbi's brows flattened, and the fingers pulling at his beard relaxed. "You are staying with the Sullams. Had they recognized you? Do they know of anything of the envoy or his secret?"

Belladonna shook her head.

"That is good. Be careful with their servants, who take advantage of them. Any information that comes to their ears, they will be eager to peddle. What do you need from me?"

Diana spoke up. "Isaak mentioned an English lord who was supposed to meet with Roderigo, a powerful man who has the ear of the king. Upon his arrival in Venice, the English lord was attacked by a Spanish assassin and nearly killed, but for the fortuitous intervention by the artist Mattia Correr. I was called in to attend to his wounds, and they were not life-threatening. As soon as he recovers, it is more than likely he will wish to move to the residence of the English ambassador."

Sir Henry Wotton, the English ambassador to Venice, was a patron and friend of the rabbi, who often attended his lectures in the Ghetto. Rabbi Modena stroked his beard, nodding. "So, you wish me to contact Sir Henry about this English lord. What should I tell him?"

Belladonna preempted Diana's response. "You must reassure the English we have the map, and therefore the means to get to the treasure."

The rabbi brows furrowed as he uttered an "Oy". Rubbing his eyes, he added, "Mentioning 'treasure' is a certain path to trouble."

"It is our only course," said Diana, placing a comforting hand on his shoulder. "We have to dangle the promise of treasure to keep the English interested. Otherwise, Jamaica will fall to the Spanish, and all the Jews there will be subject to the Inquisition."

The rabbi looked from his daughter to Belladonna, before he departed. "I will do what I can. May the Lord aid us in our endeavors."

Chapter Twelve: Belladonna

B elladonna followed the sea of brightly colored dresses of the women entering the synagogue, her eyes peeled for the dark hair and graceful profile of Diana. Angling her way through the throng, she finally located the rabbi's daughter, climbing the long flight of stairs to the women's section on the next floor.

The grills had been pulled up to enable the women to gaze down unimpeded at the speaker in the men's section below. Belladonna took her place beside Sarra, and hoped Diana would find her.

"Sarra!" Diana leaned to embrace her, pretending, for the sake of the other women who were listening, to be surprised to see Belladonna. "I see you have a guest."

Sarra adjusted her turban and made the introduction for the sake of the listeners. "My cousin, Raquel di Mendoza, from Livorno. Raquel, this is Diana, the rabbi's daughter."

Belladonna inclined her head towards Diana, "After the death of my husband, I felt so alone, and I appealed to my cousin Sarra, who kindly offered to take me in." She made sure to speak in a loud enough voice so all the eavesdroppers would hear it.

"Alas, we are women who share a similar fate since I, too, am a widow. I hope to be your friend while you are in the Ghetto, so you shall feel welcome and at home."

Belladonna inclined her head. "I appreciate your guidance."

"I do not believe you have heard my father's orations before."

"I have not, but there are many I know who have quoted his speeches. I am most interested to hear what he has to say," Belladonna said as Diana took the seat beside her. Together, they leaned forward over the top of the balcony to look at the sanctuary below.

A sea of yellow hats were clustered around a round podium directly below them. It was evident to her that the men in the yellow hats were men of importance. Yellow hats bobbed as men surged in, shook hands, and found their places.

How odd, they wear their yellow hats here as a symbol of authority and importance, while outside of the Ghetto, it is used as a mark of disdain. The yellow hats parted as a man in a black hat strode forward purposely to the podium. Leone di Modena, the chief rabbi of the Jewish ghetto, the father of the two people in the world she trusted most, Isaak and Diana. Though she knew him well and attended a performance of one of his plays, she had never heard one of his sermons, but had high expectations. Despite being devotedly religious, the rabbi was a rationalist, and she appreciated the sharpness of his thinking.

As if reading her mind, Diana whispered, "He will be speaking about atonement, of a return to righteousness."

Belladonna arched one eyebrow and whispered back, "I assume he will speak in Italian since I see there are nobles and churchmen in attendance."

Diana continued to speak in a low voice. "The sermons are usually in Italian, at the request of the community, despite the complaints of some of the more strictly religious, who believe they should only be in Hebrew. Of course, they also object to having Gentiles in a place of prayer."

The men below were taking their seats, and only one red hat remained on the podium along with the rabbi. As soon as he raised his hand, the hum of conversation instantly stopped among the men and the women above.

"Good afternoon, and welcome to all our members and our notable guests," the leader began. "It is a special time for us in the Ghetto, after the high holidays. Now we hope our prayers for forgiveness were heard and we will be granted a good year. With this in mind, Rabbi Leone di Modena will speak to you." He concluded his introduction with a wave of his hand, descending the few steps and leaving the rabbi alone on the podium.

The rabbi looked every one of his fifty years, though his lined face was animated with excitement, and he stood erect at the podium. His voice was strong and bold, and Belladonna was glad of it, so she could catch every word, though she was seated so far away from him.

"Atonement. Making 'good' of our sins. Returning to the path of righteousness. Asking the Almighty for forgiveness, for 'another chance'. To change our destiny over the next year from one of sorrow into success. How do we do this?"

There was a dramatic pause, and the rabbi rocked back on his heels as he raised his eyes to the balcony and adjusted his hat.

"First, we must admit to ourselves we have done wrong instead of attempting to justify our wrongdoing. If God, as judge, will deliver His judgment and a punishment to fit the crime, then we are doomed from the moment we have committed those crimes. If we have acknowledged wrongdoing and merit punishment, what good is begging forgiveness? What's done is done, is it not?"

The rabbi's rhetorical question was met with silence. There were no sounds of feet shuffling in the pews, nor coughs or throat clearings while waiting for the rabbi to continue. Even Belladonna did not shift in her seat and found she was leaning over the balcony to make sure she caught the rabbi's every word.

"But God has given something special to Man: the power to repent—the ability to change his behavior from bad to good—thereby changing himself, *so he is no longer the man who deserves punishment.* Once a man admits to himself he has done wrong, regrets and repents his former actions, and is determined to no longer act in that poor fashion, then… he is no longer the same man he was before."

The rabbi paused and took a deep breath before continuing, "It is like the man who vows to stop indulging himself in excesses of food and wine. In time, and with the determination to stay loyal to his vows, he loses his corpulence, and his clothes no longer fit him. He is thinner, a different man and a new suit of clothes must be fitted to him."

The rabbi rocked back and forth on his heels and closed his eyes for a moment. He wiped a hand across his lower face, pulling on his beard, and then said, "So, when a man recognizes his sins, is truly sorry for committing them, and changes his behavior, he becomes a different person, with his former destiny no longer fitting him."

Another dramatic pause and the rabbi adjusted his black peaked hat.

Belladonna admired the rabbi's skill in holding his audience rapt. He cast a look over his shoulder at the curtained ark that contained the Torah, on the far side of the room. The rabbi now looked tired, as if he was fading as his speech was coming to an end.

Another deep sigh. "After the sin of the Golden Calf, after Moses had shattered the tablets in anger for what they had done, the Children of Israel truly repented—as if their act of idolatry was a temporary madness. Now that they were ready and committed to achieving a greater level of connection to the Almighty, they were completely different from the people who had committed the atrocity of the Golden Calf. They had changed. And so, like the clothes that did not fit, the punishment they might have earned before no longer fit with who they had become."

Belladonna craned her neck as she watched the reaction below her to the rabbi's speech. It was annoying being so far above those who held the power, she was used to being at their center and observing every nuance to understand their underlying intentions.

At the conclusion of his sermon, men in red hats clustered around the rabbi to shake his hand. Belladonna kept her eyes on the rabbi as he made his way back to his seat beside the curtained ark, while the other women sat back. She was waiting to see if he would look up to the women's section, but he never raised his eyes up towards her at all.

Why did he choose to speak about the return to the fold and becoming a different person? Was his talk meant for her, hoping she had resumed the identity of Raquel not just as a temporary refuge but as a permanent decision? Could he believe she would identify herself as a Jew and become the victim of persecution after she had climbed to the pinnacle of Venetian society? If so, he did not realize how much the secret of her origins would endanger her.

She leaned back, unable to feel comfortable among the other women in the synagogue, despite understanding her safety depended upon pretending to fit in with them.

The women who sat around her in the balcony were friendly and welcoming, but she was pleased to see the great respect they showed to Diana. Belladonna could not tell if their deference was because of her scholarship or her beauty or simply due to her status as the chief rabbi's daughter.

Watching and listening carefully, Belladonna was determined to understand what impressed people in this strange community. The conversations were in Venetian, sprinkled with words she assumed were Hebrew, which she did not understand. The women clasped hands to their chests as they repeated key phrases of the rabbi's speech. From the quiet murmurings of the crowd and the approving glances they gave his daughter, Belladonna surmised the rabbi's sermon had met with his congregation's approval.

As the synagogue emptied, Belladonna noticed the women clustered away from their men. She kept close to Sarra and Diana, eyes and head lowered, hoping she looked docile behind them as she emulated their gestures and mimicked the words, *Shabbat Shalom*. Dressed so simply and wearing the proscribed yellow badge upon her chest, she could not imagine anyone would recognize her as Belladonna. *Hidden in plain sight*, just as Isaak had advised.

"What now?' she asked Diana in a low voice.

"The *Shalosh Seudah*, the Third Meal of the Sabbath. I will accompany you to the Sullams', where there are bound to be many guests, as Jacob is an exuberant host. Remember, though, women sit separately from the men, who will depart early to go to the synagogue for the prayers that end the Sabbath."

"Your mother will be there?"

Diana sighed. "My mother has become most quarrelsome and insulting to Sarra."

"She still harbors jealousy towards Sarra over her patronage of your father?"

"Although we are not in the same desperate straits as before, we still need Sarra's patronage," Diana lowered her voice as she continued, "however, there are many who are critical of Sarra's writing and believe she draws unwanted attention to herself and the Jewish community."

"Does she?"

Diana's nostrils flared, and her violet eyes were flashing. "Those fears are not groundless, but they should not restrict women like Sarra to domesticity. Sarra is an accomplished poet and playwright, and I am grateful she has hired me to help her with the editing of her works."

"Though I have lived with the Sullams for only a short while, I can assure you there is no hope of Sarra ever becoming domesticated. Nor, do I suspect, will you."

Diana smiled. "That is true."

"Do you think your mother will recognize me?" Belladonna asked, "I worry your mother will not be discreet if she does."

Diana bit her lip and nodded. Although Diana's mother was a difficult woman, she was an astute observer and shrewd enough to want to know the secret of the courtesan's appearance in the Ghetto.

It was but a short distance from the synagogue to the bridge that led to the *campo* of the Ghetto Nuovo. The Sullam's mansion was only one house away from it. They could see from where they stood, the elegant façade, illuminated by the light of burning torches.

"Perhaps my mother will not recognize you," Diana said, mesmerized by the dancing flames.

"If she does, how can you impress upon her she must stay silent?"

Diana gave a harsh laugh. "My mother is unpredictable, but she is doggedly loyal to her sons. She knows of your relationship with Isaak, and therefore she has become your most fearsome advocate."

Belladonna said no more, deciding she would determine her course of action if the situation arose.

Chapter Thirteen: Diana

"You must indulge me in this, rabbi," Sarra was pleading with Rabbi Modena, waving her hands emphatically, "I have promised to answer this letter, but I am unsure of what to write."

The rabbi stroked his lined and craggy face, and his dark eyes were deeply shadowed by his thick eyebrows as he scowled. "You should not answer this man. It is bound to cause trouble."

"But he speaks calumnies about us—about me! That will stir up more trouble."

Their conversation piqued Diana's curiosity, but it ended abruptly once the pair noticed her entering the hall with Belladonna at her side. Sarra's husband, Jacob, slightly overweight, but in clothes perfectly suited to his form, came bustling over to usher them all into the salon. "Come, come, our guests await."

The women followed their host into the dining room, leaving Diana no opportunity to learn more about Sarra's trouble. The rabbi had been seated in a place of honor, in a high-backed armchair at the head of the table, while Diana and her mother were led to another table set up for women. Jacob remained standing as he greeted late arriving guests, directing the men to their seats and pointing out the women's table to their wives.

Among them was the wealthy trader Avigdor Margoles, accompanied by his garishly overdressed wife. Diana grimaced as Naomi Margoles took the seat beside her before Belladonna could. Diana gave a small shake of her head to signal there was to be no revealing conversation between them while this woman sat between them.

Mordechai Maimon, the *chazzan*, complained loudly as he was shown to his seat, that as cantor, he should be given the place of honor as a leader of the community, along with the rabbi. He paid no attention to whether his young and very pregnant wife, Esther, had found a seat at the women's table. Belladonna shivered at the thought of having to manage children and a household under the critical eyes of a man such as him.

Water jugs appeared, along with bowls and towels, so everyone could wash and say the blessing over the bread. Jacob signaled to the *chazzan* to begin a tune, and he was instantly no longer peevish as he began first to hum and then to sing loudly while banging his open palm on the table to its catchy rhythm. Despite the serving staff offering cold fish and challah, the other men joined in, singing and pounding the table with their enthusiasm, ignoring their food.

The women were served special fare: a parade of savory dishes, little cakes and sweets, chickpeas pickled with peppers, and salted fish. Small porcelain cups patterned with bright blue scenes were placed before each woman guest.

"Have any of you tasted coffee before?" Sarra asked as a servant returned bearing a large, covered pitcher wrapped in a cloth. The other women watched as the servant carefully held the cloth to protect against the heat and poured a steamy, caramel-colored liquid into first Sarra's cup and then Diana's.

"It is kosher?" asked the *chazzan's* young wife, her question directed at Diana.

"Yes, it is," Diana nodded as she fanned the steaming cup to cool it. "Coffee is a plant-based brew. I have partaken of it before, and there is reference to it in the writings of many great rabbis and scholars, who had access to it from trade with the East."

Diana often brewed coffee with her father, who used it medicinally, often as a tonic to soothe her mother. Her mother loved to drink coffee and held out her cup as it was served. Their family was able to have a steady supply, thanks to the generosity of the Sullams.

As the singing finally abated, the men attacked their plates with gusto, and the servants moved around the table, pouring coffee into the cups of those who called for it.

Jacob Sullam addressed the rabbi. "Now that we have partaken of the meal, and our physical well-being has been taken care of, it is time to satisfy our spiritual needs with words of Torah from our rabbi—."

From the women's table, Sarra stood and called out, interrupting her husband. "Wait, dear friends. Before we hear from our learned rabbi, there is something that I have discovered during my studies that I would like to share."

The rabbi closed his open mouth and nodded, deferring to his hostess. Diana knew Sarra had great passion for the study of the Torah, but was oblivious to the discomfort she caused in preempting the rabbi. Diana's mother made sure to convey her disapproval with a snort, but Belladonna looked up and arched one eyebrow at Diana.

"The Talmud speaks about three of the most beautiful women ever created in the world. Do you know who they were?" Sarra's question was addressed to Esther, the *chazzan's* wife, who looked down at her cup, biting her lip. Diana knew the answer, but did not volunteer it.

"Sara, our patriarch Abraham's wife?" offered the *chazzan*, his voice impatient.

Sarra nodded. "Yes, Sara was one of the great beauties of the world. The second was Rahab, who hid Joshua's spies on her roof and later joined the Israelites. The third was Queen Esther, in the Purim story."

"Rahab was a harlot." Diana's mother made the statement, and Diana shifted uncomfortably in her chair.

"Very good, and thank you for helping to lead me to the point," Sarra said, cleverly acknowledging the rabbi's wife. "Rahab is not disparaged because of her profession, nor is Esther for hiding her true origins, or Sara for lying and pretending to be Abraham's sister instead of his wife. That is why the rabbis of the Talmud discussed each woman on this subject. You see, these three women were uniquely beautiful because of their bravery and the nobility of their souls."

"Too often, we assume that a pleasant face indicates a nobility of spirit,"

Naomi Margoles mumbled, as if her own unpleasant face must be a sign of a beautiful soul.

A down-turning of Avigdor's mouth, as if he had just tasted something disagreeable, signaled his disapproval of Sarra's commentary. "You cannot be suggesting that the Torah approves of the vices of adultery and promiscuity, are you?" he asked, directing his question not to his hostess, but to the rabbi.

The rabbi cleared his throat noisily so he could answer in the strong voice usually reserved for his sermons. "Humans have their vices, and it is each individual's challenge to overcome them. That is the concept of *Teshuva*, repentance, which, as you are aware, as we say in our prayers, can ease the severity of God's decree on one's destiny."

Diana heard the guests around the table shifting in their chairs, leaning in closer, like hounds picking up the scent of controversy. Avigdor snorted again loudly as he laced into the rabbi.

"There is none more qualified than our rabbi to speak of vices, or so I gather. Tell us, rabbi, have you been successful in overcoming your gambling habit? Have you done the proper *Teshuva*, for the coming year?"

Diana's mother folded her arms and glared at her husband, as if she completely supported Avigdor's challenge.

It was Jacob's voice which boomed, and he slammed his fist on the table, rattling the delicate teacups. "I will not have you talk to the rabbi with such disrespect in my house and at my table."

Avigdor opened his mouth, ready to retort, but Diana saw his wife give him a discreet glance, and he seemed to reconsider. "Apologies, Jacob, I did not intend to insult, only to warn our rabbi."

"Warning the rabbi of what, Avigdor?" Sarra jumped in to ask.

Surprisingly, it was Avigdor's wife who answered for him. "It is never good for one of us to mingle too much with the Gentiles. Any problem, and it would be a danger to us all."

Sarra rolled her eyes, but Jacob gave her a pointed look, so she held her tongue.

The rabbi spoke in his own defense. "These are modern times, and although we live with restrictions, there is greater tolerance in our city than ever before. We are permitted to print our *seforim*—our holy books for the first time and distribute them across all of Europe. This is only possible because the Gentiles have come to know us from our presence in their palazzos and their attendance at sermons in the Ghetto."

Diana spoke up in her father's defense. "In essence, the more we interact with them, the less danger we should have from them."

Jacob and Sarra looked expectantly at their guests, waiting for someone to challenge or commend Diana's assertion, but there was only an uncomfortable silence. When Diana looked at the cantor's wife, the young woman glanced away. Was her father at risk once again of dismissal for his unorthodox views and behaviors? How much had the rabbi's views of women, art, or mysticism alienated him from men like these, established leaders of the Ghetto?

Sarra's bold and unusual ways were straining the tolerance of the community, and her patronage of the rabbi might hurt rather than help him.

Diana was not surprised when both the physician and the young cantor did not protest when Avigdor attacked the rabbi. They kept their eyes averted from her, and she hoped it was due to their shame for not defending their spiritual leader.

Thankfully, Diana's father did not seem to be disturbed by the shifting gazes or the unnatural silence and calmly made his final pronouncement. "It is our duty to question and challenge; that is the purpose of immersing oneself in the study of Torah. Therefore, I can only encourage you to study more and always be prepared to question and challenge my thinking."

There was a grunt from Avigdor, but no other comments from the table. Rabbi Modena signaled to the cantor, who took up another tune, and soon the men were singing, and the women returned to their gossip.

Diana could sense Belladonna's rising anger at the discussion at Sarra's table. Belladonna had not lived with the Sullams for many years, and she was not used to Sarra's foolish attempts to demonstrate her scholarship in public. Sadly, no good ever came of a woman flaunting her superior knowledge among men.

Growing up as the rabbi's daughter Diana was too conscious of the dangers of drawing attention to herself, especially when there was murmuring against her father. Though his scholarship and knowledge were revered, the congregation had tired of their rabbi's weakness for the gaming tables.

Out of the corner of her eye, Diana noticed Mirabella hovering, her eyes flicking to Belladonna every once in a while. Knowing Sarra's weakness in managing her own household, Diana worried it would not bode well for all of them if this servant were to overhear too much.

Chapter Fourteen: Diana

Diana walked home from the Sullam's slowly, holding her father's arm. Her mother had marched on ahead, muttering and complaining once again about the behavior of Sarra Sullam. Diana took the opportunity of being alone with her father to ask him about the desperate-sounding plea Sarra had made to him.

The rabbi frowned and tried to dismiss the topic. "Sarra looks to me to guide her in almost every decision. Sometimes it is best I stay away from her issues."

"What issue is Sarra having?" Diana persisted. When her father did not indulge her, Diana pulled him to a stop, preventing him from escaping into their rooms. "Well? Any issue Sarra has may affect my friend Raquel, and I must know of it."

The rabbi sighed, and he relaxed his rigid stance. "Sarra has been accused of heresy against the Church."

Diana's hand rose to her lips to suppress a gasp. "How can such a thing be? Sarra is not involved in polemics, nor has her writing ever crossed into theological topics."

Her father's lips twisted, as if he had tasted something bitter. "That is the rational answer. But attacks on us do not have to be based on facts or truth or reality to hold sway. You should know that by now."

Diana's hand quivered as she reached for her father's sleeve. She had always tugged on her father in times of fear, as if the mere touch of his arm could dispel any threat. "You are not going to distance yourself from her, are you? It would be the safest course, but you know Sarra...she lives in the clouds. How can she defend herself without you?"

Her father patted her hand, "You underestimate Sarra. She does not write of theology or engage in polemics, but she has a sharp mind, and I believe she will write a response which will dispel the accusation and cast doubt upon the motives of the accuser."

"The accuser is someone she knows?"

The rabbi nodded. "The cardinal of Treviso, who had been a frequent guest at her salon. He accuses her of denying the immortality of the soul, which is heresy."

"Why?"

The rabbi shrugged. "He has tried many times to convince Sarra to convert. It would elevate his status greatly to influence the famous Jewess to become a Christian. When Sarra realized what he was after, she broke off communications with him."

Diana shuddered. "This is not the time to have such accusations against Sarra. We must find a way to defend her, and if you will not, I will."

The rabbi took his daughter's arm and proceeded forward towards their rooms. "I have never said I would not come to Sarra's defense, but nevertheless, I welcome your help."

* * *

Diana could not rest and, after tossing and turning, lay flat on her back, staring at the painted faces on the timbers of the ceiling. Unsettled by the accusation against Sarra, it seemed as if a wave of ill-will was rising against the people of the Ghetto, like a wind whipping up before a big storm. The gates of the Ghetto had been constructed long ago to contain its citizens but also to protect them, and now they were relying on them to keep their secrets. Rumors were their enemy and in the past, had caused expulsion and death.

She must not think of such things, or her eyes would never relax their vigilance, and her legs would remain tensed, ready to spring. The words of the prayers from Yom Kippur came unbidden to mind:

Who will live, who will die? Whose life will be cut short, and whose life will not?
She willed herself not to think of the rest of the prayer, which proposes other possible dire outcomes for the upcoming year. She rubbed her temples, as if to erase the worry over Sarra, over the discovery of Belladonna, over the mounting criticism of her father and the likelihood it would cause him to assuage his fears by a return to the gaming tables.

Why had she remained in the Ghetto while her brothers roamed the world in search of adventure and free from the burden of caring for her parents? *It is a daughter's duty.* She could almost hear her mother's reply, especially since she had no husband or children to care for. Her father never asked her to stay with them; it had been the logical solution to where she could live after her husband's death, and with no means of support. From the worry in his eyes and the words she had seen in his diary, her departure from the Ghetto would devastate him. Ironically, had she chosen to become Belladonna's protégé, she would now find herself back in the Ghetto, seeking its sanctuary.

She turned on her side and tried to calm herself with pleasant thoughts. Mattia. The artist who had first drawn her out of the Ghetto and into a new world of beauty and art, filled with glittering jewels and tantalizing conversations. When he had to leave Venice as a result of his commission from the Earl of Arundel for his gallery of beauties, she had despaired of him ever finishing her portrait. He had eventually finished her portrait upon his return, and Diana was resigned to never having it, but only visiting it in Belladonna's palazzo. Though her father felt that a portrait did not transgress rabbinic law, there were others in the Ghetto who did not hold so liberal a viewpoint. Besides, where could she hang such a thing in their tiny, cluttered rooms?

If she were to be honest with herself, perhaps it was not only for the completion of her portrait she had wished for Mattia's return. As another year passed, the face of the husband she had loved and lost had begun to blur, and the emptiness could no longer be filled with the study of the Talmud. Mattia had stirred new feelings as she posed for him. She had fooled herself into believing such was a part of the mystical connection of an artist to his subject, but now she knew it was to share his passion for his work, just as she had shared Yaakov's passion for study.

When Mattia had sent for her to tend the Englishman, she hoped he had not noticed her cheeks were more flushed than usual. She had felt a fluttering whenever the artist came close to her, which she had suppressed by focusing solely on the wounds of the Englishman. Now, Mattia had returned, and she would not sleep the entire night if she continued to wonder what the future might bring for the two of them.

Chapter Fifteen: Belladonna

Belladonna was not expecting the news Diana had come to share. "An Englishman, a lord such as Arundel, has just arrived and been stabbed—with a Spanish dagger."

Belladonna bit her lip to keep herself from voicing her worry. It was as Isaak had feared; the Spanish knew of Roderigo's outreach to the English and were determined to stop it.

"Is he alive?"

"Yes, Mattia Correr found him and sent for me to attend to his wounds. Though he had bled profusely, the blade had not penetrated his heart, and he seems strong enough to recover."

Belladonna smiled. "I hope he was not fully conscious to appreciate it was a woman, and a Jewess at that, who tended his wound. Most men of his kind would gather any strength they possessed to run from you."

"He had been fully conscious by the time I arrived, although I suspect Mattia had plied him with enough wine to dull any resistance."

Diana looked at Mirabella, hovering at the threshold, and Belladonna frowned when she followed her gaze. They must be rid of the servant for this conversation. "Mirabella, would you please bring some wine for our rabbi's daughter."

Mirabella did not acknowledge the order verbally, but did comply, and was soon gone from their sight.

"Villiers is asking to see Sir Henry."

Belladonna, unable to indulge her habit of fondling her pearls, twirled the ends of a stray hair. "I shall see him first. He will not know me as Belladonna, and I may learn something of the English intentions regarding Jamaica."

Diana's eyes widened for a moment before she nodded. She was quick-witted, which Belladonna appreciated, as well as brave. Belladonna had no doubt Diana would volunteer to accompany her to the artist Correr's rooms to visit the Englishman.

"We must think of something to dangle before him, to maintain his interest while keeping him out of the clutches of the Spanish," Belladonna said while repeatedly tapping a long finger on her lower lip as her mind raced through many scenarios. "I have an inkling of an idea, but we will need some help."

She could not elaborate as Mirabella had returned, carrying a decanter of wine, two green and gold filigreed glasses, and a small dish of sweets.

"Thank you, Mirabella," Belladonna nodded and repeated, "Thank you, you may go," as the maid seemed to be inclined to linger.

Mirabella shuffled her way out, and Belladonna began a trivial conversation in loud enough tones for the maid to overhear.

"How do you like the sweets?"

Diana nodded, conveying her understanding of the need to have a silly discourse over food and wine until they were certain the maid had finally departed.

Belladonna picked up the thread of their previous conversation by asking, "Have you heard anything from Morosini?"

Previously, Diana had caught the fancy of a nobleman, Bardon Morosini, one of the powerful men on the Council of Ten, a man who could be a fearsome enemy, but who they presently counted on as a friend. Diana reached for a sweet, which she popped into her mouth before answering.

Licking her fingers, she said, "No, I have not, and I am relieved. His wife is dead, and his mistress has moved on, and I do not want to find myself the center of his unwanted attentions. Why do you ask?"

Belladonna sipped her wine and then replaced her glass on the tray before them. "I am sorry to ask you, but I am afraid you will have to go see him."

Diana's eyebrows rose halfway up her forehead. "Why?"

"We will need his help."

Diana fell back against her chair and rolled her eyes. "What help can he possibly provide? Besides he hates the English for stealing the design for his fast ships."

"They paid him generously for it, if you recall. Besides, he hates the Spanish even more. Bardon is an opportunist who will follow any path that leads to gold, and the promise of the lost treasure will entice him just as it has the Englishman."

Belladonna was beginning to feel more like her old self as if power was once more at her fingertips. Power seemed to be an elusive quality to possess in the Ghetto, and in her masquerade as 'Raquel,' she had been falling too much into the mindset of a vulnerable widow.

Diana inhaled and exhaled deeply. "So, you want me to go to him."

"I do not want him to know I am still in Venice yet; it is too dangerous—to me and possibly to you." Belladonna clasped her friend's arm. "I will tell you exactly what to do, and have no fear. He will not hurt you."

"I am more concerned with stirring his passions than his animosity." Diana patted Belladonna's hand. "But I will do as you ask. We must all face our demons sometime, and I suppose it is the time for me to face mine."

Chapter Sixteen: Villiers

Pain awoke him. He must have turned onto the side of the wound in his sleep. He cried out as he flipped onto his back and was gratified it did not bring in a servant or the artist. The light was weak and grey, and he supposed it was barely dawn. Disappointed he had slept for so few hours, he leaned back again and closed his eyes.

Venice was filled with temptation, and he had no intention of resisting any of them. Now, he would have ample opportunity to indulge his vices, subsidized by King James. All he had to do was to find the man who would lead them to victory and treasure in the Caribbean island of Jamaica.

Villiers had learned his quarry was in Venice to see the notorious courtesan, Belladonna. Treasure and a beautiful courtesan seemed a quest tailor-made for him, and he should not complain, but it seemed as if the Spanish were right on his heels. An attempt on his life, which nearly succeeded almost as soon as he had arrived, should be taken seriously. The Spanish needed the treasure even more than he did; it was rumored their navy had not been paid or provisioned in months, and their crews were ready to revolt. Jamaica was the prize of the Caribbean both countries were after, and he had promised the King he would ensure England would triumph.

He had been in such a haze of pain and weakness; all seemed a blur. He did recall a woman's touch, and he had a vague impression she was beautiful, unless she was a dream, or all women in Venice were beautiful. There were women last night at the gaming tables with luscious chests spilling out of their gowns, their scents equally seductive. They had brought him luck, and he had won enough to pay for a new doublet, and he was far from the most threatening of his creditors. A beautiful woman and buckets of gold were ready for the taking, wound be damned, and he must get on his feet to pursue them.

He swung his legs down and staggered to his feet, only to see he had no breeches on. Nor stockings, nor boots. He squinted as he swiveled about to take in the room. Swaths of fabric, square canvases, small tables, and a host of glass jars surrounded him. Ahh, he was in the artist's studio. No sign of his clothes, and a draft found its way up his long shirt and made him shiver. Back to the divan and keeping warm under the coverings until the maid could be pressed to bring back his clothes seemed like the best idea. He carefully lay back loaded as much of the coverings as he could over himself, and was resigned to spend the next hour or so staring at the coffered ceiling. There was nothing else to do but make plans, though such an act was contrary to his usual method of jumping in and rolling with the dice.

Taking stock of his situation, Villiers realized for once luck seemed to be on his side. He had survived a nearly lethal attack, the wound had been expertly cauterized, and the money he had won at the gaming tables at the Monte Carlo was still in his possession. By default, he had found a satisfactory place to lay his head without cost. Villiers liked his companion, Mattia, a gentleman artist acquainted with the English ambassador, who also had a bevy of beauties eagerly pursuing him to pose for his portraits.

Now he must focus on finding this elusive gentleman from Jamaica. The first step must be Sir Henry, who, though a plodding and dreary old man, would have the resources to chase his quarry down while he, Villiers, used his own expertise to pursue the courtesan.

From what he gathered from the chit-chat at last night's tables, her palace was supposed to be magnificent, and the plan would be to become *her* guest for the rest of his sojourn in Venice. Then, through his well-proven powers of persuasion, he would have her find the map to the treasure in Jamaica while Sir Henry negotiated with her brother about the English support against the Spanish.

The studio seemed to be growing lighter; he could make out more definition among the canvases and cloths, and as he turned his head towards the window, it seemed it was going to be another bright, glorious day. It would not be long before the maid appeared to stoke up the fires and bring him his breeches. His fingers probed the site of the wound carefully, managing to cause enough pain to make him howl.

Running footsteps got closer while his head was still enveloped in a fog left from all the pain. He did not have the strength to turn or respond to whoever had arrived. Taking deep breaths, eyes closed, until the pain subsided. When he opened them, the artist hovered above him, eyes bloodshot and hair wild.

"…has the wound reopened? I will send for Diana," were the only words Villiers caught.

When the artist reached towards the coverings over his wound, Villiers grabbed his hand and held it in a tight grip. "Stay. Give me a moment."

Correr fell back as Villiers took another deep breath. The pain had subsided, and now, he knew his limitations. The courtesan might have to wait a bit, but not the ambassador.

"Have you sent for Sir Henry?"

"Not yet," the artist called over his shoulder as he turned away. Before Villiers could chastise him, he returned with a glass of wine as an offering.

Villiers struggled to raise himself without inciting the wound, took the glass gratefully, and drank it down. When he returned the glass to the artist, Mattia Correr was grinning.

"Prodigious thirst, eh?"

"Pain will do that to you." He answered.

"I will send for Diana. That wound needs to be looked at." He gestured to the glass, offering a refill.

Villiers nodded and gave an appreciative sigh as he held the full glass once more to his lips. "Good wine."

"I am relieved you approve."

"Fetch me my breeches, it's damnably breezy without them. And send for Sir Henry."

The artist raised an eyebrow and then nodded. "As you wish, my illustrious guest. Are you thinking of leaving, then?"

"It is the duty of the ambassador to house the emissaries of the King," said Villiers as he took another gulp and gave a satisfied sigh. The wine was truly a superior vintage. "Appreciate your hospitality –"

"And saving your life."

"Yes, that too, of course. Would not want to impose upon you by taking residence in what seems to be your studio?" Villiers could not stay supine. He was sitting now and ran a hand through his tousled hair. "You do not have a man to do for you, help you bathe, tend to your doublet, and such."

Mattia Correr shook his unruly mop of hair, as if to emphasize his lacking. "My maid can help you with the chamber pot and draw you a bath, although I would wait a bit on the bath," he gestured to the wounded side with his chin. "As I mentioned, Diana will come and clean the wound, and provide a new bandage."

Villiers shrugged his shoulders. "I suppose that will have to do for now. I do appreciate your kindness and all that, however, I do really want those breeches."

"And the pouch of coins with them, no doubt," said the artist as he departed.

Chapter Seventeen: Belladonna

Belladonna has set her trap for Mirabella. Jacob had already left to tend to his affairs at the docks while Sarra was still abed. Her announcement to the staff to inform the mistress she was going to call on the rabbi's daughter had earned barely a grunt from the footman, but Mirabella's face had perked up and ignited a gleam in her eye.

Though Mirabella seemed to do her best to accomplish the minimum, Belladonna was certain she would make the effort to do some chores in her chamber this morning. The cupboard seemed the most likely place to hide treasures, so she had stashed a brooch and a necklace there, wrapped in a linen shift. One benefit of the maidservant's search for her valuables was her room would be thoroughly cleaned.

It sparkled, and it was gold. No doubt it would catch the rat.

* * *

Belladonna walked along the main thoroughfare of the Ghetto with many other women, young and old, dragging buckets, parcels, or children. They greeted her as if she knew them, and she smiled back, hoping the minimal response would not encourage further conversation. Her dress was more elegant than theirs, thanks to the Sullams' generosity, and stood out among the drab greys and brown shapeless gowns most of them wore. She had joined them, wearing the yellow brand upon her chest, marking her, like them, for exclusion from genteel society.

Her feet, in the common leather slippers, felt every groove and bump in the stone pavement, reminding her of how much she missed her platform shoes and the feeling of being above the common crowd. It was but a short walk from the Sullams' to Diana's rooms in the campo of the Ghetto Nuovo, and she took a quick look at the cluster of women around the well to see if either Diana or her mother were there. Luckily, it was Diana's mother who was seated on the stone bench beside the well, so busy in conversation with her cronies, Belladonna was certain she had not been noticed.

It was good news indeed to be able to be alone with Diana because she wanted to discuss Isaak with her friend, a topic she could not discuss in front of his parents. Diana sat by the fireplace, sorting and shaking a mass of beans or chickpeas or some such stuff in her lap.

"What brings you so early? Have you received any encouraging news?"

"Wishful thinking," said Belladonna, shaking her head and drawing up a stool beside her. "I have received no word about my brother from anyone and nothing from Mattia about the Englishman."

Diana brushed a few peas or beans off her fingers and then offloaded the entire mass in her lap into a large bowl. "You have a plan about the Englishman?"

Belladonna snorted. "The Englishman is the kind of man who is not difficult to manage. He is an overly self-confident opportunist who only questions a benefit that comes his way if it is too easy to obtain. Therefore, though we know how to find him, we must allow him to make the first move."

Diana tilted her head and paused, still holding the bowl. "Oh. I had not thought of it in that way. However, having tended to the man when he was most vulnerable, I do see the wisdom in what you are suggesting."

Belladonna sat up very straight, which was a challenge sitting on such a rickety stool, as she primed herself to bring up Isaak with his sister. "I had wondered how Isaak would react to me after so many years."

Diana raised an eyebrow, "And?'

Belladonna exhaled, her posture collapsing and her back rounding. "Nothing has changed. At least for me. When he saved me from the Berber pirates, bound to be sold as a slave, he won my heart, as well as my eternal gratitude. He has come to my rescue once again, but I am not certain he comes to me out of love or a sense of duty."

"How does he act when you are with him? Does he betray any of his emotion?"

Belladonna scrunched her eyes to withstand the onslaught of her emotions coming to the surface. "He took me in his arms…." She found it difficult to say anymore, even to Diana, a friend she trusted more than any other.

Diana promptly put her bowl of peas and lentils on the floor and took both of Belladonna's hands into hers. "Listen. I know my brother. He is a strong, tough man who has hardened himself to withstand beauty and avoid love. If he has taken you in his arms and held you with tenderness, even without a kiss," Diana smiled as Belladonna's eyes widened at the last word, as she inhaled sharply. "He has lost his control, and he showed you feelings he has not divulged to a soul since he was a child. Cherish it, especially if that is all you can get from him now. It has cost him dearly to show his feelings for you, and you should appreciate it."

Belladonna exhaled once more, as if she had been defeated. "His return to me has made me reconsider my whole life, and my future."

"What can you mean?"

"Maybe I am better off leaving Venice. Starting anew."

"With Isaak?"

"If you think he will have me."

Diana took her shoulders and gave her a warm hug. "He will ask you to come with him this time. I do not doubt it. I have seen the way he looks at you. He has never looked at a woman in such a way before."

* * *

Though Diana's assessment of her brother was heartening, Belladonna succumbed to a weariness which had been kept at bay until now and collapsed on the large bed in her chamber at the Sullam mansion. She stared into the tufted fabric of its canopy and felt the comforting softness of the coverlet under her. As luxurious as the Sullams had made their home,

Belladonna still craved her own large bed and home. So many of the items she had collected and treasured, such as a headboard exquisitely inlaid with mother-of-pearl, she had left behind in her palazzo. It was not just the many ducats she had spent on its furnishings. The palazzo was her own accomplishment, chosen by her and furnished with her personal taste. She had carefully saved the gifts and bequests she had received from lovers, turning them into enough gold to last a lifetime.

She might never be able to return to her home, but must not think of what might be lost, or what dangers must be overcome, or whether she would be able to outwit her enemies. Time would tell, and the future must be earned. She should take comfort that all through her life, she had always prevailed.

She rubbed her hand along the bed linens, appreciating how fine they were. The Sullams' mansion was furnished with the very finest and would put many an aristocrat's palazzo to shame. The bed was carved of walnut and draped with tapestries that would keep out the drafts in winter and soothe the soul as its occupant sought their rest.

Beside the bed was a small table with its candle, and on the opposite wall, a washstand with a large white porcelain pitcher with painted flowers and a gilded handle. The linen towel which rested on its handle was white and crisp, and the mirror inset in its backing gleamed. The walls were covered with a red moiré, and the draperies around the tall windows were of the same color and style, now tied back with a golden cord to let in the light and air.

The wardrobe in burled walnut caught her eye, and she noticed its door was not quite closed. Had she not closed it firmly before she left? Curious and suspecting her belongings had been explored by Mirabella, she rose to investigate. She felt around the bottom of the cupboard and found the linen where she had hidden the jewels. Empty.

Belladonna smiled. Now she would be able to prove Mirabella was a thief. She would wait for the appropriate moment to expose her. Soon, Sarra should no longer be plagued by such a surly, incompetent servant.

Belladonna sighed when she remembered her many trusted servants, most of whom had been with her for several years and whom she had trusted with her life. Zancani. What had become of him? Not many would tolerate his slovenly appearance and his loutish demeanor, but he had protected Belladonna with the fierceness of an emperor's praetorian guard. She was unable to warn him of her need to disappear. He would search for her in his own brutish manner, which could land him in the prisons beneath the Doge's palace.

Since there was little she could do for Zancani or any of her servants now, she brushed such thoughts aside.

Chapter Eighteen: Diana

Diana felt like Daniel entering the lion's den, and although she was no prophet, it would not be difficult to predict the reaction she could expect from a powerful nobleman like Bardon Morosini by her visit. She was stirring the pot, possibly reactivating the lust he had expressed for her. Months ago, when she had first met him, he had invited her, with a threat to her family as an incentive, to become his mistress. When she had not taken his offer, he had postponed acting upon his threat after his wife had been poisoned, and he feared the poison had been intended for him.

Under Belladonna's patronage and guidance, she had discovered who was responsible for his wife's death along with the other beauties of Venice, earning his respect. Along with unmasking the murderer, Belladonna had made other discoveries, which had swayed him into becoming her ally. How would he behave towards her without Belladonna's protection? Did he have enough loyalty to the courtesan that could be leveraged to acquire his support now?

Smoothing her skirts and drawing her shawl to cover the yellow badge on her dress, she waited for the servant to admit her into Morosini's grand palazzo.

The servant did not return for her, but the master himself, Bardon Morosini. He held out his hands and clasped her own in greeting. The warmth of his welcome surprised her, but the cold, calculating look in his eyes did not.

"I confess, a visit from you was not an event I had anticipated, despite the friendly terms on which we parted. How does your brother Zebulun fare? I know better than to ask after Isaak."

Diana retrieved her hand from his grasp and pointed to the staircase. "Perhaps we should speak in a more private setting?"

Morosini grinned and beckoned her to follow. Lifting her skirts and summoning her courage, she did.

He led her to a room that had all the signs of a sanctuary. The odor of his cologne was strong enough to make her wince, and the room was as dark and handsome as its owner. Morosini gestured for her to sit on a beautifully carved chair before the desk. She hesitated to sit down, admiring the burled leather of the cushion, which was the same as the design on the leather paneled walls. Instead of taking his place behind the large desk, Morosini pulled its chair alongside hers and sat beside her.

"I am all ears, my dear. I am certain it is a dire situation that has brought you here, and not your desire to bask in my presence." He crossed his elegantly clad legs and rested his chin on his hand, appearing at ease while his eyes were wary.

"It is Belladonna—"

Morosini leaned forward, all his languidness disappearing as his brows furrowed and his hands clutched the arms of the chair. "Have you spoken to her? Do you know where she can be found? All Venice is obsessed with her disappearance, and oddly enough, I find myself concerned for her welfare."

Momentarily, Diana hesitated to reveal anything of Belladonna's whereabouts. She did not trust the nobleman and believed his concern for the courtesan must only tie into his own interests. Nevertheless, Belladonna had instructed her to elicit his support, so she would have to provide him with enough information to keep him engaged. "She is safe and is in hiding and will remain so until the threat against her can be removed."

Morosini leaned back and tented his fingers before his lips. Diana did not underestimate this man, whose machinations and network of informants had kept him in power and a member of the Council of Ten, the men who controlled Venice.

She allowed him time to absorb her news, but she must pry out of him anything he had learned of the Spanish plot against Belladonna. "Surely, you are aware she has become the target of Spanish assassins."

The nobleman's black brows raised high over his piercing blue eyes. "I cannot keep track of all those considered the enemies of Spain. Lord knows, there are so many these days. But no, I had not heard the fair Belladonna had earned a place on their list. Whatever for?"

He cocked an eye at her, signaling to her he was lying. He was testing her to see what she knew of the enemy and what she knew of Belladonna. She feared of telling him too much, but knew he was clever enough to understand more than her words. "The Spanish are seeking an envoy from the New World who holds the secret to a great treasure. They have tracked this man to Venice and have learned he has come to see Belladonna. However, he has since disappeared."

Morosini's lips widened into a smile. "Treasure, you say? How interesting. Your brother Isaak would have no hand in this matter, would he?"

Diana straightened her spine and tensed her jaw, ignoring his question. "We do not know what has become of the envoy, but we should be able to find him. But we must first ensure the Spanish will be kept at bay. With your help."

"I see." Morosini rested his tented fingers upon his lips. For once, he shifted his gaze away from her and looked towards the tall windows, which were the source of most of the light in the room. "I envy Isaak, you know. To sail off into the horizon, not knowing what the next day will bring, living by his wits and his sword." He sighed. "Well, we must all fall into step and learn to survive the life allotted to us."

Diana pursed her lips at the nobleman's assertion. He must have noticed her expression because he suddenly laughed. She said, "You do not believe Belladonna is your concern."

He raised a finger and pointed it at her. "Do not make assumptions. You see, treasure is always my business, and if Belladonna will be the means for me to acquire it, I am at your service."

Should she trust him? He would make a powerful ally, and with his network of thugs and spies, he could not only help them find Roderigo, but thwart the Spanish assassins. Shrugging off her concerns like an old shawl, she leaned forward. "Use your resources. Find the envoy. Listen to the rumors, the whispers about Belladonna. Learn what the Spanish know and what they plan."

"I am not used to taking orders from a woman, but I quite like the experience." Morosini leaned closer to her and rested his hand on her shoulder. "I have always held you in high esteem."

Diana stood, shrugging off his hand. "Let us not revisit old scenarios. You know where I stand, and let us be partners in this endeavor. No more."

She let the heavy door fall back into place with a thud as she left the lion in his den.

Chapter Nineteen: Belladonna

Belladonna joined Sarra in the library, where the poetess was perched at the edge of her chair, scrawling furiously on a curling sheet of paper. Sarra did not look up at Belladonna's approach, so she dragged a heavy-looking chair, which squeaked loudly across the floor until Sarra did.

"Raquel? Is there something you require?" she wiped away a stray lock that had fallen across her forehead, leaving a smudge of ink.

Belladonna leaned back in her chair. "I must learn what is expected of me here. As a widow, a woman, and as a member of your family. My life—and yours— may be at stake if I am noticed to be different. If I am suspected of not being who I say I am."

Sarra put the pen back in its stand and tented her ink-stained fingers as she regarded Belladonna. "There are many who come to the Ghetto who had been hiding their Jewish origins and know very little of the traditions they had been accused of practicing. You do not appear any different than you had several years ago when you first came to us."

Belladonna smoothed her skirts, hoping with each stroke of her hand, she could settle her temper. "I am quite different, Sarra, and now as then, I am not familiar with your customs."

"Yours, and not ours," Sarra murmured. Belladonna arched an eyebrow. "It is from the Passover Haggadah. It is a comment describing one of the Four Sons—who symbolize four types of Jews: the Intellectual, who wants to know all about his heritage and his people. The Scoffer, who asks: what is *your* religion about, clearly excluding himself because he wants no part of it."

Belladonna smiled. "Point taken. I do not identify as a Jew, but I must understand the society I find myself in, or I will be conspicuous."

"Mmm, I see." Sarra's eyes strayed back to her writing, and it seemed as if she was resisting the temptation to pick up her pen once again.

Belladonna plowed forward with her questions. "What is expected of a widow? Should I be dressed in some sort of mourning? Are there certain activities I should refrain from?"

Sarra shook her head. "According to Jewish law, a wife only mourns her husband for thirty days. During that time, it is customary not to buy new clothes, or cut one's hair, or seek musical entertainment or parties. After thirty days, however, it is over. Since you have been a widow longer than that, you are not expected to be in mourning."

"Interesting," Belladonna tapped her lip. "I had looks from the women in the synagogue and thought I may have acted or dressed in a manner inappropriate for a widow."

"They are always curious about a new arrival, especially one as lovely as you. Although widows are not required to wear mourning, it is the custom for many widows to continue to keep their hair covered by a turban or veil even though it is no longer a requirement since they no longer have a husband." Sarra paused, watching Belladonna's reaction.

Belladonna frowned, "Diana is a widow and the rabbi's daughter, and yet she wears no turban or veil."

Sarra shrugged. "It is an individual's choice. It is hoped by all that Diana will marry again soon. She was only married to her husband for a short time, and she is still very young."

Belladonna straightened her back, her pride prickled at the inference—*you are too old to have many prospects*—but forced a smile. "It might be better if I wore such a turban, since there would be less chance of being recognized."

Sarra nodded. "The yellow turban will not only signal you are one of us, but will blind many to the face beneath it. I have many of them, and Mirabella can help you find one to your liking." She stood, ready to call for her servant, but Belladonna laid a hand on her wrist to stop her.

"Please, let us talk in private for a little more. There are matters left unspoken for too long which I would like to discuss."

When Sarra hesitated, Belladonna thought she might refuse, but Sarra reseated herself, though her eyes shifted again to her writing. Belladonna sat beside her and took her hand. "I have been troubled by the way we parted ways years ago—"

Sarra interrupted her. "There is no need for you to feel remorse. We were saddened you felt compelled to leave. We believed—we still believe—that you are one of us and belong with your people."

Belladonna's nostrils flared, and she took a deep breath before responding. "Why would I belong? Neither my parents nor I had been brought up with your beliefs or practices, and only through birth are to be considered Jews. I was raised a Christian, and your traditions are as alien to me as mine are to you."

"There are others who have come to the Ghetto under similar circumstances," Sarra raised her chin and met her eyes. "Escaping from the Inquisition, refugees from the persecution which claimed your parents' lives, for not being True Christians. Many have decided to return to practice the religion of their forefathers."

Whether Sarra had intended her words to sting or not, they had. The course of this discussion was not going in the direction she had intended, and she needed to make her point. "Men use religion, like any other weapon, to achieve their aims. The Inquisition came to the New World to plunder it. Since New Christians like my family had amassed great fortunes, they had become a ripe opportunity. Roderigo and I have taken different paths in life as a result of where our escape had taken us. I do not know what has shaped his beliefs, or what religion he has chosen to follow. I only know I have none. My beliefs revolve around self-preservation, and therefore, taking up a religion that will put me in the path of persecution is contrary to my beliefs. Do you still accept me as I am?"

A heavy silence remained for a few moments before Sarra responded by shaking her head. "I do not understand your beliefs, but I do accept them. I have not had to face evils and overcome them as you have." She swiped a stray hair from her forehead and sighed. "You must think I am a sheltered, pampered idealist, and I admit that I am. The Almighty has blessed me with the good fortune of a loving husband and comfortable surroundings. I can write of noble acts and heroic deeds and expect only good of others."

"I did not intend to hurt you with my departure. You had given me more than refuge—a home, an education, and a new family. However, I could not remain in the Ghetto, restricted and hated, where the Inquisition still loomed as a threat. I chafed for freedom as if I was still fettered by Barbary pirates. I had to leave, much as it pained me to discard the love you had shown for me."

"Now, circumstances have brought me back to the Ghetto and to you. Though I wish to reclaim our relationship and be counted among your family, you should not consider me a Jew."

Sarra had lowered her eyes to her hands, which plucked at the lavender silk of her dress. She nodded.

Belladonna let out a long deep breath and leaned back. Her emotions back under her control, she said, "What of the Sabbath? I am not quite certain of what is permitted and what is not. I remember that you do not cook or light fires on the Sabbath, but the food we ate on Sabbath was warm."

Sarra gave a long dramatic sigh. "It is a strange concept for those who have not grown up with our logic, born out of scholarly discourse. There are thirty-nine activities that are not permitted on the Sabbath—"

"Thirty-nine?" Belladonna repeated, her eyes widening and alert. "Will I have to know all of them?"

Sarra cheeks were becomingly flushed, and her face animated. "You should not have to. Many do not. Customs are in place, handed down by each generation, so there is familiarity with how things should be done. Although fires are not to be lit, we may partake of their warmth if they have been lit prior to Sabbath. So many bring their stew pots to the bakers' ovens to keep warm since their heat is retained from the previous day's baking. It is also permitted to task a non-Jew, who does not have the restrictions of the Sabbath, to ensure fires do not go out."

"Similar to Venetian law, then, your laws have many exceptions, which is a concept I can understand."

Sarra's eyes had become glossy and dreamy, and there was wistfulness in her voice as she asked, "You have had the opportunity to learn from such great minds, and I envy you. It was my dream to bring such thinkers and writers, and artists to the Ghetto. In fact, I had convinced Jacob to fund an Academy, under the leadership of the great philosopher and poet, Baldassare Bonifacio—"

Belladonna interrupted her with a sharp laugh, "Never trust a man such as Bonifacio Baldassare, and certainly do not give him any of your money. Not a noble thought or deed will ever come from him, and your gold will only go to his tailor and to stock his wine cellar, with perhaps a little left over for the gaming tables."

Sarra's eyes misted, and her mouth pursed, and Belladonna regretted her candor. Sarra said, "It is all to naught, now, the Academy. Despite my efforts to establish unity among us all, I have been accused of heresy."

Belladonna bit her lip. If she had been in her usual position and in her palazzo, she would have the influence to ridicule such an accusation and make short work of Baldasarre. Besides the danger to Sarra, if Bonifacio knew she was in the Ghetto, he would extort more gold from the Sullams before selling his knowledge of Belladonna's hiding place to the Spanish. *How frustrating it was to be powerless!*

"I have heard of writers and theologists accused of heresy before," she took Sarra's hand, so thin and delicate, and hoped her words would be reassuring, "and nothing came of it."

Sarra drew her hand from Belladonna's and placed it over her heart. Her eyes widened. "Were they able to avert the charge or the punishment?"

Belladonna forced a small smile. In truth, she did not know, but her mind raced to plot a potential strategy for Sarra. "I believe they took their case to the people. They penned a clever response, arguing heresy had not been intended nor implied, and distributed their treatise widely. Yes, that is what they did, I am certain. The Church did not want to make a cause out of the defense, so instead chose to ignore the entire matter."

Belladonna was surprised at how easily she was able to concoct and elaborate a strategy to extract Sarra from a difficult situation. Her suggestion seemed to make Sarra straighten her back and instigate a determined look in her eyes. "What you say makes perfect sense. I shall begin re-drafting my response immediately."

She turned to her writing table, and the pile of notes smattered with lines of ink. Taking up a handful, she gazed at them for a moment and closed her eyes. Several moments passed before she reopened them. When she did, the notes were squashed into a ball to be discarded. Then she picked up her pen, dipped it in the inkwell, and began writing.

Chapter Twenty: Diana

Diana stood in the traghetto, turning her face to catch the warmth of the rising sun as the little boat crossed the Grand Canal, following a path dappled with orange and gold. If Isaak had returned, would he stay away from them, since there was a price on his head? Knowing her brother, he would venture into Venice in disguise while keeping his ship ready enough to enable a quick escape if needed.

She was bound for the Moorish quarter, knowing her brother was in contact with a man known as the Turk. The Turk was a longtime friend and associate, and although neither of them ever revealed the source of their relationship, it seemed as though they had once sailed together as corsairs. Once she alighted from the traghetto in the *séstere* of the Cannaregio, she made haste to the bridge that connected the Moorish quarter to the Ghetto, since only one canal separated each settlement. Isaak, usually in the Moorish garb of a white caftan and turban, could enter the Ghetto, and in this disguise, even their father would not recognize him.

It had been so long since Isaak had come home. The last time her brother had ventured into Venice was at the death of her husband, Yaakov. There had been a bounty on his head then, too, but he had risked capture to comfort his sister and be present at his brother-in-law's funeral.

Isaak seemed to respect Yaakov for his dedication to the study of the Torah. It was not difficult to see how studying the Torah filled Yaakov's life with purpose, but Isaak, like her younger brother Zebulun, had never enjoyed the esoteric discussions of the rabbis. Despite her father's many attempts, he had failed to ignite such a passion for Torah in his sons, only his daughter.

Though the rabbi knew his son had bravely dedicated his life to rescuing fellow Jews from the continued persecutions of the Spanish, he still spoke to Diana of his disappointment in him and Zebulun for discarding their traditions like old clothes. She had argued for Isaak that he had found his purpose in rescuing Jews, not in study, and though it was not a traditional route for a chief rabbi's son, there was no justification for being disappointed in him.

Diana hoped Isaak would not sail away this time without seeing his family. She paused before hurrying across the bridge and squinted at the gates of the Ghetto, visible from this distance. She wondered if anyone would see her as she entered the Moorish quarter and possibly question about her purpose there. She shrugged off such worries; she had her justification; she came to this quarter many times to purchase herbs that could be used for many remedies, which could not be found in the apothecary shops.

She hoped to send word to Isaak of Morosini's potential to help them for an interest in the treasure of Christopher Columbus. If anyone could reach Isaak, it would be the Turk, notorious for his expertise in gathering intelligence and sharing it for a price. Besides supplying the apothecaries with exotic and hard-to-find ingredients for remedies, the Turk was a central figure in the dealing of fine spices and silks, as well as gemstones 'liberated' from Spanish vessels. Venetians appreciated luxury, and most had no love of the Spanish, who were the allies of their traditional enemy, Genoa.

The Turk's activities were never challenged. The Council of Ten knew the Turk could be relied upon to perform favors when required.

Diana was hoping to arrive before the Turk's business hours, which were late in the afternoon when many of the Turk's various contracts would be negotiated over thick, hot coffee. Relieved she did not merit a glance from the exotically-dressed men and women who passed her by, Diana knocked boldly on the Turk's door. Subsequently, she was admitted into the courtyard and the center of activity for the Turk's deals and trades.

The gentle gurgle of cascading water from a marble urn into the basin of a fountain at the center accompanied the chirping of birds as they flitted from trees to the beds of flowers arranged in well-tended plots. Diana was charmed by the beauty and serenity and could imagine remaining in this spot to empty her mind of concerns and wild imaginings.

Isaak had spoken to her of meditation, a skill he had acquired in the court of the sultan of Morocco. He attributed his success in the most daring endeavors, both on land and sea, to the focus provided by meditation. He explained the key was to focus only on the means to accomplish a goal without cluttering one's mind with self-doubt. Diana could understand lack of self-confidence could be disastrous, especially if sensed by the men under Isaak's command.

Diana did not allow herself to linger in the seductively serene courtyard; she was here for the Turk's help. Diana heard the murmur of voices and realized she was not the Turk's only visitor. She held back from entering the courtyard, taking refuge in a vine-covered pathway where she could see and hear the other guests without being spotted.

Despite his costume of flowing white robes and white turban, Diana recognized Isaak immediately, who was receiving a comradely kiss on both cheeks from the Turk. The smells of the thick Turkish coffee wafted towards her as a slim veiled woman emerged from the shadows, bearing a tray with the steaming, fragrant brew.

Isaak had joined his host as they seated themselves on colorful cushions beside small intricately carved tables where the veiled woman left the tray and coffee. Diana was about to reveal herself as she listened to the two old friends banter, gossip, and sipping their coffee, but stopped at the sight of another visitor who had just appeared and must have come through the garden right before her. Bardon Morosini bowed to the two men and settled himself comfortably among the cushions beside them. He gave Isaak but a cursory glance and nod, which Diana found amusing, since her brother's disguise had shielded him from being recognized by his former patron.

There was no longer any purpose for her visit, and Diana was about to retrace her steps and depart when she peaked through the vines once more. The nobleman had upended a small purse into his hand and was now stacking a handful of golden ducats onto the small table before the Turk. The Turk snatched the coins away immediately, just as the slim woman, her face veiled, returned to serve him coffee. Morosini sniffed at the aroma of the drink and seemed to enjoy it as he sipped his cup, although his eyes never left the face of the woman who served him.

"Come now, is it really necessary for you to remain veiled?" Diana overheard Morosini ask the woman. "After all, I am no stranger to this house. And I assume," he waved at Isaak, "your other guest is equally well-known to you."

The woman glanced at the Turk and vehemently shook her head, and scurried away. The Turk came to her defense. "Our customs do not permit the unveiling of a female of good character to any man outside of her family. Because you are a *friend*," he emphasized the word with his mouth curving into a slight grimace, as if he dreaded using the word, "I have allowed her to serve you. Otherwise, she would be hidden in her rooms in another part of the house."

Morosini withdrew more golden coins from his pouch to offer to the Turk, but the bushy brows descended over his host's glowering eyes, and understanding dawning, the nobleman stayed his hand.

"It was not my intention to offend," Morosini was about to replace the coins in his purse, but, instead, handed them to the Turk, who nodding, accepted them. He must have felt compelled to explain himself to Isaak, who he assumed had similar sensibilities, "I meant to commend my host on his lovely servant and thought to see her face for that purpose. I must apologize to you as well if I have taken a cultural misstep."

Isaak waved a hand in dismissal, but did not speak. Instead, he raised his coffee to his lips. He must fear his voice would be recognized by Morosini, who he had met when the nobleman had invested in several of his voyages.

The Turk sipped his coffee and watched both his guests over his cup. He said, "I am certain you have far more interesting women to capture your attention."

Morosini replaced his cup on the small table and smoothed his doublet with his elegant hands. Diana recognized the gesture as Morosini's way of preparing himself for a negotiation. She wondered if Isaak would be asked to leave, and if so, should she risk discovery by remaining to hear Morosini's agenda? If Morosini's proposal was solely in the Turk's interest, would Isaak trust his old friend to share it if he did not remain?

Morosini gestured towards Isaak. "Perhaps your guest will allow us some privacy to discuss our business?"

Diana was gratified that Isaak made no move to depart, and the Turk did not seem inclined to dismiss him. "My friend should not disturb you. His interests coincide with my own."

The nobleman sighed and waved a hand at Isaak. "I must assume he understands, as you do, that my business should not be shared and that I have the ways and means to deal with anyone who chooses to disregard my wishes."

The Turk leaned closer to the nobleman, and he spoke in lower tones, so Diana could not hear all that was said. She did catch the Turk's final comment, which was made in his usual booming voice. "You have made your point, and I shall make mine. You have dangled your gold and have made your threats. Now let us talk business."

"Actually, it is because of your knowledge of the surreptitious comings and goings of this city I have come to you," said Morosini, smoothing his well-groomed mustache, "I want information about a woman who is missing and is of great importance. No doubt you have heard of her and even been in her employ. She is known by the name of Belladonna."

Chapter Twenty-One: Diana

"**B**elladonna the courtesan? I had not heard of her disappearance. Perhaps she has just gone away and does not want to be found?" the Turk angled his head and squinted at the nobleman.

Morosini barked a laugh. "A woman like Belladonna would never leave her palazzo in such a manner, and certainly not for a man, as you imply. If she left of her own free will, it was for a good reason, and it would be important for me to know why. If she has met with foul play, I would know by whom and why." His eyes narrowed once more as he regarded Isaak. "Of late, my interests have aligned with Belladonna's, and I would know the enemy who lurks at my door."

Isaak was busy lifting his cup, although nearly empty, to his lips. Diana assumed it was to avoid speaking.

Isaak's action made Morosini take notice of him, and in a suspicious tone of voice, he asked the Turk, "Does your friend understand our language?"

"A bit, but he does not speak it at all," said the Turk, and as if to demonstrate, he unleashed a discourse in Arabic, a language Isaak would understand, but both Diana and Morosini did not.

Isaak managed to answer in Arabic in a low guttural voice, which seemed to satisfy Morosini.

"I assume you are asking for his aid in your investigation," said Morosini, as he tapped his fingers on his knee, an obvious attempt to control his agitation.

The Turk clapped the nobleman on his back and grinned. "My friend says it should not be difficult to discover if this woman has sailed from Venice, and I agree. Our men proliferate the harbor, and they will keep a vigilant eye to all comings and goings, especially of the Spanish. If this lady is seen boarding any ship in the harbor, I will be aware of it."

The Turk's answer seemed to mollify Morosini, and pulling a lace handkerchief from his sleeve, he swiftly mopped his forehead. The Turk rose along with his guest, who was saying his farewell. Before he departed, he gave Isaak a mock salute and added, "Tell your friend if he notices anything unusual on any Spanish ship now in port, he should send word to me directly."

The Turk gave Isaak a sharp glance before acceding to Morosini's demand that word should be sent to him within the week. Satisfied, Morosini took his leave, his well-shod heels clicking loudly as he followed the marble path out of the courtyard.

When Morosini was safely out of earshot, the Turk's fawning attitude dropped, and he raised his bushy eyebrows at Isaak. "I suppose you have an idea of where the lady is?"

Diana stepped out of the vine-covered enclosure and ran to her brother, flinging her arms around his neck. The Turk's bushy brows shot up to his cap. As Isaak disengaged himself from her arms, he spoke to her in the scolding tone of an older brother, "Diana! Whatever are you doing here?"

"I came here to ask the Turk to help me contact you." She smoothed her hair and gave a smile to the Turk. "I have known Zebulun to come here when he needed to reach you, so I decided to do the same." Their younger brother had recently sailed away from Venice, and though Diana did not know where he was, she assumed her older brother might.

Returning to the Turk's question, Isaak said, "If I did know where to find the lady, I would not be simple-minded enough to share it, now would I?"

The Turk laughed heartily. "You are swimming in dangerous waters, my friend. Morosini is a devil, though one we may count on from time to time. The Spanish, they are vicious and not likely to give up easily when they have set their sights on their prey. Have you heard of Antonio?" the Turk tented his fingers before them, as if preparing to recite a tale, "Antonio the Assassin. He is often in the employ of the Spanish ambassador. However, I know more of Antonio than his employer. Antonio is clever enough to have purchased a vineyard in the Veneto, because the Spanish, who do not pay their soldiers at all, pay their assassins not as well as they should. Therefore, Antonio has a nice business going, as he is open to negotiations from his targets to delay their execution long enough for them to escape."

"Interesting. However, it is never wise to underestimate the Spanish. I never have, which is why I am still alive." Isaak said. He turned his attention back to Diana. "So, what has led to such great urgency that you had to come here? And tell us, how much have you overheard of our discussion with Bardon Morosini?"

The Turk gestured to the cushions and invited Diana to sit. Awkwardly, she angled herself down to a large cushion and found it quite comfortable. Isaak sat nearby, and the Turk clapped his hands loudly. Emerging from the shadows was the lovely woman swathed in veils. She carried another steaming pot of aromatic coffee on her tray. "My daughter," the Turk introduced the veiled woman, who bowed her head in deference to them and then served the coffee. Diana refused a cup, as she adhered to the Jewish dietary laws and would never partake of food or drink outside the Ghetto, even in the home of her friend, Belladonna. She inhaled the rich aroma and then answered her brother's question. "I had met with Morosini at Belladonna's request. He will lend his support to our endeavor to find Roderigo and to keep Belladonna out of reach of the Spanish." Diana was unsure of how much to share with the Turk about their plans.

"It must have been quite a shock to see him here." Her brother gave her a short nod and then gave the Turk the full explanation. "The Spanish know of the treasure of Christopher Columbus and the existence of a map to pinpoint its location. The heirs of Columbus hold dominion over the island, but they are eager to relinquish it to Spain, expecting a good price for their cooperation. The Spanish are determined to annex the island of Jamaica, and the Inquisition must already smell the opportunity of looting its New Christians and Jewish settlers."

The Turk's brows descended into an angry frown. "The Inquisition. What they did to your people, they had done to mine in Spain. They continue to attack ships belonging to Morocco or under the sultan of Constantinople, slaughtering the crew or turning them into slaves in their galleys. Now, they wish to spread their evil to the New World. You have my attention and my help, of course."

Isaak clapped his friend on the shoulder and explained that he had become involved when the Jews of Jamaica had sent word to the Brethren, the brotherhood of Jewish corsairs, sworn enemies of Spain. The plan shared with the Brethren was ambitious and optimistic; its goal was to lure the English into taking the island of Jamaica, adding the promise of an undiscovered treasure to the benefit of acquiring a key asset for trade in the West Indies.

"If Morosini is willing to expend his resources to support our efforts and protect Belladonna, we should consider letting him 'find' her. Your help is needed in a matter of greater importance, of keeping watch for the envoy, Roderigo Mendoza, the man who holds the key to the treasure and the island of Jamaica."

Now, Isaak had the Turk's full attention. He leaned forward, a grin on his lips and a gleam in his eye. "You can count on me to call upon all my resources."

Diana supposed Isaak trusted the Turk enough to share so much with him. Doubtless, it would not hurt their cause to have the Moors as their ally. In case the English could not be persuaded to come to the aid of Jamaica, perhaps the Berber pirates would. Vast stores of gold were a delight to any Corsair, no matter where it was located. Isaak fed him the tale of the lost gold of Christopher Columbus and how its location was entrusted only to the descendants of the young men who had saved him from the mutineers and had been the first settlers in Jamaica. "The man who is missing, Roderigo, has been entrusted with the secret of those descendants. The treasure is to be offered to the English, which can only be obtained when they invade Jamaica."

The Turk chuckled. "A noble cause and a lost treasure. All the right ingredients. Now, tell me what this missing man looks like and when he was last seen in Venice..."

Chapter Twenty-Two: Diana

The next day, Diana was on a different mission. Her leather slippers were stained with wetness even though she had tried her best to avoid the puddles in her path. She was wearing her best day dress, which had been a present from Belladonna, and she was headed to the rooms of the artist, Mattia Correr. Though her purpose was to check on the Englishman, she was glad of the excuse to see Mattia again. As she approached the bridge leading to the Ca Vendramin where the artist lived and worked, her breath quickened, and her heart pounded in her chest.

The door to the inner courtyard was open, as if someone had just exited. It was odd to find the doors unlocked and no sign of anyone within. Mattia's housekeeper was usually lurking, but there was no sign or sound of her presence.

Diana slipped inside and up the stairs towards the *piano nobile* where Mattia had his studio. The double doors to the large salon he used as his studio were open as well, and she navigated her way through the clutter of canvas, cloth, glass jars, and pots of paint, calling out the artist's name. She touched the back of the chaise where she had once posed for her portrait and, more recently, had been the place she had tended to the wounded man. Now, it was empty, its damask coverlet puddling on the floor.

Perhaps the Englishman had been moved to Mattia's bedroom? She called out the artist's name once more and stopped short of the artist's inner rooms. Whether Mattia was alone there or the Englishman, she could not venture further alone. Her scalp prickled. Could the men responsible for the attack on the Englishman have discovered him and in his weakened condition, taken him away? If so, what would they have done with Mattia?

No matter what had happened, Diana sensed this was not the place for the rabbi's unchaperoned daughter to be found. She retraced her steps through the cluttered salon and was about to make her escape when a large man blocked her path to the staircase. He grabbed her by the arms, and she squirmed to wrest herself free, but he held her tight.

"Diana!"

She froze at the sound of the name and, looking up into the man's face, was astonished to discover Isaak. This time, dressed in the clothes of the common laborer, wearing a cap pulled low over his face and covering his curly dark hair. In this guise, Isaak appeared broader and sturdier than the day before when he wore the flowing robes of an Arab.

"What are you doing here?" brother and sister spoke at the same time.

Before either could answer, a voice called out to them from the stairway below.

"Who are you?"

Mattia had returned. In a few seconds, he had bounded up the stairs and now stood glaring at Isaak. "I repeat: who are you and what are you doing here?"

Diana placed a warning hand on her brother's arm and was relieved when he unclenched his fist. "Mattia, meet Isaak, my brother."

The artist's face softened into a smile. "Then I must welcome him and ask to what I owe the occasion of your visit?"

Isaak answered in his usual manner, using as few words as possible. "The Englishman."

"Where is he?" Diana added.

Mattia shrugged. "The fool insisted on leaving. He claimed he had a mission to fulfill and must be off to Sir Henry. I went out to find a gondola to transport a wounded man discreetly, only to see he had left on his own."

He ushered them into the salon, kicking away a tousle of fabrics in their path, which he pointed to. "Left quite a mess in his departure, as you can see."

After inviting them to take any seat they could find, Mattia went to the sideboard where the shapes of various decanters towered over jars of colored powders and liquids. "He finished my best brandy, too." Mattia sighed, "Ah, I wish him well. My experience of Englishmen has demonstrated I do myself no good by associating with them."

Mattia's reference was not lost on Diana or Isaak. They knew he was referring to the events of the spring, when his commission from an English lord to paint the portraits of the most beautiful women in Venice had turned out poorly for him and forced him to flee the city. However, as the wise rabbis of the Talmud argued, often out of terrible events, there is found some good—at least for Diana. It was due to the artist's selection of her to be painted for the Englishman's "gallery of beauties" she had been introduced to Belladonna and Venetian society.

Mattia handed a glass of wine to her, which she refused, and then to Isaak, which he accepted. The walls of the salon were all mirrored, and she could not resist glancing at her reflection. She had never thought about her appearance until Mattia had begged her to sit for her portrait for the Gallery of Beauties. She had spent her life studying with her father and her husband, and though both men always lavished praise upon her, it was not for her beauty but for her erudition. She had always valued herself as a scholar, not as a woman of beauty.

From the moment she had met Mattia, she had felt herself change. It was more than the lavender dress he had given her, but the way he looked at her when he was painting her. Perhaps, as the kabbalah suggested, there had been some transference of souls as he brought her image to life on his canvas. She glanced sideways at Isaak and was glad her completed portrait did not hang in the artist's rooms, but in the palazzo of Belladonna.

The two men had seemed to have lost interest in her, and Mattia's eyes were wide as he listened to Isaak's explanation of Villiers' appearance in Venice and Belladonna's need to disappear from her palazzo and into the Ghetto.

Isaak concluded with, "By coming to the aid of the Englishman, your actions will save many others. The Spanish are well-informed and determined, as their attempt on Villiers occurred as soon as he stepped foot in this city. It was our good luck, since you happened upon Villiers at random. The Spanish would have no inkling of where to find him. It is unfortunate the Englishman has departed, for I am certain the Spanish will be waiting for him at Sir Henry's, and he is at risk of another attack."

"Perhaps that is his strategy," Diana interjected, and both men turned to her with raised eyebrows. "To be obvious, in plain sight, would force the Spanish to show their hand, creating an ugly incident which would require action from the Council of Ten."

"I would agree with Diana," nodded Mattia, "this Villiers seems as sly as a fox."

"His wound was significant, yet he was not deterred from going out again. I would guess he is no stranger to such attacks," added Diana.

"My little sister surprises me," Isaak said, squinting as if to see her more clearly. "It seems you are not only an accomplished healer, but have become more knowledgeable about the ways of the men who come under your care."

Diana felt her face flushing. "I confess, I did not expect the Englishman would be able to walk so soon. It is a wonder he was able to leave on his own. "

Mattia grinned. "I noticed the Englishman was quite charming to my housekeeper. No doubt you have noticed her absence. I believe she lent him her more than ample shoulder to help him on his way."

"If he has made it without incident to Sir Henry's perhaps, as Diana suggests, he is safe there. As Sir Henry is a friend of our father, we have access to the Englishman when we are ready."

Mattia had leaned back in his chair and stretched his long legs before him, wine glass in hand as he posed his next question. "And when will that be?"

Isaak sniffed the contents of the glass before drinking from it. "When we have the envoy, Roderigo Mendez. The Spanish are searching for him, and we must find him before they do."

"You are a nervous fellow."

"It is why I am still alive, my friend."

Isaak rose to depart, and Diana had to follow his lead, disappointed she would not have the opportunity to speak with Mattia alone. Even a renegade such as Isaak would not allow her to remain alone with the artist. Mattia stood and made the offer to show them out, but Isaak waved him away. Isaak escorted Diana through the outer door and closed it with a resolute click behind them.

"Do not think you will escape a visit to our mother," she said, grabbing Isaak's sleeve so he could not escape her, "No one will recognize you dressed as you are, so there is no excuse—"

"I have every intention of visiting our parents," Isaak interrupted her, "It will give me the opportunity to see you safely home and hear more about how you have become acquainted with the artist, Mattia Correr."

Chapter Twenty-Three: Villiers

G eorge Villiers felt much more comfortable in his new surroundings. Though the artist was a good fellow, and they might have enjoyed a bit of carousing together, the spacious and well-appointed palazzo of Sir Henry Wotton was more to his taste. The gondola ride over had not troubled his wound much, as he had been cradled in the ample arms of the housekeeper, who helped him up the grand staircase to the *piano nobile* of the ambassador's residence.

Sir Henry had not expected him, an amusing irony since their enemies, the Spanish had. However, like a good English nobleman, Sir Henry had ensured his new guest was shown to the very best room and given the utmost attention by his servants. His bags arrived miraculously intact from the inn to which he had originally sent them, and he was able to bathe and change. Now, feeling more like his regular self, he was seated in Sir Henry's book-lined study, a decanter of excellent wine before him and a newly poured glass in his hand.

What he appreciated about Sir Henry, most of all, was his wine. Sir Henry really was a good sport, not raising an eyebrow when he asked repeatedly for another bottle to be brought from the wine cellar.

Villiers ached to go out and explore the glories of this fair city. The Venetian ambassador—whatever the poor fellow's name was—was quite right when he moaned at having to leave the festive city of his birth for the grey muck of London. His ending was quite poetic, once you consider he could have just been stabbed in some hallway. No, the poisoned cloak was clever and had delivered a glorious death that would be remembered for years to come.

Villiers cursed himself for allowing himself to be stabbed on his first night in Venice, and after a lucrative night at the gaming tables, no less. He should have heeded the unspoken warning of the Venetian ambassador's spectacular death—but he had been way too cocky and spoiled by being a favorite of his King. Fate had taken his bravado down a peg, now, had it not?

He squinted a bit, and gulped a mouthful of wine as he remembered the spectacular death of the Venetian ambassador at the Hampton Court Masque. It had spurred his King to send him to Venice, at the court's expense, in pursuit of the treasure and the envoy. With the dying man's last words, it had also directed him to "Belladonna."

An Italian word, meaning "beautiful woman." In this city, it referred to a specific woman, an elite courtesan who had particular appeal not only because she was rumored to be beautiful, but also extremely rich. At the present, it was the lady's fortune that had awakened his desire, as well as the secret she knew which promised an even greater yield. A poor run of luck, so when he arrived, the lovely Belladonna had disappeared. No word or hint of where she had gone or any clue to locate the envoy who had come from the New World supposedly seeking her.

"Have you been contacted by the envoy?" Sir Henry's fingers did a dance across the papers on his desk, and his brows were creased in a frown.

Villiers took a long sip and a deep swallow of the wine before answering with a simple, "No."

"I fear the man has been captured or killed, and this will not bode well for our interests in the Caribbean."

Villiers touched the wound at his side. "The Spanish have much to answer for."

Sir Henry's thick eyebrows rose over his eyes as he pointed a warning finger at Villiers. "We cannot afford to escalate this now. At the moment, the Council of Ten are clearly aligned with us, and the Spanish have lost favor, but I do not want to risk a confrontation that can sway them to the other side. To the Venetians, commerce is king, and if the Spanish make it more lucrative to align with their interest, England stands to lose, despite our contracts with them for Arundel's swift ships."

Villiers swallowed a large gulp of wine loudly at the mention of Arundel. Enough about his rival's acquisition of the Venetian design for the swift ships! Arundel had trumpeted this accomplishment at Court, about how these ships could literally run circles around older vessels, perfect for engaging in a bit of piracy when there was a well-laden Spanish ship on the horizon.

His attention had wandered from the conversation, so Villiers now tuned in to what Sir Henry was saying. "Our two nations are in a dance of aggression which we do not want to escalate into war. Remember, there are those at court who wish for an alliance by positioning the prince as a bridegroom for the Spanish princess," Sir Henry said, causing Villiers to snort loudly at such a possibility. Sir Henry was scowling as he warned, "We must watch our step, Sir George, or we could easily lose the King's favor."

Ahh, so that is what has this courtier so fidgety. He had thought Sir Henry secure in his statesmanship, having the pedigree and, what is most important, a great fortune behind him. It was beginning to concern Villiers that his own position at court may be shakier than he imagined, and it would be best to end this adventure as soon as he was able. With the likes of Arundel parading his success with the fleet, it was wise to get back to the King's side quickly, with the results His Majesty expected.

"Where the devil is this man with the treasure map!" the words came out before he could stop them. He lowered his head sheepishly and peeked up at Sir Henry to see if he had offended him.

Luckily, the ambassador was smiling. "I am gratified you are eager to get to the matter at hand. Although the Spanish must be handled with finesse, we should not hold back any means to locate the envoy, get his promised treasure, and his people's assistance in Jamaica."

"If Jamaica is so bloody important to the Spanish, why should we be hesitating? Why not just take it?" It must be the wine, which was excellent, which was removing the polish from Villiers' words to state his thoughts so bluntly to the ambassador.

The ambassador's face lit up as he answered. "I agree. It is the gateway to all the trade of the West Indies—sugar, and spices like nutmeg, which are worth more than their weight in gold. Whoever controls Jamaica has the keys to the wealth of the New World. But, as I warned, there are others in Court who do not want to antagonize the Spanish."

Villiers put his now-empty glass down on the desk with a resolute bang. "A pox on the Spanish! Time is not on our side, and we need this man. Now. You have lived here long enough, so you must have an idea of how to locate a missing visitor. My wound is on the mend, thanks to the ministrations of a pretty little woman—"

Sir Henry's eyebrows shot up instantly. "A woman healed you. Was she a Jewess?"

Villiers pursed his lips, trying to remember. "How the devil should I know? The painter fellow, Correr, brought her to my aid. Why?"

Sir Henry tented his fingers before his face and smiled. "The Hebrew people are quite knowledgeable in the medicinal arts, and many prefer to come under their care. I have built a friendship with the leader of the Jews, who is skilled in healing, as his daughter, who is also a lovely woman. If Diana has tended to you, they will already be aware of the danger we face. These Hebrew people are key to the search for the envoy."

"Why is that?"

Sir Henry gave him a curious look. "Did you not know? The envoy is a Jew."

Villiers pursed his lips. "Ah, well, I know nothing of Jews or Hebrews or whatever they are called. I do not believe we have any of them in England. But returning to the courtesan. The artist, that Mattia fellow, he has to have painted Belladonna as she is considered one of the most beautiful women in Venice. He seems to know the women he paints quite well, so he may have an inkling as to where she has gone. I will invite him here to thank him, formally, for saving my life. With his help, I will pursue Belladonna, and you will go after the envoy with the help of your Hebrew friends."

"Mmm. It is possible…. Although Correr has been traveling and only recently returned to the city." He turned his gaze to the ceiling, and his fingers tapped one well-shaven cheek. "Although…perhaps…he might have some information on where in the Veneto she might find sanctuary. I shall send him a note."

The ambassador took out some paper and his quill and began scratching rapidly.

Calling out to his servant, Sir Henry put down his pen and folded the note. He pulled open a drawer in the small desk and retrieved wax, which he held over the candle, then applied it to his note and fixed it with his seal. He handed it to his manservant, who bowed and disappeared.

"Very well. We shall see."

Villiers smiled. "While we await his arrival, perhaps some more of your excellent wine?"

Chapter Twenty-Four: Diana

The light was fading, the shadows deep enough in the recessed doorways to hide an enemy. Diana was grateful for an escort through the less traveled *calles* she would have had to navigate alone to the Ghetto.

Isaak's rough work boots striking the stone pathway was the only sound disturbing their silent progress. Isaak was never one to chat or make idle talk. He used words sparingly, bluntly, and only with purpose. They had not seen each other in too long a time, and there was an awkwardness between them as if they were strangers.

"Much has changed since you were last in Venice," she started, intending to openly address the questions her brother must have about her.

Her brother arched one eyebrow and tilted his head. "The gates are still closed at nightfall. Our father still manages to gamble away all his earnings?"

She smiled at his teasing tone and answered him with a bluntness he would appreciate, "I suppose then it is I who have changed."

Her big brother surprised her by sidling up close and placing a protective arm around her shoulders. "It must be for the better, for when I left, your cheeks were not so rosy, nor was there the glint of determination in your eyes."

His words and his arm warmed her. "Though we live a precarious existence, I have learned we do not have to remain secluded and isolated. The world outside of the Ghetto has much to offer, and I have dared to venture out to acquire what I can. I shall not be limited by my own insecurity."

CHAPTER TWENTY-FOUR: DIANA

"How has this come to pass? After the death of Yaakov—"

Tears started at the mention of her dead husband, and Diana blinked her eyes rapidly to stop them from falling. "I found solace in the study of Torah after his death. Each day my goal has been to master a new page of Talmud. It had been my only focus, until one day, I was approached in the marketplace by the artist Mattia Correr. He begged me to allow him to paint my portrait for a commission to paint the most beautiful women of Venice for an English lord."

Isaak stopped. "And you agreed? To venture out of the Ghetto, to pose for a stranger, a non-Jew? You risked not only our father's reputation and livelihood, but imprisonment from the Venetian authorities."

Diana drew her shawl over the tell-tale yellow badge still blazing from her dress. Although Morosini had once promised her she was exempt from wearing the badge that marked her as a Jew, she was taking no chances. It had been bold enough to leave the Ghetto on her own, but she still feared being detained by a soldier from the Council of Ten for being without it. "I was barely living before. Venturing beyond the gates, my eyes were opened—to the art of painting, to the glories of Carnevale. My senses and my curiosity were awakened. I was alive again and could never return to my life as it had been before."

Isaak nodded. "We are gamblers, just like our father. Although we risk our lives, while our father merely gambles with his meager fortune."

Diana slapped Isaak's hand playfully. "Do not speak ill of our father. His gambling relieves anxiety and gives him hope. Besides his study of Torah, he has little to enjoy besides the gaming tables."

"Our mother has not changed, then. She still harangues him day and night?"

Diana looked up to her brother's weather-bronzed face. "It will do much for them both to see you once more."

Isaak did not comment, but squeezed her shoulder. "Sometimes I feel bereft, as if I have lost you all. Maudlin thoughts, which can be dangerous for one who must always be confident of a way to achieve success. It is only when I see Zebulun—"

"You have news of our younger brother? Does he live under the patronage of the English lord?" With Belladonna's help, her younger brother Zebulun was introduced to Arundel, who had helped Zebulun secure a ship and the promise of a secure future in England.

"Zebulun prefers his ship to the English shore. Besides, Arundel's patronage was contingent on Zebulun renouncing his faith, which our brother found himself unable to do."

Diana exhaled as she imagined her daring younger brother, face to the wind, standing on the prow of his sailing ship. "He finally achieved what he wanted. He is brave enough to make his own way."

They were walking in lock step now, but Isaak paused at the last bridge and the entry, flanked by the gates, to the Ghetto. Diana glanced about them, assuring herself there was no one in sight, and pulled her brother beyond the gates.

Isaak brushed his fingers against the mezuzah on the doorpost and kissed them. Diana wondered if his gesture signaled a return to traditionalism or was a remnant of it.

The rabbi was not sitting in his usual place at the table when the brother and sister entered. Their mother was sitting on a low stool by the hearth, chucking the shells off lentils and adding them to the wooden bowl on her lap. A black cauldron was heating on the fire, and Diana inhaled the tantalizing smell of cooking vegetables and spices. Her mother did not look up at the sound of her arrival, but when she saw a man behind her daughter, she jumped up, upending the bowl and scattering lentils onto the floor.

"Isaak!"

Her mother recognized her son, no matter how different he now appeared. Diana stepped out of her mother's path just as she threw herself into her son's arms.

At their mother's scream, the rabbi appeared, scowling. Lowered brows rose, almost to the rim of his worn velvet cap, when he saw his wife in the arms of a male visitor.

Gently releasing himself from his mother's grasp, Isaak addressed his father. "I have returned, Father, but not for long."

The rabbi's face flushed, and Diana hoped it was a sign of joy and not anger. The rabbi fell against the wall, directing his gaze upward. "He returns," the rabbi murmured, as if he were addressing the heavens and not his family, "but he must go again. So, what else is new? Distancing himself from us, the Torah, and our traditions."

It was Isaak's turn to scowl, and he said, "You disappoint me. I had thought you understood the path I have taken."

"I disappoint *you!*" the rabbi's face flushed again, and he glared at his son. "You could have been a scholar and perhaps a great rabbi. Instead, you go off to sea, like some ne'er-do-well with no regard for—"

"Please, Father, Isaak has risked much to return. You should be proud of him; he is prepared to face death or imprisonment to save a fellow Jew. Does not the Torah teach us "saving a life overrides even the laws of the Sabbath?" And what of *Tikun Olam*—Isaak is certainly trying to do something for the betterment of the world. He defends the defenseless—men and women taken and imprisoned by the Inquisition or Maltese pirates."

Her father did not answer at first. Then he nodded, saying, "How like you, Diana, to use logic and Torah reasoning to make your point." He opened his arms to Isaak, "Welcome home, my son."

Diana smiled as Isaak's hard-lined face softened into a smile, transforming it, for a moment, into the visage of the boy she remembered. *Isaak wants to come home.* It dawned on her that this time, Isaak's return was tempting him to give up his seafaring days. Because of his family, or maybe for his love of Belladonna? She chided herself to keep her musings to herself. It would do no good to raise hopes that were doomed to be dashed.

"What has brought you here? And, I am loathe to ask, what danger lies ahead?" The rabbi had taken a seat in his usual chair and directed Isaak to pull up the stool and sit beside him.

Diana joined her mother in gathering the precious lentils from the floor. Isaak gave his father a summary of all that had occurred and asked for ideas of where to search for Roderigo.

The rabbi had little insight into where a visitor like the envoy might be found. However, he did indicate he would do all he could to help them.

"I will speak to Sir Henry to gain some insight into the English interest in Jamaica and of this man, Villiers," the rabbi said, then he inhaled the aroma of the cooking stew and asked his son in a fatherly tone, "in the meantime, are you hungry?"

Chapter Twenty-Five: Belladonna

Belladonna was tiring of all the rituals that had been foisted upon her in the Ghetto. There were ablutions in the morning, where she was expected to toss water over her hands no less and no more than six times. Then there were blessings to be made not only over food, but after exiting the privies, to thank the Almighty for their proper function, as Sarra explained.

Like Sarra, she refused to get involved in the kitchen, for there were rituals for baking bread she did not want to know. For once, she was grateful for being a woman, so she would not be required to attend prayer services three times a day. How did a rational woman like Diana manage the duties and activities required by an invisible, absent god?

Beneath the watchful eye of Mirabella, the surly servant, she dare not expose her skepticism or her lack of enthusiasm for the Jewish customs. Before she could get rid of Mirabella, she had to be wary of what the servant might say or use against her.

Belladonna supposed her annoyance with the rituals and the Sullams' servant stemmed from her frustration at her inability to find her brother. They had expected a Jew visiting Venice would seek to be housed among his own people, so Diana had checked the guest houses in and around the Ghetto, but none had a visitor from the New World. They had to find Roderigo before the Englishman grew tired of waiting for the missing man and abandoned the whole scheme to return to England.

The Englishman made her lips curl into an involuntary smile. A type she knew well, so it should not prove difficult to keep his interest if she took it upon herself to do so. He was a man to be equally enticed by acquiring a beautiful woman as finding a treasure, as long as each proved equally elusive. However, how could she continue her search for Roderigo if she had to reveal herself to Villiers?

Would it be possible to visit Villiers at Sir Henry's under the guise of 'Raquel,' a widow from the Ghetto? Would such a visitor be so unusual it would arouse suspicion from the Spanish, who must be watching the visitors to the English ambassador? If the Spanish recognized her, and she fell into their hands....

She was treading on uncertain ground, out of her element. Isaak—where was he now? Could she call on him for help?

Without realizing it, she had twisted a yellow scarf into a tightly wound twist. She had meant to wrap it around her head as a turban, but used it to bind her hair back behind her neck instead. At the sound of footsteps, she turned away from her reflection in the mirror to find Diana had arrived.

"Have you learned anything new?"

"Well, not really, but I have an idea." The rabbi's daughter joined her, and the two seated themselves on a comfortable couch in Sarra's smaller salon. Diana's violet eyes glittered with excitement as she explained. "It seems as if your brother did not visit or contact anyone within the Ghetto. If he came to Venice to find you, as Isaak suggested, as a foreigner, he would not know where to begin looking, would he? Visitors from the Levant or Europe are often directed to one man in the Moorish quarter, who has a reputation for finding whatever is needed in Venice."

Belladonna sat up straighter, clasping her hands tightly as she felt a surge of hope. "Take me to him."

Diana pointed at Belladonna's golden hair. "It would be best for us both to cover our hair where we are going."

Belladonna followed Diana to bind her hair with a scarf as they descended down the staircase. She reminded herself to walk demurely, with her eyes down, focused only on the ground before her until they reached their destination.

Out of the Ghetto Nuovo across a rail-less wooden bridge and through another gated threshold, they found themselves in a throng of men and women dressed in bright, colorful fabrics and chattering in languages she did not understand. Diana grasped her hand and pulled her along the *fondimenta* forcing her to navigate between the clusters of humanity and the glistening puddles beneath her feet. The people and the air smelled different here, filled with scents of exotic perfumes and spices from cook pots.

They came to a *Campo dei Mori,* having gotten its name from the statues of three Moors carved into the front of the square's buildings. It was rumored they were three Moorish brothers who engaged in a great fraud and were turned to stone as punishment. A loud cry, coming out of the sky, startled Belladonna, and she stumbled and fell, but Diana caught her before she pitched into the canal.

"It is the Moslem's call to prayer. Pay it no mind." She helped Belladonna to right herself and position her shawl over her yellow badge. When Belladonna raised an eyebrow, Diana explained. "One never knows who harbors resentment against us. It is best to be discreet."

Belladonna reluctantly tied her shawl into position, although both the badge and the act annoyed her. She was tired of her role and felt like her head was being forcibly bent into submission. Diana was not timid but did not appear docile, and she admired the skill of maintaining her dignity despite being subjected to scorn.

"We are nearly there," Diana reassured her as they turned down a narrow alleyway. Cats screeched and scattered at their feet, since they had interrupted their meal of fish scraps snagged from a nearby pile of discarded household trash. Diana did not slow or falter, and as Belladonna struggled to keep up, she tried not to inhale as much as possible.

At last, they came to a green-painted door inset into a wall. Diana had located a leather cord, and a tinkle of bells followed her tug on it. The door creaked open, releasing a scent of flowers as a dark-eyed girl greeted them. The girl's voice was so soft Belladonna was not able to catch what she said to Diana. Nevertheless, she and Diana followed the girl's fluttering purple veils through a lovely garden filled with flowers of different colors, sizes, and odors, all of them pleasant. Butterflies and bees danced across upturned sunflowers, and the tinkle of water cascading from a pedestal-shaped fountain cast a soothing melody. Belladonna inhaled deeply and was tempted to stay in this hidden Garden of Eden. She slowed her footsteps and closed her eyes for a moment, and when she opened them, her heart pounded.

Before her, hands on hips and dressed like a Moor, was Isaak.

How white his teeth were against his skin! She winced when he greeted her by calling her "Raquel. Why are you here?"

Had they been alone, she would fall into his arms. In the presence of his sister and a man she barely knew, she had to respond to his question.

"I had to come."

"What do you mean?"

"Villiers has been attacked. Finding my brother has become more urgent. This whole affair will come to an end if the Englishman is murdered. We thought the Turk might be able to help us."

Isaak nodded. "I have heard Sir George Villiers is a man who will die with his boots on." When he saw Diana's puzzled expression, Isaak explained, "he is too cocky, has made scores of enemies, and is very likely to be murdered."

They were interrupted by the arrival of their host, the Turk, whose thick form was draped in an appealing saffron robe and matching turban. "Welcome again, dear sister of my dear friend Isaak." He bowed to Diana and peered up at Belladonna. "Is this another sister?"

"No, a visiting friend and a widow like my sister. Raquel Mendoza from Livorno," Isaak quickly explained, giving Belladonna no chance to speak. Acting the part of the demure widow, she inclined her head slightly in greeting.

"We have not seen each other since we were children, and we have much about our family to talk about, which will only bore you. You understand, my friend?" Isaak added, clapping the Turk on the shoulder.

"Perfectly," the Turk answered, bowing at the two women as he prepared to take his leave.

"Wait," Diana said, glaring at her brother. "We have come to speak with you and beg a few moments."

The Turk stroked the thicket of his beard, and his dark eyes twinkled. "But of course, how can I be of service?"

Gesturing them to be seated on a sprawl of cushions arranged in the shady section of the courtyard, the Turk squatted down, careful not to bunch up his robe. "What can a simple businessman like me do for the daughter of the illustrious Rabbi Leone di Modena?"

"We are looking for someone," Diana began, giving her brother a warning look to keep quiet, "who you might have encountered as a result of your business dealings."

"I assume he is a merchant or a trader from the Levant?" he said, rubbing his hands together. Isaak seemed unable to contain himself and began pacing, his white embroidered robe pulled back, exposing a short sword tucked into the black wrapping at his waist.

Belladonna was distracted by Isaak's pacing, and it took her a moment to respond. "No, he is recently arrived from the New World."

The Turk's eyebrows raised even higher, and he pursed his lips. "Aha, this is becoming very interesting. A Spaniard, perhaps?"

"Stop playing with them," Isaak stopped pacing. "You know they would not come to ask you, of all people, about a Spaniard."

"Everyone is looking for someone these days, but why must they all come to me?" he raised his arms dramatically towards the sky as if he was appealing to a god. "Morosini comes to the Turk with his own request. He is seeking a woman, a courtesan, no less. Then you come to me to ask after a foreigner. Why come to me? Do you suppose the courtesan might have been kidnapped, possibly bound for the Sultan's harem?"

Isaak's warning glance made Belladonna swallow her comment. She cleared her throat and asked, "Who was he seeking?"

"A courtesan who calls herself, 'Belladonna.'"

Was he teasing her? Had he guessed who she was?

Isaak took charge of the conversation. "Well, never mind this woman, my friend. Their purpose in coming here was to ask about a man who recently arrived from the New World. Tell them, please, if you have any word of such a visitor?"

The Turk did not answer but clapped his hands loudly. A soft swish of silk and the scent of exotic flowers signaled the appearance of the veiled girl who had opened the door for them.

"Coffee, my dear, for my guests."

"We cannot partake of any refreshments, sir, but appreciate your hospitality," Diana informed him. Belladonna wiped any signs of disappointment from her face; she yearned for the strong taste of the Turk's brew.

"Oh yes, I had forgotten," the Turk raised his hand to dismiss his daughter, "your dietary laws are more stringent than ours."

"Tell us, please, if you know where this man may be." Diana leaned forward, and Belladonna was surprised by the earnestness of her look. She would not have expected such a performance from Diana. Perhaps the young woman had learned more from her tutelage than she had suspected.

The Turk grinned. "What interest does the daughter of Rabbi Leone di Modena have in a merchant from the New World?"

Isaak answered for his sister. "The same interest we share. To prevent the Spanish from pillaging their way through another country."

The Turk's smile withered, and his mouth settled into a straight simple line. "The Spanish deserve only destruction and death. I suppose this man you are seeking, he is one of yours, Isaak?"

"The envoy is of the Hebrew faith, yes, but he has come to Venice from the New World." With an eye to Belladonna, he continued, "Let us get down to business. If you can find the envoy, it will earn you a hefty finder's fee."

"How much?"

"Five thousand ducats."

"Ten."

"I am not certain," Isaak stroked his chin, "if we can raise that much."

"Fifteen." Belladonna's voice stopped the Turk before he could make a counteroffer, and his lips broadened into a wide smile.

Isaak scowled at her. "Raquel, I do not think you understand. The Brethren must allocate funds towards ransoms in the East and funding ships like my own. We cannot demand such an extravagant allocation."

Belladonna's retort died on her lips. It would be out of character for a woman like Raquel to contradict him and could also alienate the Moor. She took a different approach instead. "I am sorry, but I fear the danger of the Inquisition and what they will do to Jamaica."

The Turk's face flushed at the mention of the Inquisition. "You are right, my dear. To stop the Inquisition is a duty which overrides profit—this one time. Very well, I will accept the first offer of five thousand ducats."

Isaak gave a dramatic bow. "As always, I am impressed by your altruism."

The Turk sighed. "I am a generous man, it is true, but I am not one to let opportunity pass me by. I can also recognize a great beauty no matter how she tries to hide herself."

Belladonna's eyes narrowed at his admission, but the Turk shook a finger at Belladonna. "Once a man sees you... Isaak's young brother had pointed you out to me at Carnevale. You wore the very same cloak. But have no fear, friends. It is an honor to keep this lady's secret, especially from men such as Morosini."

Belladonna took a deep breath and exhaled. It was good to let down her mask and speak in her usual tone. "Morosini is clever and dangerous, but at the moment, he professes to be our ally." She glanced at Isaak. "I can handle Morosini."

"He came here asking for you." Diana reminded them of what she had overheard on her previous visit.

"It is possible he is looking for me because he has learned something of value," Belladonna tapped her cheek as her mind explored possibilities. Perhaps it was best to contact Morosini through the Turk rather than sending Diana as her messenger. "I would not want to deprive our gracious host of Morosini's gold, which you are certain to receive when you tell him you have found me. Then we shall discover what he wants and what he knows."

Chapter Twenty-Six: Belladonna

The Turk was gracious enough to take leave of them, so they could talk freely among themselves. Isaak rubbed his temples. "Seeing you here alarmed me more than the sighting of a Spanish man-of-war at sea."

At his comment, Belladonna's nostril flared. Did he expect her to sit docilely in the Ghetto and do nothing to find Roderigo after discovering he was alive and in Venice? Did he imagine she would be afraid to search for her brother on her own? She was not in the habit of waiting for a man to fight her battles and had not expected him to come ashore. There was a bounty on his head, and the last time he had risked appearing in the city was for the funeral of Diana's husband.

"Why are you here?" she folded both arms across her chest, confronting Isaak. "I thought the plan was for you to remain on board ship in case we were in need of immediate escape."

He must have come because he worried for her, and she wanted him to admit it.

She did not show her disappointment when he gave another explanation. "The Brethren are concerned. The Spanish grow ever more aggressive, amassing more ships around Jamaica. Finding Roderigo and helping him fulfill his mission is an urgent priority."

Belladonna did not chide him for what he had not said, and he calmly continued, "If Roderigo is no longer alive, there are steps that must be taken."

Belladonna felt as if she had been slapped. Her hopes of reuniting with the one member of her family who had survived, dashed. Until this moment, she had not considered the possibility of Roderigo's death. He had come to Venice, delaying his mission to *find* her. Tears were stinging her eyes, and she blinked several times to keep them from falling. She did not want to consider the possibility Roderigo had been killed. However, when someone disappeared in Venice, it was the most likely scenario.

"I do not believe he is dead," Diana jutted her chin up at her brother, and Belladonna was grateful for her support.

Isaak sighed. "We must consider all possibilities and plan for the worst. If he is alive, he must be found. Villiers will not dawdle in Venice for long. In wounding him, the Spanish have slowed his departure. He is bound to Sir Henry for the time being, and with Morosini on our side, we should be able to keep him safe."

Looking away from Isaak, Belladonna addressed Diana. "The greater danger is losing Villiers' interest in the treasure and Jamaica. There is much to distract a man such as he in Venice, and we must focus on ways to keep George Villiers' interest."

Diana raised an eyebrow, but Isaak's mouth had flattened to a hard line. Belladonna hoped she had aroused feelings of jealousy, and she imagined the change of expression was a sign of it.

Isaak stood, pulling back his white embroidered robe as if he needed to let air circulate around him. "The Turk hates the Spanish, and he has eyes and ears at every dock in the city. If the Spanish attempt to bundle anyone onto a ship, he will get wind of it and alert me."

Belladonna straightened her skirts and the scarf that bound her hair while conscious of Isaak's eyes upon her. She wondered how he saw her—as the woman from the past or as the person she had become.

Diana, too, was standing, ready to depart, when she suddenly grabbed Belladonna's arm. "There is one place that comes to mind that we may have overlooked. Isaak, I have heard that many who come from the New World arrive with fevers and illness, either from their islands or simply due to the arduous trip. I can find out where they are taken."

"How?" asked Isaak, echoing Belladonna's thoughts.

"To the apothecaries, the physicians. They will know where such travelers are taken, due to the medicines ordered for their care."

"Good thinking, Diana. As our next step, you will go to the apothecaries to learn what you can," Belladonna said, and Diana nodded. Turning to Isaak, she added, "I can keep Villiers entertained, but Isaak, it is you who must be vigilant for the Spanish assassin."

"Do not think of revealing yourself," said Isaak, his eyes sharp and his nostrils flaring.

"I will go to the Englishman at Sir Henry's, and then I will determine the next course."

"Raquel, there is no need—"

She brought her face closer to his. "It is best you remember I am no longer Raquel."

He did not answer her, nor did he draw away. He reached for her hand and grasped it tightly, but did not look down at it. They kept their eyes locked on each other for several moments until Belladonna forced herself to break away. "Come, Diana. We must be on our way."

Outside, their ears were assailed by a cacophony of sounds; the calls of the fisherman loading their boats, the shrieks of wild children weaving in and out of the crowds, and the din of foreign voices in a sing-song tongue. The contrast to the peacefulness of the Turk's garden, along with her regret for her coolness to Isaak, made Belladonna consider retracing her steps, but pride and a sense of urgency to find her brother stopped her. Instead, she plowed her way forward through the Moorish quarter, aiming herself towards the Ghetto.

Diana waved as she took another path towards the apothecary shops.

Chapter Twenty-Seven: Belladonna

When Belladonna returned to the Sullams, Sarra was secluded in her room, having left word she was not to be disturbed until dinner. The day was brighter than the previous one, and the sun streaming into her chamber gave her hope her plans for the day would lead to success. Out of habit, she checked her bag of jewels, which she had secreted in a space between the mattress and the bed frame.

As she made a quick check and verified all were accounted for, she realized she had forgotten about the pearl earrings she had hidden in the bedposts. They were set in gold, with tiny pave diamonds ringed around each large round pearl at the top, followed by an aquamarine stone set in more diamond studded gold, and ending in a large tear-drop-shaped pearl. These were a marvel known by every jeweler in the city.

Each post was comprised of two halves, though the joints were barely visible, swathed in the curtain as they were. Before she attempted to unscrew each pole, she closed the chamber's door in case another servant should pass by. The post squeaked as if it protested her invasion, and she paused for a moment; perhaps she was wrong. It seemed too tight, as if it had not been moved—ever. Just to be certain, she kept turning until it loosened, and careful not to unhook the bed curtains, she disengaged the upper post from the lower. She peered into the hollow. The linen bundle was still there.

She was just straightening her skirts when there was a knock at the door, and the footman peeked in. Once he spotted her, he blanched.

"Were you expecting to find Mirabella in my room? If I were you, I would distance myself from her. Unless you are her accomplice." Belladonna came over to the door and gestured for the man to enter.

The footman was no half-wit, and there was real fear on his face, and he was quick to exclude himself from Mirabella's deeds. "She has secrets, that one, but I mind my business, and that is all."

Belladonna did not press him other than advise him that if her jewelry was missing, she would find the thief and his or her accomplices. Belladonna hoped to gain some insight from the other servants about Mirabella, but they kept silent.

Chapter Twenty-Eight: Diana

Diana knew the apothecary in the Cannaregio, close to the Ghetto, was most involved in the trade of medicines in Venice. She made her way to his well-stocked shop, slowing her pace as she passed by the bridge which led to Mattia's rooms, tempted to visit him. Fresh in her mind was the first time she had walked this way, filled with trepidation, when Mattia approached her, begging her to come to his rooms to paint her portrait.

She narrowed her eyes, squinting towards Ca' Vendramin, as if by doing so, she could reveal the ghost of her former self, trembling with every step away from the Ghetto as she was set to gamble on her future. Time had supported her decision, and she had gained much through her association with the artist. In truth, she could not resist him. There were stirrings of feelings she must have had with her husband, although perhaps she no longer remembered those types of feelings, because Yaakov had been gone for nearly three years.

Diana waited for a few moments in the shadow of the doorway for the customer within to depart. The apothecary glanced up at the sound of another customer, then scowled when he recognized her. Diana had become immune to his disdain, but she was a good customer, and he knew it, despite his preference not to have to serve her. Diana quite enjoyed his discomfort and stood before him, hands palm down on the highly polished wood counter.

"What is it this time?" he practically hissed, his jaw clenched so tight, he could barely open his mouth. "Willow bark?"

"Yes, please, but there is more I seek to purchase if," she cocked her head at him, as if assessing his worth, "you have what I require in your stock."

The apothecary scowled at her. "You know I have the best stock in the Cannaregio, and I am benevolent enough to serve your kind."

Diana gave a harsh laugh. "You are far too greedy to turn down my people's custom; you charge us double what the other customers pay because we cannot complain about it. What's more, the Ghetto is famous for its medicines and remedies, so if you want to reap a portion of our gold, you must deal with the likes of me." She tossed back her black braided hair while the apothecary pulled out a container from under the counter and measured out her usual quantity of willow bark. "Besides, the English ambassador refers his countrymen to me, and I now have customers from as far as the New World."

The apothecary gave a snort of a laugh. "Not much you or any of us can do for those poor devils."

"What do you mean by that? There are plenty of remedies for the ailments from a long sea journey. Or is it an illness you have not seen because it is from a different land?"

"I have seen plenty, dear lady, and in my experience, there is nothing to be done for what I have heard has come ashore with these fellows." He peered at her, grinning at her discomfort, for well she understood what he was implying. He lowered his voice as he uttered the word she dreaded hearing, "Plague."

"What type of plague?" Diana said without showing any signs of being as disturbed as she was by his news. "There is more than one kind. Contrary to your belief, there are some remedies that do work for some types of plague."

"Maybe your people survive the plague, but I do not know many who have," the apothecary snickered as he folded and wrapped the willow bark for her to take. "I suppose your clientele will also need coriander for the fever?"

Diana gave a distracted nod while a new thought arose. A new plague could have come from the New World. How would it compare to the experience of the plague here? Would it be more deadly or more benign? It was possible Roderigo had become ill and was being kept in isolation for having signs of a plague. Either he was already dead, as Isaak supposed or in some Pest House or—

"I wonder if you have any at hand. I hope your source has provided you with a fresh supply."

The apothecary stopped his searching among the jars on the shelf behind him and came forward, eyes blazing, his lower lip jutting out in defiance. "You can leave my shop right now if you are impugning my stores!"

Diana took the package and left a gold coin, remnants of the payment she still had saved from the largesse once received from another English visitor. At the sight of the coin, the apothecary seemed to have a change of heart towards her, because as his thick fingers grabbed the gold, he said, "You have a client, you say, a foreigner who needs some remedy for the plague?"

Diana smiled. "With more gold than you have ever seen, to pay for it."

The man raised a finger of one hand and disappeared behind a thick curtain into the back of the store. Diana looked out the large window, angling to get a better glimpse of Ca' Vendramin with the vague hope of catching sight of Mattia Correr.

The shuffling of the apothecary's shoes across the wooden floor heralded his return, and Diana, reluctantly, turned aside from the view to the grumpy man. "Here it is, a special mixture concocted by the nuns of Giudecca. Coriander, a bit of mint, and wormwood. Perhaps it will work, perhaps not. Nevertheless, you will get your coin, and I will get mine, although yours will come later, and mine must come now." He dangled a sachet of herbs of which the strongest smell was mint in one hand, while his outstretched palm reached out for her gold.

"Giudecca, you say?" Diana trickled out a few coins, but the apothecary shook his hand for more. As she upended more of its contents into his palm, she added, "Are they the same sisters from the convent which sells herbs for perfumes and soaps?"

The apothecary's fingers were stained and cracked as they closed around her precious coins as he answered, "The same."

Taking the packets and stashing her near-empty purse inside her cloak, Diana exited the shop, passing two servants and taking one last longing look towards Mattia's rooms.

Chapter Twenty-Nine: Diana

As soon as Diana entered the rooms she shared with her parents, and before she could remove her shawl, her mother had pulled the stool beside her at the table and motioned for her to sit.

"I warned him, but would he listen? Do you listen? Now we shall be excommunicated, that is what will be the result of your folly and his."

Diana was used to her mother's melodrama, and rose to heat some water for tea, which always worked to calm her. Her mother grabbed her arm and pushed her back down. "It is time you both listened to me. You are heedless of the tongues wagging against us, because you spend so much time outside of the Ghetto. First, it was that artist, oh, yes, I do know about that, and then the courtesan, who appears in my very house!"

"You did not mind when Belladonna introduced your son Zebulun to the Englishman who funded his last voyage? I seem to recall you beaming with pride over the clothes he wore and the life *he* was leading outside of the Ghetto," Diana's voice rose along with her anger.

"Shhh, quiet! The neighbors need not hear our family squabbles. You and your father, always with your friends from outside of the Ghetto. That Sullam woman, inviting outsiders into her home, into the Ghetto. It is raising eyebrows and building a hum of discontent that will land on your father," the older woman pressed her hands to both sides of her head. "Ooooh, it makes my head ache to think of it."

This was not the usual rant, and Diana wanted to know what had brought it on. "Why are you so fraught with worry? Has something happened?"

Her mother sighed, "My life is filled with sorrow. Both my boys are gone. My daughter with a courtesan, and my husband spends his time with another woman. Why do I deserve such problems?"

Diana rose abruptly, knocking over the stool she had been sitting on. She opened her mouth to unleash words laced with anger, but realizing it would only make the situation worse, clamped her mouth shut. Her mother, with her head in her hands, did not seem to notice the fallen chair. Diana kissed the *mezuzah* at the doorpost as she departed, shutting the door firmly behind her, setting off to find her father to learn what new trouble awaited them.

When she arrived at her father's office, her concern increased. The rabbi paced the small open area between his large desk and cabinet, a clearing among the piles of papers and books. He did not look up at her or greet her, though he must have heard her arrival; the large studded wooden door creaked noisily when opened.

"What is it?" she asked, remaining cautiously by the door. If her father did not answer, it meant he was not to be disturbed.

He waved a hand at her, but did not respond. She bit her lip, stopping herself from protesting. It would do no good when her father was like this. She pivoted on her softened heels and, instead, headed to the mansion of the Sullams.

Sarra Coppio Sullam was idling in the salon, the smell of strong coffee coming from the steaming cup she was raising to her lips. She sipped, and then the lips parted into a welcoming smile as she gestured for Diana to take a seat beside her on the golden damask of the divan. She placed a delicate red glass cup on the small table before them and gestured to Diana to take the additional cup and pour the steaming coffee from the silver pot. Diana gratefully complied, hoping strong coffee would dispel a sudden feeling of light-headedness.

"What have you learned?" Sarra asked, leaning close and lowering her voice, for once conscious of the risk of a servant overhearing their conversation.

"I have come from the apothecary, who has given me an idea of where to find Roderigo. I will wait until Raquel is present to reveal it," Diana placed her nearly empty cup down on the table, adding, "However, what I wanted to discuss is not a matter for her ears."

Sarra's delicate eyebrows rose almost to the edge of her yellow silk turban. "Is it Roderigo? Is he no longer among the living?"

"No, it is not about Roderigo. I must speak to you, but about my father."

Sarra's face held a puzzled expression. "Your father?" she repeated.

"My mother seems to believe our family has incurred the wrath of the community due to our habit of fraternizing with Gentiles. Inviting them into the Ghetto. As you do in your salon and my father, with his sermons. Has Jacob spoken to you of such complaints?"

Sarra waved her hand dismissively. "There is always such talk, but it amounts to nothing. Your mother has a tendency to be...overwrought."

Diana leaned back and released the breath she had been holding, and along with it, the tension in her chest. "I was not certain if there was some news causing her distress. I am relieved to hear there is naught to cause me worry."

Her father had been pacing. Sarra was in her own world and did not perceive beyond what was written in a book. Diana clasped her hands tightly together and asked, "Where is your husband? Perhaps he has heard mutterings among the men in the synagogue?"

"Yes, he is here, in his study. Shall we go to him?" Sarra rose, and Diana followed her through a long corridor to a pair of large wooden doors. Pulling at the handle of one of them, Sarra ushered Diana into a cool dark room, its walls covered in tooled leather up to the wainscotting of dark wood. There was a rich smell of tobacco and spices, and as Diana's eyes adjusted to the dimness, she saw Jacob standing by the window gazing into the bright light of the outside world.

Though considerably older than Sarra, Jacob had merry eyes, a man filled with so much vitality it seemed his small stature could barely contain it. He pulled a thick curtain across the window, snuffing out the bright daylight, leaving Diana with the impression he had been veiling his true feelings with a bright smile and a warm greeting. When Sarra posed Diana's question to him, the smile dimmed, and he sat down abruptly in the chair by the desk, his eyes lowered to some papers on top of it. He handed one of them to

Diana.

It was a pamphlet written by her father's colleague, Rabbi Simon Luzzatto. Although they shared similar views about the popular misinterpretation of Kabbalah, it seemed they did not share the same opinion about inviting non-Jews to sermons in the Ghetto.

"Very odd that he has taken this position, given he is a Modern Thinker and has pupils who are Gentiles," said Diana. "He and my father collaborated on various treatises, and I thought they generally tolerated each other. This seems to be an indictment against my father, does it not?"

Jacob nodded and gave a pointed look at his wife, who fidgeted under his gaze. "Your father is not the only one who will suffer from this. I believe Luzzato was pressured into writing this pamphlet."

Diana read the last line of the pamphlet.

"Those who have a good knowledge of human events know that the quality of evil is much more perceptible than the quality of good. The former is a deviation from and disturbance of order, and a departure from habitual, well-known rules, while the latter is in continual progress and conforms to a series of already established issues, which even the wisest men are seldom able to observe."

Diana agreed with Luzzato's observation, and moreover, she recognized it from his *Discourse on the State of the Jews* which he had written to dispel prejudice and defend the value of the Jewish population to Venice. He had not written it as an attack on her father or Sarra Coppio Sullam.

"Who is behind this?"

"Moshe Arye Kalmansen." Jacob tented his fingers and rested his lips on them, waiting for Diana to absorb this intelligence.

"He should not be casting aspersions on others when he himself is not beyond rebuke. Moshe Kalmansen is a businessman, not a scholar. Why should he be concerned about matters of philosophy?" Diana ran a hand through her hair, as if she could rid herself of this problem as if it were head lice.

"Attacking others is Kalmansen's way to deflect attention away from his own wrong-doing," Jacob said as he pulled out a leather-bound book from a desk drawer and flipped it open. "Kalmansen owes me quite a sum of money, which I have not been able to collect, and I am not the only one. If he has the gall to attack the rabbi, others will overestimate his importance, as if he is a *g'vir*, one of the wealthiest in the community."

"He is from the German community, and so how has he come to my father's synagogue?"

Jacob Sullam sighed, and his eyes were still on his wife, who could not meet his gaze. "He bluffed his way to a high position in the German congregation, where he was able to befriend the wealthiest families in the German community. His inability to make good on his promises has put many family fortunes in jeopardy."

"Including the Luzzato family." Diana understood at last. "Who have somehow been convinced by Kalmenson that allowing outsiders into the synagogue and our holiday celebrations could be dangerous to their investment."

"Or he could have threatened them that he would withhold their payout if they did not do as he says."

Diana frowned. "I had thought Kalmenson was motivated to stir the pot, to make himself important, but I did not expect him to behave like a robber baron or to take up a vendetta against my father."

"He is not the first, nor will he be the last to attack your father for his forward-thinking, "Jacob sat down on a tufted damask bench beside the divan where Sarra was sitting. "Too many people these days are turning to mysticism, believing it to be the means to magically provide both power and meaning to their lives. Your father has spoken out against relying on kabbalistic practices to predict and wrangle the future. These are the same fools who now believe in Kalmenson's schemes which he has been peddling along with kabbalistic numerology.

Jacob's eyes shifted to his wife. "Though Kalmenson is vile, we must take the blessing out of the curse. Let this serve as a warning to us, and one which should not go unheeded. There *is* danger in bringing outsiders into the Ghetto, or engaging too much with the Gentiles, as you both have learned."

Diana felt her face flushing. Besides his hints about the dangers of her friendship with the artist and posing for her portrait, he was gently reminding Sarra of her misplaced trust in Bonifacio Baldassare, who had betrayed her by instigating the charge of heresy to be brought against her.

Sarra raised her chin defiantly and gave a small, forced smile. "I am prepared to defend myself. Remember, it is because of my relationship with the Patriarch of Venice, who has enjoyed the theatricals he has attended in our home, that I have been given the opportunity to provide a written response."

"We can only hope men of reason, like the Patriarch, will be swayed by logic and not prejudice," Jacob said, laying a comforting hand on Sarra's shoulder.

Diana was not so easily reassured. With Sarra under a charge of heresy and the rabbi under censure for his relationships with Gentiles, what would happen if it was discovered that they had allowed a courtesan into their midst?

Chapter Thirty: Diana

Once the apothecary had mentioned the convent, Diana did not want to waste time looking for Belladonna before exploring her clue to its end. She wanted to be able to surprise Belladonna with having found Roderigo alive. If the worst had happened, it was better if she discovered it first and then could manage how to share the bad news with Belladonna.

Her face to the wind as her boat plowed towards the island, Diana realized her decision to go without Belladonna was clouded by the excitement of her discovery. The voice of reason, usually the dominant voice, now raised many concerns, and she had been foolish not to consider them.

How could she be certain she had found Roderigo? She had no idea what he looked like. *What if he was too ill, or not cognizant of his identity?*

The wind was whipping her hair into a frenzy which only aggravated her more. As the gondola plodded forward towards the island of Giudecca, she chided herself again for going off unprepared. She had rarely gone to this part of Venice, which was reserved for large residences with extensive gardens belonging to the wealthiest families of Venice, and did not know exactly where to find the convent.

The only time she had set foot on the wide promenade, fronted by the beautiful church Santissimo Redentore was on the Festival of the Redentore, when she had joined the crowds crossing the pontoon bridge made up of aligned boats, stretching from Venice to Giudecca. The convent was supposed to be not far from the famous church, and it was probably well-known enough so that a local could point her in its direction.

There were whispers that the nuns in this convent had the knowledge and the means to care for those with strange illnesses, and had many who had been stricken with plague in the previous decade had survived under their care. Anticipation of learning more about such medicines spurred her into a gondola with the desire to get to Giudecca as fast as possible. She wished to spend some time alone with the nuns to learn of their methods for treating the plague.

A spray of sea washed across her face, and she wiped it away. The waters were choppy, the skies were gray, a storm seemed to be brewing. She hoped she could get to the convent's door before a downpour. Her ability to get back to the Ghetto she pushed out of her mind, as it was too late to turn back.

Racing across the cobblestone of the wide promenade, she was grateful to see the convent's name painted on a section of the long wall of pink brick. A painted arrow pointed to a narrow passageway alongside the church. Large droplets of rain splashed on her head, and she raised her shawl for shelter as she hurried along the passageway. Her shawl was nearly ripped out of her hands by the wind, and the rain doused her dress and hair thoroughly before she reached the sign for the church and the covered entranceway that kept her out of direct contact with the heavy rain.

At her banging on the thick wood nail-studded door, a middle-aged woman dressed all in white invited her inside. Their footsteps echoed loudly as she followed the woman through a large white stuccoed hall and into a sparse reception room, where a warm fire was blazing in the hearth. Diana gratefully basked in the warmth of the fire, momentarily forgetting what she was supposed to do. When the nun returned, bearing a steaming bowl of food, Diana was tempted to take it. Instead, she politely refused it, since she was unable to drink or eat any food that was not prepared according to Jewish law.

The nun seemed surprised by her refusal, and her eyes narrowed. "You are from the Ghetto?"

"I am."

"Why have you come here?"

136

"To buy some of your herbs." She rubbed her hands to warm them, adding, "lavender, primrose, and oleander abstract."

"If you have come in such weather, your needs must be pressing."

Diana did not want to raise the nun's protective guard by asking directly about the patients in the convent's infirmary. "Travelers in a guesthouse in the Ghetto have developed a strange illness that may be of great concern."

Her hint caused the woman's face to soften, and her shoulders relaxed as she shared her knowledge as one concerned with treating the sick should. "We, too, have such a traveler here. The primrose and lavender will not be enough, if your visitors suffer from the same symptoms."

Diana hid her excitement by frowning. "Primrose will not work, you say? What of willow bark? Do you find it effective enough to bring down the fever?"

The nun gestured for Diana to sit beside her on a wooden bench by the hearth. "Willow bark does lower the fever somewhat, but it is not enough. We add soaking cloths infused with juniper and rosemary to his chest to diffuse the miasma."

Diana raised her eyebrows. "I have heard of this, but have never attempted it. Have you tried chamomile?"

The nun barked a laugh. "Of course. We brew lavender and chamomile, and all of us make sure to be adequately dosed with Four Thieves Vinegar, as protection. If you suspect a similar illness, it will not hurt for you to do the same."

Diana was immediately alarmed. She had heard of the concoction of herbs brewed with vinegar and used as a preventative for the plague. "I suspect you must have stores of meadowsweet. That should help with the pain."

The nun smiled. "I see you know your medicines and eschew the practice of blood-letting and leeches as we do."

"Women usually choose the gentler course, often proven to be more effective. It seems you have quite a thorough capability for dealing with these illnesses," Diana was still cautious not to use the word 'plague.' There were still some among the clerics who blamed the Jews for starting the plague. "I should very much like to see how you minister to these cases, if you have one present."

As Diana expected, the discussion had earned her acceptance as a fellow nurse. The nun, whose demeanor had evolved from suspicious to kindly, rose and nodded towards a darkened corridor. "Come along, then, we do have one such patient. He came to us with a stiletto embedded in his thigh, but when his fever would not abate, and the wound did not ooze, we considered there was another illness present. He is not fully recovered, mind you, but he has improved greatly. It will be of interest to you to see how we have been able to keep him alive—despite the wound and complicated by this very serious illness."

Diana's breathing quickened as she kept up with the nun who led her towards the infirmary. They passed through an arched gallery that ran along an inner courtyard. At its center, a stone urn overrun with climbing vines was a small bubbling fountain. The air was fragrant with lilac, roses, and lilies of the valley as they passed through a flower garden. Then, the scent of cooking garlic and stewing vinegar took over as the path turned into another arched corridor along another stone building. Diana wrinkled her nose as the smell grew more intense as they mounted stairs to a bare whitewashed corridor. The nun paused before a single door at the corridor's end and raised a hand in warning.

"As quiet as possible, please. Take care not to disturb the sleep of a patient."

Diana signaled her agreement and allowed her guide to lead her into a surprisingly airy and light-filled room. Although it reeked from herbs and spices, most of it stemming from a boiling kettle on the hearth, the whitewashed room seemed clean and the solitary patient well-cared for. The man on the bed looked ghastly white, his chin grizzled with a few days' growth of beard, his long black hair stringy against the white linen of the pillow. His eyes were open, dark and large in his gaunt face, and they still had the glossiness of fever upon them.

"Keep your distance," she whispered loudly, "I have survived the plague before and seem to be immune, even to this one, but there is no need for you to risk contagion."

"Water..." the man on the bed croaked. His lips were cracked and dry, and his tongue was white. Another woman in white hurried over with a ladle filled with water and lifted the patient's head to gently trickle it through his parched lips.

Diana had one question. "Will he live?"

The nurse shrugged. "There are two types of plague, one with large sores or black buboes under the skin and one which immediately affects the lungs and makes it difficult to breathe. With this strange plague, he seems to exhibit both, although, for the past few days, he has had no new sores and no new buboes. His breathing has improved, but as you know, those whose illness has affected breathing have less chance of survival. We do not know if the same is true of this plague." The nurse had the thoughtfulness to keep her voice low, so the patient would not hear.

"Do you know where he is from?" When she saw a wave of suspicion cross the nun's face, Diana quickly added, "I am curious to know which travelers may be likely to have the same infection."

"Understood. He says he has come from the New World."

Diana raised her eyebrows. "There have not been many of such travelers to come our way from the New World."

The nurse gave the man on the bed another look. "He does not seem so now, but when he arrived his skin was quite brown, as if he was a common laborer. But I understand in those islands across the sea; the sun turns everyone to a darker shade."

"Did he tell you his name, or how he came to Venice?"

The nurse shook her head. "We found some papers in his clothing, stating his name is Roderigo Mendez, from the island of Jamaica. Other than that, we know nothing about him. The fever has kept him either unconscious or raving. We do not know if he came here for family, or to find a bride, since many times he has called out one name, *Raquel*."

Diana clenched her hands at the name. The nun must have felt her tension and looked at her curiously. "Do you know this man?"

Diana did not see any reason not to reveal the truth. "It is possible he is the brother of a friend."

The nun's mouth tensed into a straight line. "From the Ghetto?"

Diana was glad she did not have to lie in order to gain this woman's support. "No, she is not from the Ghetto. If the storm has passed, I will go and bring her here. She has been searching for him and will be grateful to see he is alive and under your excellent care."

Chapter Thirty-One: Belladonna

When Belladonna returned to the Sullam mansion, her thoughts were elsewhere—but mostly on Isaak. After each encounter, her insides trembled, and it took every ounce of her self-control not to display the turmoil of her emotions. If Isaak could disguise himself so effectively dressed as a Moor, she wondered if they both could escape their pasts, find a new identity and live in peace in a far-off Moorish place like Constantinople. Even though Belladonna could occasionally indulge herself with such fantasies, she was a realist and doubted Isaak would be able to give up his life as a corsair as much as she would be able to give up all she had become in Venice.

Up in her chamber, as she undressed to her shift, her mind swirled with images of Isaak. *No!* She must focus on Villiers. Villiers was not a man to be teased but to intrigue. She lifted her chin, regarding her image with a critical eye in the gilded mirror above the basin. It was certainly one of her skills to keep a man entranced, and she must use her talents to ensure her face would haunt his dreams.

Pulling off the yellow scarf, she shook her hair free and was about to wash when she noticed the pitcher was empty. Searching the room, all was not as she left it; the wardrobe door was slightly opened, and the bedcurtains pulled too widely aside. She hurried over to the bedposts, now turned to a different position than before she left.

Mirabella!

Belladonna had no doubt the surly housekeeper had been thorough in her search. She unscrewed the bed posts and reached into its hollows, confirming the earrings were gone. She smiled. Now she had Mirabella. Those earrings were distinctive, and Mirabella would not be able to explain how she had them in her possession by accident.

Belladonna was ready to catch the woman red-handed. She left her room and headed for the back stairs and the servants' quarters. She would search Mirabella's room and no doubt uncover her earrings as well as a treasure trove of her mistress's "lost" jewelry.

The servants' quarters were freshly painted and clean, smelling pleasantly from lemon oil and lavender. Sarra did not have many servants, but the few she did were treated well. There were feather beds and small washstands that mimicked her own in every room. The windows had been left open and let in bright light and fresh air aplenty. Belladonna drifted in and out of each room, conducting a quick review until she reached a much larger room which she was certain was Mirabella's. As she opened the burled wooden door, her eyes narrowed, and her lips pursed. It was completely empty. All signs of its former inhabitant were gone. Mirabella had already fled, along with Belladonna's earrings.

Now it dawned on her why the ewer in her washstand was empty. She gave a great sigh, certain Sarra would feel the loss of her housekeeper greatly. Unwisely, her hostess had delegated the running of her household to a disloyal and conniving woman. Sarra had given the keys to a thief, and the woman did not delay seizing her opportunity for plunder. Mirabella would not worry about being sacked without references, since she had stolen enough to never need work again.

In a way, Belladonna could not blame her. Mirabella had desired a better life, and had taken the initiative to achieve it. Still, it did not warrant Mirabella any mercy from Belladonna. An unforgivable line had been crossed when she stole from Belladonna.

To find Mirabella and reclaim her jewels, but without her usual resources, such as Zancani, she would not have much success in finding either the thief or her property. Nevertheless, she was determined to get her revenge and her jewels and considered the Turk would likely have the resources to help discreetly.

While descending the narrow stairway that led to the kitchens and pantries, Belladonna stopped in mid-step. Mirabella would hurry to pawn her booty, and Belladonna's earrings were very distinctive. Any jeweler worth his salt would know this. She clenched her fists. Damn that thieving woman! She had underestimated her. She had not expected her to find these earrings, but the less expensive set she had stashed in the wardrobe. Mirabella had taken advantage of her absence in the household to abscond before she could be confronted.

Now, inadvertently, Mirabella had gotten the upper hand—by revealing Belladonna's hiding place with the Sullams. Was it too late to stop her? Once the jewels were in the hands of the pawn shops, it would not be long before the Spanish would come sniffing around the Ghetto.

Belladonna continued her descent to the kitchen. Her best chance of locating Mirabella was through her fellow servants. Something of Mirabella's life outside this house must be known to them and might provide her with some knowledge of associations and predilections to aid in hunting for her.

As Belladonna expected, even though Mirabella displayed a complete lack of interest in her work, all was in chaos without her leadership. The scullery maid refused to take her post to peel the vegetables, claiming it would sully her uniform—having now informed everyone she had decided to take on the position of upstairs maid. The former upstairs maid had assumed Mirabella's role, although she did not seem suited for additional responsibility, throwing up her hands and her bundle of keys, while her eyes were wide with panic.

Belladonna had dealt with upheavals amongst servants before and calmly stepped between the confused and the disconcerted, assigning tasks and organizing. The scullery maid was given an apron and a peeler. The cook returned to her pots, and the footman back to sorting the silver and dishes to be taken up to the dining room. As soon as everyone had regained their confidence and were certain of their responsibilities, Belladonna leaned back and wiped her brow. "What an awful thing for Mirabella to do, to leave in such a sudden way."

Belladonna had directed her comment to the competent cook, who seemed the most loyal of Sarra's servants. The large woman grunted and pounded roughly on the dough she had been kneading before responding. "Good riddance to her, I say. She was always in my larder, pilfering. Selling it on the side, she was. I confided in the mistress the stores were always missing, but…." Her voice trailed off.

"I know," Belladonna sighed, "my cousin has no mind for such things, and the worst people are able to take advantage of her. I was going to demand Mirabella's dismissal, for I, too, found her stealing. My earrings are missing, a gift from my dead husband. I would give anything to get them back."

The cook scowled. "They should cut off her hands if they find her!"

"I wish I knew where she would sell those earrings. At least I would have the opportunity to get them back." Belladonna added a soft wistfulness to her tone.

The cook cocked her head towards the old footman, and Belladonna noted his shifty eyes and a surliness to rival Mirabella. "Thick with him, Mirabella was. Always thought she needed help in her pilfering, and he was the one to give it."

Belladonna nodded, and when the man stepped into the kitchen, she called out to him. "A moment, please. Join me in the pantry."

He was a cool one; if her request unsettled him, he took great care not to show it. He was tall and stooped slightly as he led her into the pantry. Of middle age, his eyes, underscored by dark shadows and pouchy folds, signaled a more dissipated life than his clean uniform suggested. He tried to widen his eyes, as if he were innocent when he looked at her. "Yes, Missus?"

"Your name?"

"Paulo, Missus."

"Well, Paulo, Mirabella is gone, and she has taken something of mine. I am determined to get it back and will reward anyone who helps me handsomely." With no honor among thieves, Belladonna was betting on the man's betrayal for profit.

At the mention of a reward, Paulo's eyes narrowed instantly. He was on his guard. "Send me where you wish. I will be sure to *convince* that whore to give it back." He bared his yellowed teeth as he grinned for emphasis.

"You never suspected Mirabella was thieving? A smart man like you would naturally be suspicious of a spiteful woman like Mirabella. Surely you must have followed her when she was out on her errands, just to be certain, no?" Belladonna tilted her head at him, hoping to disarm him with compliments rather than cornering him with threats.

Paulo was too experienced to make an admission of complicity. He played his role as loyal servant, but could not fully suppress an opportunity to grab a few extra ducats by peddling some information. "Sorry, Missus, I never believe such as she would be pilfering from our good mistress."

When Belladonna raised an eyebrow and jingled some coins in her hand. "Well, if you cannot think of anything to help me—"

"Wait!" The footman screwed up his mouth and squinted, as if he were trying to remember something. "It seems I do recall Mirabella going on about some ring she once saw in one of the pawnshops right there in the Ghetto Nuovo. So mebbe she was going to go there?"

"Which one?" Belladonna opened her fist to reveal a coin in her palm, but closed it as soon as the footman reached for it.

"It is in the alley coming off the campo, right beneath the sottoporto leading to the Ghetto Vecchio." He waited for her to open her palm, almost like a good dog.

"Do you know the proprietor?" she asked, knowing he would lie, but she had to play a part as well.

He shook his head vehemently. "Well, why would I? It is not like I got what to sell."

Belladonna withheld a sarcastic reply. "No, I suppose not." She opened her palm and allowed him to seize the coin. She doubted a pawnshop or an alleyway existed where he described, but at least he had given away Mirabella's likelihood to frequent pawnshops in the Ghetto.

Somewhere to start, at least. Diana would know pawnbrokers in the Ghetto due to her father's frequent losses at the gaming tables.

Dismissing the sneaky footman, Belladonna searched for the newly appointed housekeeper and ordered water to wash.

When she was rejoined by Sarra and Jacob in the salon after having washed and changed, she heard voices. Belladonna gave a soft moan. She had no strength left to settle her face into the pleasing, wide-eyed softness for her role as Sarra's cousin, Raquel. She clasped her hands before her and relaxed her shoulders into a more submissive pose as she entered the salon. At the sight of Diana and the rabbi, she straightened her back and sharpened her gaze, ready to face their news—good or bad.

Diana's announcement made her forget all about the missing earrings and Mirabella. "We've found him. We found Roderigo."

Chapter Thirty-Two: Belladonna

Belladonna's hands had flown to her neck, missing the comfort of the pearls that usually hung there. She took a deep breath as she prepared for the worst; she did not know if Roderigo was alive, but the look on her friends' faces gave her hope.

"Where?"

"On the island of Giudecca, in the care of the Sisters of the Convent of San Beneficiato," said Diana, and gestured for Belladonna to take a seat beside her as she continued, "When a guest is found sick at an inn, they are sent to be cared by the nuns at this convent, who are highly skilled in herbal medicines. They will take any sick traveler, regardless of religion."

Sarra reached for her hand. "You see? Thanks to the Almighty, your brother has been found, alive, and at last, you will be reunited."

Belladonna pursed her lips at the mention of Divine intervention. After all, where was the Almighty when her parents had been burned at the stake? "Is there hope of recovery?"

Diana glanced quickly at her father before answering. "He had been stabbed, but is recovered from his wound. However, he is very ill." She lowered her voice, "With the plague."

Belladonna jolted back, as if she had been slapped. Now she understood the presence of the rabbi. Roderigo was dying. She swallowed before asking her next question. "Is he conscious?"

Diana nodded, but looked away. "He is very weak."

The plague was usually a death sentence. Thirty years ago, not long after her birth, a plague had spread throughout Venice, leaving thousands dead before it mysteriously ended. The rabbi possessed *The Medical Compendium*, a compilation of the learnings of Moorish physicians on illnesses and treatments which both he and Diana had studied. Whatever type of plague had infected Roderigo, perhaps they had the understanding to treat it? It could not end this way, discovering the one member of her family who had survived only to lose him now, when they found each other? She had none of Sarra or Diana's faith and felt cheated by Fate, who had dealt both her and Roderigo a trick card. "I wish to see him. Immediately."

Diana opened her mouth to protest, but the rabbi put a hand on his daughter's arm and said, "Of course."

"I will hire a gondola for you," Sarra offered and, without a word, went out to arrange it.

Belladonna rose. "I am ready to go." She looked to the rabbi. "You will join us?"

Rabbi Modena nodded, and though he offered no words of hope, Belladonna would be comforted by his presence at Roderigo's bedside.

The three friends sat in the gondola in silence as the boat made its entrance into the Grand Canal, heading towards Giudecca. It was dusk, and the setting sun had cast a shimmering path of gold to ripple across waters of violet and dark blue. Torches blazed from the many grand palazzos they passed, illuminating facades and balconies that were then duplicated by their reflection in the water below. A strong breeze whipped Belladonna's hair from the scarf she had attempted to confine it and stung her eyes to tears. Or so she pretended. The wind, the smell of the sea, brought back memories of a sandier shore where she had taken refuge with Roderigo, huddled in the bushes, hiding from their enemies.

The irony was not lost on Belladonna that, once again, she was in hiding with Roderigo. This time they were not defenseless adolescents, but have the experience, the knowledge and means to defy the Spanish. However, for all her wealth and influence, she was powerless against the plague. She knew little of sickness or medicines, but she could rely on Diana and her father, who were skilled in such matters and had mastered the creation of the most complex remedies they kept in a heretical book, *The Medical Compendium of ibn Saud.* Rome may have designated such books heretical, but in Venice, they were honored and shared with those who had the skills to use them. Belladonna wondered if the rabbi could find a magical treatment for her brother's plague in its pages.

"Have you the knowledge of how to treat my brother's ailment?" She hesitated to use the dreaded word.

Diana jumped to answer. "There are many herbal remedies that have been useful in such illnesses, and the sisters at San Bonifacio are known for their herbal gardens and are treating him with those herbs. It is probably why he is still alive."

"That is good to know, that he is safe in their hands." She kept her eyes focused on the horizon, since she did not want her companions to study her face too closely.

Breaking the uncomfortable silence, the rabbi added, "Willow bark for fever, and lavender and oleander leaves. I have seen patients recover with these remedies. If the sisters have kept him fever-free and alleviated his breathing, he should be out of danger."

Belladonna nodded and brushed away the hair that had blown across her face, but did not speak, and once again, the boat was silent, with only the sounds of the slushing water as they progressed across the lagoon towards Giudecca.

The gondolier pointed out the campanile of their destination, the *Chiesa* of Santa Croce. "The convent became well-known during the time of the Abbess, Eufamia Giustiniani, who was the niece of the first patriarch of Venice, because only four nuns died during the plague of 1446. Legend has it that Saint Sebastian himself drank from the well there, and it is believed that the waters have miraculous healing powers."

"I have not partaken of the water, but their garden is filled with many herbs that are sought after and usually difficult to find. I have often bought many of the ingredients for my own remedies and can attest to the quality of their product." The rabbi spoke as he held down his turban with both hands while the wind seemed determined to blow it from his head. The wind had grown fiercer, and the gondolier struggled against it as he docked their craft. As they disembarked, the wind whipped the women's skirts about their legs, and they held onto their hair coverings as much as the rabbi. Diana hurried ahead, and Belladonna and the rabbi followed not far behind her, navigating a rough cobblestone path interrupted by weeds until they faced the chapel and campanile and the wall with the doorway to the convent.

The wind had chilled her, and Belladonna was shivering, although her companions did not seem to be suffering as she was. Perhaps it was not the cold, but her apprehension about Roderigo; she had last seen him as a youth, now he was a middle-aged man. They both may look at each other as strangers. What caused her to tremble even more was the thought of her brother being taken from her once again, although not by the Inquisition but by the plague. Belladonna pounded on the door without mercy, her patience had been taxed for too long.

The door opened slightly, and then wider, when the doorkeeper seemed to recognize Diana.

"I am Sister Maria. You were here before, were you not?" asked the round-faced nun, whose cheeks dimpled as she smiled.

"Yes, we have come about the patient from the New World. We have brought a member of his family and a religious leader of our faith."

Chapter Thirty-Three: Belladonna

The nun pulled the door open to its full width and welcomed them inside. They hurried past her, grateful to be out of the wind, and glancing back at the sky, Belladonna thought it was likely a storm would soon arrive. It would affect their trip back across the lagoon, and with the choppy waters, it would be unsafe for Roderigo's condition to accompany them.

Belladonna was surprised at the pleasant smells of lilac and lilies of the valley instead of the odors of refuse and privies as they traversed the courtyard path. Inside, the air of cleanliness prevailed; the walls were freshly whitewashed, and the floors scrubbed clean and strewn with sweet-smelling rushes in the large wardroom. The nun led their party to a door in the back which opened to another long corridor that ended at another door. Belladonna took a deep breath to prepare herself for her first sight of Roderigo.

Sister Maria halted them at the threshold. "Though he is no longer feverish, it is best to keep your distance and avoid contact, especially if you have any bodily weakness." She looked pointedly at the rabbi, who shrugged. "If you will wait, but a moment, I will see if he is conscious and well enough to converse."

She moved forward with light steps that hardly made a sound and leaned over the supine form on the bed. Belladonna was grateful for the convent's obvious commitment to cleanliness. There was no odor of sickness in the room, only the faint smell of roses, most likely stemming from the rose petals scattered among the rushes on the floor. A porcelain basin in which rested a large white pitcher was right by the bedside, and a fresh linen towel hung from a peg on the plain wooden stand that held it. The nun ushered them in, and as they entered, another small Sister slipped by them, carrying a covered pail.

The man on the bed turned large sunken eyes towards her. They widened when they saw her, and the pale lips parted and said, "Raquel, you have become a beauty." It came out barely louder than a whisper, and he smiled and lifted a hand towards her. "All these years, I had believed you were dead."

"And I you," she said, coming closer but careful to keep distance between them. "You had returned to our home in Jamaica after… after…." She still could not bring herself to speak of their parents' death.

His hands reached for her, and Belladonna worried he was becoming agitated. "We have found each other at last. I give thanks to the Almighty for granting me the comfort of seeing you before I…"

"Shhh! You are going to recover," Belladonna took a step closer, but Sister Maria gave her a warning look, and she kept back. Though he had no obvious signs of the plague, he looked like a man depleted of life. His eyes were black and shiny, but he squinted at her, as if he could barely see her, and the hand that had reached for hers fell back on the bed.

"I have brought my father, Rabbi Modena, who is skilled in the healing arts. He has a book with the remedies of the great Moorish physicians, and you will come back with us to the Ghetto, where he will help you rebuild your strength," Diana added. She had taken a place beside Belladonna, but the rabbi hung back, joining the Sister who had cared for Roderigo. The two of them began a whispered conversation, in which they frequently cast their eyes on the patient.

"Raquel," came the hoarse voice of the patient. "God has granted me the privilege of seeing you again before I die. I knew this mission would be dangerous, but it is a noble one and crucial to the survival of the Jews of Jamaica." He paused and beckoned for water. Diana fetched some, and Belladonna held his head as he sipped. "I had never imagined you had survived, and now at last I have the chance to beg your forgiveness."

"My forgiveness?" Belladonna repeated, furrowing her brow.

Roderigo nodded, his eyes filling with tears, which trickled down his cheeks. "For not saving you. I saw you being taken aboard that ship, and I knew I should have gone with you, but I was too afraid. I was rooted to the spot, hiding, smelling the burning flesh, and terrified I, too. would be taken. But I should have gone with you."

"You were young, Roderigo, and right to be afraid. There is no need to ask for forgiveness; you did me no wrong. We each had to make our way in the world, and where Fate has sent us, it seems we have both survived."

Roderigo shook his head and wiped off the trail of tears. "No, it is not Fate, but God."

Belladonna did not want to argue with her brother about his beliefs, so she turned the conversation away from the past. "There is no predicting the future. We do not know how we will be able to save the Jews of Jamaica and avoid the Spanish assassins, but we must try. You must tell us about the map and the gold. An emissary from the King of England, George Villiers, has arrived, and he needs to receive the map to guide him to the treasure you promised."

Roderigo gave a short laugh. "There is no map. It was meant to stir the English interest in taking over the island of Jamaica before the heirs of Columbus sell it to the Spanish. It seems to have succeeded, since Villiers has followed me here to Venice."

Her brother's voice shook as he continued, "They tried to kill me in London, when I first begged an audience with the English king. Sir Henry Wotton had arranged for me to stay in one of the unused rooms allocated to the Venetian ambassador. Before I left for Venice, I questioned him about a woman named Belladonna, your new name, which Isaak had revealed to me. As a parting gesture, I advised him to help himself to all I had left behind, including the cloak I was to wear for the King's Masque. He donned a poisoned cloak meant for me. The palace was rife with Spanish spies, and they must have overheard our talk."

"Do they know why you were seeking Belladonna?"

Roderigo shook his head. "I do not believe so. I never revealed the reason for my interest in you."

"Then why are they hunting me?" she asked.

"They must think we had...a relationship," he coughed out the last word, "and that perhaps I had confided in you the location of the treasure or my plans with the English."

It seemed the urgency in Isaak's warning had not been overplayed. The Spanish would not hesitate to employ torture to learn what they imagined she knew. Diego di Rivera, the Spanish ambassador to Venice, would relish the opportunity to 'chasten' her for what he deemed her immorality.

"Well, we have found you, and Villiers is here, sent by the English king, and he is impatient to find you and get his hands on the treasure—"

She put up a hand to stop her brother from protesting. "I understand. We must maintain his interest and ensure to incite some urgency for England to move on Jamaica."

"But how? The Spanish will be watching Villiers and will be ready to intercept you if you attempt to make contact. I do not know you well, dear sister, but now that I have found you, I do not want to lose you." Roderigo's pale, thin hand reached for her.

Belladonna's eyes narrowed, and she regretted she could not come closer, nor take his hand. "Do not worry. The Spanish have their eyes out for a courtesan, not for a Jewish widow. As for Villiers, leave him to me."

Roderigo closed his eyes, and Sister Maria gestured for them to take their leave.

Belladonna's mind raced with possibilities and means of escape for her and Roderigo. If they came before dawn in a fishing boat, could they remove Roderigo discreetly? But where would they go? Belladonna did have an estate in the Veneto, but it was common knowledge, and her enemies would certainly look for her there. She sighed. Isaak was right; the Ghetto was the best place for them to hide.

Belladonna moved to the window and opened it wider to lean out and look up at the sky. "The storm seems to be clearing, and then we shall be able to take him with us."

"I do not think it would be wise to move him from here at this time."

With a glance at Sister Maria, who nodded in support, the rabbi had come forward.

"What if the Spanish discover him here?"

"There is little likelihood of that occurring. They would have no reason to suspect a Jew would find shelter in a convent," said the rabbi. "He is too weak, and the care and cleanliness here will give him the best chance for recovery."

"They know this place takes in travelers who have become sick—" Belladonna did not want to leave Roderigo.

Diana put a hand on her shoulder. "They do not know he is sick."

Belladonna had to acknowledge the logic of her friends' arguments, but she was reluctant to leave without Roderigo. Perhaps, if she did, she would never see him again. Looking at Roderigo's wan face, Belladonna realized it was best for her brother if he remained here. Besides, if he was a carrier of the plague, no one would be safe if he were taken into the Ghetto.

As they set off across more turbulent waters towards the Ghetto, Belladonna wondered what would happen if her secret was revealed and others learned of her true relationship with Roderigo. If her origins became known, she would lose everything she had achieved in Venice. Her hand had shot up to her chest, where she could feel the pulsing of her blood at the thought of leaving Venice, her palazzo, her lifestyle behind.

Isaak. A new life with Isaak.

Whether it was her brother's God or her Fates who had taken the helm to guide the course of her life, she still had her wits and enough of her fortune to survive. Now she had no reason not to go off with Isaak, if he still wanted her.

At last, she would have what Diana once had—the love of her life.

Chapter Thirty-Four: Antonio

A ntonio had taken up a position outside the residence of the English ambassador, and he smiled as his vigilance was rewarded, when the Englishman arrived and staggered into the palazzo.

He had one critical piece of the puzzle at hand, and he was confident that one way or another, the Englishman and not the courtesan would lead him to the envoy and the treasure. As long as Di Ribera kept his distance and did not attempt any confrontation with the English, Antonio estimated he had a high likelihood of success.

He still had one other avenue to pursue, and he decided to leave his position to explore it. For a fall day, it seemed like the golden sunlight had intensified as it was reflected across the water, and he threw back the folds of his thick cloak to allow access to cooler air as he seated himself in a hired gondola. He lay back to enjoy the colorful facades of the palazzos they passed and imagined himself one day studying the view from one of their balconies. Spain, be damned. He would amass as much of Diego di Ribera's gold as he could, take something from the envoy to keep him from the Spanish and haggle with the English lord for a good price for the location of the envoy and the scope of di Ribera's plans.

As for the rumored treasure, Antonio did not hold much belief in its existence; it seemed a nice spicy story to get the game going between Spain and England. He would much rather take the gold in the Old World than bet on the gold to be harvested from the New World. Then, of course, he would retire to the obscure but pleasant vineyard he had purchased in the Veneto, far enough from di Ribera's tentacles and the plots and poisons of the Council of Ten.

As the gondola followed the curve of the Grand Canal towards the Misericordia, Antonio planned his next move with the Turk. He was not a regular visitor to the Moorish quarter and like most Spaniards, disdained their ways and the smells of their enclave. They were strange people, clever and disloyal, and he would have to be on his guard, especially when venturing into their realm.

His usual threats would not work with the Turk, who had a strong alliance with the Council of Ten, Constantinople, and the Barbary Pirates. Antonio recognized a fellow opportunist, however, and knew the best way to get to the Turk was through his pocket. The man always had information to peddle, and thanks to di Ribera, Antonio had the means to purchase it.

He let his index finger trail along the comforting hilt of the stiletto tucked into his waistband. His hand would never be far from it, and he managed to scout around for anyone or anything suspicious as he disembarked at the threshold of the Turk's residence.

Antonio inhaled the scent of the Turk's garden and relished the soft murmur of the fountain and the smell of the wet stones that bordered it. Someday, he vowed, he would have a garden such as this. There was the exotic tinkling of bells, or maybe it was the soft clanks of bracelets that announced the presence of a slim, veiled young woman who emerged from the shadows of the gallery. She beckoned, and he followed, and soon he found himself before a man whose white teeth flashed like a beacon in the dimness of the room.

The room was swathed with fabrics, but the windows had shutters of lace-like Moorish design, which allowed some light but not enough to make out the colors of the cloth.

"Sit, sit, my friend, and tell me what I can do for you." Large hands, palms up, gestured towards a lute-like chair, which Antonio was surprised to find very comfortable. He crossed one leg over the other and faced the Turk, ready for the game to begin.

Antonio tossed a bag of coins into the lap of the Turk, whose eyes widened as he felt its weight. Fumbling with its opening, the Turk's wide, fleshy mouth widened into a broad smile after he had removed one of the coins and bit it to verify its authenticity.

Holding the bag in one hand, the Turk waved to someone behind Antonio, and with a swish of veils and the scent of exotic spices, the bag of coins disappeared from sight.

"Bring coffee, my dear," called out the Turk to the departing figure. He winked at Antonio. "You have captured my attention, and from the weight of your purse, I surmise your needs are…shall we say, not in the way of ordinary trade. So, is it opium or powder of the poppy? Or perhaps an undetectable poison?"

The Turk's insinuations were not lost on Antonio, and his blood surged. "Why do you make such suggestions? What do you know of me?"

The Turk raised his eyebrows. "Have we met before? If so, I must apologize for I cannot recall it. I usually judge a man by his purse. The heavier the purse, the more secrets he has to hide. You have presented quite a large bag of coins…hence my assumptions."

Antonio snorted, "I will not challenge you on your methods. Employing our instincts is all we have to rely upon, is it not so? Though you may not know me, I have heard of you; your reputation has guided me here. I have not come to you to buy items I can find at any shady apothecary. I have come for information. You know much of who arrives and departs from this city. I am seeking information on a man who recently arrived from the New World."

The conversation was interrupted by the young woman and the rich smell of the freshly brewed coffee from a small silver urn on a decorative tray. She pulled over a small table and rested the tray upon it, and the two men watched with anticipation as she poured them each a steaming glass. Alongside the coffee were shavings of a dark substance, which the Turk's daughter had sprinkled across the top of her father's drink before passing it to him.

The Turk sipped the fragrant brew, and Antonio did not hesitate to do the same. Antonio had always thought it a shame when Spain purged itself of the Moors, for the skills of brewing seductive beverages such as coffee and tea had been lost. Another benefit of living in Venice was its food and drink, rewards Antonio would ensure he would never be denied.

"You should try some of this," said the Turk pointing to the shavings.

"What is it?" Antonio was curious, as a strange new aroma was coming from the Turk's glass.

"Another bounty from the New World. It is called chocolate, and it is prepared with sugar. There is nothing like it, and I predict it will be the true treasure to come from the New World."

Intrigued, Antonio used the silver spoon to sprinkle a small amount into his cup. Tentatively, he took a sip, breathing in the rich new smell as the strange exotic sweetness seemed to melt into his tongue.

He put down the cup and spooned in more of the shavings, and drank. He closed his eyes as he savored the sweetness. "I will want more of that, but I am not distracted from my purpose. My purse will open wider for information."

"A man from the New World, hmmm. Let me ask you this, how certain are you this man is in Venice? He may never have arrived or may have already moved on?"

Antonio could not help himself and grinned. "Oh, he is here, and I doubt he has moved on," he pulled aside his cloak to reveal the hilt of his dagger, "I witnessed one of my daggers landing in his leg."

The Turk's eyes widened, registering fear, but for a fleeting moment, so that his voice betrayed only a mild curiosity. "If so, perhaps he is dead."

Antonio shook his head. "Not so. The man had the energy to launch himself into a gondola and make his escape. Now, I come to you, sir, to ask you where would he go?"

The Turk tented his fingers beneath his chin and nodded. "I should be able to find the whereabouts of a wounded man, a foreigner yet, in this city. If you return in a few days, I will have something to tell you."

The blood rose in Antonio, pounding in his ears, as he rose and grabbed the Turk by the throat, "Do not toy with me. You shall not barter my information to someone else."

"I advise you to let go of my father," came a soft voice in his ear. He felt the cold of a steel blade on his neck and smelled flowers and spices. "One little scratch of this blade, and I promise you will die a very painful and ignoble death."

Instantly, Antonio released his hold on the Turk, who smoothed and straightened his garments. "These are dangerous times, my friend, and one's family must always be prepared to defend themselves. Yasmina has been well-trained, and she does not like Spanish men."

Antonio waited until she moved the dagger away from his throat and the scent of flowers receded. He turned to study his assailant, but she had already melted into the shadows. Antonio regained his seat, ready to resume the conversation.

"I can assume her experience of my countrymen under Diego di Ribera has formed such an impression."

"You take orders from the ambassador, no?"

It was Antonio's turn to wink. "I hear his orders, and I take his gold. As for fulfilling his orders...that is up to me. Which is why I have another request for you. I wish to locate the courtesan known as Belladonna."

Antonio's words arrested the path of the refilled coffee cup to the Turk's lips. The Turk set it back down on the table, and sat back with his arms folded across his chest. "Why Belladonna?"

"Is she a friend of yours? You sound very protective of her."

The Turk's eyes narrowed as he answered. "It is just you are not the first to ask about her. I do not understand the sudden interest in such a woman. A courtesan is at the beck and call of her patron. If her patron has called her away from Venice, no doubt she would go, and very discreetly."

Antonio sought to reassure his adversary as to his purpose. "Di Ribera is eager for me to find her as well, although I have gathered it is for his own purposes. He hates her and wishes to have her in his power. I want to know why."

The Turk nodded, as Antonio knew he would. A man such as he understood the advantage of knowing more about di Ribera. The enemy of my enemy is my friend.

The Turk unfolded his arms and leaned forward. "Such a request will require more gold. I trust Di Ribera will be able to afford it?"

Antonio rose to depart. "Undoubtedly. I shall return in two days to see what you have for me." His eyes turned to the shadows, "send my apologies for my rude behavior to your daughter."

As he made his way through the luscious garden, he sensed eyes upon him. Was it only the Turk's daughter, or another?

Chapter Thirty-Five: Belladonna

Later, back in her room at the Sullam's, Belladonna lay her cheek against the coldness of the windowpane. Storm clouds still hovered, and occasionally a streak of lightning cracked across the sky. She felt like a somnambulist, walking in a dream since finding Roderigo, reliving the last moments they had been together on the beach in Recife before their lives had been torn away from them.

They had been crouched among the tall grass watching the loading of the ships. The sun beat down hot on their shoulders, and she could feel sweat trickling down her back. The air was thick and smelled of the smoke of the fires in the main square, a warning of what would befall them if they were not able to board one of the ships.

There was no sign of the soldiers who had overrun their cousin's wedding, dragging off the bride and groom and many of the guests, including their parents. She and Roderigo had been bored with the long ceremony and snuck away, with bread in their hands, to feed the fish in the small river flowing through the property. They were too far away to hear the shots and screams and returned to find blood and death and the wreckage of a family. Roderigo had covered her mouth to stifle her screams and pulled her away into the safety of the trees. Then, together they ran towards the beach and to the docks, to the ships that had brought them to Recife only a few weeks ago, and now were their means of escaping the Inquisition. There was no hope for them here, now that the Inquisition had arrived; what their family had experienced had happened to many others in the territories Spain controlled in the New World.

"We will be safe in Jamaica, out of reach of Spain or the Inquisition," Roderigo

said.

"Our parents thought we would be safe in Recife," she said. "Enemies seem to be inescapable."

"Jamaica is close. Where would you have us go?"

She had no answer. Waiting in the tall grass, her skin prickled with goosebumps as if she were cold, despite the heat. They watched the ships load their cargo, not daring to look away for an instant, vigilant for any sign of soldiers. Roderigo had taught her to be practical, reassuring her with his plans. "Do not succumb to fear. We need our wits about us to survive. We shall escape, do not worry. We have a few sovereigns and your rings to pay for passage."

Roderigo would go first; to find the right ship to take them away from this horrid place. He was supposed to return for her, but he never did. She had waited until dawn until she heard the cries of the seamen as they pulled on ropes and chains, and she knew the ships were preparing to set sail.

If Roderigo had not returned, it was because he had been caught. The realization she was alone and the last of her family was gone hit her like a blow. Remembering Roderigo's last words to her, she could not fall apart now. She could not afford to grieve, and she had no belief that any God could come to her aid. She was on her own. She had to make her move, or she would not survive.

Her choice was a ship flying a French flag, bound for France. She had her rings, but she was not sure it would be enough to convince the captain to take her onboard. Time was running out. She was never a flirt and never practiced using womanly charms on a man, but this time, she must. Roderigo had warned her they must not look desperate, or like they needed to escape, so, brushing the sand and grass from her dress and smoothing her hair, she straightened her back and strode over to the captain like a queen. She played to the captain's sympathies, about not wanting to marry the suitor who had sent for her, to be doomed to remain in such a backwater colony. Luckily, her story and offering her rings as payment, was enough to convince him to take her onboard. As the ship pulled away from the scene of her family's death, she did not allow herself to grieve. It was not relief she felt upon her escape, but triumph. She had taken Roderigo's last words as a lesson, and she had learned to survive.

Her life had taken another unexpected turn after the ship had been attacked by pirates off the coast of Gibraltar. Her fate as a slave to a Moorish caliph seemed certain if she had not been rescued by Isaak.

Her thoughts had wandered from the beach in Recifewith Roderigo to the days of blinding sun and the caws of seagulls circling above her on the deck of Isaak's ship. She had slumped down on the deck, while he stood on the deck above her, a bold strong silhouette against the purest blue sky. Isaak shouted commands to his men, and the ship tilted as it turned towards its new course. She remembered that moment when she first heard their destination, "Venice."

With reluctance, she let go of her memories and forced herself alert. She sat up. The candle was still lit, but it was flickering. Pulling aside the thick drapes, lightning flashed in the storm-darkened skies, illuminating the room with a flash of light. Thunder rumbled. For a moment, she lost track of where she was; she had expected the expansive view of the Grand Canal, but here, locked within the Ghetto, she could catch only a glimpse of water from a small canal behind Sarra's mansion. How she longed to return to her own home! It was not the time to be sentimental. She must find a way to keep her brother safe, the Spanish at bay and stir Villiers's enthusiasm for an invasion of Jamaica.

She tapped a finger to her cheek. She could handle Villiers, but she must enlist Isaak to watch over Roderigo and ensure he was safe. Finding her long-lost brother had unnerved her, but she could not let her fears for him make her incapable of the kind of thinking and action necessary to accomplish her goals.

A small voice inside nagged at her, wishing for all contrivances to end and the desire for her secrets to be revealed. Could she close one era of her life and enter into a different existence—this time, with Isaak and her brother?

She shook her head violently, as if to rid her head of such troublesome thoughts. An impossible dream, as years of experience with men and women had shown. Could she and Isaak ever find a place where they could coexist together, or had life forged them to become too different?

She turned away from the wrathful clouds and slashing rain to the quiet domesticity of her room. The large, comfortable bed, surrounded by thick velvet curtains to keep out cold air, the rich coverlet, and puffy, feather-filled pillows. The small table beside the bed, the flickering candle, the washing stand. The hand towel was missing, and the water to wash. Mirabella! She had forgotten the perfidious maid. By now, it was most likely she had found a pawnshop to trade the jewels pilfered from Belladonna. With gold lining her pocket, it was doubtful she had remained in the city and was probably on her way to a new life. Regardless of the maid's whereabouts, Belladonna wanted those jewels back. Could she enlist the rabbi's aid in finding where they could have been pawned? He was familiar with the pawnbrokers from his own struggles to pay off his debts.

Satisfied with the course of action she had planned, she stoked the embers of the dying fire, then retreated back to the bed, hoping to find peace and much-needed sleep.

Chapter Thirty-Six: Diana

Stooped over the well in the campo of the Ghetto Nuovo, Diana was filling her bucket with water when the Men in Dark Cloaks arrived, stomping across the *campo*, heading towards her family's home. The bucket clanked, and water splashed as she ran towards her father, who was now striding quickly across the square, ignoring the men and women who called out to him, including her. Diana hoped she could divert him before he was seen by her mother or the men sent by the Council of Ten.

Her feet made loud squelching noises, and she shouted, "Father!" but he was lost in some reverie and did not notice her. Kissing the *mezuzah* at the threshold as he entered, the rabbi was oblivious to what awaited him. Diana hurried after him.

Men in cloaks and caps pulled low over their eyes. Her mother by the hearth, chafing her hands in her lap. One man held several of her father's papers in his gloved hand. He held it close to his face, and his nostrils flared as he sneered at them. He held it to the candle on the table, where it caught the flame and flared.

The rabbi lost his composure and reached for his papers. "What are you doing? There is no call for that. Those are but notes for my upcoming sermon. The Patriarch of Venice attends my sermons so—"

"You will not be needing any sermon this week, my friend," the man said. He flicked his gloved hand to the men on his left. They immediately stood on each side of the rabbi and each took one of his arms.

The rabbi looked from side to side. "What is this?"

"Rabbi Leone di Modena, you are summoned by the Council of Ten."

Diana took a step towards her father, but he warned her back. "If the Council of Ten has sent for me, I must go." He addressed the man who gave the orders, "Have no fear. I will not try to escape you."

The leader smiled. "Of course, you will not, especially if you are restrained." He nodded towards one of the guards. "Tie his hands."

Her mother moaned. "What have we done to deserve this?"

Diana swallowed and summoned the courage to raise her voice. "He is the leader of this community and should not be treated like a common criminal. If you treat him poorly, we will send word of it to Bardon Morosini."

The guard's eyes were shadowed under his cap, but his lips were curled into a snarl, and she felt more menace than his words conveyed. "I have heard the women of the Ghetto practice witchcraft, casting spells over good Christian men to ensnare them. You would not be one of those, would you?"

Diana bit her lips to suppress another protest. Her mother did not hold back and wailed loudly.

"Quiet! We shall be gone in a moment, along with the rabbi." The man holding her father's right arm was pulling him towards the door. The man holding his other arm snickered, "We shall return, do not worry. To search this hovel and the rest of this infernal Ghetto."

Diana put a hand on the stool and wished she had the courage to throw it. "What accusation had come against us now? We do have friends among the Council of Ten who will champion the truth."

The leader shook his head. "The truth? Tell us the truth about the courtesan Belladonna, then. She has been missing for many days, and her jewels have surfaced in the Ghetto."

One of the other men had circled close to Diana and placed a gloved hand on her shoulder. "Perhaps we should not take the old man with us to the Doge's Palace, but this one, eh?" he asked, "I would wager she would know more about the jewels than he would."

Diana clenched her hands and kept her arms tightly to her sides, ready to resist them. But the leader had other plans. "Our orders were clear. The rabbi is summoned, not the girl." He tilted his head towards the door.

One by one, the men filed out, following their orders. They pushed the rabbi ahead of them, but despite their threat, they did not tie his hands. With her mother's cries still ringing in her ears, Diana ran after them, stopping when she saw them depart in a long black gondola waiting outside the gates of the Ghetto.

There was no time to lose. She debated whether to get in a boat and head to the palazzo of Morosini to beg his help or to continue along the *fondimenta* towards the bridge of Trei Archi to the Moorish quarter to find her brother. To enlist Morosini, she needed a plan, so Isaak seemed the better course of action.

Pivoting on her heels, she retreated back through the Ghetto gates. First, she must calm her mother; then, she would hurry to inform Belladonna of the turn of events.

Chapter Thirty-Seven: Belladonna

Without Mirabella, the pounding on the door went on for some time before one of the other servants took it upon themselves to respond. Belladonna did not wait to be summoned by the still disoriented maids; she imagined a caller at this time of the evening meant important business or imminent trouble.

She put on a wrap over her night dress and descended the stairs. Though it was only a few hours past sunset, she was certain Sarra was already in her bed, either writing or sleeping and would not rise to see who had come to her door. From her perch on the staircase, when she saw Diana, Roderigo's safety was Belladonna's first thought. Her fingers clenched on the banister, and she took a deep breath, preparing for the worst.

Diana was nearly breathless, using one hand to support herself as she leaned into the doorframe. Belladonna gestured towards the stairway and into the salon. As soon as they were seated and the servant was out of sight, Diana burst out. "They have taken my father. The Council of Ten. They accuse us of your abduction and robbery!"

"How could they—?"

"Your jewels." Diana interrupted her, telling the rest of the story in staccato gasps, "Found in the Ghetto. Recognized as Belladonna's."

"Mirabella!" Belladonna stamped her fist into her open palm. "I should have dealt with her much, much earlier."

Diana needed to explain the threat hanging over them in the Ghetto. "It is a blood libel. A lie applied many times to Jews everywhere throughout our history, although in Venice, thank God, not often. Usually, it is a child who is missing or murdered, and fingers are pointed to the alien in their midst, the Jew. The claim is that we Jews have murdered to obtain their blood for our rituals or our food."

"That is a ludicrous accusation." Belladonna hugged her arms, as if she were cold, but it was Diana's words that had chilled her.

"Some, like the Patriarch of Venice, know that blood is not part of any of our rituals and that it is forbidden and not to be consumed, even if still in the meat of the animal. But that truth does not stop many from believing in the blood libel, and it can be used as a means to persecute us," Diana bit her lip to keep it from trembling. "So, it seems you have been deemed our latest victim, and if we cannot dispel the rumors of your death, the reaction will be dire."

Belladonna frowned. "If I reveal myself and return to my palazzo, I and the Jews of Jamaica will fall victim to the agents of the Inquisition. If I remain in hiding, it will be the Jews of the Ghetto who will suffer the consequences. Not a very good choice."

"There must be an alternative, some way you can reveal yourself without exposing yourself to the Spanish," said Diana, her hands clasped tightly, as she began to pace.

Footsteps announced the arrival of their hosts, Sarra and Jacob, both dressed for bed and blinking repeatedly as if they had just come awake. Glancing at each other in confusion, Sarra and Jacob did not seem pleased at the sight of a visitor, though it was Diana.

"It is the rabbi," Belladonna informed them and beckoned for the couple to be seated, "he has been taken by the Men in Dark Cloaks."

The Sullams followed obediently, with Jacob keeping his arm around Sarra protectively. Diana quickly described her father's capture by the Men in Dark Cloaks and summarized the danger to the Ghetto.

Jacob peered at the women in the flickering candlelight and patted his wife's hand as he spoke in a reassuring tone, "We will find a plan to avert this threat."

"Mirabella was the cause of this all," Belladonna muttered, "she was an insidious enemy, biding her time to strike."

Sarra swallowed. "It cannot be. Why would she ever do this? We had always treated her with kindness."

"Kindness is not the way with such a woman. She had been stealing from you and corrupting the other servants where she could."

Diana raised a hand. "We must find a way to prove to the Council of Ten that the people of the Ghetto are innocent of any crime. The evidence against us is far from conclusive. The discovery of the jewelry should not lead to conviction; it is well-known that pawnbrokers in the Ghetto receive most of their goods from noblemen and merchants outside of it."

Belladonna shook her head. "Will you never learn? Though it is the Age of Reason, there is no logic or reason in the accusations against you. Ever. I do not fathom the reasons behind it, but there is deep-routed hatred against the Jews, and it is always ready to resurface at the slightest provocation. The discovery of the jewels and my disappearance are the latest sparks to ignite a torch-bearing mob."

Sarra clutched her husband's hand and looked from him to Diana. "I had heard we have friends among the Council of Ten. Surely, with their help, we can avert this threat. After all, they have helped before, when there was a call for the Ghetto's charter to be revoked."

"The blood libel is a very powerful calumny and not so easily dispelled. Even the Patriarch of Venice, who scoffs at such nonsense, will have to mind his words if he speaks out on our behalf. We still have many powerful enemies who would like nothing more than to drive every Jew from their midst," Jacob Sullam said. Sarra sat with her back arched like a cat sensing danger.

Diana looked at Belladonna. "We must find a lucrative enough proposition to sway allegiances." Belladonna had no doubt Diana had Morosini in mind.

However, she had a different idea. "Or leverage old secrets," Belladonna was thinking of Niccolo Contarini and the deeds she knew he wanted kept hidden. "Both strategies have merit, depending on where they are employed." Belladonna tapped a finger to her temple, and her lips settled into a determined smile.

Diana could not sit still, her feet tapped incessantly, and her fingers tore at her skirts. Belladonna wished she could alleviate her friend's distress and persuade both Morosini and Contarini to have the rabbi released. However, Roderigo's life was at stake, as well as her own.

She placed her hand over Diana's. "I know you are aching for action, but we must be very cautious of our next step. Painful as it may be, we must wait. We do not know what the Council of Ten wants, and the last time, the rabbi was released after they had informed him of what they needed. It is likely they will do the same this time."

She looked to Jacob and Sarra, but their eyes shifted away. It was Diana who said, "This time, we know what they want. You."

Chapter Thirty-Eight: Diana

Before Diana left the Sullams', they had collectively decided the best course of action was to contact Morosini. As a leading member of the Council of Ten, he was privy to their plans for the rabbi. Had the rabbi been sent for because of his skills with medicine or poison as before? Or because they truly believed Belladonna was being held captive in the Ghetto?

Diana had volunteered to go to the nobleman to enlist his help, which she was thankful the others had declined. "There can be no direct communication to Morosini from the Ghetto. Especially you, as the chief rabbi's daughter. Your presence with Morosini could compromise his abilities to help us, if you were observed."

Instead, it had been determined to have word sent through the Turk. Diana was to go home to comfort her mother and to keep her from spreading her panic throughout the Ghetto. If the chief rabbi was being held by the Council of Ten, the whole community would be on alert. The Committee for the Redemption of Prisoners would be called to meet, and they would be ready to amass the ducats required to free their rabbi.

Though she appreciated their ability to quickly muster support, it was not yet clear that it was needed. The last time the Men in Dark Cloaks had come for the rabbi, he had not been arrested and had been summoned only to fill their request. Diana was still hopeful this was a similar occurrence, although, from the manner of the men who took him, she suspected this time, if Morosini could not help, she would need the Committee's support.

When she reached the threshold of their rooms and reached up to touch the *mezuzah*, she closed her eyes and added a special prayer for its protection over her family. The prayer parchment wrapped inside contained the *Shemah,* a prayer recited for centuries as an affirmation of faith in the Almighty's protection and written on amulets for the same purpose. Protection. The gates of the Ghetto were for their protection. As she finished the prayer, she included her wish for less need for protection for her people.

Her mother's stool by the fire was vacant, and it was eerily quiet, the only sound the bubbling and occasional burping of the stew on the fire. From the smell of it, it had been cooking too long, and she grabbed a cloth to protect her hands from the heat of the pot as she moved it away from the heat.

"Mother!" she called out. It was not her mother's usual practice to leave good food on the fire to burn. A knot of unease began to form in her stomach. Where had her mother gone? It was late, and no one still lingered in the *campo* of the Ghetto Nuovo for gossiping.

Diana sat down on her mother's vacated seat. She felt tears beading in her eyes and blinked them away. It was no time to feel sorry for herself. She stood and hurried to the back room and was relieved to see a lump on the bed and the sound of snores.

She would wait a few minutes to ensure her mother was deep in sleep before she would address her fears, and consider what new trouble awaited them all.

* * *

Belladonna donned a woolen cloak to face the dampness and cold that seemed to have suddenly enveloped the Ghetto like a fallen cloud. She had assured her hosts she needed no footman to accompany her to the *Campo de Mori* since she had felt confident of finding her way on her own to the Turk. But once she saw the heaviness of the fog over the bridge before her, she decided to ask the servants to find an intrepid boatman to take her there.

Although it took some time until a boatman could be found, Belladonna was grateful when at last, she was able to seat herself inside and could enjoy the journey in peace. Reclining in the seat, she closed her eyes as she relished the time to consider the events alone, without the input, no matter how well intended, of her friends. The gentle lull of the water would put her to sleep if she let her mind wander too much, especially if it roamed to Isaak and the bright blue skies of other voyages.

Think. Belladonna had always prided herself on her ability to strategize, plot, and plan her way out of any disaster the Fates tossed her way. What was most important to her was Roderigo. She could dangle herself before the Spanish and lead them away from her brother and her friends in the Ghetto. She knew how to play the song the Spanish ambassador would most like to hear. As she imagined such an encounter, she tried to smile, but inside, a knot of fear was forming. Diego di Ribera was not a kind man, and he relished the sufferings of others. He would very much enjoy using the whip on her, claiming he was purging her soul. To avoid getting into his hands would be wiser.

A distraction? It had worked before, when the intrigues around the Gallery of Beauties thickened with menace. Perhaps she could rely on an outsider, as she had before? Morosini had been instrumental, then, in helping her. The opportunity for new trade with the English in the Caribbean should be enough incentive for him to ally with her once more.

The fog seemed to be lifting some, taking the gloom off her mood as well. Torches blazed outside one of the hostels in the main *campo* of the Moorish quarter, so it was not difficult for her to see her path to the Turk's door, despite the dimness of the still-lingering fog. She had barely touched the heavy door with her knuckles when it creaked open, and a man in Moorish dress emerged.

A hand holding a flaming torch caused a protective shadow behind it, another hand beckoned, and she followed without fear or suspicion. In the courtyard, it was very quiet. The fountain murmured, and there was the click-clicking of bats who flitted from trees to house and back again and the soft swish of the draperies of the man beside her. Before she could break the silence with her voice, the man turned and wrapped her in his arms.

"Isaak," she moaned as she let herself be thoroughly enveloped in his arms.

He did not kiss her, but placed a warning finger to her lips. With his arms around her waist, he navigated her across the garden to a small grotto, flanked by trees and hidden from view. Water cascaded from a niched wall, which had been plastered and marked with the curly-cue writing of the Moors.

"A better place to share confidences," Isaak said.

Though she would rather linger in this quiet place, nestled in his arms, Belladonna knew she should waste no time and updated him—his father had been taken to the Council of Ten. As expected, her news caused Isaak to instantly pull away from her. His jaw tensed, his brow descended into a scowl, and his face seemed to harden into granite.

Isaak paced, and Belladonna said nothing, waiting for his thinking to evolve into a plan of action. Isaak continued moving, sometimes mumbling to himself or shaking his head.

She said, "If you cannot stop this frenzy of pacing, I shall certainly lose my mind."

Isaak stopped and spoke to her, "There is no purpose in planning. We do not have enough information. However, we must ensure Roderigo's safety, and we must contact the Englishman. There is no time to be lost. Either Villiers or Roderigo will be killed if we dally."

His eyes refocused on Belladonna. "You must be the one to approach Villiers."

Belladonna raised an eyebrow. "And Morosini?"

"The Turk will send a message. He will come here, and I will deal with him." He paused, "We have had business between us before."

There was an uneasy quiet between them, and the intimacy of their greeting seemed to have disappeared. Belladonna looked away when Isaak's eyes sought hers. Though there was no doubt Villiers would be best handled by her, there was a pang of pain at her love ordering her to go to him. The magic of their reunion had been broken by the intrusion of reality. She was a courtesan; he was a pirate. Their lives were on divergent paths. The intersections where they were together were anomalies—chimeras, illusions that should not be mistaken as possibilities. Still conscious of Isaak's eyes on her, Belladonna did not allow a sigh to escape her; instead, she straightened her spine and faced him with a determined look.

"You might consider having your sister with you when Morosini arrives." She said it to hurt him and instantly regretted it when he asked, "And why is that?"

Belladonna bit her lip, "Morosini seems to have taken an interest in your sister."

His jaw tensed, and his voice was hard. "What kind of interest?"

"In her medicinal skills." This time she could not meet his eyes, as she did not want to be the one to inform him of the nobleman's lust for his sister. "Along with your father, she provided him with Venice Treacle when he felt the threat of a poisoner."

Isaak's smoothed his hand across his chin, and his face relaxed. "I suppose having a steady source for Venice Treacle makes good sense to a man in his position. It is supposed to be effective against most poisons."

As if on cue, the Turk rambled in, followed by his daughter, holding a tray with a silver pot and small porcelain cups. "Coffee?"

The Turk remained standing while his guests reclined on the cushions of a low divan, and Isaak waited until the steaming cups had been distributed before broaching the subject of Morosini.

"Send Morosini a message to meet us here."

"Are you certain the time is right for such a move?" asked the Turk, his eyes shifting towards Belladonna.

Isaak nodded. "We need his help. The Council of Ten has taken my father. It is time to bargain. Why do you hesitate?"

"Because," said their host, who looked beyond them towards the entryway, "The English nobleman has just arrived."

Belladonna stood immediately. "Is there somewhere I can listen but not be seen?"

The soft fluttering fabrics brushed her cheek as the Turk's daughter slid by her. "This way."

Chapter Thirty-Nine: Villiers

The home of the Turk did not disappoint. The exotic scents of flowers, the enticing smell of coffee, a drink he had first tasted in Spain, which had been one of his only pleasures there. It seemed this city would yield more in the way of sensory enjoyment, and he was eager to sample whatever he could. He followed the round-robed figure of his host into the shadows, who led him into a covered portico filled with brightly patterned cushions and hanging silken fabrics. He had not seen such sultry extravagance since his visit to an exotic but well-established bordello in London.

Perhaps the Turk kept a bevy of beauties like a Sultan? He took a seat on a low divan and rubbed his hands together while fantasizing about women draped over the cushions beside him. As if he had conjured her up himself, a veiled lady appeared, the gauzy fabrics that encased her slim form fluttering as she walked. He inhaled the faint scent of exotic spices and the strong aroma of coffee as she leaned forward and presented him with a steaming glass.

The Turk settled himself in a low divan facing him. Although the thick lips in the sun-darkened face were stretched in a wide smile, Villiers was not fooled. This man was an adversary to be bested, not a friend.

Villiers opened the bargaining with, "I have a proposition for you. A very profitable one."

The Turk maintained his smile, only moving his lips to utter, "You have my attention."

Villiers flashed his teeth in a return grin. "Jamaica. The entrée to lucrative trade in sugar and spices. Wrested from beneath the royal Spanish nose."

"And what would be my part in this endeavor?"

Villiers put down his now-empty glass on the small table beside the divan. "Find me the courtesan Belladonna. She holds the key."

Placing his ring-filled hand across his ample belly, the Turk chuckled. "The competition is quite fierce for the courtesan. Your offer must be... impressive."

Villiers leaned forward, as if he had a secret to share. "A partnership, although a limited one, in a new West Indies Trading Company, backed by the Bank of England."

The Turk gave a slow nod. "Your proposal has merit, I admit. However, I would need to secure your promise with gold. There are expenses..."

Villiers pretended to be distracted by the fluttering veils of the woman who caused his used glass to disappear. He took time to answer, although he was careful to be positive but non-committal. "I represent the court of King James, who will put all the resources of England behind this endeavor. Gold will flow, I promise you."

Perhaps the Turk already knew a promise from Villiers meant little. If possible, the fleshy lips of the Moor widened further. "Unfortunately, my friend, I do not trade based on promises. Only gold."

Villiers gave a dramatic sigh. "Upon delivery of the courtesan, you shall have your gold."

* * *

Although the air was cold for the fall season, the sun reflecting on the glimmering waters warmed Villiers as he reclined in his seat in the gondola. Odd thing about Venice, a fall day seemed rosy, despite the brisk wind that whipped his hair and nearly took his hat away. Maybe it was his visit with the Turk which made his outlook cheerier. He had no doubt the Turk knew where to find the elusive Belladonna and that Sir Henry would provide the gold required. What made him smile was the new opportunity to pocket some of Sir Henry's gold for himself—which would allow him another turn at the gambling tables to enrich himself even more.

The Fates had dealt him a good hand when he had been sent to Venice. For one thing, he had not lied when he described the new trading company he would spearhead, once Jamaica was in the hands of good King James. For whatever was in the King's hands would find a way to trickle down into Villiers'. He had not mentioned the Gold of Christopher Columbus nor the envoy's secret map. That treasure he would claim as his own—his reward for securing the West Indies trade route for England. His place at court would be supreme, and Arundel would seem like a gnat in comparison.

Though the wind whipped at his face, Villiers closed his eyes, only feeling the warmth of the sun.

Chapter Forty: Belladonna

The Turk's daughter had led her to a curtained passageway adjacent to the area where the men were sitting, and she was able to catch every word between Villiers and the Turk. Her fingers toyed with the lace of her bodice, missing her pearls as she considered how to stage her encounter with the Englishman. She would wear her pearls again, along with the silks and lace to which she was accustomed. She exhaled and closed her eyes, almost feeling the fabric, so perfectly aligned to her form once again. No yellow turban or yellow badge to mar its perfection.

The Englishman resided with Sir Henry Wotton, the English ambassador. One threshold no Spaniard would be likely to cross. Yes, Sir Henry's palazzo would be the best place for Belladonna to reappear. The question was when? Though she was aching to return, she knew it was best to wait until they knew what the Council of Ten was planning.

Isaak should be pleased that one part of the mission had been accomplished, as Sir George Villiers seemed to be eager for his King to annex the island of Jamaica. His greed had certainly overcome any qualms of political repercussions of antagonizing the Spanish with such an act. The lust for treasure was a powerful motivator, and she must continue to dangle the fabled map that Roderigo was rumored to possess to keep him in thrall. Belladonna smiled. Keeping men in thrall to their passions was her specialty.

Isaak. She peeked around the curtain, but only the Turk was visible, still reclining across the cushions, drinking his coffee. With nearly silent steps, possible in the leather slippers Jewish women wore, she slipped out of the passageway and into the garden. There was no murmur of voices, only the

181

splashing noises of water cascading from the spout of the fountain. No sign of Isaak.

Had he gone himself to meet with Morosini? She hoped not. Morosini was an ally, but there was a price on Isaak's head, and it might provide the nobleman with added leverage he could use against her. How much of her secret did Morosini know? If he knew of her true relationship with Roderigo, her life in Venice could not be the same as before.

She paused on tiptoe, still in shadow, at the sound of a loud knock on the gate. The Turk launched himself from the divan and waddled towards the green door. She held her breath, but released it in a hiss at the voice of the Turk's new visitor. Morosini.

It seemed her message had been received, but Isaak had not delivered it, for Morosini had arrived alone.

She followed the two men to the same cushioned area where Sir George Villiers had been sitting just minutes earlier. Her laugh rang out, echoing across the courtyard, causing the men to turn around.

"Belladonna?"

"Bardon?"

His eyes took her in from tip to toe, and he brushed the tip of his moustache with his fingers. "Admirable transformation. At first glance, I did not recognize you."

"It is always gratifying when I can surprise you, Bardon."

The Turk interrupted their banter. "Perhaps you would prefer to speak in private. It is evident you both are well acquainted and do not require my facilitation."

Belladonna nodded to the Turk, and he gave a deferential salute as he departed. Out of the corner of her eye, she caught him entering the curtained passageway where she knew he could hear their conversation.

Belladonna sat directly opposite Morosini. Morosini arranged the colorful pillows behind him and leaned back. He took a deep breath, which he exhaled slowly, before asking, "So, shall we discuss your disappearance first, or why you are so overjoyed to see me?"

Belladonna decided to get to the point. "Rabbi Modena. Why has he been summoned to the Council of Ten?"

The nobleman's eyes narrowed, making his face more snake-like. "Because of you, Belladonna."

Belladonna raised her eyebrows, and he continued, "First, you disappear from your palazzo, leaving all your possessions behind and without a word to your servants or friends. Then, your earrings. Very distinctive and known to any jeweler of quality. A Ghetto pawnbroker, who was not as knowledgeable, attempted to sell them, leading to the suspicion you were being detained in the Ghetto."

"Detained?" she repeated, scowling. "Could they possibly believe I, Belladonna, could be held by the people of the Ghetto? For what possible purpose?"

Morosini rolled his eyes. "Please, have you become like your friend Diana? You should know better. In the halls of the powerful, rational argument holds no sway. Only profit does. There are those who feel the competition from the bankers in the Ghetto and would like to see their charter revoked and the Jews expelled."

"That is an old story. Every ten years or so, there is another vote on the charter. I thought it was just approved. Why now?"

"You have generated a great deal of interest of late. Perhaps that is why you thought it best to leave so suddenly. But leaving as you did, started the hounds sniffing for opportunity. Pointing the finger at the Ghetto will meet with little opposition and possibly result in a windfall, if a Jewish trader or banker can be put out of business."

Belladonna flexed her fingers to keep them from shaking. "So, the rabbi is being held in retaliation for my 'abduction'?"

"Precisely," Morosini flicked away a leaf that must have fallen on his shoulder during his passage through the garden. A tone of annoyance crept into his voice, "Messengers are being sent to the leaders of the Ghetto as we speak. The ability to obtain his freedom rests on whether or not you are delivered to your palazzo unharmed. As you may have expected, the members of the Council who always bring up the expulsion of the Jews have brought it up again. Rumors of a nefarious end for the now beloved

Belladonna at the hands of the Jews is the excuse for a massive search to be made of every dwelling in the Ghetto."

A wave of dizziness assailed Belladonna as the scenes of the soldiers' invasion at the wedding party in Recife flashed through her mind. When soldiers searched, nothing was sacred, and no one in the Ghetto would come out of their intrusion unscathed.

Suppressing her fears, and in her usual tone of voice, she asked, "Has it become too difficult to protest the ludicrous charges made against the people of the Ghetto?"

Morosini gave a dramatic sigh and smoothed his mustache with a heavily ringed hand. "You know how much I detest the medieval prejudice against the Jews. But I shall not be their defender; it would risk too much to do so. The best I can do is to vote against banishment when the time comes."

"When the time comes," repeated a voice from the shadows of the corridor. Isaak stepped forward, and gave a respectful bow to the nobleman, adding, "is not reassuring."

Now dressed like a Moor, in flowing white draperies and a tightly wrapped white turban, Belladonna had to admit she could barely recognize him. From the scowl on his face, it was evident Morosini was annoyed by the interruption and did not understand why this man had come forward.

"Need I introduce myself? We are well-acquainted." Isaak's teeth flashed brightly as he smiled.

Morosini's eyes widened momentarily and then fell back to their usual half-lowered position. "I must confess, your disguise is quite effective. I was only moderately suspicious of you on my previous visit, but only because I was fairly certain you were able to understand my conversation with the Turk."

Isaak placed an open palm on his chest and gave another small bow. "Ostentatious it may be, but it distracts from too close an examination of my face." He turned stiffly to Belladonna, acting as if he barely knew her. "His insight into the Council of Ten forces us to act. The rumors of your disappearance have become a blood libel against the Jews which could result in banishment and death. You understand which course you must take."

Belladonna lifted her chin and gave each man, in turn, a hard look. "I am ready to reveal myself. But first, a plan must be put in place for the escape of the envoy."

Chapter Forty-One: Antonio

Antonio smelled intrigue. There was a fluttering of hands and papers at the home of the Spanish ambassador, as if a furious wind had blown in. He sat on a velvet-covered bench in the ornate entry hall and none of those rushing by paid any mind to him. Even when he removed his trusted dagger from its sheath and held it up to allow the light of the chandelier to reflect on its well-honed blade.

Spanish functionaries are used to weapons of death—another element contributing to a state of constant fear. The threat of being condemned, of being dismissed, or if, you were important enough, being assassinated was omnipresent in Spain. Antonio was glad he had been assigned to this city, a much safer place for his retirement.

Couriers, servants, and soldiers flashed by. Antonio toyed with the idea of flinging his dagger among them, just to see who or what he might hit. He was still smiling at the thought, when someone stopped in front of him.

"His Excellency will see you now."

Antonio was slow to replace the dagger back in its sheath. The messenger waited, dancing from one foot to the other. Antonio liked making him nervous. The man kept much space between them as he led Antonio into the wood-paneled office of Diego di Ribera.

The Spanish ambassador stood by the large window, which provided most of the light into the dark-paneled room. It was early enough in the day for the glimmers of sunlight reflected off the canal to quiver across the ceiling. Di Ribera turned away from the window at his arrival.

"The courtesan has been found."

There was a flicker of triumph in his smile, as if it was he who had found her and brought her back, which Antonio was certain was not the case. He took a seat on the edge of the large walnut desk, unconcerned when his movement caused a cascade of papers to fall to the floor. Antonio waited for the annoyance to register on the ambassador's face before asking the question the man was waiting for him to ask.

"How do you know?"

"I have received a report. Her jewels were seen in a pawnshop in the Ghetto. An anonymous note placed in the *Boca di Leone* reported it."

The Venetians had their own way to turn in their neighbors, in the guise of good citizenship. All that was required was a note slipped into the mouth-shaped slot on the side of the Doge's Palace, the *Boca di Leone*, and it would be brought to the Council of Ten for investigation. It bothered Antonio that Di Ribera's spies had ferreted out this intelligence while his own had not. His finger traversed the length of his dagger. His informants would pay for their sluggishness.

"Does that mean you know where to find her?" Antonio did not bother to keep the scornful tone out of his voice.

Di Ribera shook his head. "Not exactly. But the Jews know where she is. It is likely they may have even taken her for some unspeakable ritual." His hand adjusted the large ruff around his neck, as if it had suddenly become too tight. "You know they need Christian blood."

Antonio did not bother to challenge this insane belief. It was a story that justified the capture and torture of those who might come under the scrutiny of the Inquisition as 'Judaizers'. He was no lover of the Jews and once kept a Jewish merchant as prisoner for a few days while awaiting the delivery of his ransom. The merchant, who had been a pleasant fellow, had shown revulsion when Antonio had generously offered him a portion of his joint of lamb. The man had refused it, informing Antonio of his religion's prohibition from eating meat that had not been soaked heavily in salted water to get the blood out of it.

"They have Belladonna?" Antonio kept words to a bare minimum, asking but avoiding answering questions.

Di Ribera clasped his hands together and smiled. "It has worked out very well, you see. If the courtesan does not appear, the Council of Ten will have the Ghetto searched and, with luck, its inhabitants banished. If she does appear—well, then we shall have her!"

Antonio's brows rose. This was interesting news. He cursed his informants again, for not having brought this information to his attention. Having Di Ribera distracted by his hatred of the Jews and Belladonna was good for Antonio, who would keep his efforts focused on the envoy.

Let Di Ribera gloat. He had gleaned some useful information, so the visit was not a total loss. If the Council of Ten suspected the people of the Ghetto knew where to find Belladonna, it was logical to assume they might also have knowledge of the envoy. Di Ribera really wanted to get his hands on the courtesan, and eliciting information about the envoy was his excuse for torturing her.

Her earrings had been pawned in the Ghetto. It was likely there would be more jewels to be found. Antonio was determined to find them and ensure they ended up in his pocket.

Yes, all the signs pointed him in one direction. To the Ghetto.

Chapter Forty-Two: Diana

D iana had tossed and turned the entire night, unable to stop worrying about her father. He had not returned. She envisioned him in the chamber of the Council of Ten. The carved statue of Justice, above the portal into the next room, the chamber of judgment, where the *I tre babài* or The Three Inquisitors would be waiting. Two would be dressed in black and one in red. Under an exquisite ceiling painting by Veronese, the Red Inquisitor would sit in the middle, and the two Black Inquisitors would flag him to the right and left, waiting to hear the story and judge the trembling man or woman brought before them.

Rabbi Leone di Modena had previously appeared before the Council of Ten, and according to his own report, had answered their questions without trembling. He had never been directed through the portal beneath the Statue of Justice. This time, if they did not listen to the rational argument of his friends, like the Patriarch of Venice, would he be sent to the prisons, the dreaded *Pozzi*? How long would he be held hostage for Belladonna?

Her father could stand before the three judges, and if two out of three donned a black hat, another door would open. He would be led from the rich paneled, beautifully appointed rooms of the chambers of the Council of Ten into the bleakness of the Doge's prison, with light diminishing along with his freedom.

Belladonna had spoken of her visit to the prison; of the dank smells and cries of despair that had filled her ears and her nightmares for many days afterwards. If her father had been sent to the prison, she prayed he had been placed in the upper level, the *Piombi*. There was light there from windows and access to a yard. Jews were segregated among the prisoners, and the community could buy privileges for them, such as providing food, a clean bed and laundered clothing.

It would depend on the vindictiveness of their enemies. If men like Niccolo Contarini, the leader of the Council of Ten, was one of the Three Inquisitors (their identity was a closely guarded secret) or could influence them, her father might be sent to the prison's lower levels, the Wells, known as the *Pozzi*. There would be no light there, no chance they would allow him any comfort, including his books. The cells were cold and dank and were rumored to sometimes flood or be swarmed by rats. Prisoners placed in the *Pozzi* were usually placed there for long periods and likely forgotten. It would be more difficult to provide food or linens for those in the *Pozzi*, and less chance of redeeming them. She shivered and curled into the thickness of her old bridal featherbed. This time its warmth, and the memories associated with it, did not give her comfort.

She should not assume mistreatment of her father. He may not even be in the prisons, but detained somewhere else. Though she did not want to encounter Bardon Morosini again, she could not wait for Belladonna or Isaak to learn what had happened to her father.

Her decision to take action settled the turmoil of her thoughts. She must have drifted off to sleep, because soon, she heard the sounds of the morning, of her mother preparing the fire to heat water. She washed and dressed in a gown of deep green velvet, given to her by Belladonna and missing the yellow badge. She tended to her hair as best she could, with one hand holding the mirror, conscious and careful this morning of her outward appearance. Her beauty was all she had to disarm a powerful nobleman.

Donning a black veil and wearing her red velvet cloak, Diana moved quickly through the gates of the Ghetto, hoping she would not be recognized. She found a gondola to take her down the Grand Canal to the Palazzo of the Morosinis. Trailing a hand in the cold waters of the lagoon, she remembered that this coming Sabbath, they would be reading the Torah portion of *Chaye Sarra (the Life of Sarra)*, which described the first time Isaac had met his bride-to-be, Rebecca.

Diana learned that when Rebecca caught sight of her groom for the first time, her first reaction had been to veil herself. The rabbis' interpreted the phrase "veiled herself" as having seen her future success in tricking her husband into delivering his blessing to Jacob instead of Esau. Diana could identify with Rebecca now.

Like Rebecca, she was prepared to use subterfuge and do battle with Morosini if it would mean freedom for her father.

The cold water on her fingers made them feel numb. She hoped the numbness would remain and infuse her completely so she would feel invulnerable, ready for anything she might have to do.

Grey clouds hovered along the horizon line, and the sunlight seemed too weak and pale to brighten the journey. Even the coral walls of the Morosini palazzo seemed washed out, its white-accented windows and doorways pallid and gloomy. Diana mustered her courage as she lifted her skirts and stepped onto the dock of the palazzo. There was no one in attendance. It must be too early for a nobleman whose evening must have lasted into the morning hours. A voice in her head warned her to go home and wait for the others.

Despite her misgivings, Diana made her way up the stairs to the *piano nobile*. There stood a servant immaculately clad in the yellow and green Morosini livery. He looked her up and down through half-lowered lids, a poor imitation of his master, and asked her to state her business.

"I am here to see your master," she lifted her chin and pulled the red velvet cloak closed, adding, "At his request."

The man snorted and blocked her entry. "The Master is not in. Perhaps you are mistaken in his invitation?"

Diana was about to reply when there were footsteps, and a voice boomed out from behind her. "Do not be such a dullard, and let the lady pass."

The servant's eyes widened, and he immediately bowed to the voice of his master and gestured for Diana to follow him into the grand salon.

"No, not here. You can bring wine—" After Morosini gave her a quick glance, he added, "only one glass, for me, into my study."

Diana accepted the nobleman's arm as he escorted her into his private rooms. She hoped he could not feel her trembling. She must banish thoughts of their previous private encounters, when he had made advances and threatened her family, and keep calm.

Morosini gently took her cloak, gesturing for her to take a seat in the beautifully carved chair placed before a massive, dark wood desk. He was being solicitous and kind, two characteristics she would not normally associate with Morosini.

"How interesting my days are becoming," he said as he took his seat behind the desk. "Last evening, I had the pleasure of your brother's company, and today, yours. Relax, Diana, I know why you are here."

Before she could answer, the rude servant appeared with a decanter of wine and water and despite his master's admonition, two glasses. He laid down a cloth and poured both wine and some water into a glass, which he placed before Morosini. Morosini took the glass, swirled it, and sniffed before taking a deep drink. He waved the servant away.

"Wine?" Without waiting for her answer, he said, "I did not think so. You still cling to those archaic beliefs. They are shackles, my dear, and they will hold you back from where destiny can take you."

Diana had to be careful in her response not to antagonize him. "This is not a new argument, but it is not a simple matter to disengage from one's people or one's family. Isaac and Zebulun will not stay in Venice, and so the responsibility for my parents must fall to me. You must know it is for my father's sake I have come to you."

Morosini lifted the glass and took another deep drink. "I should expect nothing less, you have proven yourself a brave woman. But you know me, so what is your proposal?"

She drummed her fingers on the hard wood of the desk to delay her answer. "My proposal is the same as Isaak's. My *appeal* is personal, to you. I cannot rest while my father is confined in the *Pozzi*."

Morosini smiled, and he smoothed his mustache with his thumb and index finger. "Your appeal is moving, but allow your mind to rest. I had suggested to the Council of Ten your father should be the guest of the Patriarch of Venice, instead of the Doge's prison. The rooms within the

Patriarch's palazzo are far more comfortable."

Knowing of the friendship her father had with the Patriarch, Diana's tightly clenched fists opened. "I thank you for your help."

Morosini waved a ringed hand and took another swig of wine before continuing, "You see, Diana, I can be a very powerful advocate. You have only to discard your origins, and the world shall be yours."

"As your mistress?"

"Perhaps as my wife. My coffers are full, and my first wife is dead, so I have the freedom to marry whoever I wish." He rose from behind the desk and stood before her. The smell of wine and sandalwood accompanied him as he brought his face close to hers.

She forced herself to meet his gaze, though she cringed at his suggestions. He must have sensed her feelings. He backed away and seated himself on the edge of his desk, reaching once more for his glass of wine. His usual bantering manner had returned as he said, "Allow me to believe I have some chance with you. Although I have my suspicions that it is that artist, Correr, who distracts you."

"I loved my husband and still mourn him."

Morosini sighed, "And I loved Theresa. But they are both gone. It is time for us both to move on. I am willing to leave Venice if you are willing to leave your people. I have a hankering to explore the New World." His eyes stared far off beyond her, far from the room. "I, too, would be starting over. Adventure beckons, if you are willing to join me."

She did not answer. He drank the rest of the glass. "Surely you can understand. I envy your brothers' freedom, you see. I am tied down to this city," he brushed a hand across the heavy wood of the desk, "by this palazzo, by generations of prodigal sons whose duty it is to maintain and continue the dynasty. But I seek to find my true self, not the descendant of a dynasty. And I believe with you at my side, I can."

Diana was afraid of offending him, but she could not feign an emotion she could not feel. "I cannot see replicating the love I had with my husband."

Her answer seemed to satisfy him. "I admire your loyalty. Another quality I appreciate." He sighed, "Perhaps your feelings will change with time. And once we are better acquainted."

He reached for the red velvet cloak, which had been tossed on a nearby chair. He held it out to her, "I have reassured you about your father. It is not good for either of us for you to be seen here at this time. It is best you go."

The nobleman's fingers lingered as he arranged the cloak about her shoulders. She turned to leave, but he took her arm and held her back.

"Just know, Diana, that I am at your service. At any time. I will wait for you to feel the same."

She forced herself to meet his eyes and gave a slight nod. He released her, and as soon as she was out of his sight, she released a long-held breath.

Morosini's gentleness had surprised her. When he had first expressed his interest in her, it had been lustful and leering. Now, he had seemed wistful, and his interest in her seemed to go deeper. He was looking for a woman he could love and trust to be loyal. He wanted to turn over a new leaf and become a new person. A jaded nobleman like Bardon Morosini might need something to excite him. The more exotic, the better. The New World, hand in hand with a Jewess, would seem like the adventure of a lifetime.

She respected Morosini, but he was not a man she could ever grow to love. Though he had seemed gentler, he was hard as granite inside and not a person she could ever trust. He could never understand the desire for *tikkun olam,* of making the world right, which was the essence of all she had been taught. She could imagine Morosini sneering at the concept, for he believed what is right for Morosini is then right for the world.

Chapter Forty-Three: Belladonna

Belladonna had once vowed never again to cross the threshold of a Contarini after she and Niccolo had parted with a truce. Since then, they had been keeping an eye on each other, circling each other like disgruntled pugilists, aching for another fight.

Her appearance at his doorstep would be counted as a triumph by Niccolo, but knowing the man's bitterness, perhaps it was better to approach him when he felt he was the victor. Long ago, when they were very young, she imagined she could love him, but he disappointed her with his anger when she published a small book of sonnets. Her accomplishments were seen by him as an attempt to overshadow him. Since then, she had bested him too many times and had risen in prominence despite him. He had never forgiven her and seemed dedicated to bringing about her downfall.

He was not purposely evil, but hungry for power and did not care who might be harmed in his procurement of it. Both his daughter and wife had been disregarded, allies and friends betrayed all for the sake of his ambitions. He was no longer admired and held onto his leadership of the Council of Ten through fear.

Belladonna's appeal to Contarini to free Rabbi di Modena was for the sake of justice, not as a favor. Niccolo did take his position as magistrate and judge seriously. He would not permit the search of the Ghetto once she appeared to disprove the rumors of her abduction.

The somber-faced servant in the red and gold livery of the Contarini did not flinch, but regarded her with half-lowered haughty eyes when she asked to see his master. He did not keep her waiting for long and had the gall to sneer at her before turning his back to her to lead her to the salon on *piano nobile*.

"Belladonna, in my home? I had thought Zaccaria had been in his cups when he announced you. I had to see for myself. I have been mistaken before, as you well know, by appearances, when viewed from a distance."

The salon was cold and not very bright, though there were many tapers in the crystal chandelier and sconces around the large room. Wine-red curtains were closed around the windows, letting in no outside light, and tapestries allowed very little of the ivory walls to show above the dark wood wainscotting. It was a room for men, never for a ball filled with the sounds of music and the tinkle of laughter. A few austere benches were placed in intervals along the wall, and instead of divans for sitting, there was a large desk, with one chair before it and one behind it, in which Niccolo sat.

He pointedly did not rise at her entrance, which she ignored, as she removed her gloves and cloak and handed them to Zaccaria. "I assume you are too stunned by my presence to invite me to sit?"

He acknowledged her comment with a thin-lipped smile and gestured for her to settle herself in the chair before the desk. As soon as she had comfortably arranged herself and her skirts, she rested her elbows on the bare surface of the desk and said, "Let us get to business, shall we? As you stated before, I am here. I am well. I am unencumbered by chains, and I move freely."

"As I said before, your presence here astounds me. So many had assured me you were dead."

Belladonna sat back and laced her fingers together demurely beneath her chin. "And you are sorry to see the rumors are not true?"

Contarini's smile evaporated, and his thin lips returned to their usual tense straight line.

"What do you want from me? Why have you come here? The last time you came..." His voice drifted off, and his eyes stared off beyond her. "You stated your terms for our future encounters. I have upheld them."

Belladonna rose and, perching herself on the edge of the desk, leaned over to close the gap between them. "Promoting an accusation against the people of the Ghetto of complicity in my abduction is not in the spirit of our agreement. If you promote lies that hurt me and the people I care for, why should I not do the same to you?"

Spots of red flared in her opponent's thin, pale cheeks. Barely opening his mouth, he muttered, "I sincerely hope you are not threatening me."

Belladonna pulled back, rising from the desk and standing alongside him. She placed a hand on his shoulders, causing Contarini to flinch. "The difference between you and I is that I would not lie to defame you, and I do not threaten. I have also never spoken what I had learned about the deaths of the women of the Gallery of Beauties, and I never intend to."

The shoulder beneath her hand seemed to relax, and she lifted it. She sauntered over to the chair and stood behind it, allowing her eyes to lock with the man who had been her enemy for so long. "I know you well, Niccolo, and though you are a slave to your ambition and ache to become the next Doge, your leadership will not be unjust. You have attained a great deal of power and should have no need of the Spaniards. They are corrupt and will seek to corrupt you, and they wish to bring the Inquisition into this city. This accusation against the Jews, it stinks of their practices, and you should not sully yourself or this city with a blood libel."

Contarini closed his eyes, as if he were suffering from inner pain and then opened them, blinking several times, before responding. "You should not make a habit of entering the Lion's Den and expecting a miraculous outcome. This time, however, you do have a point. You are here, alive, and not being held captive. Do I have the right to ask how your earrings came to be in a pawnshop in the Ghetto?"

Belladonna felt the knot in her stomach loosen. She had convinced him. "The usual way. I was away with a friend—never mind where—and left them behind. They were stolen by a maid, who has since been dismissed, and, I presume, is long gone. I had given up hope of ever seeing them again, but now I shall have them back?"

Contarini raised a hand. "I shall have them sent to you."

She was prepared to leave. "My cloak and gloves, and then I shall take leave of you. I am glad we have come to an understanding."

"An understanding?"

"Yes, about dismissing the charges of abduction. And releasing the chief rabbi?"

"Ah, yes, the rabbi's daughter is your…what is she to be called, your protégé? He was grinning now, confident in that he held a card against her.

"Both she and her father have great knowledge of medicines, in particular, the antidotes to poison. They have been invaluable to me and to the Council of Ten. If I recall, the man you now detain had been commissioned by the Council of Ten to concoct large quantities of a powerful antidote to poisons. Is his detention, then, some manner of repayment?"

The smile faded from Contarini's lips, and his nostrils flared. He was too much in control to let his anger get the better of him. In a cool but gracious tone, he replied, "I am not the final word on the matter of the rabbi or the Ghetto. It must be decided by a vote from the Council. I am merely an administrator and do not make unilateral decisions of justice. Good day."

Chapter Forty-Four: Belladonna

Belladonna wanted word to spread of her appearance at the home of Niccolo Contarini, and she had not been discreet in her arrival or departure. She had called first at her own palazzo to the delighted sobs of her servants and had dressed in her usual finery. The antagonism between Belladonna and Contarini would ensure her visit to him would cause many tongues to wag and dispel the last of the rumors of her abduction.

However, next on her agenda was to appear at Sir Henry's to begin her assault on Sir George Villiers, and she could not risk traveling there as openly. The Spanish will be watching Sir Henry's palazzo and would not hesitate to waylay her before she could reach safety inside.

This time her cloak covered her golden hair and gold satin dress and draped down to the bottom of her platform shoes. She had donned a white Bata mask to hide her face and had Zancani find a gondola for hire to transport her near the palazzo. She had planned to arrive on foot and approach the back entrance, expecting the Spanish to be watching only the front.

From the moment she entered the salon, the Englishman could not take his eyes off her. Belladonna posed beneath the crystal chandelier in the center of the room, which made her seem luminescent in the light of the many candles above her. The pearls in her ears were studded with diamonds, and her favorite strands once again graced her neck. Her golden honey-colored hair was piled high and glinted with gold. Artfully turning, she cocked her head to bathe the planes of her face in soft candlelight, as if she were listening to a secret being whispered in her ear.

It was a relief to come out of hiding, to dress and stand as herself and not the downtrodden widow of the Ghetto. Even though Morosini had revealed that the rabbi was not suffering in the Doge's prison, there was still the danger of a household search of the Ghetto if she did not come forward. With searches such as these, the soldiers would enjoy the destruction, and the violations against women would be rampant. No such suffering should occur on her behalf. Roderigo had been found, so she held the cards. Restored to her position as Belladonna, she had the gold and the influence, and she hoped it would be enough to prevail.

The English ambassador's party was opportune for her to reappear in Venetian society. As George Villiers' practiced eyes traveled down her figure, she felt vindicated in her decision. The fish was hooked. Their host, Sir Henry Wotton, cleared his throat loudly to reclaim Villier's attention. The Englishman reluctantly shifted his gaze to the ambassador while accepting a filigreed goblet being offered to him by a servant. After taking a deep swallow of the wine, he lifted Belladonna's hand and brushed it gallantly with his lips.

Sir Henry stood by Villiers's side, and Belladonna's smile was also for him. "I am Belladonna. I have heard you have been inquiring after me."

"Belladonna? Is it not a poisonous herb?" Villiers raised one eyebrow provocatively.

"Precisely."

Her tone was light and teasing. Villiers eyes narrowed like a cat's, assessing her, but she held their gaze. She had honed her skills with men such as him.

Sir Henry intervened. "Where have you been, Belladonna? Your disappearance has spurred all manner of rumor,"

"Rumor often serves its purpose. More flexible than truth, is it not?" She had answered Sir Henry, but kept her gaze on Villiers.

Villiers collapsed on a divan and invited her to sit beside him. After draping a hand along its back, he deposited an empty wineglass on the tray of a liveried servant. "Ahh, at last, a woman who sees the world as I do."

Belladonna circled the Englishman, tantalizing him with the swish of silk and the scent of perfume. When she had completed her circuit, she took the seat he offered.

"What brings you to Venice, sir?" she said, speaking slowly and carefully in his language.

He cocked his head sideways, peering at her, but if he had hopes of discomforting her, he would be mistaken. "You do not know?"

Sir Henry, who had taken a chair and pulled it alongside them, coughed purposely, shifting their attention to him. "I believe the lady is aware of the situation in Jamaica."

"The New World. It is where our mutual interests align. Have you been there?" She was curious of his answer.

"Not yet," Villiers smiled, flicking a tiny piece of lint from his fine black doublet. "but I intend to travel there quite soon."

"I have heard much of the Spanish exploits there, but little of the English. The last visitor from England came to our city to commission new ships. Are those ships now to be used for travel to the New World?"

He paused, perhaps a natural inclination to be wary when asked a question.

"My mission in Venice is to meet a gentleman recently arrived from the New World. Sir Henry is to help me find him," he paused and raised his eyebrows as he continued, "unless, of course, you may be of service?"

Belladonna's laugh tinkled like music; it had taken a great deal of practice to make it so. Instead of responding, she carefully smoothed the folds of her luscious silken dress to build his eagerness for her answer. "I will not deny I know of the man you seek. However, I would like to know why it is to my benefit to help you find him."

For a man like Villiers, what was too easy to obtain was not worthwhile. She would have to entice and beguile him, and sparring with him was part of the game. First, he must believe she had something to gain from their collaboration; altruism was for fools. Second, he must never know how desperate she was and the danger she faced. Greed overcomes cowardice, but not when survival is at stake. She had to keep his interest until Roderigo was recovered enough to meet the Englishman or send him on his way with the map and the urgency to intervene in Jamaica.

Villiers cocked his head at her and grinned. "Treasure, of course. Hard-won, which I wager you would appreciate more because it means outwitting the Spanish to find it. So, are you game?"

The conversation with the Englishman felt like she was stretching her legs after being restricted to being seated in a small space. After so much time in the Ghetto, the banter of civilized conversation no longer bored her—on the contrary, it was refreshing. Among the Jews, she had no opportunity for such talk.

Her mind was wandering, and she must stay focused. Villiers was a shrewd man, and he must not doubt her control of the situation. She could anticipate his next question, and she needed to be prepared to explain her disappearance and where she had been. A joke? Hiding from a lover, she wished to discard? No, none of those would convince him.

With half an ear, she had been listening to Villiers talk about the English ships bound for Jamaica. She was prepared when he asked the question she had been anticipating.

"Before falling victim to the Spanish determination to find the envoy and the gold, I took the precaution of removing myself from the field of play. The Ghetto presented the perfect place for me to hide in plain sight."

"Clever. I suppose you were privy to the deception, Sir Henry?"

The English ambassador's eyes shifted away from Villiers and sought reassurance from Belladonna. "Er, yes. However, at the time the lady vanished, I did not know where she had gone. I learned of her whereabouts only a short time ago."

Belladonna turned her head ever so slightly to catch the gleam of candlelight so it would highlight the perfect lines of her profile. Out of the corner of her eye, she caught Villiers's appreciative assessment. "I have friends in the Ghetto who can be counted on to help us find the map and the man who carries it. Their people will be your allies when you surround Jamaica with your ships, and with their help, you can be assured that the island will fall to the English—along with its treasure."

"You have planned this most carefully, I see. Well, that is gratifying. It is not every day one is gutted by an assassin, mended by a beautiful Jewess, and then asked to place one's entire trust into the plotsof a notorious courtesan." He shook his head, clicking his tongue as if he were admonishing her. "Well, dear lady, I place myself, metaphorically for now, in your hands. Lead on, and I shall follow wherever you take me. Have you any clues to lead us to this fellow with the map?"

He asked the last question so casually, and she answered him just as breezily and indirectly. "I hope you have regained your strength sufficiently to accompany us."

Villiers widened his eyes and wiggled his brows comically. "Have no fear, I am a soldier first, and the wound will not compromise my instincts for action."

Belladonna wanted to laugh; playing with the Englishman was becoming very amusing. "Very well. I will send word to you tomorrow of where and when we are to meet."

Chapter Forty-Five: Antonio

Antonio had kept continued surveillance of the Ghetto, studying those who came and went through the gates every day. At least he was free at night, once the gates were closed, since only Christians or Moors were permitted in and out. There was a lively tavern along the Fondamenta Misericordia lit up by fiery torches. The quiet night was disturbed by the laughter and boisterous shouts which came from it. Antonio liked it there; he could drink and eat in peace while all attention was focused on the rowdy bar maids and their crude patrons.

Belladonna. He liked the name, another term for deadly nightshade. A woman who called herself after a poison would captivate his interest. He had not much use for women, but indulged with them when he felt desire, which was not often. However, a woman who tantalized and tortured that pompous bureaucrat, Di Ribera, must be clever and manipulative—two characteristics he admired and rarely found in a woman.

Her jewels. He had done some prodding of his informants, eager to assuage his anger for their failure to do their job, who told many stories about the courtesan and her collection of large gemstones. Antonio hoped to entertain this woman and convince her to part with some of her gems. He looked forward to such an encounter. Now, all he must do is locate her.

He finished his meal amid the raucous company, which had become tedious, and decided to go back to his rooms earlier than usual. It was such good luck he had done so, because he had noticed a cloaked figure of a woman slipping out of the Ghetto gates. She must have bribed the gatemen. She moved with grace and the studied gait befitting a courtesan.

He wiped his mouth with his sleeve; he had literally been drooling over the woman. Shaking awake a gondolier who had been leaning idly by the canal, he pointed out the woman stepping into a gondola and gave instructions to follow them.

Seated comfortably in the boat, he pulled his dagger from its shaft and turning it from side to side, admired its blade. He would not be using it on the courtesan, but was satisfied it would be effective for threatening her. He needed her alive and cooperative and had other items to make it easier to bring her along—a black sack-like hood, a length of strong hemp rope, and a woolen scarf that could be doubled into becoming an effective gag. The gondola they were following turned into a small canal, where many boats were pulling alongside a landing pier. That was good. He instructed the gondolier to pull in so they could wait. The gondolier was warning him that waiting would cost more, but when Antonio handed the man one gold coin, he was quieted.

He watched the gondola pull inside the water gates and then exit shortly after, empty of its passenger. He tracked the empty gondola until it found its place among the other boats, to wait for their fare's departure.

Antonio was a patient man. He could wait. He was in the right place; it was just a matter of time before the woman would fall into his hands.

Chapter Forty-Six: Belladonna

Belladonna did not want to stay too long at Sir Henry's. She had spent enough time with Villiers and was aching to return to her palazzo, to sleep in her own bed for the night. Her hands wandered to the soothing roundness of her pearls and their calming effect. She judged it a good time to make her departure, as Sir Henry's entertainment, a performance by the two talented sisters, Gaspara and Cassandra, was about to begin. Cassandra gave her a shy smile as Belladonna passed. The two had made their debut at her palazzo last spring, and since then, were in constant demand for performances.

The palazzo was well-lit with torches, and the gondoliers, including the one who had brought her, were clustered by its dock, waiting for Sir Henry's guests to depart. She was so deep in thought as she exited through the palazzo's gate, she did not notice the sound of footsteps on the flagstones, or sense someone close behind her. Suddenly, there was hot breath on her neck and the smell of mustiness as black cloth covered her eyes, nose, and mouth.

Cursing her own cockiness and her failure to remain alert, she reached for her dagger in the pocket of her skirts. As soon as she had it in her hands, she pressed the special lever so that the point was now amply coated with poison, and slashed out in every direction. The hood had blotted out all light and was wrapped tight against her throat, making it difficult to breathe.

A hand was creeping around her waist, and she slashed at it, but the dagger was forcefully knocked from her grasp. She heard it clatter to the ground. Why did no one come to her aid? Growing more and more lightheaded, she sucked desperately at the wool of the hood to glean more air. Writhing and fighting, until her cloak was wrapped tightly about her, restricting her movements. Unable to move or shout, strong arms lifted her, and her feet left the ground. With the lack of air, consciousness was ebbing. She stopped resisting, resigned to waiting to see where she was being taken and to save her strength for the next scenario. No one had ever gotten the better of her before, and she vowed now would not be any different.

* * *

"Belladonna!" a deep voice jarred her awake as it called her name.

She could breathe freely again, and when she opened her eyes, she could see—the hood had been removed. She glanced quickly around. She was in a dark paneled room that seemed to sway. A boat? Her heart pounded, and she bit her lip to keep herself from crying out.

"Belladonna," the voice said again, softer. Her head was lifted, and a cup tilted to her lips. She attempted to take hold of it with her hands, but to her dismay, she could not. They were bound before her. She had hoped her abduction had been a dream, but unfortunately, it was reality.

The man giving her water had uttered only her name. It had been a highly skilled abduction; he had come upon her quickly and must have pulled her out of sight of the gondoliers, where he wrapped her up for easy transport. This kind of efficiency pointed to an assassin, most likely the same one who had been after Roderigo and was working for Spain.

From the light streaming in through the window, she assumed it was now morning. Belladonna tried to sit up straight, and the man helped her. His arms were well-muscled, and he did not smell unclean. He was also too well-dressed to be a soldier. He wore a cap pulled low over his forehead, which was successful in shadowing his eyes. Still, he had the look of a Spaniard.

She held out her bound hands. "You work for Diego di Ribera? I should have expected better treatment from a man who has been a frequent guest at my palazzo."

Her captor did not respond, and when he did not make any move to free her hands, she dropped them down into her lap.

"I am not controlled by Diego di Ribera." The man raised his chin higher. "I am Antonio."

"You are Spanish?" Belladonna asked, as her forehead creased into a frown.

He did not answer and offered her the cup. "More water? Or wine?"

She did want to keep him talking. "You are kind. Perhaps some more water."

He paused at her first phrase, as if he had never heard it before. As he tilted the cup to her lips once more, she studied her captor's face. Pockmarks. Heavy-lidded eyes underscored by half-moon bags. Sharp angular cheeks and nose. A hard-set mouth framed by a pointed mustache and goatee, a mouth not accustomed to smiling. This was a man who had not known mercy. Or would show it.

"Why am I here?" she asked.

He stood a distance away from her. In response to her question, he picked up one of the pearl earrings she had been wearing and held it up to the torchlight. She bit her lip.

"You seem a clever woman and keen on survival. Perhaps it is best to tell me now where to find the envoy and spare yourself a great deal of trouble. And pain."

He pulled her pearls out of his tunic, and she winced as he pulled at the long strands. It would pain her too much to give up those pearls.

He examined the pearls carefully, assessing their value. Each pearl was perfect in shape and uniform in size and color with the others. It was long enough to loop more than once around her neck and cascade down to her waist. They would fetch an enormous price, and this man knew it.

"I suppose the Spanish pay well?"

Shrewd eyes flicked to hers. "Why do you say that?"

She gestured towards him with her chin. "Your tunic is of thick, tooled leather, not easily found. You appreciate fine jewels. You must demand a high price for your services." She gave a dramatic sigh, "How Di Ribera must gnash his teeth every time he must pay you."

He put down the pearls and pulled out his knife. He came closer and placed the finely honed blade against her throat. She did not flinch nor swallow. He ran the blade alongside her cheek, so she could feel its sharpness. She kept her eyes steady and did not allow herself to imagine how such a knife could scar her face. She swallowed and said, "Perhaps your services are worth more than he can afford."

The blade was lowered. She dared not even exhale to give him any sign of how afraid she was.

His eyes seemed to ignite with new interest. "I am open to counter offers."

Her adversary leaned back expectantly, replacing the dagger into the sheath hanging from this belt, but keeping his hand close to it.

Belladonna continued, using their mutual foe as a means to build an alliance. "To know Diego Di Ribera is to despise him. You seem to be a sensible man, so I would expect you to chafe under his administration and desire your independence. You will need enough gold to acquire the freedom from his demands."

Antonio's fingers wandered away from his knife to massage his chin. "More than enough. I desire to retire in comfort."

"Of course. Understand that I have the means to provide you with a more comfortable freedom. If you join with me, you will be able to act on your better instincts sooner than you think."

"Jewels?"

This Antonio was a man of few words, but he did get his point across. He had still not untied her and needed more of an incentive. "That thieving maid took my most precious earrings but not the brooch, the necklace, and the hair combs. Donated to me by a most gracious friend, they are worth a fortune."

The Spaniard was frowning; perhaps he did not believe her. She added, "They are in a leather sack, well hidden."

Belladonna offered up her bound hands with an expectant look. Antonio unsheathed his dagger, but could not resist flashing it once more before her face. She did not flinch, and keeping her eyes on his, she held her bound hands higher, towards the blade. In one quick swoop, he cut through the thick ropes.

Hands now free, she rubbed her wrists, hoping to alleviate their soreness, while keeping her eyes steady on Antonio's face. There was no telling how quickly he might shift, and his dagger was still within reach.

Though she had a feeling the Spaniard would not be charmed, she treated him to one of her most winning smiles. He gave her a wolfish smile, as he pointed to her earrings and pearls. "You already have the means to provide first payment. Now, about the balance."

The floor groaned and shifted beneath them. The ship was moving.

She looked towards the windowed side. "Perhaps now that we have come to an understanding, you can tell me where we are. And where we are bound."

The smile Antonio gave her was cold enough to make her shiver. "We are on a Spanish vessel, still in the lagoon. Do not worry, they are not setting sail for Spain. Yet."

He seemed full of good humor, but he was prodding her, watching her reaction for signs of desperation.

"The crew leaves you in peace, so I assume I am not the first captive you have brought here."

He ignored her comment. "It is better to set anchor in the lagoon instead of the docks. It makes for an easier departure, especially when there are guests aboard."

He lifted her pearls high in one gloved hand, then let them dribble into his other. "This cabin used to be the first mate's, but I have claimed it for my use. We shall not be disturbed."

Belladonna recognized his methods, designed to unnerve her. Dangling the possibility of freedom and hinting at an openness to bribes. An ideal way of eliciting more offers from his captive.

She wondered if they were close enough to swim to shore. Having spent her early years in Jamaica, swimming was as natural to her as walking. It could be an option, if she had the opportunity to get on deck. Antonio had made no promises and given no signs he would release her.

"Do you always negotiate with your 'guests' before turning them over to the Inquisition?" Belladonna asked.

'Depends on what they offer." He had his knife out again, turning the blade to reflect patterns of light. What had happened to hers? She valued that blade almost as much as her pearls and had equal hopes of retrieving them both.

Step by step, she would work on this man, as if they were dancing, instead of sparring.

Chapter Forty-Seven: Belladonna

A man of few words, but she had been able to pry something of his plans out of him. Antonio admitted he had been instructed not to kill her, which left him room to negotiate. He could protect her from Di Ribera's men, so she could return to her palazzo, where he expected her to gather more of her jewels for him. Antonio did not hesitate to remind her that if she reneged on her promises to him, he could disfigure her before he delivered her to Spain.

Belladonna stood, arching her back and flexing. Antonio's eyes never left her, and she was conscious of them as she sauntered over to the bunk slotted into the wooden cupboards surrounding it. She ran her hand along its velvet cover, assessing it, before reclining on it, tucking the ends of her gown beneath her.

"Well, what is our next step?"

A knock at the door preempted Antonio's response. He called out, "What is it?"

"Setting sail in an hour."

"All good."

If she were to make a move to escape, it would have to be within the hour. Belladonna estimated her chances of breaking away successfully and without injury were slim. The best she could do was keep to the promise of more treasure awaiting at her palazzo to incentivize an immediate departure from the ship.

"Besides my jewels, I have a cache of gold which is reserved for dire occasions. This qualifies, does it not? There should be enough for you to keep di Ribera's men busy in another direction?"

Antonio's smile widened. "Now I think we can come to an understanding. Where is the gold?"

"Hidden. In a safe place in my palazzo." Belladonna stood.

A knock once more. Antonio called out, "What is it now?"

There was a mumbled reply, and leaving his dagger on the table, Antonio strode to the door and flung it open.

A boot kicked out, and Antonio was propelled backwards. A tall soldier landed on top of Antonio, straddling her kidnapper after flinging the door shut behind him. He held a blade to Antonio's throat and warned, "Utter one syllable, and it will be your last."

Despite the leather doublet and helmet of a Spaniard, Belladonna recognized the voice and the face. "Isaak."

"Take off his belt and bind his hands," Isaak ordered. "Then take off your skirts."

Belladonna gave him a puzzled look, but did as he asked. First, she bound Antonio's hands. He did not resist as his eyes shifted from Isaak to her. "A pity. Just as I thought we were seeing eye to eye."

"This will not change the business arranged between us, Antonio," Belladonna said as she reached into his doublet and retrieved her pearls, "just the terms. You will be more than amply rewarded, and we will both get our revenge on di Ribera."

Isaak pulled a rag from his worn leather doublet and shoved it into Antonio's mouth. He pointed to a bundle he had dropped at the entry. "Clothes for you in there. Put them on. Then remove your skirts and help me get them around this fellow."

"We do not have much time," she said as she removed her skirts, "They are readying to set sail."

Isaak's white teeth flashed. "Not really, most of the men are ashore, and those left aboard are still half asleep. It was I who made the announcement of sailing, so he would open the door a second time without hesitation."

Belladonna moved quickly, shedding her own garments and changing into the rough and ragged breeches and shirt. A length of rope left from her bonds was long enough to cinch the breeches at her waist. The sleeves of the shirt were overlong, but she rolled them up.

Antonio was slender and not very tall for a man, but the skirts still would not close around him. Tearing the waist of the underskirt and folding it over, Belladonna used it to bind the overskirt far enough below his hips to cover his boots. Isaak pulled the cover from the bed and wrapped it around Antonio's upper half as Belladonna placed the black hood over her former captor's head.

Isaak stepped back to survey their bound and wrapped captive. "That should do. My man and a boat are waiting."

Belladonna tucked her hair into the cap. She was glad to see Antonio did not struggle with his wrappings or when Isaak picked him up and laid him across his shoulder. Staggering under the man's weight, Isaak mounted the stairs to the main deck with Belladonna following him, now dressed like a man in breeches and tunic.

As Isaak predicted, no one paid any attention to the soldier and his companion as they lowered themselves and their captive over the side into the waiting skiff.

Chapter Forty-Eight: Belladonna

Instead of heading towards the far end of Giudecca, where Isaak's ship lay, Belladonna realized their skiff was headed into the Grand Canal. In a bundle of wraps and skirts lay Antonio in the space between their seats, and he did not move. Antonio was clever enough to realize it would do no good to struggle and was probably conserving his strength for when he would be freed.

Though wrapped in a warm cloak, Belladonna shivered. She had faced powerful enemies without trepidation, but Antonio's calculated ruthlessness was unnerving. Could they persuade the Spaniard to truly switch his allegiance to their side? Though he professed he could be motivated by the right price, trusting in Antonio to help them seemed like trusting a viper not to bite at a bare ankle.

Isaak, facing her, must have noticed her shiver, for he took off his own cloak and draped it across her. She handed it back to him, asking, "Where are we headed?"

Isaak hesitated before accepting the return of the cloak and put it back on. He looked away from her, the sharp angles of his nose, cheekbones, and chin silhouetted against the bright sunlight. Luckily, the wind had died down, or the two of them would be struggling to keep hold of their caps. The air was cold enough to see faint white clouds when they spoke.

"Morosoni." The one word came out in a cloud worthy of a dragon.

Aha. Once again, Belladonna admired Isaak's quick thinking. The nobleman's power and riches should engender better cooperation from their captive. Then they both kept silent, following the rhythmic swoosh of the boatman's pulls at the oars.

Their path became more difficult as more gondolas, adorned with the colors of their owners, cut across their path, eliciting a curse from their oarsman.

Belladonna recognized the distinctive facade and the color of the Morosini gondolas, even before the oarsman called out, "Up ahead, sir." Her fingers played with the pearls in the leather pouch tied onto her rope belt.

She tried to imagine Antonio's reaction to Morosini. The Spaniard was not like the pitiful physician, Fornari, who had been tricked into becoming their enemy, and who was willing to do whatever they wanted to make amends. Antonio must be persuaded, and Morosini would know the best lever to push to ensure his cooperation.

"Get back to the ship, and wait. I will send word of our next course," Isaak directed the oarsman, who saluted after helping Isaak heft their bundled captive onto the dock. Servants arrived immediately to help them, ushering them up the servants' staircase to their master.

A melody being played on the pianoforte drifted across the well-appointed entry hall, but the thuds of their boots on the marble floor caused it to stop. The servants deposited them and their bundle into the leather-paneled office perfect for their purpose, since its austere opulence could be intimidating.

After the skirts and wraps and the rag in his mouth were removed, Antonio surprised her with his silence. No threats, no protests, no demands. Just the cold stare, unblinking, like a reptile, on his face.

Morosini flipped off Belladonna's cap, and her honey-colored hair came tumbling out over her shoulders. "You still look quite fetching, my dear, even in those rags." The nobleman glanced over his shoulder at the prisoner. "Ahh, Isaak, forthright at last, without the flowing draperies of the Moors. And who have you brought?"

"Antonio." The man growled out his name.

"Just Antonio?" Morosini had gone to the sideboard and poured a generous amount from the decanter into three filigreed green and gold glasses. He handed one to Antonio, who held up his bound hands. "I suppose from your coloring and the style of your doublet you are Spanish.

My guess is that you are the man sent in pursuit of the lovely Belladonna, who somehow has turned the tables on you, hmm?"

With bound hands, Antonio still succeeded in tossing down his drink, then holding out the empty glass for more. Morosini took his glass but did not refill it. Belladonna perched on the edge of the desk while Isaak kept his back to the wall and his eyes on the exits, as if scoping out every possible means of escape.

Belladonna was not surprised by Isaak's silence. He was clever enough to reveal as little as possible of himself to anyone but his most trusted friends. Morosini did not qualify as one. She took the lead in informing the nobleman of their agenda, "Antonio had been treating me to the hospitality of a Spanish ship while we negotiated a possible collaboration. Then Isaak arrived and thought it best we continue the discussion under your guidance."

Morosini took his half-filled glass and his seat behind his large desk, facing them. He stretched out his long legs and cocked his head at Antonio. "A collaboration with someone such as yourself could present advantages to all of us."

"Such as?" The Spaniard met Morosini's eyes, and his bound hands were relaxed and unclenched, a good sign. Isaak took out a knife and cut his hands free.

Antonio rubbed his wrists while Morosini poured him another drink. Morosini kept one eye on Antonio, and as he sipped, a smile on his lips. "Gold. A stake in an upcoming shipment from the Dutch East India company."

Antonio said, "As I informed the lady, I have a great wish to retire here in this lovely city and not to return to Spain. I am looking forward to a comfortable retirement."

Belladonna moved away from the Spaniard and was gratified when Morosini took the lead in the discussion. "There will be a nice pile of gold for you to start, and since I suspect you are a talented fellow and could be of great use to me, a generous retainer will be paid to you every month you are in my service."

"I am currently under retainer from Spain. So, what have I to gain?"

Morosini snorted. "The paymaster in Venice pockets half of what is supposed to be distributed to men like yourself. I know, because he is in my employ and must give me a percentage of it. In essence, you are being paid the full amount of your contract instead of less than half."

Morosini smirked as Antonio sat up straighter and his lips curled into a snarl. Isaak folded his arms across his chest, but he did not lean back and did not seem to have relaxed his guard. *Isaak did not trust the Spaniard.* Neither did she, but Belladonna pushed her visceral loathing of the man aside. They needed him on their side if they were to succeed in thwarting the Spanish.

Morosini leaned forward towards Antonio. "You see, there is little that goes on in this city that I do not have some hand in. Your vineyard in the mainland will be under my protection and out of Di Ribera's reach if you are in my employ."

Antonio tipped an imaginary hat in her direction as he answered Morosini. "I see it is in my best interest to accept your offer."

Isaak moved to stand before the assassin. "What does di Ribera know of the envoy?"

The assassin grinned. "He knows nothing of the envoy and is more focused on finding her." He gestured towards Belladonna. "Once he learned she had surfaced, he could not contain his excitement and sent out every man, including me, to find her. I was the only one who did, of course."

"Does di Ribera know you have her?"

"Undoubtedly. News travels fast, and the men on the ship will talk. Di Ribera might keep his hounds at bay if he thinks she is still in my hands."

"Why?"

"Because he knows as long as I am missing, the Jews of Venice will be held accountable," Belladonna added. "Di Ribera considers himself a holy warrior against the evils of courtesans and Jews."

Isaak unwrapped his arms, and his fists were clenched. The assassin stiffened and seemed poised to strike. Then tension in the room was alleviated by Morosini, who said, "Di Ribera was always a fool and will continue to be one. Venice is not Spain; we will not allow the Pope's

Inquisition to impose its medieval rules and prejudices upon our city."

He pointed a ringed finger at Isaak as if to halt him. "Your father was released under the request of the Patriarch of Venice, who has further detained him only to share his latest rare book acquisition."

Belladonna slid off her perch at his desk and scratched at the itchy breeches gathered under the rope belt, which captured Morosini's attention. "Apologies, my dear. You must long for a bath and a change of clothes. My servant will take you to Theresa's rooms, which should have everything you need." He wiped at his brow, "I have not been able to have her things removed as of yet."

Isaak, without saying a word, had moved towards the door. Belladonna called to him and then to Morosini, "We are in need of a plan, and each of us can contribute to it, but only with a clear head and a sharp mind. I assume without Antonio at my heels, I will be safe, for now?"

"Di Ribera's men believe you are with me on the ship," Antonio confirmed.

"Then I will see you all later," she said as she left them.

Chapter Forty-Nine: Diana

The night seemed overly long to Diana, who had slept fitfully, imagining scenarios of her father's detention. She worried, too, over Roderigo's condition, which she feared may have worsened. What if Roderigo died? It would likely increase the danger to Belladonna as the only remaining connection to the treasure of Jamaica. Each time she drifted off to sleep, she would awake suddenly, a sense of foreboding about Roderigo so strong, she wanted to jump out of bed and head to Giudecca immediately to check on him.

Finally flinging off the covers, Diana shivered as she rose quickly to wash and dress, just as the beadle began rapping on the shutters, calling out the time for early morning prayers.

The lagoon bobbed with transport to and from Giudecca, so it was not difficult to find a boat to take her. The wind blew fiercely, and she pulled her cloak more tightly around her. She did not want it blown open, revealing the yellow badge sewn onto her bodice. Despite the wind, the boatman plowed forward across the canal at a brisk pace, arriving at Giudecca within a short time. Diana kept her hood up and her cloak closed as she hurried through the passageways to the covered doorway of the convent hospital.

The pleasant Sister Maria was not the one to greet her but a thin nun who needed considerable persuasion to allow Diana in. Diana feared the nun's displeasure with her visit would only worsen if she were to see the tell-tale yellow badge upon her chest, so she kept her cloak closed tight. She asked about any changes in the patient from the New World, claiming she had new intelligence about his family in Venice. After a short consult with her superior, the thin nun motioned Diana to follow her to Roderigo's room.

Roderigo's room was much warmer than the rest of the convent, and a cloudy steaminess, attributed to a large porcelain heater in the corner, hovered over Roderigo. A splashing of water. Soft footsteps and a hand touched her shoulder. Diana turned, and a long-nosed plague mask was thrust at her.

A muffled voice, which she recognized as Sister Maria, was saying, "Please, put it on. He is at his most contagious when the fever burns."

"He has worsened?" she asked through the mask, the last syllable spoken high and soft, dissipating like smoke.

"He rallied somewhat and was able to sit up and eat. However, the fever is rising, and his breathing grows worse."

Diana took a few steps closer to the figure on the bed. Roderigo's mouth hung open, emitting wheezing noises. He was plied with coverlets up to the neck. Sister Maria placed a cool cloth on his sweaty forehead.

"How long does he have?"

"I do not know. Sometimes, the fever breaks, and he may recover." Sister Maria removed her mask and wiped her forehead. Grey, damp hair straggled out of her wimple. "It happened to me. Near death's door, I was, but then, here I am."

Diana appreciated the kind words, but based on her own assessment, she doubted Roderigo would improve very much. If he died, those who were after his secret would focus their attention on Belladonna.

"I will advise the family."

Diana was about to make her departure, when, taking one last look at Roderigo, his eyes opened wider, and he stared at her. His lips were moving as he tried to communicate, though his words were so soft she could not hear him.

Immediately, Sister Maria was at his side, holding his head as she lifted a glass of water to his lips. After he had drank, his eyes seemed to focus, and when he spoke, his voice was stronger.

"Raquel?" He licked dry lips.

Diana lifted the mask so he could see her face.

"You are Isaak's sister. Why are you here? What has happened?"

"There is nothing to concern yourself. I came to purchase more herbs and to see how you fare. You must rest, I shall bring Raquel." Diana took heart that despite the fever, Roderigo was able to recognize her.

"There is not much time," Roderigo pushed his covers down and struggled to sit up. Sister Maria was quickly at his side, helping him and tucking the bedclothes around him to keep him from getting chilled. "The English ambassador. He must know of..."

He fell back with a heavy sigh, wheezing. He swiped a shaking hand across his mouth as if to stifle it. "Raquel must go to him—if I cannot."

Diana did not want to agitate him anymore. "Raquel has already met with the Englishman and will come here soon. Rest. I will bring her, I promise."

She backed away and removed the plague mask, handing it to Sister Maria.

She moved as quickly as possible through the halls of the convent towards the quay, although she felt like running. Time was running out for Roderigo and perhaps for her father.

Diana entered the gates of the Ghetto breathless, having run from the moment she had disembarked from the boat from Giudecca. It was still early in the day, but the fishermen had sold all their fish and were sluicing off the muck right beside the Ghetto gates as they packed up their gear to depart.

She leaned against the Ghetto wall, stopping to catch her breath, inhaling the strong smell of fish, but catching the worried stares of women who passed her by. Diana straightened her skirts and smoothed her hair, which had come loose from their braids, and composed herself. Though time was running out for Roderigo, it would cause alarm in the community if the rabbi's daughter appeared to be panicked. They had much to worry about; their rabbi was taken by the Men in Dark Cloaks, and there had been an accusation of heresy against Sarra Coppio Sullam.

The Sullam mansion was her destination, hoping Belladonna had returned there. Her hope dimmed when she had to bang on the door repeatedly until an annoyed manservant appeared and informed her that 'the Cousin' was not in residence.

What now? Would Belladonna be in the Moorish quarter, with Isaak at the home of the Turk? Or, despite the danger, had she returned to her own palazzo? Her feet were like the arms of the compass, turning first towards Campo di Mori and then shifting towards the Grand Canal. Diana preferred to take the chance on the Turk. The gates toward the Moorish quarter lay across the campo of the Ghetto Nuovo, and her guilt forced her to stop at home to see her mother. This time, her mother had reason to demand her daughter stay by her side, but years of complaining had dulled her to her mother's complaints. Diana imagined how her mother's lips would tremble when she made it clear she would have to go out again.

Pressing onward, she moved quickly across the *campo* towards her home, ignoring the greetings from acquaintances gathered by the well. Tapping the *mezuzah* and bringing her fingers to her lips as she entered, she was stunned by the sight of her father seated at the table, with her mother beside him.

"Sit down, Diana." His brows were lowered, and there were deep shadows beneath his eyes, but otherwise, he did not seem to have suffered from his detention. In contrast, her mother looked wan and ill; her eyes red and puffy, her cheeks sunken and pallid, causing Diana regret for not remaining at her side. Obeying her father, she took a stool and sat beside him.

"I know the toll my absence has taken on you all," the rabbi said, looking at his wife, who sniffed in confirmation, "although rest assured, I was treated with respect by the Council of Ten, and was in the good hands of the Patriarch of Venice."

"What do they want of you? Is it that infernal book of poisons you possess, which I begged you to get rid of?" his wife clasped her hands tightly before her.

"They wanted the courtesan Belladonna," he was speaking to Diana, ignoring his wife's frown, "and they released me when your friend Morosini testified that she is now his guest and can be found in his palazzo."

Diana jumped up from her chair. "She is with Morosini? I must go to her. We have little time."

"What has happened?"

223

"Roderigo is failing, and he wants to see his sister before..." she coughed to hide her emotion and headed towards the door.

The rabbi closed his eyes and nodded. "I had expected this. There is not much I can do, so I will stay here with your mother." In an unusual gesture, he took both his hands and clasped them around his wife's. "Now, go. The danger to the Ghetto will be averted if Belladonna stays away from us and remains alive."

Chapter Fifty: Diana

The long, eventful day was coming to a close, and the shadows cast from the Morosini palazzo reached across the dock to chill her. It felt like an omen. She had not wanted to come here, but after not finding Belladonna anywhere else, it was worth consulting with the nobleman to find her. Formidable as a fortress, Diana boldly marched past the servants towards the *piano nobile,* where she hoped to find Belladonna. She was not disappointed.

The aroma of strong coffee filled the room, along with the clink of glasses placed on trays and the swoosh of expensive fabrics. Servants in green and gold flashed in and out, placing and removing trays before the four people who sat on furniture arranged, horseshoe-like, under a large chandelier that glittered in the fading afternoon light.

Had they just awakened? Belladonna, dressed in pale green silk, toying with the pearls around her neck, had deep shadows beneath her eyes and seemed wilted and less than alert. Diana had not expected to see Isaak only in a white linen shirt and rugged-looking breeches, as if he had been summoned in the midst of his slumbers. A sharp-faced man with a pointed beard dressed all in black, appeared as relaxed as Morosini, who also seemed too tired to move any muscle but his eyebrows at her entrance. Had they all stayed with Morosini overnight? She suspected they had.

Diana stood before her friend and tried to relay her news in as gentle a way as possible. "You must come. To Giudecca."

Belladonna shook off her lethargy like a cloak and was instantly standing and clutched Diana's wrist tightly. "What has happened?"

Diana looked into Belladonna's eyes. "He wishes to see you. Time is our enemy."

"Then let us go."

Morosini snapped an order to his servants, and cloaks were brought. Diana was grateful when Isaak's footsteps followed theirs, for as the day turned to night, she did not like to travel to Giudecca alone.

Morosini's gondola awaited them at the ground floor's private dock, and Belladonna, Diana, and Isaak took their seats inside the covered cabin. The gondolier raised his oar and navigated the boat into the Grand Canal towards their destination.

"Morosini claimed our father has been released." Isaak directed his comment to Diana.

Diana nodded. "He arrived home having come to no harm. He is with our mother now."

Isaak shifted his attention to Belladonna. "You must be prepared for some difficult decisions."

Belladonna did not respond. She kept her eyes ahead, watching the rhythmic rise and descent of the oar.

"There must be something we can find to heal him," Diana said softly, reaching out to take her friend's hand. "Sister Maria knows much of this disease, and under her care, he may rally."

The boat bumped against the dock. Isaak helped her and Belladonna out while instructing Morosini's man to wait there for their return.

Sister Maria handed each of them a plague mask, which Belladonna tied on and quickly advanced to Roderigo's bed. He lay quiet, his sunken eyes closed, his mouth open, lips parted to emit a raspy breath. One thin hand lay across his chest, which rose and fell in a normal rhythm.

As Belladonna leaned over him, her shadow fell across his face, and his eyes fluttered and opened. They widened at the sight of the long nose and grimace of the plague mask. She worried when Roderigo's breath came faster, and she gestured for Belladonna to raise the mask so he could see her face.

The brows descended, and then he recognized her. "Raquel? Yes, Raquel, thank God, you have come."

"I advise you to put back on the mask when you come so close," called Sister Maria, "and do not touch him, or allow him to touch you."

Belladonna's fingers played with the ribbons and seemed as if she would toss the mask away, but Roderigo nodded. "It is for the best, Raquel. I do not want the sickness to spread to you. Or any of our friends. For the Spanish, however, I would not mind."

Roderigo's pale lips tried to stretch into a smile, but did not succeed. Then his eyes widened as if something had just come to mind. He lifted his head, his neck muscles straining, and looked beyond Belladonna. At Isaak. He clenched his hand into a fist and banged it, though weakly, against the bed. "The solution to our problem, and it is so simple."

"Is he feverish?" asked Diana of the nun.

"His fever has diminished but his forehead still burns somewhat hotter than it should. I have given him a drink made with willow bark shortly before you arrived. It may be having an effect, as he seems better."

Roderigo kept his head raised and his eyes on Isaak. "Isaak, you must listen to me. It is the way out of this, the way to save Raquel from them. Have you made contact with the Englishman?"

Isaak glanced at Belladonna. "We have."

"He is going to help us?"

"He wants the map," Belladonna interjected. "He salivates for the gold. He will return to England once he has it and will then set sail, with the blessings of his King, to retrieve it."

Roderigo barked out a laugh that evolved into a cough. Hand at his throat he tried to catch his breath and muttered, "The map is but a pretense designed to heighten his desire for Jamaica."

"The treasure…it does exist?" Belladonna's words were slightly muffled by the mask.

Her brother asked her to repeat it before answering, "Perhaps it does. No one knows. The map exists, and the cave is real. But many have followed the map, entered the cave, and found nothing. Nothing at all. The map has accomplished its purpose, and my mission has been successful if what you say is true. You know this from the Englishman?"

Belladonna nodded. Roderigo looked for further confirmation from Isaak, who also nodded. He exhaled deeply and closed his eyes for a moment. When he blinked them open, they seemed to burn. "Then give him the map. It is with my belongings. Then, we will end this matter with the Spanish. You must take me to them."

Belladonna stiffened. "Do you realize what you are saying? What would happen to you? They will try to extract all they can from you, and then they will kill you."

Roderigo pursed his lips. "I am already dead, and once I am aboard their ship, they will all be dead as well."

"No!" Belladonna shouted, "not again! You will not offer yourself to save me." She threw up her hands. The muscles of her neck strained as she stretched her head forward.

Diana took the courtesan's hands in her own and lowered them. "Let us take a moment to compose ourselves and think. There is much to be discussed and understood before we take the next step."

"Raquel, allow me to have my revenge. I will sing a lullaby of treasure to fill their Spanish dreams. In a short time, I will die, and they will have the plague, so they, too, will die. Is that not so, Sister?"

Sister Maria did not respond.

He directed his gaze towards Diana, "Do I look like I suffer from the plague? Could they be fooled into thinking I am failing because of my wound?"

Diana had lowered the plague mask and flicked a gaze to the courtesan and then to Isaak.

"You look feverish from an illness. You have been wounded, and your appearance is consistent with infection from a wound." Diana was growing more confident in Roderigo and his plan.

"Once they have me, they will no longer need you."

To Diana's surprise, Belladonna squeezed her hand, and when she replied, her voice was shaky with emotion, "You cannot do this, Roderigo. There must be another way."

Roderigo turned his face towards Isaak, who hovered behind his sister. "Tell her, Isaak. It must be this way. Can you help me?"

Isaak shifted from one foot to another, and he spoke softly as if he were afraid to voice the opinion Belladonna would not want to hear. "You must show yourself, to stop the ugly rumors of your disappearance, but you know you cannot remain with Morosini. You can leave Venice—"

Roderigo's eyes were brimming with tears as he interrupted Isaak. "Please, it is my dying wish. You must."

The courtesan let go of Diana's hand, turning away. Isaak took a step towards Belladonna, but when his sister raised her hand before him, he stopped, mid-step. They both jumped when Belladonna's mask clattered to the floor as the courtesan bowed over, covering her face with her hands. No sobs or wails, but a deep shudder overtook the courtesan. The tremor passed through her, and then Belladonna straightened. Her cheeks were filled with color, and her eyes blazed as if she, too, had a fever.

"Leave us alone."

Isaak seemed rooted to the spot, but Diana forced him to turn, and they exited, along with Sister Maria, leaving the brother and sister alone.

Chapter Fifty-One: Antonio

Antonio admired the palazzo of Morosini. Such a richness of color and the lavishness which only wealth could bestow. He reclined on a chaise in a brightly lit room with lightly shaped gilded chairs and divans in the French style instead of the heavy dark wood and red damask he was used to seeing in this city. His vineyard home in the Veneto had the same lightness, not through design, but because it was not bogged down with draperies or furnishings. Antonio anticipated it would not remain bare nor empty for much longer once he threw his lot in with this group instead of Di Ribera.

A soft melody filled the air, released from the burled-wooden pianoforte Morosini played like an expert. The nobleman was dressed in sky-blue satin today, with silver buttons and elaborate ecru lace at the throat and cuffs. Sometimes, the music would stop, its last note lingering like a trail of perfume, as Morosini paused, hands lifted in the air as if he was debating which chord to strike next. The stop and starts annoyed Antonio, but he did not dare to complain. A snake steers clear of a scorpion when he sees one.

Antonio's annoyance with Morosini was minimal compared to the animosity he harbored for Diego Di Ribera. A fool like Di Ribera had not the brains nor the skills for his position. It was merely the accident of birth that denied Antonio the power and prestige of being an ambassador. The 'Purity of the Blood' should not be a valid excuse for appropriating power and riches from those who earned or deserved them. So, philosophically, Antonio had more respect for the pirate who had gotten the better of him than both the Spanish and Venetian noblemen who were bidding for his loyalty.

Antonio regarded the dagger that Morosini had restored to him. A small voice egged him into unsheathing it and throwing it at the nobleman. He did not like Morosini, but he did respect him. He hoped to gain as much as possible from Morosini, before he would need to kill him.

Antonio leaned back and sipped the excellent wine provided by his host. Time, that most precious commodity, was on his side, and he could wait for his prey in luxury without worrying about Di Ribera's men watching his every move. As far as Di Ribera was concerned, he was still on the ship, interrogating their captive. At some point, he would have to find a body to identify as the courtesan or the envoy, to bring this dramatic hunt to an end.

"Enjoying yourself?" the music had stopped, and the rich deep voice of his host was addressing him.

"I am." Always a man who observed a great deal, he did not feel the onus of initiating a conversation. He dared not forget he was merely a hired hand to Bardon Morosini.

"Now that we have reached an understanding, perhaps I should clarify the terms a bit." Morosoni stood, closing the lid of the pianoforte, and sauntered over to stand directly above him. Clever. Though Antonio had dealt with the very worst and the very best, he was wary enough to take anything this nobleman said with great seriousness. Morosini was the ultimate leader, the type of man who had no qualms and few morals, with the innate cleverness to use everyone and or everything to achieve his aims. It was best to get to the bottom of this now.

"What do you require of me?"

The nobleman folded his arms across his chest as he cocked his head at Antonio. "When Belladonna and her entourage return, I am fairly certain either she or Isaak will have the map in their possession. If so, you will make sure to deliver it to me. If they do not have the map in hand, find out where it is, and then get it to me. Very simple, really."

"I suppose you will leave it up to my discretion on how I obtain the map?"

Morosini unfolded his arms and clamped one large be-ringed hand on Antonio's shoulder. The strength of the nobleman's grip was meant to impress, and it did. "I trust you as a professional to achieve your purpose. I do not question your methods, and you do not speculate on my motives. As long as we understand each other, I am certain we shall each reap the rewards we desire."

Antonio pried the hand from his shoulders and rose to his feet, standing eye to eye with his new master. "In the spirit of understanding, it is worth remembering I am thorough and not impatient. I will wait to achieve my goals, and I am ever so persistent in reaping my rewards."

Chapter Fifty-Two: Villiers

Villiers first taste of the courtesan Belladonna made him yearn for more. She was unlike any of the women at Court. She sparkled like a goddess. Maybe it was her magnificent jewels seducing him, not her smile.

He could barely wait for the next contact with her, but it never turned out in his favor if he let his anticipation show. A few hours at the gaming tables seemed the best course of action to calm his restlessness.

Villiers donned a brown velvet waistcoat with collar and cuffs embroidered with gold. He smoothed his red-gold mustache and long wavy red hair. "Dashing, am I?" he asked his reflection before he made his departure. His wound gave him a pang when he twisted too suddenly to his left, reminding him to take his dagger and to belt on a sword. He did not want to test Fate for luck at the tables as well as keeping him from an assassin's blade.

Sir Henry blocked his path. "Sir George? If you are going out, I will accompany you."

Villiers waved a hand to dismiss the older man, itching to swat him if he continued to get in his way. "Do not trouble yourself. I can manage on my own."

Sir Henry called out for a servant, who instantly appeared with cloaks, one of which was placed on Villiers shoulders. "I insist. While you are in Venice, you are under my guardianship, and I must be absolutely certain you suffer no harm."

Villiers raised an eyebrow, and the older man bowed his own and added, "I had been derelict in my duty, and you were attacked. It shall not happen again."

Villiers shrugged himself into the cloak, resigned to the ambassador's patronage. As their gondola pulled into the Grand Canal, he considered the added benefit – risking Sir Henry's gold instead of his own when placing his bets.

Sir Henry took him to one of the larger, more respectable casinos on the Grand Canal, though he had in mind somewhere a little more decadent. No matter, the clinks of coin and dice and the sight of cards being flipped by jeweled hands was enough to ignite his blood. The hum of so many voices punctuated by shouts of joy or despair was music to his ears, and he flung himself, without hesitation, into their midst.

Baccarat? Dice? Backgammon? Lotto? Villiers sorted through the tables, and the guests clustered around them, inhaling the aroma of wine, sweat, and heady perfume. As long as Sir Henry kept up with him to sign the notes of credit, he was ready to play.

Villiers was following a cluster of ladies in lavish dresses, their feather headdresses tickling his neck, to a table that seemed to have a most appealing crowd.

"Birribisse is quite popular, and it is like the Lotto—no skill required, only blind luck," said a voice nearby. Standing very near to him, holding a small glass of wine, was the artist Mattia Correr.

"Ah. You have arrived just in time to save me. Not from an assassin, but from taking my gold to the wrong table."

Mattia gestured to the growing cluster of jewel-studded ladies and well-dressed gentlemen. "There is where you take the biggest gamble."

Villiers grinned, "Then there I must go. Have no fear, I only risk the gold of others, and tonight my losses will be paid by Sir Henry. He does not mind. Service to the King and all that."

"Suppose you win?"

"Then we all go home happy. Perhaps even you, my friend." His pointed finger rested against Mattia's plum velvet doublet. He rubbed his fingers against the fabric. "Hmm, very nice. You must be a very good artist, since you already exhibit such good taste."

"And I shall make you a good guide tonight." Mattia smiled. "Shall I explain the game to you before you place Sir Henry's gold at risk?"

"Please."

"There are thirty-six squares on the board, each with a distinct figure. You see, on this board, it looks like they are a range of playful-looking animals." Villiers squinted and leaned to the side to see before nodding. "Each player places their money upon a square. The gentleman bank-holder pulls one of the balls from the pouch and calls out the corresponding number, and figures out loud."

"The winner is the lucky fellow with the gold on the corresponding number, correct?" Villiers asked rhetorically. "I should like to play. Come along, I can follow most of the talk, but could use a translator when the speech is too quick."

"What of Sir Henry? Is he here?"

Villiers waved his hand dismissively as he pushed through the crowd surrounding the table and managed to take the seat just made vacant by a sobbing lady. He glanced over his shoulder and grinned at Mattia, who had made it through and stood behind him.

"I am here." Sir Henry said in answer to Mattia.

"All is well, then." Villiers opened his palm. Sir Henry pulled a pouch from his austere velvet doublet and emptied its contents into Villier's hand.

"Now, which of you lovelies will prove me lucky?" Villiers's hand hovered over several numbers while other hands reached beyond him to place a claim on a square. "Ah, thirty-six, with the lively-looking fox." He stacked all of the coins upon them.

Villiers was wiping his brow, and looking over the tittering ladies, so was wholly unprepared when the banker announced, "Thirty-six!"

"Bedad, sir, you have won!" Sir Henry pounded a lace-edged wrist in the air. "You have more than tripled my gold!"

"Calm, Sir Henry, do not be ready to count your profits. Unless Villiers is finished and has no wish to stake his winnings?" Mattia raised his voice above the din, loud enough for Villiers to hear him.

"Of course, I am not done." He passed a stack of coins towards Sir Henry, adding, "But I am not an utter fool. Here, Sir Henry, hold onto this. It may be all we have by the end of the night."

After his piles of coins were swiped away at another play, Villiers gave a hard slap to the table and relinquished his spot to another delusional player.

"Nothing lost, nothing gained, if you count the pile I left in Sir Henry's hands," Villiers said as he and Mattia moved deeper into the assembly in search of the next game.

Sir Henry turned up beside them again, standing in their path with a hand out to stop them in their path. "Do not go any further. We must depart."

Villiers rolled his eyes and fanned himself with his hand. The further they went, the thicker the crowd and the warmer it was becoming. "But I am just getting the hang of these games, and they are so very diverting. What if I promise to take no more of your money?"

"It is not your loss, I worry about. Di Ribera has arrived with enough men to cause me concern." Sir Henry gestured towards the large end of the hall, where a black-clad man with a pointed beard and a stiff white collar stood, perusing the crowd. Two burly men, dressed in tooled leather flanked him, followed by a few more behind them.

"This way," said Mattia, directing them to windows that opened onto a balcony, "there is a stairway leading down to the water from there."

"Oh, come now, the man would not be so bold as to waylay me in such a public place." Villiers did not want to go.

"He knows Correr and is quite familiar with my face," said Sir Henry, glancing nervously over his shoulder, "It should not tax his faculties to guess who you might be. Do not underestimate the Spanish ambassador's determination. His men must have followed us here. They will find an opportunity to slip through the crowd unnoticed to get close enough to persuade you, with the tip of a knife, to accompany them."

Villiers directed his hand to the hilt of his dagger. Cocking his head in the direction of the balcony, he said. "I will follow your suggestion, since I have no wish to play cat and mouse with some burly Spaniards for the rest of the night. Lead on Correr, and I shall follow."

"It is pure chance that we meet here tonight," said Mattia. "but it will be to your benefit once more."

Why are the blasted Spanish so determined to kill me? Was Jamaica or the treasure so great a prize for the Spanish ambassador to risk war for an attack on a member of His Majesty's court?

Chapter Fifty-Three: Villiers

The artist navigated them through clusters of gamblers very quickly, and Villiers had to be especially careful of his wound at the twists and turns he was forced to make as he followed in the artist's wake. He wrinkled his nose at the heady scents of strange perfumes and swatted away feathers from ladies' headdresses. Glancing back, he saw the Spaniards fanning out in the crowd. Were they looking for him? Or were they just looking for a good spot at one of the tables?

A gust of cold air, refreshing against his sweating face, signaled they had reached the exit. A gold-liveried footman held open the heavy door, Mattia snatched their cloaks, and they were out. Gondoliers lazing by their boats looked up with anticipation, and Mattia headed in their direction, but Villiers arrested his progress. "Spanish. Waiting behind the boats in the shadows. Is there another way?"

Mattia tilted his head to the left, and Villiers followed him round the palazzo to a narrow alleyway that snaked from the torchlight into utter darkness. Unsheathing his sword, Villiers said, "Just in case."

Mattia, his dagger leading the way, plowed ahead, and there was just enough space for Villiers to be at his side. They moved slowly until their eyes acclimated in the darkness, and they were able to make out the curve of the walls and hollows of the rear doorways of darkened palazzos. A clatter up ahead. Both men stopped, listening. All was quiet, and Villiers put a finger to his lips. A light flickered above, briefly illuminating the uneven stones and piles of refuse but no boots or the glint of metal. The two men inched forward. Yellow eyes and a cry from a cat, arching its back as it crossed their path, was a warning they were not alone. Instinctively, Villiers thrust his sword forward, and, surprisingly, felt it penetrate. A shocked cry and then the pounding of boots as the would-be assailant ran away.

Villiers held up his sword, wondering if it was stained with blood, for it was too dark to see. "I wonder if the cat that crossed the Spaniard's path was black. Bad luck for him, eh?"

"I do not believe it was a Spaniard. These *calles* are known to harbor low-level criminals hoping to capitalize on a drunken soul staggering out of a gambling den. You would think it a poor target, since anyone walking in a *calle* would undoubtedly have lost every ducat they had."

The two men kept their weapons up, but now moved at a quicker pace. Darkness receded as the *calle* widened into a large campo, the torches from taverns along its perimeter making it bright. From ominous to merry in just a few paces.

Villiers sheathed his sword and rubbed his chin. His mouth was dry, and the taverns were tantalizing. Dare he? "I confess all this danger has awakened a deep thirst. Perhaps you can choose the best of the bunch before us to slake it?"

The artist's face was temporarily veiled by a curtain of his wavy hair as he bent to the task of securing his blade back in the sheath at his waist. When Mattia looked up, he was grinning. "Follow me."

The *campo* was dominated by a large octagonally-shaped church that was so majestic, even Villiers found himself tip-toeing as he passed by. Mattia waved a hand and said, "Santa Maria Formosa. Very old. A thank you to the powers that be for the victorious rescue of the fair maidens, the "marias" of Venice who had been kidnapped by some invading Goths. This campo also hosts the best places to raise a glass to their memory. We shall not go wrong in any of these taverns."

Villiers followed the artist through a brightly lit doorway, where the sounds of laughter and the hum of conversation were a welcome change to the previous gloom. Taking their seats at a rough wooden table, a dark glass carafe with two small glasses was placed before them with a resounding thunk, by a fair-haired and voluptuous lady who was clearly no longer a maiden.

"Thank you," Villiers nodded to the lady, who only had eyes for Mattia. The fellow had quite a way with the ladies, it seemed, as the serving woman refused the artist's offer of coin for the wine.

"I should be so lucky," muttered Villiers to himself. It seemed his own Fate was to nearly bankrupt himself on spending for his ladyloves. Out loud he said, "You have not only saved my life, but you make a most amiable companion."

Mattia acknowledged his comment with a slight nod, while pouring wine into each of the glasses. "Well, tonight you saved mine."

"You see, my friend, I am no stranger to sudden attack, and I am quite able to defend myself. Despite my wound." He raised the glass to his nose, swirled it, and inhaled.

"I led you into the seamier side of my city, so now I must show my gratitude by sharing its riches, one of which is this wine. Taste it, and you will agree this tavern has earned its reputation as one of the best in Venice."

The wine did indeed satisfy Villiers and live up to expectations. "Speaking of reputations, Venice is known for its beautiful women. That bore, Arundel, keeps going on and on about his aborted attempt to collect them, via their portraits for his gallery. I must say, this courtesan, Belladonna, she is quite breathtaking. Tell me more about her."

Mattia drank some more of his wine and gave a satisfied sigh. "She first appeared in Venice over ten years ago, and though she never revealed her origins or her true name, it was assumed she had come from a noble house, possibly in the Veneto. She has been well educated, and besides her ability to discourse on Plato or quote from the Iliad, she is known to have great wit and self-composure. She drew patrons from the most powerful, and it is no wonder they never hesitate to seek her perspective."

"She is a mystery, then. There is nothing more alluring about a woman than an aura of mystery." Villiers found the topic more enticing than his wine, which did not happen often.

"Though she has not been linked, recently, to any great man, at one time, she was quite close to a man who is the leader of the Council of Ten. Unlike most of her former lovers, who often watch and wait for an opportunity to renew their friendship, this man bides his time like a tiger, waiting to pounce."

The conversation was growing even more interesting. Villiers decided to share his own perspective. "A woman can learn many secrets from a man. Perhaps she has learned his. Evidently, the Spanish believe she has milked the envoy for the secret of the treasure."

Mattia flicked his long hair away from his face. "The lady is not usually one to play with fire. She has earned a great deal of respect because of the way she has conducted herself." He glanced around, avoiding the bar maid's stare from across the room.

Villiers began tapping his fingers on the table, signaling his impatience to Mattia, so the man would get on with his story instead of staring over his wine glass. Mattia took a long drink before continuing, "She is a most unusual woman, so difficult to fathom. I have tried to paint her, but I never could quite grasp her essence. She keeps her true self too well hidden."

Villiers had heard enough. "Well, all in all, you have incited my interest in this courtesan even further. Let us not delay, I have seen her for but a fleeting moment, and I would like to know this woman better."

"For the sake of the gold and the island of Jamaica?" asked Mattia, in a jesting tone.

Villiers grinned. "Of course."

Chapter Fifty-Four: Belladonna

Belladonna took a step closer to her brother and lowered the plague mask so he could see her clearly. The sisters had not shaved him, and his beard had grown, wispy but curly black beneath his chin. The face she knew from childhood was here, hidden behind the deathly pallor, the sunken cheeks, and the dark beard. His long hands were folded across his chest, and each breath looked like it pained him, as it struggled to rise and fall. A hissing wheeze issued from his mouth filled her with dread.

Belladonna felt a knot at her core, and she pounded a fist into her stomach to dispel it. She took a step closer, but Roderigo held up his hand to warn her back. "Please, stay. I will not have you sicken. Listen to me, Raquel. My time is coming to an end—"

She started to argue, but he stopped her. "Please. I am weakening, and I do not know how long I will be able to speak. That is why you must act now. I came on this mission knowing full well I might not survive it. I had made it clear to my family that in all likelihood, I would not return to them."

"Your family?" Belladonna repeated, her eyes widening, and her mouth gaping.

"I have a wife, Mariella, and a son, Moises." His mouth widened into a true smile, and his eyes brightened. "They are the blessings from the Almighty. After I escaped Recife and returned to Jamaica, I had nothing. No family, no one to turn to. Mariella's father, a good man, a leader of the community, took me into his own home. I was treated like his son, and soon I took on the role, officially, when I married Mariella."

Roderigo paused again, inhaling deeply, only to cough violently as he exhaled. He was weakening, and talking was wearying on him.

"Do not stress yourself. We can speak later."

Roderigo coughed himself into a sitting position as he struggled to control it. When at last the coughing stopped, he lay back on the pillow, facing the ceiling.

"There is not much time, and you need to know this. Give the real map to the English lord, and make a fake copy to leave with me. Then have the Spanish 'find' me with the fake map," he tried to sit up again. "Then they will be satisfied. They will cease to search for you."

"How do you expect me to do that? Have the Spanish found you here in Giudecca?"

"No, no, not here. I would not expose these kind Sisters to their brutishness. You must take me to their ship. Make sure that Di Ribera comes on board."

Like the ship of her would-be kidnapper, Antonio. Perhaps now was the time to put Antonio's usefulness to the test. With the black hood, the wraps, Roderigo's condition would be hidden until it was too late. If they kept him bundled up the way she had been during her abduction, those who transported him should be safe from contagion.

Roderigo nodded, but his eyelids were drooping. He had reached the end of his strength. Belladonna softly stepped back. She slipped out and gave her thanks to Sister Maria.

Chapter Fifty-Five: Belladonna

Isaak and Diana were waiting for her outside Roderigo's room, but did not ask her what was said. She could not have responded if they had. She needed some time to accept so many things—Roderigo's imminent death, learning of his wife and child, and the terrible decision he had forced her to make, to turn him over to the Spanish before he expired.

Belladonna marched through the convent with the siblings trailing behind her. She caught their glances at each other, and it angered her. The relationship between them was an irritating reminder of what she could have had with Roderigo. It was not until she was sitting on the prow of the gondola, face to the wind, she could exhale deeply, releasing the breath she had been holding for a while. The wind battering her face and hair felt refreshing, and Belladonna kept to the prow, away from her friends. As her eyes stung and tears formed, she wiped them away before they could trickle down her cheeks.

Isaak had directed the gondolier toward the Ghetto, and she supposed Diana had chosen not to accompany them back to Palazzo Morosini. The irony did not escape her that it was Isaak who had brought Roderigo to her and would now mastermind the plan to separate them forever. Isaak was steadfast and true to his ideals, and Belladonna believed he still loved her. Could his love be enough? If she was prepared to leave Venice forever, leaving everything behind, could Roderigo's wife and child fill the holes in her life left by the deaths of her family?

For Belladonna, sailing away with Isaak should remain a nice dream, but one without the possibility of ever becoming a reality. If she ran away, her disappearance would cast suspicion upon the Ghetto for enemies like Contarini to use against the Jews. The Men in the Dark Cloaks were to be feared, and a ransack of the Ghetto would be inevitable if she did not appear in public, or at her palazzo, on the morrow.

Belladonna leaned back into the seat, listening idly to the rhythmic splashing of the oars. The motion of the ship and the splashing water were soothing, and her eyelids lowered and then closed. It could not be for long, but she needed a few moments to rest.

Her eyes did not open until she felt the jolt of the boat hitting the poles of the dock. Isaak was helping his sister alight. Diana waved to her and hurried off towards the gates of the Ghetto.

"Diana is worried about my father. He has just been set free by the Council of Ten," Isaak explained.

"Has he come to any harm?"

"No, but I am sure my mother is distraught, and my father will have little patience for her. It is best for Diana to be with them." The gondolier had turned their craft and was poling away from the Ghetto towards the Grand Canal and Morosini's palazzo.

"There is no choice, you know," Isaak said, taking her hand and cradling it in his.

Belladonna sighed. "Understanding the course that must be taken does not lessen the pain of taking it."

His hands were rough but so warm, and she nestled closer into him under the covered section of the gondola. Arms came around her, comforting her with the feel of his strength.

"I will take care of everything," Isaak whispered in her ear. "You should not have to be the one to do this."

She closed her eyes. Someone to take the weight from her shoulders. It was a relief she felt too guilty to enjoy. "I am about to take my own brother to the Inquisition. The same institution killed our parents and destroyed our lives. I cannot avoid the guilt and shame of this act."

"There is no room for such emotions when people's lives are at stake. Roderigo understands this and is prepared to face the Inquisitors. Make no mistake, he is doing it for your sake as well as for the Jews of this community and those on the island of Jamaica."

Belladonna looked into Isaak's fierce, sapphire blue eyes. His gaze did not waver as he held her close. *He understands, because he would do the same as Roderigo.* She was not so noble. She would do anything to succeed, but her goal was always either self-preservation or to vanquish her enemies. Roderigo had spoken of his family, a wife and a son. If she sailed off with Isaak to the New World, they would be her family. She would *belong* truly in their world, on the island of her birth, with her family.

She must not entertain such thoughts. There was still much to be done, and neither her survival nor Roderigo's family's future would be assured until all was settled. In Isaak's arms, she believed he was her champion and could set it all to right. However, much as she wanted to, Belladonna could not suspend her cynicism, even for Isaak.

Chapter Fifty-Six: Villiers

Despite the late hour and their mission to find Belladonna, Villiers wanted to linger in the tavern to finish a second bottle of wine. Although he did not want to be drunk at the next encounter, a bit of inebriation seemed in order after the confrontation in the alley. His drinking companion did not seem as committed to relaxation as he and Mattia barely finished the wine in his cup from the first bottle. The fellow was preoccupied with drawing, had pulled out a small chalk, and now was sketching a likeness of the barmaid on a slip of paper he must have pulled out of his doublet.

Villiers leaned over to watch and found he was rather fascinated as the artist's strokes became the defining lines of the plump face. He had truly captured the squint of the lady's eyes and the merriment of her dimpled smile. Impressive, really. The lovely barmaid was enchanted and begged Correr for the sketch. Though he sighed as he parted with it, the artist handed it over to her, who hugged it to her chest, dancing off with it to share with her friends at the bar.

"I believe it is time to go," stated Correr, gathering his cap.

"I suppose so," said Villiers, downing the last of his wine and rising. He adjusted his sword, made sure his dagger was also near at hand, and straightened his doublet.

Villiers gave a mock salute to the men and women who looked up at their departure. The torches still blazed, and the square was still bright, but there were fewer people milling about, which sobered him into vigilance. He kept his hand on the hilt of his sword until they had settled themselves into the comfortable seats of the gondola and were on their way to the Grand Canal.

"Where to now?" asked Villiers.

"It is time you met one of the most powerful men in Venice. He has the resources to protect your safety, and besides, his palazzo is even grander than Sir Henry's. You should be very comfortable under his care."

Villiers was duly impressed as they arrived at white-columned portico of the Morosini palazzo. He was pleased with the efficiency of the servants, and envy stirred in his breast as the servant guided him up a majestic marble staircase to the *piano nobile*.

A tall nobleman awaited them at the entry to the salon. "Mattia, besides being a master at your craft, you have the grace of perfect timing. I expect the others to arrive momentarily. Now, please do me the honor of introducing our guest."

The lavish décor of the salon, with its marble fireplaces, gilt-edged mirrors, crystal chandeliers, and wall sconces amplifying the candlelight, was impressive, even to a favorite of the King of England. Villiers gave a most civilized bow and announced his title and his representation of the Court of King James. His attention shifted to take in the gilt furniture, delicate porcelain, and intricate tapestries signaling his host's abundant wealth. He was so taken with the room's appointments it took him some time to notice a man in black reclining on an elegantly curved blue and gilt divan. Villiers eyes widened, and a dagger appeared in hand.

"Is he the fiend who stabbed me?"

Within a few steps, Villiers had his blade beneath the assassin's throat. The man did not seem perturbed, and responded with a burning, defiant stare. Villiers pressed the knife into the flesh, cutting the skin. A trickle of blood descended beneath the man's collar. He kept up the grin and had no other reaction.

Gems flashed in the candlelight as the nobleman's fingers closed over Villiers' hand. Firmly, he pressed his hand away from the other's throat, saying, "Let us allow yesterday's travesties to be forgotten. Today's realities have forged new alliances. More lucrative to us all."

Villiers, his eyes still on the man in black, gave a righteous sniff, but

248

restored the blade to his scabbard. "Unfortunately, I am reminded of this fellow's dark deed every time I twist to my left. But I am a reasonable man, especially when it comes to possibilities for my purse."

"It was nothing personal, sir," said the man in black, "it is the Spanish ambassador who should be the target of your ire."

Villiers ignored the blighter and instead turned his attention to the delicate glass of amber liquid being offered by an impeccably liveried servant.

"A brandy, recently acquired, which I reserved for my most discerning guests," said Morosini.

Villiers gave a swirl and then took a sniff before drinking it, savoring the rich flavor as it swirled around his mouth. "Ambrosia," he said in conclusion. His host nodded his head appreciatively.

The sound of voices and footsteps thudding across the terrazzo floors turned their heads.

"You see, just in time," Morosini said, nodding towards the doorway, "Belladonna has returned."

The nobleman's announcement heralded the entry of the beauty Villiers had met at Sir Henry's.

The courtesan marched in, flinging her cloak off into the arms of a waiting footman. Her cheeks were aflame from the briskness of the cold, and her eyes burned with determination, making her even lovelier.

"Antonio," her commanding voice seemed to have an effect on the man in black, who lost his languor and stood to attention. "We have need of your services."

A dark-skinned man, his cap pulled low over his long hair, put a hand to her shoulder. "Wait. There is little chance of succeeding if the plan is not worked out completely."

To his surprise, those words seemed to deflate the woman's spirit, and she drooped her head and pressed a hand to her forehead. She allowed herself to be led to a divan opposite Villiers and took a deep draught of the brandy Morosini himself handed to her.

As she drank, her eyes fastened on him for the first time. "Oh."

Smoothing her hair, which had broken free of what must have been an elegant coiffeur, she straightened her posture and held out her hand to him. "Sir George Villiers. We meet again, although under most unusual circumstances."

Villiers raised and brushed his lips against the thin leather of her gloves. "To be sure, it seems I have come at a most opportune time, if I can be of service to you."

The woman graced him with an amused smile, and the other voices seemed to fade away. As he gazed into Belladonna's beautiful amber eyes, his desire for her was overwhelming.

"Now, Belladonna, stop toying with the Englishman. You know where the envoy is and where the map to the treasure can be found," said Morosini, taking a commander's stance before her.

Chapter Fifty-Seven: Belladonna

Morosini had settled the four men and himself on two couches facing each other, with Belladonna seated in a gilded chair between them. A liveried servant appeared, offering her a glass of deep red wine. After taking a fortifying sip, she closed her eyes until she felt in full control of her emotions. Morosini would lose confidence in the enterprise if the unflappable Belladonna seemed overwhelmed.

"We have found the envoy. He had been wounded, thanks to Antonio, and is under the care of the sisters in a convent on Giudecca. The envoy is dying, but still wishes to both fulfill his mission and kill as many Spaniards as he can. Sir George, you are the means to fulfill his mission when you convey to King James the map to the treasure and the promise of the assistance of the Jews in your conquest of Jamaica." She paused a moment to ensure they were following, before she continued, "When the envoy is delivered to the Spanish, they will receive more than they bargained for, since he is dying of the plague."

Plague. The very word conjured images of pure horror. Stunned looks and audible gasps. Even Morosini took a deep breath and put down his wine glass.

"Leave it to you, my dear, to always catch me unaware. None of us have been exposed to it, I warrant?"

Belladonna's eyes met Isaak's. "No. We have kept our distance."

"Good. Well, then, may I ask how you propose to get the plague-ridden fellow to the Spanish? I cannot allow one of my men to risk exposure, and I warrant...." He pointedly looked at Antonio, who shook his head, "none of us is willing to either."

Isaak spoke up. "Leave it to me. All has been arranged. The rest of you must play your parts and follow my orders to the letter."

Antonio did not look pleased with this announcement, and his eyes shifted under her gaze. Belladonna was unsure if they could fully trust the Spaniard, though their plan depended on him. She stared into her wine glass, which she clutched in both hands to keep the others from noticing their trembling.

"We do not expect the envoy to survive the journey for very long," Isaak had risen from his seat, and Belladonna put down her glass and joined him. Isaac continued, "We must act quickly. Tonight. By tomorrow Belladonna must return to her palazzo."

"Quite right," nodded Morosini, as he, too, stood. "It is difficult to stave off those rabid instigators on the Council of Ten for much longer. They are salivating at the chance to loot the Ghetto, and only Belladonna's reappearance will keep them back."

Mattia finished off his wine and staggered a bit when he stood. "What is my role in all of this?"

Belladonna reached between the folds of the bodice and retrieved a folded document, which looked like weathered parchment. "The map to the gold of Christopher Columbus in Jamaica."

Villiers immediately rose from his seat, ready to retrieve the map, but Belladonna held it out of his reach and passed it to Mattia. The artist studied the lines and scribbles on the parchment. "They have never seen this, have they?"

Isaak shook his head. "They have not. How long will it take you to make a counterfeit one?"

"A few hours at most."

Villiers asked, "Why does he need it? It was supposed to come to me." He stuck his hand out, and his lip protruded belligerently.

"The Spanish expect to find a map with the envoy. They will not know the one they find with him is false." Turning to Mattia, Isaak added, "Take it. Two hours will have to suffice. Be ready when we come for it."

Mattia rolled up the map and nodded before he strode out of the room.

His footsteps could be heard rapidly descending the staircase.

Morosini clamped his hand to Villiers's shoulder. From the expression on Villiers' face, it was not a soft touch. "You will receive the map as an incentive to your King to take the island of Jamaica for England. A key location to regulate the trade routes of the West Indies, the island will bring your country, and yourself, a great deal of wealth. Just make sure you and your King recognize that I retain the right to retrieve and retain a portion of any treasure found."

Villiers unhooked one ringed finger after another from his shoulder and brushed off his doublet where they had been. Scowling, he said, "If Jamaica becomes the property of England, then why would I—we —need a partner to harvest its riches?"

Morosini frowned, and Belladonna was afraid he would lose his temper. She jumped in to offer an answer that would serve their purpose. "Because you need more than the map if you want to find treasure on Jamaica. The secret to finding it has been passed down from the times of Christopher Columbus, shared by the descendants of the loyal men who saved Columbus from mutineers. The Jews of Jamaica have the means to decipher the map. If the Spanish get to Jamaica before you—"

Morosini interrupted her. "Thank you, my dear, for clarifying the overall operation. Now, Sir George Villiers, let me *clarify* why I merit a portion of this enterprise. If you wish to get out of Venice *alive*, you can pay up now, or later, with shares of the treasure."

Villiers glanced at Belladonna, who shrugged. He treated Morosini with a broad smile and spread his arms wide for emphasis. "Well, I suppose now, we are partners."

Morosini pursed his lips. "I was certain you would see it my way. Now, I would advise you to follow this man's," he pointed to Isaak, "instructions to the letter. He has outwitted the Spanish more than once, and I am certain he will succeed. But you must follow his lead. No bravado, or you will die."

"I intend to die," Antonio said. "In order to retire, I must be presumed dead by my countryman, and it must be convincing." He bowed his head deferentially to Isaak, "Please consider how I must meet my death in your arrangements."

Isaak gave a solemn nod, and Belladonna grabbed hold of a black sleeve. "Antonio, you are key to this enterprise. You must follow Isaak's orders, or we will not have to stage your death, I promise you."

A smile came to the assassin's lips, but he answered. "I understand. Have no fear, I am a good soldier, and I am used to following orders."

Villiers had stepped up close to the Spanish assassin and gave him a sneering grin. "Happy to be of service to make your 'death' convincing."

"Quite a cut I made on you, no?" Antonio's hand had traveled to the hilt of his blade, just as Villiers had migrated to his own.

"Gentlemen!" Belladonna stood between them and stamped her foot for emphasis. "This is not a time for squabbling." Their confrontation gave her an idea, which she offered to Isaak. "Villiers could attempt to board the ship to retrieve the envoy, and Antonio could launch himself into the invader's boat to stop him. It would give Antonio the chance to leave the ship and provide the scene of his death to the Spanish audience when Villiers strikes him down."

Antonio raised one eyebrow as he considered her suggestion. "Must I fall into the lagoon?"

"Do you know how to swim?"

"Yes."

"Then make sure not to wear your best boots," she said. Excitement bubbled within her; this plan had revived her spirit. Isaak frowned, but she continued, "Once Di Ribera has witnessed Antonio's death, he should make great haste to sail out of the lagoon."

Villiers, listening to her every word, made a face with the twist of his lips, "Not a bad plan. I especially like dumping this fellow in the lagoon. As long as our black-clad friend does not get overenthusiastic or decide his loyalties truly lie with king and country, and use our trick to run me in."

Antonio was quick to respond, but he did not sound angry at the charge. "Since the Englishman's survival is necessary to make my fortune, I will make certain he comes to no harm. "

Isaak dismissed them all, each with their specific instructions, including

Morosini, "We meet in three hours."

* * *

With Isaak, they returned to the home of the Turk. Though it was late, lights still burned, and a brazier in the courtyard gave off heat and a soft light.

"What can I do for you, my friends?" asked the Turk as he ushered them to the familiar cushioned corner.

"We require a man from *Lazzaretto Vecchio* to man a boat. Tonight," said Belladonna.

Isaak and the Turk shot looks at each other, and then raised their eyebrows. "The Leper Colony?"

"And the plague hospital. There are those who have had the plague and survived it. They would now be immune to it, just like Sister Maria," Belladonna explained and was relieved when Isaak seemed to catch on.

The Turk's brows furrowed, and he twisted his hands. "The *plague*? I cannot risk exposure. My ships, my business, no, it is too dangerous."

Isaak hastened to reassure the man by explaining where they had found Roderigo and what state he was in. Then they explained Isaak's plan to send the plague victim into the arms of his enemies.

"The envoy will consent to this?" was the Turk's only question. When their full plan was explained, he agreed to help. "I will find such a man." He leaned back on a cushion and gave a broad smile, for his people had originally come from Spain, and he enjoyed nothing more than to see the Spanish suffer. "How long will it take for those Spaniards to die, I wonder?"

Chapter Fifty-Eight: Villiers

Isaak had thought it best for Villiers not to return to the ambassador's dwelling, but to remain with him aboard his ship. Villiers did not complain; he was greatly interested in learning more about this very successful corsair. Perhaps what he gleaned could be shared with the Royal Navy? He would love to see Arundel's smug face crumple when he, Villiers, guided them to greater victory at sea.

There was something about the corsair's face that seemed oddly familiar. His eyes, with their dark brows and pupils and the strange shade of blue in their irises. Unusual, never seen before until...

Ah yes, the ministering angel, the Jewess, Diana. Could they be related? Why, that would mean the corsair was also of the Hebrew persuasion. How odd. Never having met any of their kind before, Villiers did not know if their eyes or their dedication to noble causes was common among them.

The Corsair seemed to run his ship with efficiency. The men looked at their captain with admiration and seemed eager to do his bidding. Villiers followed Isaak around the deck, watching him supervise or comment to the men at work. It seemed they were readying the craft for a long departure, since men came up to Isaak asking about storage of victuals and making sure below decks was ready. Isaak was called to examine one of the short boats, which Villiers wondered if it was to be used to transfer the envoy to the Spanish.

When it seemed all the arrangements were complete, the corsair invited Villiers to his cabin to wait for word of the arrival of the man from *Larrezzeto Vecchio* or for the messenger from the artist with the maps—the false copy and the original. Villiers rubbed his fingers together in anticipation of feeling that vellum once more. Gold at the tip of his fingers. Isaak invited him to take a seat across from him, and Villiers complied.

Isaak removed his cap and tented his fingers, before his chin. "How is your aim?"

Villiers raised his eyebrows. Not a question he was expecting. "I have been the winner of more duels than I care to count."

"You will not need to shoot from a distance. I just needed to confirm you know how to aim and fire."

"These days, most courtiers in the court of King James are well trained on such scores. It is necessary to survive. Shooting a pistol, being good with a sword, and having enough gold to bribe your way out of most anything." Villers grinned. "Not much difference between us, you see. Perhaps you need to shoot more from a distance, as well?"

"There are similarities in the way we survive perhaps, but not likely in the way we were reared." Only one side of the corsair's mouth rose in an odd, crooked smile.

"That reminds me, the beautiful Jewess, Diana, is she of some relation?" asked Villiers as he watched the man's eyes. He had always been able to tell from a man's eyes if he was lying.

"What concern is it of yours?"

"Curiosity. I do not often study faces, unlike my friend Correr, but your eyes and hers—they are distinct. I have not seen any other eyes such as yours in England." Villiers kept his eyes on Isaak's as he waited for a response.

Isaak sighed. "How observant of you. Yes, Diana is my sister. Convinced now, that our origins are quite different?"

Before Villiers could answer, there was a knock at the door, and upon Isaak's permission, one of his men entered bearing a tray and a silver pot. Coffee. Villers hoped it was not as thick as the Turk's, or it would not only thoroughly sober him, but might turn his stomach to bring up the wine.

The sailor poured out two steaming cups. The aroma was delicious, and Villiers took the cup that was offered. "Your man brews it well. Better than the Turk."

Isaak bade the man to leave the tray and leave. "I make sure to always have coffee on hand. It keeps the men sharp, especially before a battle. We do not have enough time for rest, so I thought it might do us both some good."

Villiers had not detected any sense of worry in the corsair, so assumed he was confident in the plan. As Belladonna had said, they each had a part to play and he knew his. He also knew very well how to survive, but he did not like putting his trust in a Spanish assassin.

Before taking another sip, he wanted to know the Corsair's perspective. "Do you trust this Antonio fellow?"

Isaak's lips flattened as if he had tasted something sour. "Not in the least. Since Spain has been my enemy for so long, it may be difficult for me to be unbiased about any Spaniard. I do trust in one thing, however, his greed. His loyalty, like most of his kind, is up to the highest bidder. Morosini has offered much more than Diego Di Ribera, and if he wants to collect it, he has to play his part. Without accident, I might add."

Villiers nodded. "If my gun should go off accidentally..."

"I would save the bullets for the Spanish who will be firing at you. Let your vengeance be satisfied by consigning Antonio to the lagoon." Isaak blew at the steam rising from his cup and took a tentative sip. "After all, you will have the map."

"When?" the thought of the map made him want to leap out of his seat and go find it.

Isaak sighed. "I have found the key to my successes has been patience. I wait, plan, and assess before I make a move. Logic must drive my actions without them being colored by emotions. Perhaps you would benefit from the same approach."

Villiers chuckled. "I do act too much without thinking, especially in matters of the heart." Villiers recalled his reaction to Belladonna at their first meeting. He would have offered to marry her then; he had been so smitten. He was shrewd enough to see the courtesan had not been equally smitten with him. In fact, Villiers sensed a connection between the corsair and the courtesan, which he wanted to probe. "What of you? Have you found your heart racing at the sight of a woman such as Belladonna, as I did?"

"Belladonna works her magic on many," said the corsair. An answer that revealed little.

Villiers yawned and drank more coffee. It would be a long wait, if the man proved to be so coy.

Chapter Fifty-Nine: Villiers

Despite the coffee, Villiers must have fallen asleep, because he awoke with a pressing urge to relieve himself. The chair opposite was empty. Isaak must have gone on deck, perhaps for the same urgent purpose. Villiers staggered to his feet, bound for the stairs and fresh air. There was no sign of the corsair, nor of anybody else. As he unloosed his breeches for relief of his urges, he looked up at a cloudless starry sky. Nights such as these seemed like a good omen.

"I am glad you are awake and ready," Isaak's voice startled him, and he almost lost his footing. Villiers buttoned his trousers and leaned over the rail. It came from below, where Isaak sat in the lowered smaller boat.

"Make haste. Grab your sword, for we need to be off."

The boat wobbled as he climbed aboard. Isaak was not alone. Antonio, swathed in a black cloak, hat, and gloves, blended into the night and was seated aft.

Villiers shivered in his cloak as the air was damp and cold. Isaak handed him a pistol, which Villiers carefully tucked into his belt.

Villiers had two questions for Isaak, "Where is the map? Has the envoy arrived?"

"The map is with Correr. The envoy is on his way with Giacomo, the man from the Lazzaretto."

"And the Spanish ship?"

"At the far side of the lagoon, moored by the island of Murano."

Villiers had heard of Murano; it was the island of the glassmakers. Villiers did not comment or ask any other questions. Both the Corsair and the

Spaniard did not seem in the mood for conversation.

The boat plowed onward in silence, with only the sound of the water swooshing against the oars to disturb it. Isaak used the oars efficiently to guide their craft through clusters of barges, boats, and gondolas bobbing and moving through the Grand Canal.

"Before you ask," Isaak was addressing Villiers, "we are headed toward the Canal of the Cannaregio, which ends at the Grand Canal. Mattia awaits us there with the maps. I will pull close enough to shore for one of you to take them from him."

The promise of the map must have triggered some inner spark, for Villiers felt as if he had been suffused with so much energy he could not be still. He took the pistol that lay across his lap and lifted it, squinting through its sites and making sure the chamber had been loaded correctly. One bullet, ready to fire. He kept it in his right hand, resting on his thigh.

It was well after midnight, and the half-moon was swallowed by large clusters of clouds limiting its light. They passed very few boats, since this narrow canal was mostly used by tradesmen and locals who had long been in their beds. The flickering light of candles in the windows and the occasional fiery torches of a tavern were their only sources of illumination, since Isaak had ordered no lantern to be lit in their boat.

The Canal of the Cannaregio was much narrower than the Grand Canal, and flat walkways, or *fondimenta*, ran right alongside it. Isaak had no trouble navigating the narrow canal, even in the bleak light, and brought them close to the shore. Villiers squinted through the dimness, his eye out for the figure of Mattia Correr.

The boat had slowed down. Isaak had put down the oars and stood at attention in the prow. Would the artist see them? Could he reach over to hand over the maps without dropping them into the canal?

"It is so bloody dark," mumbled Villiers.

"The better for us tonight," Isaak said and retrieved his oar to push them towards a set of moss-covered steps leading into the canal. "We could not do this under a full moon."

"Why not?"

"*Acqua alta*. The canal waters rise and overflow at full moon during the fall and winter. It would not be safe for us to meet Mattia here."

A light moved towards them in the darkness. Emerging from the shadows, beyond the mossy steps, was Mattia Correr.

Isaak held the boat at bay with the oar. Mattia held one map in each hand. "This," he held up his right hand, "is for England. And this one," he held out his left hand, "is for Spain."

Villiers rose too suddenly from his seat, rocking the boat, as he reached for the artist's right hand. Antonio took the map from Mattia's left.

Quickly, Villiers stowed his treasure within his doublet, so he could feel it was close to his heart. His fingers lingered at the open doublet; he had the urge to take the map out and examine it more closely, but suppressed it.

Villiers was so fixated on the bundle resting against his chest, he forgot about his companions and what lay ahead. Isaak nodded to Antonio, who stood and used an oar to push them on their way. "Make sure it lands in the hands of Diego di Ribera."

Isaak rowed, and his passengers kept silent. As they neared the end of the Canal of the Cannaregio, a misty rain started. Villiers grabbed a ratty blanket from between the seats and draped it from his hat. No use ruining a good hat.

The waterway was widening, and Isaak bent to his oar to steer them into the lagoon. As they advanced into the Venetian lagoon, Villiers could see the dark shape of land, dotted with little flares of light. He supposed it was the island of Murano, where the Spanish ship lay. Isaak had stopped using his oar, and the boat bobbed softly in the current. Antonio pointed to the horizon where the crisscross of rigging and the silhouette of a ship could be seen. An arc of light appeared out of the darkness. Villiers thought it might be lightning, but when it appeared again, knew it was some kind of signal. Was it their man, or one of Di Ribera's crew?

"Did you see that?" he asked Isaak, raising his pistol in readiness.

"It is the boatman and the envoy. They await us." Isaak lay a hand across the pistol so it pointed away from the approaching boat. To Antonio, he warned, "Get ready to board."

Antonio protested, "You expect me to get into that boat full of plague?"

"There is no danger, the Sisters assured me. The envoy is hooded and wrapped. He will sit at the far end with the boatman. You will sit aft, the other side." Isaak's last words had the ring of a command.

The Spaniard's jaw tensed. "It is not what I had bargained for."

When Isaak turned back from his oar, he had his pistol cocked under the Spaniard's chin. "You have a choice. Either get in or swim."

Several tense moments passed. Grumbling, Antonio turned up the collar of his cloak and wrapped his scarf almost completely around his face.

Isaak hailed the approaching boat as soon as it was close enough. In the quiet, they could all hear the boatman call. Within minutes, they had pulled up alongside the other craft. Isaak had his pistol out in one hand and held the side of the other boat in the other. Antonio rose and kept his hands raised to gain his balance. He lifted one leg and lost his balance as the boat rocked, and he fell into Villiers.

Immediately, Villiers pushed the man in black away, and, to alleviate his fears, checked to see the map was still in his doublet. It was.

Isaak grabbed the Spaniard by the arm to steady him. "Giacomo will carry your prisoner aboard the ship. Make sure he is placed comfortably, and then you can give Di Ribera his map."

Isaak guided the assassin into the other boat. Antonio scurried aft, as far from the men in the prow as he could.

"Hold fast to the boat. I must have one last word with the envoy," said Isaak to Villiers, tucking his pistol into his belt and stepping into the adjoining boat.

Villiers held onto the second boat with both hands. The last thing he wanted was to lose his navigator and oarsman in the midst of a dark lagoon. Isaak was back on the other craft, crouching beside a swathed and hooded man. *Must be the envoy.*

Isaak removed the hood. The envoy looked unkempt and, from the pallor of his complexion, unwell. His eyes were so deeply shadowed they were like dark holes in his face, and the only signs of life to be seen were the muscles protruding in his neck, as he struggled to speak to Isaak.

263

Their voices were too low to make out, but a thin pale hand shot out from the layers of fabric wrapping the envoy. Isaak's gloved hand was quick to grasp it and hide it in his doublet. Villiers glanced at Antonio, wondering if the Spaniard had noticed.

"Di Ribera and his men will be arriving soon," Antonio called out with a note of impatience. The assassin's eyes seemed glued to the horizon for a sign of another boat.

Isaak rose and nodded to the envoy and then replaced the black hood. In three moves, he had stepped back into the boat with Villiers and directed him to let go of the other craft. The boatman picked up his oars at the same time as Isaak, and both launched their craft through the waters, separating and going in two different directions.

Isaak drove their craft *away* from the Spanish vessel. Confusing, since the plan Isaak had outlined earlier was to approach the ship and then fire away, so the Spaniards would think it was an attempt to rescue the envoy.

"Is there a change of plan? What is our next step?" Villiers asked.

Isaak stopped, resting the oar and attempting to catch his breath.

"We wait here until Di Ribera arrives. Then we will circle back, close enough to shoot several guns. Shoot back, close enough to Antonio, then pick him out of the lagoon, if he has acted according to plan and row like the devil to the Canal of the Cannaregio, where they cannot follow."

"Sounds like we are kicking a sleeping dragon."

The corsair smiled, flashing enviable white teeth. "A good metaphor. The goal is to kick di Ribera into making way to open sea, as he will fear a continued rescue attempt."

Isaak leaned forward as his hands felt under the seat until they retrieved a large sack. From inside it, he pulled out more pistols, handing Villiers half of the arsenal and retaining the other half for himself. "You told me you were a good shot. Now will be the time to test your skill. We will pull alongside the ship, get the men on deck in your sites, and fire."

"What if Di Ribera decides to fire back? We would be an easy target."

Isaak wiped the sweat from his forehead and picked up the oar again. "It should still be dark enough to hide us, but it is a chance we have to take. I am betting Di Ribera is more likely to turn tail and run than stay and fight."

Isaak examined each pistol to ensure each was properly loaded and ready for firing. "There will be no time to reload, so just one shot a piece. It should be enough for our purpose."

Chapter Sixty: Antonio

In the distance, the crisscross of rigging and masts and the silhouette of a ship were dark lines against the deep purple sky. Antonio's black-gloved hand clutched both sides of the craft. The oarsman from Lazaretto raised his oar and launched the boat forward into the lagoon.

He could see the outlines of the big ship ahead. Good. The sooner he was away from this pestilence, the better. He considered using the gun to shoot a hole in the bottom of the boat to sink it once he had gained the rigging to climb on board. He expected the craft to sink within minutes, and then he would not risk any contamination. After all, he held the map. The real map, not the copy. He had always been quick with his hands and spent his youth as a pickpocket before learning the skills of murder. He had switched his copy for the real map after rocking the boat to fall across the Englishman.

No, he must follow the corsair's plan. di Ribera would not be satisfied with the map alone, as the noble ambassador looked forward to an interrogation with the envoy. Antonio did not abide with torture; the intelligence received through it was questionable. A man or woman would mutter anything to make the pain stop. Offering the avoidance of torture was far more productive.

He did like the poetic justice of exposing di Ribera and his men to the plague. A very tidy solution to disposing of di Ribera, with the added benefit of never being considered as the cause of his death. It would probably take a week or two for the ambassador to sicken, but by then, he should be at sea in a plague-ridden ship.

All he needed to do was to make sure to take the map back from di Ribera before he jumped ship. If he could swipe it from the Englishman, lifting it from a fool of a Spaniard would be a simple matter, especially during a gun battle.

As they came alongside the large ship, the watch called out a challenge in Spanish. Antonio called out his name and was instructed to approach.

He launched himself onto the deck and directed the seaman to help the man from Lazzaretto bring the bundled envoy on board. He kept his scarf around his face until the envoy was placed in the room usually reserved for his hooded guests, and the oarsman from Lazzaretto departed.

Antonio patted the map inside his doublet and smiled as he heard the crumple of canvas at his touch. Facing the horizon, he remained on deck to await the Spanish ambassador and his men. All in all, his alliance with the Venetians had proved highly lucrative. He had learned enough about the Corsair and his allies to satisfy the Master of Spies, and he could blame the disaster of this mission solely on Di Ribera.

After the death of the envoy, he would point out that the English would no longer be receiving any intelligence from Jamaica. Besides, there would be other, bigger plots to plan after he shared his intelligence on the corsair and his allies.

The sky seemed to be changing to a lighter shade of purple, as the clouds blanketing the moon shifted. The corsair and the Englishman were relying on complete darkness to mask their attack, but they had dallied too long. Perhaps di Ribera's men would discover them, as Antonio would be helpful to point them out?

He stretched and pumped his fingers to prepare them for the next phase of this adventure. Another glance at the horizon, and a tiny spot of light in the distance, growing larger, announced the imminent arrival of di Ribera.

"The prisoner?" were the ambassador's first words upon his arrival. Antonio gestured to the hatchway. The ambassador pushed him to the side and strode promptly to the door, snapping his fingers at the two lackeys in dull, unpolished helmets who hurried after him.

He imagined di Ribera's reaction at finding the poor man hooded and wrapped, obviously in poor condition. It did not take long for the ambassador to return.

"The man's half dead."

"You did not specify he had to be in good condition."

"He cannot be interrogated now about the treasure," di Ribera rubbed his lower lip and tapped a foot as he seemed to be rallying his thoughts. "What else can we do?"

"The map?" Antonio held up the folded parchment by one of its corners.

Di Ribera snatched the map out of his fingers. "Ahh, yes, the map. You have done well. I shall commend you to your master. Where did you find the envoy?"

"With the courtesan and a corsair who seems to make it a habit of plundering Spanish ships. They were meeting at the palazzo of a nobleman, Bardon Morosini."

The ambassador's shaggy grey brows shot up high on his forehead. "Morosini has been harboring the courtesan? And with a corsair? I shall demand his ouster from the Council of Ten. I shall see to it that—"

The ambassador was interrupted by the sound of a shot. Instinctively, both he and Antonio ducked down.

"Fool! You have led the English straight to us. They are attempting to rescue the envoy!"

"Then see that they do not get him. Make for open sea." Antonio had to shout at Di Ribera, as seaman and soldiers began to run for cover, shouting and cursing as more shots were volleyed.

Di Ribera was clambering to his feet again, keeping his head down but leaning over the railing to see where the shots came from. Distracted thus, he should not notice Antonio's fingers as they freed the map from his doublet.

But he did. Slapping away Antonio's wrist, he snarled, "Scoundrel! I knew you could not be trusted. Over my dead body, you will get this map!"

"Happy to oblige," said Antonio as he pulled out his own pistol and shot the Spanish ambassador in the head. He could claim it was an Englishman's bullet.

He retrieved the map and stood up in triumph. He shouted at the sailors to hoist the sails and make way out to open sea.

Just as the blast from Isaak's gun hit him squarely in the face.

Chapter Sixty-One: Belladonna

T he maid pulled back the thick curtains to a sun that seemed too bright for a November day. When Belladonna opened her eyes, she was grateful to see she was back in her own bed, in her own chamber.

Zancani slept directly outside her door. It was a wonder the maid had the temerity to step over him, for he was fierce and a loyal protector. Until she had confirmation from Isaak that the danger to her was past, Zancani would be by her side at all times.

"Madame has returned, and we are so happy," said the young woman as she stoked more wood in the fireplace to raise the fire's intensity. "There is a man here to see you." The maid offered Belladonna a thick silken robe, which she put on. "An Englishman," she added.

Villiers? "What is the time?" she asked.

"It is noon, madam. The Englishman has been shown into the Morning Room? "

Belladonna nodded. "Help me wash and dress, then. And kick Zancani awake."

When the maid's eyes widened, she explained, "I did not mean that literally. Just shout to him that he must awaken. I do not want to greet any guest alone."

She had left Morosini's palazzo at dawn without word from Isaak. Despite her fears for the future, she had been exhausted and must have fallen into a very deep sleep, from which she had just awoken. With so many hours elapsed, what had happened? Was Isaak safe? Was her brother gone?

Belladonna's hair was arranged in a high braid at the crown with wispy tendrils descending in curls to her eyes, her bodice was of a rich brocade of green and red and gold, and beneath her wide dark green satin skirts, she stood tall in her gilded platform shoes as she entered the Morning Room. She felt more like herself than she had for the past few weeks and kept her back straight as a queen's.

As she suspected, it was Villiers. The Englishman stood, cap in hand, admiring the large portrait which hung over the marble mantlepiece.

"Correr's work, I presume. Of the Jewess, Diana?"

"You are correct on both accounts. Please take a seat."

When he was seated on a settee covered in gold damask, she took a seat opposite him in a matching settee.

"When first we met, I thought you were one of the most beautiful women I had ever seen. Today, you take my breath away." He rotated his plumed hat in his hands, obviously unable to remain still, and kept his eyes locked on hers.

"Thank you. But I do not need your praises. I need to know the outcome of your excursion last night."

She followed his eyes to the entry, where Zancani hovered. "You can speak in front of my servant. He is most loyal, and I trust him with my life."

"Trust?" Villiers's mouth pursed as if speaking the word left a sour taste. "A word most overused and underachieved. However, I must say that the only man I have ever thought worthy of it is that corsair Isaak."

Belladonna could feel the thump of her heart and the pulsing of the blood in her veins at the mention of that name. Keeping her voice at an even tone, she asked, "Where is he? I see that you came through last night's ordeal unscathed. I suppose he has as well?"

"He is better than the Spaniard, who he had the good wit not to trust."

"Antonio?"

Villiers's mouth flattened into a flat line at the sound of that name. "He switched the maps, the blackguard. Swiped the real one and left me the artist's copy. We started firing, then heard a shot—but it was not directed at us. It must have been Antonio who shot Di Ribera. After an excellent shot by Isaak, from quite a distance, I might add, next went Antonio."

"So, things did not go exactly to plan, did they?" As her anxiety increased, her fingers flew to her pearls. Playing with their cool smoothness had a calming effect. "What of the envoy?"

The Englishman shook his head. "We do not know. During the shooting, the ship made sail, and off they went. The man who carried him on board, however, said he was near death when he left him."

Villiers cleared his throat and looked down at his hands. "I saw the envoy speak to Isaak last night and hand him something in the boat. I assume it was for you."

"Thank you," she managed to say. She coughed to clear her throat of the rising sob threatening to erupt. "Isaak is unhurt?"

"He is finishing up some last items of business, and then he will be on board his ship. Readying it to sail. He is taking me back to England tomorrow to advise the king on the annexation of Jamaica." Villiers lowered his eyes. "He asked if you would come to see us off."

Her fingers twisted the strands of pearls. Isaak was leaving. Would he offer to take her with him? To England, or to the New World? Could she leave Venice and all this behind? Without betraying the turmoil inside, she changed the topic, "What of the treasure?"

Villiers shrugged. "The map may be worthless, or it may not. But I have since learned of another treasure to be had in Jamaica. One which will be an ongoing source of riches for years to come."

Belladonna roise one eyebrow. "Oh?"

"Chocolate. Have you ever had some?" The Englishman's eyes sparked with excitement, and he rubbed his hands. "It is a growing delicacy, especially among the royals. It is some kind of nut or bean, grown from the ground, which is ground into powder, mixed with sugar and some other magical ingredients, and it becomes *ambrosia*. The Spanish have made it into a hot drink, and it is truly worth its weight in gold. The envoy has delivered the true treasure: a ready source of this chocolate plant and the expertise of his family in Jamaica to harvest it. Truly a gift of the gods."

Belladonna blinked several times to keep the tears from falling at the mention of her brother's family. She managed to smile. "How very opportune, for you."

Villiers grinned back. "It is. I grant you the next time I come to Venice, I will be a very rich man, ready to acquire as many portraits such as these," he pointed to the portrait of Diana, "as that wooly old goat Arundel."

Belladonna rose, and Villiers followed her as she led him to the door. "Please let Isaak know I will be at the ship at sunset."

Villiers gave her a courtly bow before marching off, the plume of his hat bouncing on his head.

Chapter Sixty-Two: Diana

The last day Isaak was to spend in Venice, he surprised Diana by appearing at her door. He came after midday prayers when her father had returned home for the midday meal.

"Ahh, the fragrant smell of chickpea and lentil stew," said Isaak as he raised his head and inhaled deeply.

"It has probably been a long time since you have eaten anything so kosher," grumbled the rabbi, as his wife dropped the bowl of stew before him and went to embrace her son.

Diana was grateful Isaak ignored their father's jibe and that he was not dressed in flowing Arab garb, certain to raise eyebrows among the many who clustered outside the well and within sight of their door.

"How are you, father? Fully recovered from this last encounter with the Council of Ten?" Isaak asked, taking the seat beside his father and accepting stew from his mother.

The rabbi adjusted the worn red velvet cap and as in his usual manner, answered his son's question with a question. "I suppose I have you to thank for my release?"

"It is Belladonna we have to thank for that," Diana broke in. "She risked her life to publicly reappear at her palazzo and at great personal sacrifice."

Isaak's brow lowered as he agreed. "It is true. She acted solely for the benefit of our people, to prevent the Ghetto from what could have been a devastating attack."

"Our people? You still count yourself as one of us?" asked the rabbi, his tone skeptical.

"Stop it! Stop it, I say!" his mother banged the metal ladle against the wooden table before her husband, causing the liquid of the stew to erupt over the sides of his bowl. "Can you, for one moment, greet the son you have not laid eyes on for three years with warmth and affection? Must you continually chastise him? You are no saint yourself, gambling our rent money away time after time. Isaak serves the Almighty differently, but what he does is important. If not for Isaak, how many Jews would be dead or rotting away in a Spanish or Maltese prison, hmm? How many? So, stop treating him like a ten-year-old boy who is skipping afternoon prayers!"

The rabbi raised a hand and opened his mouth to defend himself, but seemed to think better of it and said not a word.

"Thank you, mother," said Isaak with a grin as he placed a heaping spoonful of stew into his mouth.

The rabbi gave a deep sigh and was about to speak again when Diana cut him off. "It is a great blessing, is it not, to find one's purpose in life? I have found mine in the study of Torah, which is categorized as a *mitzvah* between man and God, while Isaak found his purpose in saving victims from the cruelty of their fellow man, categorized as a *mitzva* to better the relationships among people. According to the sages, and contrary to what many believe, a *mitzvah* to better human relations is of a higher level than those between man and God, because it is a more difficult accomplishment. Is that not so, Father?"

The rabbi adjusted his cap again and raised an eyebrow at Diana. "You are correct. In the Sabbath prayers, we recite: *Whoever occupies himself with the needs of the community in good faith will earn himself a reward from the Almighty in the world to come.*" Turning to his son, he cleared his throat and said, "I am in error, and I must beg your apology. Know that I am proud of all you have accomplished, and recognize your sacrifice. As a father, I still wish you could stop embroiling yourself in such danger and stay here, in Venice, with your family." The rabbi blinked several times in succession, and Diana believed he was fighting back tears.

Isaak took the hands of both parents. "I wish I could be the son you had wished for, who would learn at your side and have children for you to enjoy.

My life has taken a different course, and I cannot change it now." The look he gave Diana was filled with hidden meaning as he added, "Perhaps one day, when this era of reason takes hold, the persecutions will be at an end, and I shall be able to settle down."

"A wish we can all pray for," the rabbi said. "When must you go?"

Isaak gave a deep sigh and lowered his eyes before answering. "Tomorrow."

"Always my children go, and hardly ever they come," said her mother, refilling Isaak's bowl.

Considering how dramatically her mother usually reacted, Diana was relieved she was taking her son's departure so well.

The time passed too quickly with Isaak. The shadows lengthened in the campo outside their door as the day waned. The rabbi reluctantly pushed himself away from the table. "It is time for afternoon prayers. I must go."

Isaak rose along with him and suddenly wrapped his father in a tight embrace. It happened so quickly and was so uncharacteristic of her older brother; she hoped she had not imagined it.

Likewise, he embraced their mother in the same manner. Diana was wondering whether she, too, would be swept into his arms, until Isaak asked, "Diana, will you walk with me to the gates?"

Diana felt as if her heart had crept into her throat, as they crossed over the bridge from the Ghetto Nuovo, and Isaak stopped her with his question. "Do you believe it possible she would come with me if I asked?"

Diana did not know how to respond to her brother's question. He was as tremulous as a young boy, and for the first time, it dawned on her that Isaak had never had a courtship. His life had been interrupted when he had gone to sea at such a young age. By his question, he was acknowledging her superior expertise in this manner and, more importantly, the close relationship she had with Belladonna.

She had to answer his question without causing him to lose faith in himself or in the value of such relationships. "Truly, Isaak, I do not know how she will respond, but I believe you must ask, or you will lose a once-in-a-lifetime chance for happiness. I know she cares deeply for you, and I have seen her searching the horizon for signs of your ship. But even if you do love each other greatly, it may not be enough to overcome the challenges you would face in being together."

Diana realized that she was echoing her own feelings about Mattia. The strange sensations which drew her to the artist were different than the love she had experienced with her husband. Though she was tempted to pursue a deeper relationship with Mattia, to do so would result in alienation from her family and a transgression punishable by Venetian law. Of the restrictive laws created for the Jews, this one was zealously enforced.

Though Belladonna was really a Jew by birth, it was her secret, so as a Christian, her relationship with Isaak would evoke the same law. Diana would not speak of this complication with Isaak. There were far greater differences between the courtesan and her brother, necessitating both emotional and practical sacrifices.

"You must give her the chance." Diana took her brother's arm before adding, "You will always regret it if you do not."

Isaak reacted to her words in a manner she had not expected. Her intrepid older brother first recited a silent prayer and then embraced her. "Thank you. You have shed some light into a murky path."

Chapter Sixty-Three: Belladonna

Belladonna, wrapped from head to toe in a thick black cloak, looked back at her palazzo as the gondola moved forward into the Grand Canal. The last rays of afternoon sunlight left a dappled path across the waters and traversed the carved faces of the sphinxes in the friezes of the palazzo's windows, dancing around the long columns that reached from the top floor to the ground. Designed by Palladio, it was one of the most elegant private residences and had been a gift to Belladonna from a generous patron who had lost his sons in a naval battle with Genoa and had no other heirs.

How she had loved this home! She had taken special care with all that was inside, from furniture to servants, to ensure it would become the most popular salon to engage Venetian society. She had enjoyed being hostess to dignitaries and ambassadors, to famous poets and artists, but of late, nights that had once glittered were becoming tedious. The preparation of her hair, of her face, and figure had become more and more of a chore. A crackling of wrinkles had appeared at the corners of her eyes. Though still in her prime at the age of twenty-nine, she was old enough to retire and refused to complicate her life with any other lovers.

How many times had she raised her eyes to the far-off horizon and dreamed of Isaak's return? Pined for him, wished for his ship to come to the lagoon to take her away.

Now he had come. If he should offer to take her with him, should she go? *Could* she go away from Venice?

The first eighteen years of her life, she had spent in the shelter of her parents' villa in Jamaica. She had never expected to ever be separated from them or from Roderigo.

Man plans and God laughs. It had been one of her father's favorite expressions. Her father had always expected to remain in Toledo, where his family had lived for over two hundred years. The Inquisition, the random imprisonments of friends and family had led her father to move to Jamaica. With their deaths, all had changed, and she had boarded a ship bound for France that never arrived.

Isaak had entered her life when she was in need of a savior. He had bargained for her and redeemed her from the Barbary pirates who had captured her ship and had designs to sell her to a Turkish pasha. Isaak had brought her to Venice and had found her a place with the Sullams. Sarra had welcomed the young refugee into her home, taught her how to think, and disciplined her to study philosophy, literature, and poetry. She had absorbed all of Sarra's teachings, but had rejected her religion. Though she may have been born of Jewish parents, she had no desire to accept a heritage limited by hatred and persecution.

She envied Isaak's freedom to sail wherever the winds took him. At sea, he was no longer a rabbi's son, and if she went with him, she would no longer be a notorious courtesan. They could settle in a place where no one knew their origins, choose who they wished to be and how they wanted to live. She could imagine herself without the constraints of braided hair, tight bodices, and billowing skirts, and without having to banter with men like Morosini or keep vigilant for enemies like Contarini.

The gondola plowed through the glimmering waters, and as she drew nearer to Isaak's ship, its masts standing tall in a rosy, orange sky, she imagined herself on its prow, facing miles of ocean, her hair dancing free to the whipping whims of the wind.

Seagulls shrieking overhead awakened her from her daydreaming. The gondola drew up close to the side of the large ship. A rope with a seat attached dropped down from above. With the help of the gondolier, she angled herself into it and felt herself rising as the sailors pulled her to the deck.

Isaak was waiting for her, and his sapphire-blue eyes seemed to glow beneath his heavy black brows. The men on deck paused in their tasks and watched as Isaak took her hand and led her to the privacy of his cabin.

Is this to be our farewell?" she asked, removing her cloak.

His linen shirt was rolled up to his elbows, revealing his muscular, sun-darkened arms. He stood before a table strewn with maps and papers, tamped down with large navigational instruments. He took a folded packet from among the clutter and handed it to her.

"Your brother asked me to give this to you."

Belladonna's eyes studied his and then shifted to the folded paper he had placed in her hands. Carefully, she unfolded it, and read Roderigo's final words:

All my life, I have been haunted by what might have become of you. The chance to see you alive and well was so powerful it forced me to stray from my mission. I never considered it would place you in danger. I am sorry for it and hope I can save you now, even as I could not in Recife.

My only wish is for you to meet my son and my sweet Marietta, so they should know someone of their father's family.

"Have you read this?" she held up the note.

Isaak shook his head. "It was meant for your eyes, not mine."

Her eyes roved around the cabin, from the efficient bunk that nestled within one wall of cupboards to the thick-paned windows, where the captain could keep an eye to the horizon on the other.

"The ship must sail at dawn," he said softly before adding, "You can come with me."

"The destination?"

"First, to England, to fulfill Roderigo's mission and deliver Villiers. Then to the New World. Possibly to Jamaica. Or wherever you wish to go."

She could fulfill Roderigo's last wish and set sail for Jamaica with Isaak. A new life and a new family. Perhaps a child of their own?

Wishes are dangerous. Or so she had come to believe. A wish proposes to attain the impossible. A plan is made to accomplish what is possible.

Belladonna nodded. "There is much to do if I plan to leave with you at dawn."

Without a word, Isaak swept her into his arms.

Chapter Sixty-Four: Belladonna

Belladonna had ordered the staff to join her in the salon, which had been prepared, as usual, for an evening of illustrious guests. The footmen stood at attention, impeccable in their golden livery, while the maids, in their neatly pressed gowns, sat decorously and with some trepidation on a cluster of divans.

There were a few gasps and stifled sobs when she announced her intention to leave Venice. Belladonna blamed her departure on Villiers and his invitation to join him in England. The length of her stay could not be determined at this time, but she reassured them they would not be dismissed or the palazzo shuttered in her absence.

Belladonna stunned them with the news that the artist Mattia Correr would take up residence, and she wished the salon to be converted into his studio. Though his paintings hung on the walls, she could tell that the artist did not seem adequate, in their eyes, to be master of her magnificent palazzo.

Belladonna then revealed her appointment of a manager to oversee both the maintenance and the budget of the palazzo and its staff, who would keep her informed of how things fared until her return. Her choice was a merchant, a man well-versed in managing finances and who managed his own elegant palazzo. No one recognized the name of Jacob Sullam or knew he was from the Ghetto.

Belladonna also advised them that her trusted friend, Diana, a frequent guest, often on the arm of the artist, would have free reign to her wardrobe or to any of her possessions and would be equally welcome to stay in the palazzo with the artist.

Now she had only to inform Mattia, the Sullams, and Diana of her plans. She would go to the Ghetto first and then send for Mattia upon her return after she had sorted through her possessions. She had decided not to weigh down her new life with too much baggage from the old.

* * *

The gates to the Ghetto were already closed when Belladonna arrived, but that would not be a problem. She, like anyone outside of its residents, were welcome in and out of the Ghetto at any time, even at night, with the payment of a small fee to the men who manned the gate.

She was greeted by Jacob Sullam as he met her at the door of his home. He was just returning from evening prayers, and the rabbi was at his side. Both were surprised to see her in the Ghetto. After all the trouble her presence had caused and the fear of further repercussions, Jacob quickly ushered her into the house, while Belladonna asked the rabbi to return with Diana.

At the sound of their entry, Sarra had descended from her chamber, still adjusting a bright gold turban to cover her hair. At the sight of Belladonna, she smiled and gestured enthusiastically for her to come into the salon. Belladonna warned Sarra and Jacob to keep the servants away, knowing how likely they would be to peddle any information they might overhear.

"We are so glad to see you are safe," said Sarra, "and appreciate how you have risked your life on our behalf."

"I have been treated with great kindness by you, first as a penniless refugee, and these past few weeks, when you have welcomed me back."

Belladonna asked if she might return to her room to collect what remained of her possessions there. She did not want to share her news until the rabbi and Diana arrived.

She opened the wardrobe and surveyed the shifts, bodices, and skirts Sarra had purchased for her. She would leave all but a few shifts and a pair of leather slippers. She checked the corners of the wardrobes, and beneath the mattress of the bed, for any items of jewelry, she might have hidden there and found a pair of golden earrings and a delicate golden bracelet she had left behind. She decided she had enough jewelry and would give them to Diana.

When she returned to the salon, the rabbi and Diana were already seated and waiting for her. Diana gave her a warm smile, and the rabbi nodded to her in greeting.

"I have news I must share and favors I must ask of you," she tented her fingers before her and took a deep breath before saying, "I am leaving Venice. With Isaak."

Her eyes shifted from one face to the other. Eyebrows raised. Mouths hung open. Only the women settled theirs into a smile. Diana clapped her hands excitedly. "At last! I am so happy for you."

Jacob's brows had descended and curved down in a puzzled frown. "He sails into danger."

"Then so must I."

"Do you love him?" Sarra asked.

"I do." Belladonna looked to the rabbi, who had remained silent. "Have you nothing to say?"

"It is not for me to say anything. You seem to have made your decision, and it seems Isaak has made his." The rabbi clasped his hands together tightly. "I can only wish the Almighty should protect you."

"Amen, rabbi," nodded Jacob, "but what favor do you need from us?"

Belladonna quickly told him of her plans for the palazzo and asked Jacob if he would manage it in her absence.

"When do you plan to return?" he asked when she finished.

"If all goes well, I hope to never return. In that event, I shall send word of how to dispose of it." She turned to Diana. "If anyone will appreciate the beauty of my home and the view of the canal, it is Mattia, which is why I have decided to let him make his residence there. I hope it will inspire him to create great works of art. However, Diana, I want you to consider it your home as well. You are welcome to my clothes, my furnishings, any of my fine things. You are, and have always been, my one true friend."

Diana embraced her. "Where will you go?"

Belladonna repeated Isaak's intended destination, adding, "My brother's family is still in Jamaica. With Villiers' persuasion and England's intervention, they will be safe from Spain and the Inquisition. It was his last wish that I should return to Jamaica and meet his wife and son."

The rabbi sighed, "Your brother was a goodman. We are grateful for his sacrifice, and we will say *kaddish*, the memorial prayer for him, at our services. May you be successful in fulfilling his last wish."

Chapter Sixty-Five: Villiers

At last, they were underway, and he could set his sights for home and his soon-to-be-found fortune. It was a bit disconcerting to have a woman aboard, and he could tell the men who swabbed the decks and climbed up the riggings agreed with him. Still, she was glorious to look at, and he could not complain of her conversation, which was always entertaining.

He was astonished she had abandoned Venice and her palazzo, especially since she had left it in the artist's hands. What was it about Mattia Correr women found so fascinating? He was not a hero, nor a man of power. All he did was swirl paint around, and the ladies clamored for his attention. Now, the lucky dog had just landed himself a magnificent palazzo!

As the last sight of Venice faded from view, Villiers gave it a silent salute. Although he had acquired a new scar, courtesy of the Spanish assassin, his pockets were now filled with gold, thanks to Sir Henry, who had collected his winnings from the gaming tables. He had bested the Spanish, always rewarding, and seen the beauties the city was famous for, like the Jewess who had healed him and the former courtesan who now graced the deck of this ship.

In this city, his luck had changed. Someday, he was certain, he would return.

Epilogue

Diana was disconcerted to hear giggles coming from the salon as she came up the stairs. She was reassured when she heard Mattia's angry shout, which stopped the female tittering immediately. *He is working again.*

She placed a hand on her chest as she caught her breath and a smile on her face as she entered the large, airy room. It had undergone great change since the nights when Belladonna had made it the most popular salon in all of Venice. If she closed her eyes, perhaps the piles of canvases stacked against the pale gold damask walls would disappear, as well as the bundles of rags, the jars of pigments, and brushes. Maybe Belladonna would appear, shining and luminescent, bedecked in pearls and gold satin?

"Stay still, you silly geese; I need more time to capture your pose." Mattia stood behind his easel, like a captain at the helm of his ship. His eyes blazed, and his nostrils flared, and his brush dashed furiously from palette to canvas.

Opposite him, on a podium covered with dark plum velvet, two young women stood, while a third reclined on a divan before them. Their hair was undressed and rippled around their shoulders, and they wore lavish satin dresses in pale colors of lavender, green and blue, all likely from Belladonna's wardrobe.

"My shoulders ache, Mattia," said a fair-haired woman in pale green, whom she recognized as the singer Gaspara. Her sister, Cassandra, with dark hair and in lavender satin, reclined on a divan and held a lyre in her lap. The third young woman wore a crown of flowers and ribbons on her dark hair and looked at Diana with curiosity, as if she must know her.

"Stop pouting, Bettina. I am working on your lips right now," Mattia called out. Bettina immediately complied and softened her mouth into a sweet smile. "Much better."

Diana recognized all three of the women, though they did not seem to know her. Like Diana, they had been the subjects of the Gallery of Beauties, and Diana was glad they were still a source of inspiration for the artist.

The great windows filled the room with a bright cold light, reflected from the canal waters even though it was a cloudy spring day. Belladonna had been gone for months, and though Mattia had settled into the palazzo almost as soon as she had gone, it was not until today Diana had seen him pick up a brush to paint.

Most often, when she came to visit him, he would be sprawled on a divan, staring at the half-finished portrait of Belladonna. Every time, with a glass of wine in hand, he would ask, "Do you think she will return soon?"

Diana would assure him she would, and he would nod and drink more of his wine. Belladonna's palazzo seemed empty and cold without her, though Diana and Jacob Sullam tried their best to keep it up as she would. Both of them had no word from Isaak or Belladonna since they had arrived in England. Sir Henry received news of Sir George Villiers, who had delivered the map and his message to King James. He had not led the launch of the King's fleet for Jamaica, but there had been no news of the Spanish ships surrounding the island.

All was as it had been for the Jews in Jamaica and in Venice, where danger had been averted. Sarra had been successful in her treatise of defending herself against the charge of heresy. The charter of the Ghetto had not been challenged, and the merchants of the Ghetto could continue to engage in trade in peace.

Occasionally, Diana would venture across the bridge to the Moorish quarter, visiting the Turk to purchase more herbs for her remedies, but he always shook his head when she asked if he had news of her brother.

Until Belladonna was gone, Diana had not realized how much she had relied on the courtesan for access to life outside of the Ghetto. Escaping from the dreariness of her chores and the bickering of her mother and father, she had come today, like so many other days, with the hope of finding some excitement. At last, Mattia had found his inspiration and was painting once more, perhaps a sign of better things to come. When he finally gave his models permission to relax, he noticed her. "Diana! Come, see what I am doing."

Diana stood alongside him to view the canvas. He had already blocked out the figures, and she recognized his skill in how he had arranged them on the canvas. "I shall call it, 'My Muses.'"

"You have taken the structure of Da Vinci, the triangle composed of three figures."

Mattia raised his eyebrows, "You have learned much of art, then, have you?"

Diana smiled. "Mostly from you. When I plagued you with all of my questions, I listened to your answers. It is good to see you inspired and painting again."

He shrugged. "I could work much faster, if only they would stay still for longer."

He looked up and continued staring at his canvas, "I can envision just how it will look when I complete it."

He looked over her head at the young women who were stretching and talking and clapped his hands. "Please, resume your positions."

The models resumed their pose, and Mattia's eyes locked onto them as he resumed his furious brushstrokes. Diana thought she understood how he struggled with his desire to finish the portrait of Belladonna. He could see it in his mind, but was unable to complete it without her.

Diana wondered if Belladonna would ever return and if he would have the chance to finish it.

Glossary

- *Talmud*—the central text of Rabbinic Judaism and the primary source of Jewish religious law.
- *Torah*—primarily the Five Books of Moses, but refers to the whole body of Judaism's religious literature.
- *Mitzvah*—a good deed, a positive commandment.
- *Teshuva*—atonement, literally, returning to the just path.
- *Pirkei Avot*—*The Ethics of the Fathers* is an excerpt of the Mishnah, and a part of the Talmud. It contains a collection of ethical and moral principles, passed down from generations.
- *Shabbos*—another term for Sabbath.
- *Challah*—special braided bread eaten at the Sabbath meal.
- *Kabbalah*—the study of Jewish mysticism.
- *Mezuzah*—a small roll of parchment with a special prayer, secured in a metal or wooden case upon the doorposts of Jewish homes, which serves as a reminder of Divine protection.
- *Gvirim* or *G'vir*—important people or person in the community, usually the wealthy.
- *Ilui*—a genius or prodigy.
- *Kvitels*—little wish-notes, with prayers or wishes for good health, wealth or fortune.
- *Chamsa*—a hand-shaped good luck amulet.
- *Shalosh Seudot*—the third meal of the Sabbath, eaten late Saturday afternoon.
- *Tikun Olam*—literally, 'repairing the world' but connotes social action or the pursuit of social justice.

- *Shema*—considered the most essential declaration of the Jewish faith, "the Lord is our God, the Lord is one."
- *Seforim*—holy books, like the Talmud, or the books of the Torah.
- *Campo*—rectangular square in Venice.
- *Calle*—narrow street or passage in Venice.
- *Fondamenta*—walkway along the canal.
- *Piano nobile*—main story of a large house.
- *Cortega onesta*—'honest courtesan' an elite courtesan.
- *Pozzi*—underground prison cells in the Doge's palace.

A Note from the Author

This book, like the first book in the series, *The Gallery of Beauties*, was inspired by the autobiography of Rabbi Leon di Modena, a poet, a scholar, a masterful orator and a self-professed addicted gambler. In his autobiography, he describes how his writings or sermons would earn him significant sums of money, which he would immediately gamble away, leaving his family in debt. He was once excommunicated for a short time due to his inability to curb his gambling habit. His three sons gave him no end of sorrow and grief. The eldest, an alchemist, died from his experiments. The second son, likely a pirate, never returned from sea. His youngest son associated with local thugs who murdered him before his father's eyes. Only Diana, his widowed daughter, stayed with him through his old age. His study and many of the synagogues where he spoke are still in existence and can be visited in the old Ghetto.

Sara Coppio Sullam was a poetess, playwright, and actress whose fame was known beyond the confines of the Ghetto. Although confined to living there, wealthy Jewish women like Sara were able to partake in theatre, dancing, and literary salons without censure by either the Venetian or the rabbinic authorities. She was known to be what would now be termed an "airhead," and the lack of control she had over her household and her thieving servants caused her much suffering before she died. She truly had spent time and money on establishing a foundation where Jews and Gentiles could share their philosophies and learn tolerance for each other. Unfortunately, one of the scholars who had received her largess from the foundation later accused her of heresy, a charge she was able to refute with her publication of a responsa.

Venice became a haven for Jews escaping persecution from Spain,

Portugal, Germany, and other parts of Italy. Venice was a maritime city of merchants engaged in trade, and although Jews were not permitted in the guilds or to take up many professions, they had networks established in trading centers of Amsterdam and Constantinople, which made them valuable to the Venetian merchants and government. The Jews of Venice were tolerated, although not permitted to live in any other area but the small section which was the site of the former quarries, called the Ghetto. There was a long-standing edict for Jews' to wear a distinctive mark on their clothing, which in Venice was a yellow triangle. Some Jews were given special permission to forego wearing the yellow triangle, but for most Jews, being caught without it could incur fines, beatings, or incarceration. It was against Venetian law for a Jew to have relations with a non-Jew, although it was not actively enforced. If a Jew wanted to prosper and live in complete freedom, conversion to Christianity was required.

My sources for the life and customs of the Ghetto during the early 17th century come from Cecil Roth's, *The History of the Jews of Venice* and *The Ghetto of Venice* by Riccardo Calimani. In the scholarly papers from the Italian Academia Research Brief, The *Mediterranean in the Seventeenth Century, Pirates, Captive and Ransoms* was used for background on the capture of Jews on the high seas and for Isaak's feats of piracy. Isaak's purpose to free captive Jews is unfortunately based on reality; the Knights of St. John, the fierce Christian pirates of Malta, were notorious for raiding ships on the Mediterranean with the purpose of capturing Jews to be held for ransom on Malta.

For the stories of the Jews of Jamaica, including the lost treasure of Christopher Columbus and the role of the Jews in saving both Columbus and his treasure, I relied upon the excellent research of Edward Kritzler in *Jewish Pirates of the Caribbean*. According to Kritzler, as early as 1501, the Spanish Crown published an edict that "Moors, Jews, heretics, reconciliados [repentants—those who returned to the church,] and New Christians [former Jews] are not permitted to travel to the Indies." The exception was made for Jamaica, an island so bleak, Spain could not incentivize anyone to settle it save for New Christians. Jamaica had been awarded in perpetuity to Christopher Columbus and his heirs in 1494 by the King and Queen of Spain. For over a century, the heirs of Columbus kept Jamaica out of the clutches of Spain's inquisitors, which was not the case for the colony of Portuguese in Recife, Brazil. The scene of how Belladonna's parents met their deaths was also based on real events, as there was a major *auto de fé* in Recifé, in the early 1600s, which led to a boatload of Jewish refugees escaping to the colony of New Amsterdam, which later became New York.

The story of the Venice Ghetto has special significance to me, since it has always had a place in my mother's family lore. I am a rabbi's daughter, as is my mother, who is a descendant of a great rabbinical family which traces its roots to one of the leading rabbis of Venice, a contemporary of Leon di Modena. Our family candlesticks, which my mother lit every Friday night, were rumored to have come from the Venetian Ghetto, my mother claiming they had been silver torch holders sold by some nobleman in the Ghetto pawnshops.

If you enjoyed this book, please leave a favorable review on Amazon or Goodreads, and you can sign up to receive notifications of the third book in the series when it becomes available in 2024.

Acknowledgements

This book could not have come about without the support and encouragement of my fellow writers and friends from Level Best Books and Sisters in Crime. The Dames, Harriette, Verena and Shawn truly love the books they bring out, and are able to bring out the best in our writing, and I truly appreciate them.

I am grateful for a most magical childhood. My inspiration for indulging my fantasies and crafting them into stories comes from my mother, who is now unable to share in this success because she suffers from advanced dementia. My father, my uncles, my grandfathers, all of whom were rabbis, always encouraged my innovative thinking, and never questioned the rights of a woman to study Torah, philosophy or ask any questions about it.

My children, Shana, Riva, and Jake, all lent their ears and their talents to help me craft this book and promote it. I am thankful for my eight grandchildren, who cheer me on and consent to pose for Instagram whenever I ask them.

Lastly, I would like to thank my husband, for his love and support for everything I do.

About the Author

Nina Wachsman is a graduate of the Parsons School of Design, where she studied under Maurice Sendak. She is currently the CEO of a digital marketing agency in New York City. She is also a descendant of a chief rabbi of the Ghetto, a contemporary of the rabbi in the novel. She is a member of Sisters in Crime, Mystery Writers of America, and the Historical Novel Society, and has published stories in mystery and horror magazines and anthologies. *The Gallery of Beauties*, her debut novel, was an Agatha nominee for Best First Novel.

SOCIAL MEDIA HANDLES:
 facebook/gallerybeauties,
 Instagram @thegalleryofbeauties
 facebook/ninawachsman

AUTHOR WEBSITE:
 venicebeauties.com

Also by Nina Wachsman

The Gallery of Beauties